TALONS & TALISMANS II

LIBRI MYSTERIORUM II

Edited by Chris Kennedy
& Rob Howell

New Mythology Press
Coinjock, NC

Chris Kennedy/New Mythology Press
1097 Waterlily Rd., Coinjock, NC, 27923
http://chriskennedypublishing.com/

Publisher's Note: This is a work of fiction. Names, characters, places, and incidents are a product of the author's imagination. Locales and public names are sometimes used for atmospheric purposes. Any resemblance to actual people, living or dead, or to businesses, companies, events, institutions, or locales is completely coincidental.

Cover Art and Design by Jake Caleb (https://www.jcalebdesign.com/)

The stories and articles contained herein have never been previously published. They are copyrighted as follows:

Talons & Talismans II/Chris Kennedy and Rob Howell -- 1st ed.
ISBN: 978-1648552380

* * * * *

Preface by Rob Howell

Welcome to *Talons & Talismans II*! Chances are, you're reading this after reading *Talons & Talismans I*. If so, I hope you enjoy this one as much as the first one. If not, you are in for a treat, as you've got fifteen more amazing stories in that one to go with the fifteen great stories here.

When I announced this project, I received some interest from a number of authors. By 'some interest,' I mean they said, "Yeah! I want in!" and by 'a number,' I mean 'a whole bunch.' It became clear early on that there was no way I was going to be able to fit all that enthusiasm from so many authors into one anthology. Darn the luck!

So here's the second fruit off that tree. Again, I'm honored to get to work with a number of the best writers around, and I can go into superlatives about Aaron Rosenberg, Todd Fahnestock, Mel Todd, and D.J. Butler. However, you don't need *me* to tell you they can write because you've probably already read their stuff. If you haven't, you're in for a treat.

D.J. Butler, by the way, went the extra step. He actually gave me *two* stories, one for both anthologies. They're from his terrific *Indrajit and Fix* series, which I dearly love. This one might be my favorite of all the ones I've read, too.

But as I mentioned in the Foreword for Talons & Talismans I, one of the best parts of this job is to work with new writers. This includes the first published story from both Richard Hailey and Elowyn Fahnestock, and I hope I see more from them.

Michael Gants is just getting into a career as a writer after I met him as a fan and a guy who works to make fun things for other fans at LibertyCon and elsewhere. His story was so fun, I had to put his Goblin sanitation engineer on the cover. Also on the cover is C.M. DeMott's Unicorn. I loved how she took the glittery ideal of the Unicorn and filled it with steel, pride, and honor.

However, this anthology gives you something else.

Sure, it's a great collection of stories, but it's also a springboard. New Mythology Press has been working on a new shared world project called the Eldros Legacy. All five founders—me, Quincy J. Allen, Mark Stallings, Marie Whittaker, and Todd Fahnestock—contributed a story from that universe to this anthology. Elowyn Fahnestock, Sam Witt, and Jamie Ibson also added stories set in that universe. That's eight stories to get you primed for the release of Khyven the Unkillable, by Todd, coming 7 December 2021. Oh, and you can add five free short stories in the Eldros Legacy by downloading *Here There Be Giants* at: https://dl.bookfunnel.com/qabsr57lq3.

Oh, and I should mention Aaron Rosenberg and Courtney Farrell are also writing in the Eldros Legacy, though their stories here aren't set in that world. Aaron's, by the way, provides us the Manticore for the third beast on the cover and is the story that will start us off.

So, here we go. Have fun; I certainly did.

— Rob Howell

Publisher, New Mythology Press

* * * * *

Table of Contents

* * * * *

The Face of Things
by Aaron Rosenberg

I f he were being honest, Sir Roderick had no interest in battling a Manticore. They were said to be fearsome creatures, massive, furred beasts built like a great cat, but with bat wings, a barbed and armored tail, and the face of a man. Who in their right mind would wish to go up against something like that?

Yet, when the proclamation had reached Roderick, he'd buckled on his armor, strapped on his sword, hefted his shield, mounted his horse, and set out for the kingdom of Oreah, eventually joining a long, loose line of fellow knights, nobles, hunters, and others, all journeying to the same place and for the same purpose: to face the deadly Manticore and, in besting it, win for themselves a kingdom.

Why, then, had he gone? Traveling amongst these other men, ground-tying his faithful steed Patience with the other animals at night, and sharing a fire, food, and drink with their masters, Roderick had been forced to acknowledge—yet again—several facts about himself.

Namely, that he was getting a bit too long in the tooth for all this running about on a whim, riding up and down the countryside, sleeping out under the stars, seeking adventure and destiny, and all that sort of thing.

Then again, he'd *never* been much good at adventure, even when he was younger. The other squires and knights-in-training would leap at the first chance for excitement and battle, but not Roderick. He would hang back, considering, studying, assessing.

"You're like an old man already!" he remembered one of the others, a big, rowdy boy named Callum, teasing him once. "'Oh no, I might break something!' Stop worrying and have some fun already!"

Callum had died two years later, charging headlong into battle against a group of ruffians who'd been waylaying villagers. He'd fallen less than halfway to the villains, his body so filled with clothyard shafts he'd looked more pincushion than man.

Roderick had seen that the men had been carrying longbows, of course. He'd even tried to tell Callum that, but the other squire had refused to listen. For the last time, as it had turned out.

Roderick had taken down the highwaymen himself. Not by charging them, no. He'd hidden behind some bushes and tailed them back to their well-concealed hideout on the edge of a small forest. Then, while they'd slept, he'd lit the whole thicket of brambles and branches and cleverly woven reeds on fire. He'd been waiting a short way beyond as the brigands had come stumbling out, coughing and choking, and he'd shot those who hadn't thrown down their weapons at once. With a crossbow. He hadn't trusted himself with a longbow—while it might have played better in a ballad, he hadn't exactly been worried about having some bard recounting the tale.

That incident—and its successful outcome—had led to his knighthood. Since then, Roderick had continued to distinguish himself…by not distinguishing himself.

He'd never been the fastest or the strongest. He wasn't the best with sword or bow, and safest not to even mention lance or axe. He was a fair rider, but too soft with his steed, too lenient a master, or so it was said. And while of an adequate size, decent looks, and possessing a clear voice, he lacked a commanding presence or the ability to stir men with his words or his glance.

In short, he was a middling knight at best. Hardly the kind to do well against something like a Manticore. Hardly the kind to win a kingdom.

So why *had* he come?

Curiosity, perhaps. Few knew much about Oreah or its king, other than that the land was rich and fair and its king strong but kind. Despite its wealth, no one ever attacked the small realm or attempted to annex or invade it. They didn't dare. Not because of its knights, for Oreah had none.

No, all the neighboring lands feared the monster that stalked Oreah's borders, protecting it from the outside world. Everyone knew of the Manticore, though few had seen it and survived, beyond the passing glimpses traders had of the creature as they entered or exited the forests forming a natural barrier around the realm. Of those who'd sought the creature out to combat it, however, none had returned, proof of its deadly prowess, and a silent warning to all others: none shall trespass here.

Which made Roderick wonder how all these aspirants expected to enter unscathed in the first place?

Yet, except for a passing shadow he thought he saw as they ducked beneath the branches of the first trees, the Manticore didn't appear as he and his newfound traveling companions entered Oreah. Nor did it pick off any of their number as they passed through the forest, weaving their way among the broad trunks, the smell of pine and oak strong all around, the heavy foliage above blocking the sun and providing a cool respite from its warmth. Birds sang, squirrels chittered, rabbits hopped, and wolves howled as the men continued through, until finally the light filtered down once more, and Patience stepped out of the shade. Roderick squinted in the returned sunlight to get his first proper glimpse of this sheltered kingdom.

It was beautiful.

Oreah was a vast, shallow bowl, with the forest circling on two sides and mountains springing up along the other two, rivers and brooks cutting through the former and down from the latter toward a wide lake at the kingdom's center. Small towns and villages dotted the gently sloping landscape, their appearance demonstrating that the realm was far larger than it seemed when one could glance clear across. It was around the lake's far side, with the mountains at its back, that the capital city rose like a small collection of spiky foothills itself, its spires and turrets feeling almost like a miniature of the peaks behind. The land smelled fresh and clean, with hints of flowers and wheat and corn on the wind. Roderick smiled as he let Patience have her head and quicken into a loose trot, both of them enjoying the rustling of the tall grass against the horse's legs and the breeze against their faces.

Yes, the journey had been worth it for this alone. He'd be able to say, afterward, that he'd been to fabled Oreah, where few outsiders had gone, and the memory of its loveliness would brighten his days forevermore. He hoped for nothing more, and so dared to believe that he might not be disappointed.

* * *

"Name?" the stable boy inquired as Roderick swung down out of the saddle, groaning a little as he straightened, the hand not still holding the reins going to his aching back. A seneschal had been waiting by the capital's wide, arching front gates to greet the men and direct them toward the stables off to the side, where stable hands waited to take their horses, and pages stood ready to lead them toward guest quarters.

"Sir Roderick of Altmont," he answered and was surprised when the boy laughed. He was a slim lad, with blond hair pulled back in a braid and freckles across his cheeks and the bridge of his nose, and the high, clear sound made Roderick look again and reassess.

"*Her* name," the stable *girl* corrected, patting his horse's flank while still laughing, then swept into a rough curtsey. "Though it's nice to meet you, Sir Roderick. They call me Mags."

"Nice to meet you as well," he responded, bowing and feeling only slightly foolish about it, for her amusement had seemed too genuine to be taken as mockery. "And her name is Patience." He reached up to stroke his steed's nose, and she responded with an affectionate snuffle.

"Patience? Really?" The girl—and he wondered how he hadn't noticed before—smiled. "Not Thunder or Tempest or Challenger or, I don't know, Skullbasher? Winged Victory?"

That made him chuckle as well. "I find most men name their horses for the virtues they wished they themselves possessed, or the outcomes they wish to achieve," he answered, still petting Patience. "I did the same, and she has indeed helped me in that regard, for she's even-tempered and careful, and would stop me from rushing foolishly into danger, even were I so inclined."

The girl was studying him now, even as her hands were removing Patience's bridle with the ease of long practice. "You're not what I expected a knight to be," she stated frankly, but she did so with that same smile, so he hoped it was more a pleasant surprise than a sour disappointment. Especially when she dipped her head and said, "Welcome to Oreah, Sir Roderick. Good luck to you."

"Thank you." Collecting his saddlebags—a few of the others had arrived with pack steeds trailing behind, but he'd seen no reason for such—he turned toward the boy waiting patiently just outside the stables. This one was a boy in truth, stocky and with a thatch of black hair sticking out every which way. His tabard was that of the kingdom, bright green with a Manticore silhouetted in gold upon his chest, and Roderick wondered at a kingdom that would so honor its most dangerous predator. Then again, the creature served as their protector, so why not respect it?

"This way, Sir Knight," the boy said loudly to be heard over the tumult of men and horses. Roderick nodded and followed the page through the city, admiring the place even as he made sure to keep close to his guide and watch his step. The streets were cobbled, the hard stones tough under his boots but handsome in their pale gray, providing a pleasant contrast to the whitewash of the buildings and their bright doors, window frames, and roofs. It was a cheery place, and the people he passed all seemed healthy and prosperous. Many of them paused to watch him pass, and the other travelers as well, and more than a few smiled and nodded in welcome. He returned each such greeting, feeling as if he were on parade, though he realized that shouldn't come as a surprise. After all, how often had they received such visitors here?

The procession led to the palace, of course, and it was every bit as grand as it had appeared at first glance, and quite a bit larger, for it took nearly two hours to reach it. The outer walls were constructed of the same stone as the street, which Roderick could see must have come from the mountains behind. They gave the entire structure a smooth, almost cloud-like appearance, the faint shift in hues giving it depth and appeal but subtly enough not to detract or mar. Its height and the turrets atop it made the building seem light and fanciful despite its width and obvious strength. Tall, slim windows dotted the structure, and, as they entered, he found the space was well-lit and not at all stuffy, the air within as clean and fresh as without.

The page—Roderick had asked his name and been told, "Tomas, an' it please, sir"—led him into the broad main hall and then up a wide, winding staircase to the left. Some of the others were going the same way, while others had taken a matching staircase to the right. They climbed up a single level—and his knees protested nonetheless, for with such a high ceiling, it had easily been fifty feet—before reaching a long hall. Doors lined it on both sides, and Tomas stopped at one, opening it with a bow. "Your rooms for the duration of your stay, Sir Knight," the boy declared. "If you need aught, just tug the bell pull there. Supper shall be at five."

"Thank you," Roderick told him, taking the hint and entering. He heard the door shut behind him, but was too busy admiring the space to notice much. It was a fine room, warm and bright, with a pair of glass-paned doors leading out onto a small balcony. A large bed stood against one side wall, a massive wardrobe was just beside the hall door, a handsome armchair and small table took up the rest of the outer wall past the balcony doors, and a long dresser sat opposite the bed beside a smaller door that was already open, revealing a wash basin, tub, and garderobe beyond. A quick glance in there confirmed his suspicions, for there were faucets over the basin and tub, and the garderobe was in fact a toilet, complete with a pull chain to flush it. Fascinating! He'd seen indoor plumbing once or twice, but it was still a rare treat. He wondered if all Oreah had such conveniences, or if it was only the palace.

The bed boasted a sturdy mattress, soft enough but not too much so, and it was piled high with thick comforters and pillows. Yet the furnishings, while sumptuous, weren't gaudy, and everything was clearly well made and handsomely carved but lacked excessive detail. If a space's design and ornamentation were indicative of its owner, Roderick surmised that King Tykor must be a wise man, more given to comfort and ease of use than to ostentation.

That, he thought as he set his saddlebags on the dresser and then stepped out onto the balcony, letting the sunlight warm his face, was an emphasis he could appreciate. Especially as the man's guest.

* * *

Shortly before five—Roderick knew this because he'd noticed the clock tower, another rarity, on one side of the city's central square as they'd passed, and thus had been only slightly startled when it had chimed the hour at four—there was a knock upon his door, and Roderick answered it to find Tomas waiting, his hair slightly tamer than earlier. "If you'll follow me, Sir Knight, I'm to lead you down to dinner," the page said, bowing, and Roderick couldn't help but smile. He'd done such duty once himself, but he doubted it had been with such clear enthusiasm.

"Thank you, lead the way," he replied, and the boy did so at once, his quick pace more than making up for his shorter stride and forcing Roderick to quicken his own steps to keep up. "It's beautiful here," he said as they hurried down the hall, where other pages were collecting men from other rooms.

"'Course it is," the boy replied, not slowing down in the slightest as they reached the stairs and began to descend. "Oreah's the best kingdom in the world."

That could have been taken as arrogance from someone older, but in Tomas it seemed merely pride in his homeland. Besides which, Roderick was hardly one to take offense, especially when what little he'd seen so far appeared to support the boy's wild claim.

Once down the stairs, they turned back onto the main hall, proceeding with the gathering crowd toward a pair of massive wooden doors flung wide to reveal an enormous hall beyond. The ceiling here was even higher, enormous beams crisscrossing some seventy or eighty feet up, with colossal chandeliers of wrought iron hanging down and providing light by way of dozens of candles apiece. The extra illumination was barely needed, however, for the back of the room, behind the raised dais, was a sweeping expanse of windows, revealing the majesty of the mountains and, at this time of day, letting in an almost blinding amount of sunlight. Long wooden tables stood in rows to either side of the central aisle, and Tomas led Roderick to a spot along one to the right. Thanking the boy, Roderick took his place there, glad he'd set aside armor for a more comfortable doublet and breeches as he easily swung his legs over the bench and listened to the groans, curses, and creaks of men who'd chosen to come to dinner wearing chain and plate instead. He hadn't even brought his sword, arming himself with only a long dagger, and he tried to hide his smile as he watched and heard others fumbling to adjust their longer blades so as not to hook them under the bench. Did they expect armed battle to commence over the roast goose?

It took some time for everyone to file in and be seated, and Roderick spent that time studying his surroundings. There were more benches pushed back against the walls, and he guessed they would normally be set in rows along either side so petitioners and courtiers alike could attend when the king held court. The benches had neither backs nor cushions, but they matched the one he sat upon now, well-made and sanded smooth, the surface carved out somewhat to provide a more natural seat than a straight plank might. So no coddling, but some consideration, nonetheless. He saw no sign of armed guards, though there'd been a handful standing by the outer gates when they'd arrived, bearing crossbows, pikes, and swords, and garbed in breastplates and helmets. Proficient, no doubt, but it was clear Oreah relied heavily upon its reputation, its natural defenses, and its bestial protector to keep any danger at bay. Get past those, and an army would find little resistance.

His thoughts were interrupted, not by the servers who'd already filled his wine and water glasses so smoothly he'd barely noticed, but by the blare of trumpets from beside the dais. Glancing that way, Roderick watched as the musicians bowed and parted, revealing a man behind them, standing before the large, heavily carved wooden throne. This could only be King Tykor.

"Greetings, one and all," the king declared, his deep, rich, somewhat gravelly voice carrying easily across the expansive space. He was a large man, big and barrel-chested, with a squared head made even more grand by a thick, bristly beard hued somewhere between blond, brown, and red. His green tunic was simple but elegant, edged unobtrusively in gold, but over his shoulders hung a long, stiff cloak of darker red, the edges of which scraped the ground when he moved. From his belt hung a scabbarded sword to one side and a heavy, hooked club to the other—an incongruous enough weapon that Roderick wondered if it might be some ancient rod of office.

Regardless, the man was every inch a monarch, and all attention was upon him as he continued, "I am King Tykor, and I bid you welcome to Oreah.

"I am grateful you have heeded my call," he continued. "I have been fortunate enough to rule here for many years now, and a finer land and finer people you will never see. Yet I near the end of my reign and, with no wife or children, I must think of my people's future and help prepare them for a time when I will no longer sit the throne. Thus my proclamation." He turned and paced as he spoke, his cloak rustling with each step. "Over the next few days, you will be subjected to a series of tests and challenges. At the end of those, I will select my champion. He shall face the Manticore—and if he should prevail, that man shall become my rightful heir." The king smiled and clapped his hands together. "But that is for tomorrow. For tonight, eat, drink, and be merry. Enjoy!" The musicians to either side began to play, a light, happy tune loud enough to fill the air with pleasant song but soft enough to allow conversation, and servers stepped forward to set bowls of soup at each diner's place.

"Nice speech," the man beside Roderick declared, lifting his wineglass and loudly gulping down the contents before continuing. "Seems pretty easy, right? Win a few fights, take down one beastie, get a crown." He belched loudly, wiping wine from his mouth with the back of his hand. "No problem."

Indeed, Roderick thought, smiling and nodding as he sipped more judiciously from his own cup—the wine proved to be a deep red, rich and velvety. Yet why put out a call for so many if you only needed one? Unless the tests were far more challenging than his dinner companion supposed, and the final contest against the Manticore was one only a true champion could hope to survive, much less win?

Well, the food and drink were good, the accommodations excellent, and the next few days promised to be fascinating, if nothing else. He would stay and see what transpired next.

* * *

The revels that night extended quite late, or so Roderick supposed—he'd excused himself when he'd begun yawning, traipsed back to his room, and fell into a solid sleep almost the instant his head collided with the pillow, but many of the other guests had still been carousing when he'd left. Thus he was hardly surprised the next morning when, upon being summoned by Tomas and led back down to the great hall, Roderick found many of the others there groaning, wincing, and resting their heads on their brawny forearms.

"Good morn to you all, my noble guests!" King Tykor announced loudly upon entering with, Roderick thought, a certain amount of malicious glee, the monarch's eyes twinkling at the chorus of groans that rose in response to his exuberant declaration. "I trust you all slept well?" More sounds of displeasure and discomfort. "Well, today we shall start our tests, so eat up, and then we begin!" He clapped his hands together—again, perhaps more vigorously than strictly required—before retreating to his throne, where a server waited to set a breakfast tray before him.

That was something Roderick had noticed the night before, as well. The king had dined with them, in the sense that he'd eaten in the same room and at the same time, yet he'd also kept himself apart, eating alone up on the dais. He'd circled the room afterward, however, stopping every few seats to exchange words with the guests there and inquire about them. Up close, the man had been just as impressive as from a distance, a powerful, majestic figure, every inch a king.

But Roderick had noted the gleam of silver threaded through his host's beard and at his temples, and the creases along the corners of his eyes and above his nose, proof that King Tykor was indeed growing old. *How long has he reigned here*, Roderick had wondered, so last night he'd taken the opportunity to ask exactly that of the man when he'd stopped by.

A few of the nearby guests had gasped at Roderick's audacity, or perhaps it had been guards or courtiers, but the king himself had smiled. "Oh, nearly four decades now," he'd answered readily enough. "I was still but a young man when I came to Oreah." Tykor had sighed. "It was a wild land, then, dangerous and untamed, its people huddled together in a handful of small villages that struggled to survive alone."

"The king united us," one of the servants had offered, an interruption that in and of itself drew surprise from many of the guests, but that the king didn't seem to mind. "He drove off the wild beasts, defeated the brigands, and helped us grow into a kingdom of our own." The look in the man's eye had been one of near worship, and Roderick could see why that might be so. It sounded as if Tykor had singlehandedly brought Oreah to life.

"I merely led the way," the ruler had protested. "It took all of us together to make this land what it is, what it always deserved to be." He'd moved on with a smile and a nod, and talk had turned to the riches of the kingdom itself, and how fine a place it would be to rule. But Roderick had thought that, even if they succeeded in defeating the Manticore, whomever the king chose wouldn't find taking over to be so easy. Not when the small realm had only ever known one liege, and when all here loved him so.

Roderick was still pondering all this when pages appeared to guide them from the room. Their path took them in a new direction, down a side hall, then a short flight of stairs, to a heavy rear door that already stood open, letting in both the early morning sun and the scent of fresh air, nearby water, and trees. He could see the peaks beyond, but between here and there was a wide yard, the ground naught but hard dirt ringed by a sturdy wooden palisade. The space was divided by ropes into several large squares, and it was to one of these that Roderick and the others were taken.

King Tykor stood at the center of the roped-off area, regarding the men now filing in before him. "You'll now be divided into teams of four," he explained. "Your teams will compete against one another in a series of contests, bouts, and mock-battles. You'll only be able to field one person for each contest, so choose wisely. Those who triumph shall advance to the next level, until only one team remains. Good luck." He turned away, and Roderick noticed that stands rose along the far side and across the back of this square, providing seats for any spectators. It was there the king went, while heralds circulated, calling out names and assigning each man a number between one and thirty-two.

Roderick was assigned to Team Seven. When he arrived, his three teammates were already speaking—or at least one of them was. "Clearly, I will handle any contests involving combat," the man in full plate announced, dismissing his two unarmored companions with a sniff and a glance visible through his raised helm, and Roderick with only slightly less condescension. "You'll handle feats of strength," he informed one of the others, a massive man built like a watchtower with broad shoulders, thick arms and legs, and hands the size of a ham. "You—" he studied the second, who was glaring back at him, "—what can you do, precisely?"

The other man's hands were already curled into fists, and though nowhere near their hulking teammate's size, Roderick could tell that the man's wiry frame possessed its own strength. "I can knock you on your arse, for starters," he muttered, his voice rough and thick, his face reddening. "I don't take no orders from you!"

The knight started to retort, his face flushing as well above his neatly trimmed beard, but Roderick stepped in. "We're all on the same team," he pointed out, "so let's try to work together, hm? Why don't we start by introducing ourselves properly, saying who we are and what we're good at? I'll start—I'm Sir Roderick of Altmont. I'm a fair shot with a crossbow, and decent enough on horse, plus I think I can be useful for gauging our opponents." He turned expectantly to the armored figure, who huffed but finally nodded curtly.

"Yes, very well," the other knight replied. "Sir Jasper, Lord Bellamer," he declared haughtily. "And of course I possess all the standard knightly skills: swordplay, jousting, horsemanship, and so on." He set gauntleted hands on his hips with the clang of metal on metal, as if daring any of them to disagree.

"Darin of Longhill," the lean man said, nodding to Roderick. "I'm no knight, sure, but I'm a hunter, an' a good one. You need an archer, a trapper, or a runner, I'm your man."

"I'm Nat," the big man rumbled when it was his turn, his voice soft. "I work on the docks back home, and in the mill, and sometimes on the farm. I'm good with rope and with my hands."

"I fail to understand why anyone not of noble blood was included," Sir Jasper stated huffily, which made Nat hang his head and Darin spit. "Honestly!"

"Because everyone has valuable skills," Roderick argued, careful to keep his own tone mild, even though the man's arrogance was already grating on him as well. Still, Sir Jasper was hardly the first noble he'd met with such an attitude. "Now, let's find out what they've got in store for us, shall we?" He could already tell he'd have his work cut out for him, keeping the lord and the hunter from each other's throats.

Nor was theirs the only team suffering such difficulties. In many of the others, fistfights had broken out, and he saw at least three duels. The palace guards were watching but not interfering, and Roderick saw the king observing everything closely. It was only after the various scuffles had finally ended that a herald cleared his throat. "The first contest will be one of strength," the man declared in a ringing voice. "Choose your champions and send them forth into the ring to compete!"

"Good luck, Nat," Roderick told the big man, and Darin quickly chimed in as well.

Sir Jasper merely nodded and said, "Do not fail us."

While everyone had been getting ready, men had carried, dragged—or, in a few cases, used horses to haul in—crates, barrels, and rocks of various sizes. The competitors were now lined up together at one end near the smallest of these and told to work their way along, lifting each item in turn. Nat fared well, lifting all but the last three items, and Team Seven was one of sixteen teams to continue on.

The next competition was archery, and though Sir Jasper sneered, both Roderick and Nat agreed Darin should handle it. That proved to be the right choice, as he beat out all but one other man, putting all his shots in the center even when the target was a good two hundred yards away.

"Well done!" Roderick and Nat told him when the man returned to where they waited, and Jasper sniffed but grudgingly admitted the same. The field had now narrowed to eight teams.

Then came swordplay. Jasper insisted this one was his, and he proved to be a decent swordsman—but not nearly as good as he seemed to think. The man he faced was younger, taller, and more skilled, disarming Jasper after only a few exchanges.

"Damn and blast!" Jasper snapped when he returned to them, clutching his arm where his opponent's blade had slammed down hard enough to relieve him of his own sword. "That's a low blow, going for the arm like that! Extremely unbecoming! He should be disqualified!"

"It's all right," Roderick told the other knight. "It happens. You put up a good fight." Nat was quick to agree, and Darin at least refrained from rubbing in the lord's defeat. Other teams had filtered into the stands as they'd lost, and Roderick led his teammates there as well, claiming seats so they could watch the final contests. As luck would have it, they found spots not far from the king himself, and Tykor nodded as they approached.

"I'm sorry you didn't get to compete yourself, Sir Roderick," he stated. "I hope you don't feel ill-used for being left out?"

"Not really, no," Roderick replied. "I wouldn't have done half as well as Nat or Darin, or even Sir Jasper, so it was for the best."

"Well put." The king leaned in slightly, continuing their conversation as Roderick sat. "Who do you think will win the day, then?"

Roderick studied the remaining four teams. Two of them had only a single man competing at everything—both of those had been among the groups where teammates had fought for dominance. "Neither of them," he said finally. "They wore themselves out early, forcing the rest of their team to back off, and now they've got no support as a result." The other two teams were rotating through their members, and both contained at least one noble and one commoner, which Roderick suspected was no accident. "Team Nineteen," he decided at last. "I think they've got the best range of skills. But," he added, turning to face his host more fully, "it depends on what the final contests will be, doesn't it?"

"Ha, yes, yes it does," Tykor agreed with a grin. "Let's see if your prediction is correct."

The next match was jousting, and beside him Sir Jasper groaned in disappointment. Roderick didn't share his sorrow at missing out— he'd never liked jousting, and Patience liked it even less. The two dominant knights were clearly exhausted, and both lost their bouts, leaving the other two teams, Four and Nineteen, to reach the final round.

"And our last contest," the herald called out, "shall be—song! Each team's champion shall sing one song, and the audience shall judge who is the victor!"

"A song?" Nat actually laughed at that. "Aw, man. I can sing," he admitted bashfully, and Roderick believed him, for the big man's voice was clear and sweet.

On his other side, though, Sir Jasper was grumbling. "What mockery is this?" he demanded, though softly, since the king was right there. "A battle—of song? Is this contest for knights or jesters?"

"It's for kings," Roderick told him. "And sometimes you need more than a sword or lance to get things done."

Team Four's singer went first, a tall, slim man with long blonde hair who sang a sweet ballad with a lovely, strong voice. Team Nineteen's, in contrast, was a big, burly man who belted out a popular drinking song, his voice rougher but filled with gusto and good cheer. That had been the wiser choice, and Roderick wasn't surprised when Team Nineteen won the bout easily.

"But the other man had the better voice," Nat protested quietly.

Roderick clapped the big man on the shoulder. "He did," he agreed, "but Team Nineteen knew their audience. That was the real test, I think, so they earned that win."

Behind him, he saw King Tykor nod before rising and applauding the victors. "Well done, all!" the king stated. "And do not despair, the rest of you, for there will be another contest on the morrow! In the meantime, I must attend affairs of state. You're free to roam the city and the palace as you wish. I shall see you all at supper." With a quick wave, he marched without ceremony down the stands, those seated in his path shifting to let him pass, and hopped down onto the dirt of the practice yard, heading for the door and disappearing back into the palace.

"Might as well wander a bit, eh?" Darin said as many of the men rose to their feet. "Not often you get to see a place like this, am I right?"

Roderick and Nat both agreed, and the three of them headed off to see the sights together. Sir Jasper had, for an instant, seemed on the verge of joining them, but then had straightened, lifted his chin, and declared that he wished them all a good day, and would surely see them in the great hall later.

"Good riddance," Darin commented after they were out of earshot. "Don't need him lording over us, anyway." He glanced at Roderick. "No offense. For a knight, you're all right."

That made Roderick laugh. "Thanks. For a not-knight, so're you."

* * *

The next morning, after all had eaten, King Tykor called for his guests' attention. "Your next challenge," he declared, "shall be a race! Down the main street, around the palace, and back to the city's front gates. Not on foot, however—no, you will have your trusty steeds for this. Any who arrived on foot may choose from my stables instead. The race begins in two hours' time." He smiled. "Good luck to you all."

Roderick didn't leap to his feet, as some did, but neither did he dawdle. He knew from their arrival that two hours was enough time to reach the stables without having to run, so he crossed the capital at a steady pace but didn't tax himself unduly. There was little point in racing now and being too winded to sit your horse well for the actual competition.

When he finally arrived, most of his rivals were already mounted, and he found Mags the stable hand waiting for him, holding Patience's reins. "You took your time, Sir Knight," she teased as he approached, holding out his hand for the horse to snuffle—and letting Patience take the apple he'd brought along from the breakfast table. "Well, she's happy to see you, at any rate."

"And I her," he replied, resting a hand on his steed's forehead and another on her neck. "You've taken good care of her. Thank you."

"Happy to," Mags answered, patting the horse as well, and receiving a friendly nicker in return. "She's been a pleasure—not like some of her more colorfully named neighbors."

Indeed, Roderick could see what she meant as he hooked his foot in the stirrup and swung himself up into the saddle. Several of the other men were battling their own horses, struggling to control obviously high-strung, and in some cases clearly ill-tempered, mounts. "That's the problem with choosing a horse for speed and aggression," he said, as much to Patience as Mags. "You get what you ask for." He stroked Patience's mane and tapped her sides with his heels, guiding her into an easy walk out of the stables and into the yard beyond. "As did I."

The king was standing at the front of the yard, guards to either side and a herald there with a long horn. "Riders, prepare yourself!" Tykor shouted, raising one arm. "And—" he swept his hand down, and the herald blew a mighty blast, "—be off!"

Roderick nudged Patience, and she leaped forward—past several horses that had shied at the sudden noise, and some still fighting their masters. At least a dozen others had managed to retain control, however, so Patience found herself in the middle of a small pack as it coursed down the street. The residents had clearly been warned, for the cobbled avenue was clear, and people waved and cheered from upper windows as the riders raced on by.

Patience was by no means a racehorse, and she slowly fell farther and farther back as bigger, stronger horses surged ahead. But Roderick wasn't concerned, for he remembered what it appeared some of the others hadn't—that this was a race there and back again.

By the time they neared the palace, the street widening to form the semicircular courtyard at its fore, a few of the other horses were already slowing, their muscles straining and lather forming at their mouths. Patience, on the other hand, was still breathing well, and maintained her pace as they rounded the back of the building—circling the same yards where everyone had competed the day before—and, returning to the courtyard and the road beyond, began the journey back.

All along the return, Patience passed other horses that had staggered to a stop or were limping along at barely a walk, and Roderick felt for the steeds. They'd done their best; it wasn't their fault. He saw more than a few of his opponents screaming at their failing mounts, and a few kicking or whipping theirs, and winced in both sympathy and anger. But he couldn't stop, nor was it his place to discipline the men. Still, what manner of person punished an animal for doing as it was told?

He reached the stables in perhaps the second handful, and was pleased to see Mags waiting for him there. "You made it!" she declared as he reined in and dismounted, patting Patience once he did. "And she's not lamed!"

"I did, and she's not," he agreed, groaning a little as his legs protested having been stretched for so long. "She did very well, as I knew she would." The stable hand offered him a carrot, and he bowed gratefully before presenting the treat to Patience, who gobbled it up. "Good girl," he assured the horse, whose ears flicked in response.

"You did well, Sir Roderick," someone stated behind him, and he turned to find the king standing there. "Seeing your horse earlier, I'm sure some would be surprised."

Roderick bowed, then shrugged. "Patience isn't the swiftest," he admitted, "but then, neither am I. She's solid and steady, calm and good-natured, and that suits me nicely." He glanced fondly after the horse Mags was leading back to her stall. "We work well together."

"Indeed you do. I often find that you can tell a lot about a man by how he treats others—and even more by how he treats animals," Tykor remarked. He smiled and turned away, and Roderick couldn't help but think, given the way some of his fellows had behaved today, that had been a telling remark indeed.

* * *

"Your final contest shall start tomorrow morning," the king announced at dinner that night, as many of the men groaned along the tables, feeling their aches and pains and lamenting their losses. "It will be a hunt in the forest. Each of you may arm yourself as you see fit. You will have the day, and you will be judged by what you return with."

"In the forest?" one man asked, and Roderick noted that it was Sir Jasper. "But what of the Manticore? Does the beast not dwell there?"

"It has been seen among the woods, yes," Tykor agreed, "but whether it dwells there or not, who can say?"

"What if we bring *that* back?" someone else called out, a big, burly man who'd done well in the feats the first day. "That's the final challenge anyway, right? So what if we make an early start of it and bring back the Manticore's head?"

"You may hunt whatever you choose—save each other and my people," the king responded. "How you fare against your chosen prey will help determine how you rank in the final contest."

He sipped at his wine then, clearly unwilling to say more, but a great many of the others were now muttering to each other, and Roderick saw smirks and smiles on several faces. It was clear many had the same idea as the big man, to shortcut the trials by finding and defeating the Manticore now instead of waiting.

"What do you think?" Darin asked. He and Nat had found Roderick before the meal and invited him to sit with them, which he'd happily accepted. Neither man had arrived in Oreah on horseback, so each had taken one of the king's own horses for the race, which was perhaps why both of them had at least finished the course, since they hadn't wanted to risk their host's displeasure by overworking one of his own mounts. Now the hunter was fingering the bone handle of his long knife as he considered the task ahead. "I'm not worried about anyone returning with more game than me, but if someone bags the Manticore—" He shook his head.

"I wouldn't worry about that," Roderick answered. "If it were so easy to defeat, it would have been vanquished long ago. No, worry about the hunt for now. Let the rest sort itself out in due time."

His friends nodded, and the three of them returned to discussing the race, the horses, the woods, and other things, while all around them men ate, drank, and schemed. Once or twice Roderick glanced up and found King Tykor watching him, and each time he raised his goblet in salute, which the king acknowledged with a nod.

Yes, he was sure the monarch was learning a great deal about his guests from their actions tonight. Perhaps even more than he would from what they did and what they brought back tomorrow.

* * *

"That's all you're taking?" someone scoffed nearby, and Roderick turned to find the big man from the night before watching him with a sneer. He was decked out as if for battle, with a longbow and quiver of arrows slung over his broad shoulder, a brace of throwing knives across his chest, a pair of hatchets at his side, and a long javelin in his hand.

Roderick glanced down at the crossbow he'd selected and shrugged. "I'm not much of a hunter," he admitted, "and I'd be just as likely to hurt myself as anything else if I tried lugging all that, much less using it."

"Well, fine by me," the big man declared with a laugh, swatting him on the shoulder hard enough to stagger him. "The less real competition, the better." He stomped off, still chuckling, and Roderick watched him go for a moment, wondering, *What if the man's right, and I'm dooming myself to failure?*

Then again, trying to hunt with unfamiliar weapons would be equally defeating, and a whole lot more dangerous. No, best to stick with the crossbow. That, at least, he knew how to use.

"Good luck," Darin called, and Roderick nodded in return. The hunter was carrying a longbow and arrows as well, and a long knife or two at his side, but he looked comfortable with them, and still moved easily toward the palace's front doors. Nat was nearby and waved, armed only with a thick staff and a hatchet, but Roderick wouldn't want to get in the way of either of those when the big man brought them down.

They'd all eaten and been offered full use of the palace's armory to equip themselves, and now they were being shown out. The forest was all around, of course, and they'd been given no instructions beyond, "Return at dusk with whatever you've gathered from your hunt."

King Tykor had been present while they ate, then had wished them all luck and departed. Perhaps he was squeamish at the thought of his land's deer, pheasants, and rabbits being slaughtered?

The day was pleasant, just a touch warm but with the heat offset by a breeze, and Roderick traipsed out through the city gates, then turned left, his boots trampling the long grass as he made for the nearest outcropping of trees. Might as well begin.

It was cooler beneath the trees, the leaves blocking much of the light, and Roderick was glad he'd worn both a long shirt and a cloak. He waited a moment, blinking to let his eyes adjust, then glanced about, studying his surroundings.

The trees here were old, for one thing. They were tall, with broad trunks and thick limbs well above his head. A younger man—or a nimbler one—might try climbing and claiming a perch there to fire down upon whatever creatures passed below. But Roderick was not so agile. Instead, he studied the ground for any sign of tracks, and listened for any hint of creatures moving around. Over the rustling of leaves from the wind, and the creak of branches, he could hear nothing. So, with a sigh, he began to walk, keeping alert for anything he might find.

After some time he came to a small brook, and there he paused to drink from its water, which was cold and clear. He was still crouched, enjoying the feel of the cool liquid across his fingers, when he heard a sound nearby.

Not daring to move, Roderick glanced to the side, able to see despite the sudden shadows that had fallen across the brook, and beheld a lithe, dappled figure. It crept closer, its ears twitching, its large eyes wide, but either it didn't see him, or it chose to believe he wouldn't harm it, for the doe continued forward until it dipped its delicate face into the water to drink.

Carefully, Roderick lowered his hand to his side. The crossbow lay there on the ground, and he was able to pick it up quietly. A quarrel lay in the channel, the bow already cocked. All he need do was line up the shot and pull the trigger. He was astonished at his luck.

He was still raising the weapon when the bushes rustled just behind the deer—and a second, smaller creature emerged, much like the doe in miniature. The fawn toddled forward, reaching its mother's side with an awkward scramble, then also began to drink.

Roderick watched them a moment. He knew he could still take the deer, just as he knew many of his recent companions would. Perhaps even Darin and Nat. He crouched there without moving, the crossbow heavy in his hands, as the doe and her fawn drank their fill. And he remained there as they finished, lifted their heads, then wheeled about and darted off, vanishing into the bushes once more. Only then did he set the crossbow back down and relax.

His hand had barely left the weapon when the shadows suddenly shifted—and a massive figure leaped down from the trees above to land beside the water, facing him from only a few feet away.

Roderick couldn't move. All he could do was stare at this new sight, this horrid apparition. It was easily wider than Patience, and nearly as tall, its body covered in a thick, tawny fur, its paws massive, the claws as long as a good knife and far sharper, hooked like a bird's talons. Its great crimson bat wings had flared behind it as it leaped, but now furled again, their curved tips still hovering over its broad shoulders, and its tail arched up behind, waving ominously like a striking snake, the length of it segmented, armored, and flaring out before its deadly tip. But it was the head that had Roderick so paralyzed, that great thick mane—and the very human face within it.

A face he'd seen before, as recently as this morning.

"You didn't take the shot," the Manticore said, its voice a deeper rumble but still recognizable as the one that had wished them all luck. "Why not?"

Roderick studied this impossible creature, and slowly his composure returned, and with it his wits. Now he saw the hints he'd missed before: the strangely heavy cloak, the spiked club, the bristly beard. Even the name—he laughed as he got the joke, which made the monster smile. "You're the Manticore," he said softly, "yet you disguise yourself as a man. The man Tykor. Man-ti-cor." He shook his head, that bit of humor somehow allaying some of his fear, and recalled the question. "I couldn't," he answered honestly. "It had a fawn."

"But you might now return empty-handed," the Manticore pointed out, as if they were merely two men discussing such a thing, rather than a man and a monster.

Roderick shrugged. "I never expected to catch much game," he replied, straightening and rising to his feet but choosing to leave the crossbow on the ground where it sat, "and I'll not deprive the little one of its mother."

The Manticore nodded its great head and padded closer, but its eyes seemed wise and kind, and Roderick found he still felt little fear. "You're a good man, Sir Roderick of Altmont," it declared. "I've watched you. You set your ego aside to support your teammates. You treat others well, people and animals alike. You don't talk down to anyone, regardless of station. You're careful, and thoughtful, and kind." It smiled, revealing many rows of sharp teeth, yet the expression didn't seem designed to scare him. "I like you."

"Thank you." Roderick dipped his head. "I've never been liked by a Manticore before." He laughed, surprised at his own calm. "So what happens now?"

"Now," the creature replied with the hint of a growl, the sound making Roderick's knees quiver, "I must continue my rounds. Not all your fellows are as considerate, and some must be dissuaded from harming those in my care." He turned to go, but Roderick shifted, and the Manticore glanced back. "Yes?"

"I'm sorry," Roderick said. "Can I ask, though—I just don't understand. You protect these lands, clearly, both as their king and as the Manticore. Why the contest, then? Why look for an heir?" He sighed, seeing the danger that could come from winning rather than losing. "Even the best of us could never do what you do. If you leave, this land will be defenseless, and quickly overrun."

"It would," the monster agreed, "but I'm not going anywhere." It studied him, its eyes thoughtful, kind, and a touch sad. "Manticores are immortal," it said at last, "but as we age, we lose some of our reason, and some of our skills. I cannot maintain my other form much longer."

"Ah." Roderick nodded, comprehending at last. "You need someone to become king after you, but you still mean to protect the realm as well." He smiled. "Oreah is lucky to have a guardian such as you."

"Thank you." The Manticore dipped its head, and when it looked back up, it was smiling as well. "I think they will be lucky to have you as well, Sir Roderick." It bared its teeth, spread its wings, and leaped up into the trees once more, its words echoing behind it: "We will speak more of this later. Good luck with your hunt."

"And you with yours," Roderick called after it, though he didn't know if the creature heard him. After a moment he retrieved the crossbow, wiping it clear of mud. He had no intention of using it now, but he didn't want to return it in poor condition. Then, whistling softly, he continued on his trek, looking at the surrounding woods a bit differently now.

In the end, he returned to the palace with a pouch full of wild mushrooms and an approximate capful of tiny, tart strawberries, both of which he presented with a flourish to the palace cooks—except for some of the strawberries, which he was saving for Mags and for Tomas. Many of the other men—those who made it back, for not everyone did, and even some of those took immediately to their horses and fled the kingdom without another word—laughed at his poor showing, but Roderick only smiled, feeling a good deal more optimistic about his chances now than at any point before.

He had, after all, already faced the Manticore.

* * * * *

Aaron Rosenberg Biography

Aaron Rosenberg is the author of the best-selling *DuckBob* SF comedy series, the *Relicant Chronicles* epic fantasy series, the *Dread Remora* space-opera series, and with David Niall Wilson the *O.C.L.T.* occult thriller series. His tie-in work contains novels for *Star Trek*, *Warhammer*, *World of Warcraft*, *Stargate: Atlantis*, *Shadowrun*, and *Eureka*. He has written children's books (including the award-winning *Bandslam: The Junior Novel* and the #1 best-selling *42: The Jackie Robinson Story*), educational books, and roleplaying games (including the Origins Award-winning *Gamemastering Secrets*). Aaron lives in New York. You can follow him online at gryphonrose.com, at facebook.com/gryphonrose, and on Twitter @gryphonrose.

* * * * *

Beast Intervention
by Mel Todd

A Little Magics Story

"**M**oby Beast Intervention, how may I help you?" I answered the desk phone by rote, not paying much attention as I took the call. "Yes, ma'am, there's a rash of rabid jackalopes going on. No, you don't need to call us. The local were-packs have contracted out to dispose of them." I nodded, drawing doodles on my desk. "Normally I help when a unicorn fixates on a maiden, or you've got a hoop snake swarm at your place. I can get grims to back off, or if you've got a wyvern infestation, I can get them transferred to a safe tree."

Most magical animals were protected, and killing them got you in a lot of trouble, but they weren't common enough to give me a steady paycheck.

I rubbed my forehead as I listened to the woman babble. "Yes, ma'am. If you see a cerberus or drunk bear, give me a call. Thanks, you too." The phone went back on its cradle. I didn't really mind that the local werewolf pack had taken the jackalope job—rabid creatures didn't communicate well—but still, it would be nice to have a paying job occasionally. At the rate I was going, I'd need to get a second job just to afford my first one.

Time to go home. And I needed to look for gas. Leaded was getting harder to find. Well, all gas was, and it was a bit too far to walk from my house to my office. Though if business didn't pick up soon, I'd lose the office.

I shut the doors, the faded letters reading: "Jonah Moby – Beast Intervention." My magic wasn't great, not like my ex-wife's. She was a fifth-level metal bender, which meant she could work with five metals. It also meant she made much more than a lowly beast whisperer, and she'd left for greener pastures, leaving me trying to make a living without my wife or son.

That was the past. It didn't matter anymore. My son hated me, and trying to convince him I wasn't the man my ex said I was had always failed. Pizza. I should grab pizza and a movie. Maybe Blockbuster had something new in. I thought I'd seen an ad for that movie *Tron* at the video store. Fancy idea, living in games.

Pizza was easier than cooking, and Blockbuster was better than thinking. I pulled up to my house with a loaded pie and a video. No *Tron*, but something called *Clash of the Titans*. I'd heard they used real pegasi in it, as well as a cameo from a true gorgon. Pegasi were rare, while unicorns were a dime a dozen, and lecherous stalkers to boot. Walking up to my house, I balanced the pizza in one hand with the VHS tucked under my arm. I fumbled with my key, trying to unlock the door without dropping pizza or movie.

It was a small cottage, a Craftsman that I'd tried to keep up, but my skills weren't the best, and inevitably I had jobs on the weekends when—theoretically—I could try to talk someone into helping me. I needed more human friends. The neighborhood dogs were great for local gossip, and the cats wonderful for keeping my house vermin free, but none of them were much help at fixing stuck windows.

"Jonah Moby?" a voice called behind me. I turned, trying not to drop the pizza or the video. Dropped pizza was still edible, just messier, but they charged a lot if you damaged the video cassettes.

A man stood at the edge of my yard, watching me. He was about my age—which meant late forties—with dark brown hair and circles under his eyes. But the important part was the sheriff's uniform. I backtracked my gaze from him to the four-wheeled sheriff's Jeep behind him. I needed to pay more attention to my surroundings. I also suspected I wouldn't be watching my video tonight.

"Last time I checked," I said. I turned back, unlocked the door, and set the video down on the table in the hall as I heard steps from the deputy. I kept the pizza.

"Heard you were the best around?" he said, his voice doubtful as he looked me up and down. I frowned, holding my pizza and tugging down my flannel shirt, suddenly self-conscious. The last woman I'd dated swore no cool guys wore them. I didn't care. They were comfortable, had pockets, and best of all, didn't show slobber or blood stains easily.

"Best? Doubt that. There's lots of people better at the animal gig than me. In the area, though—well, probably." One of the good sides of living near the Cascades was there weren't too many people out here, but a big city was only two hours away. Granted, I didn't know of any other Whisperers within five hundred miles, but that didn't mean much when the Yellow Pages was local.

"So you do that…talk to animals, I mean." He still didn't look like he believed me. Not my problem.

"So, you need something? I've got a pizza going cold and a movie to watch."

"Yeah, Sheriff McAlister sent me to grab you. Said he's got a situation and needs you ASAP."

That gave me pause. Samuel McAlister didn't hold much with magic, but he didn't have a problem using it, or the people with it, to solve a problem. Though usually he preferred a non-magical way.

"Come on. We better get going. He's going to be pissed I've been gone this long. Get in. I'll drive."

Curiosity, and the suspicion he'd throw me in the Jeep if I didn't come, got me walking. "Bringing my pizza," I stated as I moved to the passenger side.

"Suit yourself, just don't make a mess in my car."

I opened the passenger door and snorted. This guy wouldn't notice if I left the pizza box in the trashcan that was his car. After sweeping fast food bags onto the floor, I climbed in, positioning my feet over the six inches of detritus that rode in the bottom.

The deputy had his radio pulled out from the dash. "Margaret. I've got him. Headed back that way now, fast and loud."

"Ten-four," came the response from Margaret Attworth. I'd gone to school with her, but she'd quit talking to me when I blossomed with magic and she hadn't. It was too bad. She'd been a right hotty in high school.

I pulled out a piece of pizza and managed two bites before he slammed the Jeep into gear, grinding them enough that I winced. Then he tore out of the small street I lived on, lights and siren blaring. The idea of pumping him for information flashed through my mind, but if it was odd enough to need me, I should eat now. The pizza still tasted good as he tore through Tulamac, splashing in puddles and crossing more than one small bridge with the water lapping at the top.

Between the rains lately and an early spring heat wave, the rivers had been full of melting snow. To occupy my mind and avoid thinking about being a victim in a roll-over crash, I went over what possible creatures could be involved that might have been brought in or driven out by the rain.

Kelpies were unlikely. They preferred oceans. Streams and the occasional river didn't qualify. Selkies were humanoids in their own right, but again, ocean. It could always be a water dragon, or even something non-magical like river otters. But off the top of my head, I couldn't really think of many things that existed in the Northwest, associated with water, that would require my unique skills.

Granted, I was making a lot of assumptions, but it kept me busy, and not paying attention to how the deputy drove. I closed my eyes and focused on the pizza. Three slices had disappeared into my now much happier stomach, and I was debating the merits of eating a fourth when he jerked to a stop.

"Sheriff's over there. Hope you can help."

I gave him a side-eyed look as I got out. There'd been too much worry in his voice. I brought my pizza box with me. Sometimes these situations were like a firehose. Other times they were like watching a boring baseball game. That's why I prefer hockey.

We'd stopped in one of the areas where construction companies had been building nicer townhomes on the side of the hill. They were much more than I could afford, but right now three of them were sliding down the hill in a river of mud. They made my little two-bedroom, one bath house seem like a palace. The building had slipped down the hillside and fallen over backward, the base of it exposed to the air. It looked like a sad toy house knocked over by a toddler's temper tantrum.

"I need that damn animal out of here now!" a man in a fire jacket with the word "Captain" across the back yelled, facing down the sheriff. "I don't care what you do, I want it gone *now*."

"Bert, I get that, but if you don't quit yelling in my face, I'm going to toss you in the back of a squad car to cool off." Sheriff Samuel McAlister was a long, lean man who looked like he had to stoop to get through any door in town. I'd never had a problem with him, but at the same time, I'd also never shared a drink with him.

I looked around, trying to see what animal they were talking about, even as my gut twisted in knots. Situations like this almost always meant one thing. They wanted me to get the animal far enough away they could kill it and get on with rescuing humans.

I hate jobs like these. Most of the time I had more sympathy for the animal than the humans. Even peering around, I couldn't see what animal it was, and I weighed the odds of if I'd be able to walk away right now. When you could talk to the critters, it made it hard to help kill them.

I watched the fire engines and firemen standing and staring at the building, as well as the cops. It struck me as funny that no one moved toward the house. With a shake of my head, I made my way over.

My feet stumbled to a halt as a man stuck his head out of one of the windows near the top of the building facing the sky, yelling. "She says her water just broke! What am I supposed to do?"

The panic in the man's voice wasn't what stopped me, it was that I recognized the voice.

"Peter?" I barely whispered the word, talking more to myself. When had I last seen my son? I'd received a notice he'd gotten married. At least I didn't feel bad about not being invited to it, since they'd gotten married in Vegas. One of the Sphinxes ran a marriage chapel down there, and my ex had sent pictures of him and his bride. I assumed it had been a spur-of-the-moment thing, though his wife's dress had been pretty.

If she was going into labor now, it put things in a different light. But he still wouldn't want me here.

With a shake of my head, I approached the gaggle of men standing there, catching sight of a few people standing by, looking shook up. When had this building collapsed, and how long had they been standing there? Based on the outfits of the people standing around—no one was in bathrobes or nightshirts—that placed it at earlier today. I checked my watch, an old Timex that still worked. It read 7:48. Probably happened this afternoon. The rain had let up about three hours ago. It was summer, so at least another hour before it got too dark.

"Sheriff McAlister? You had a deputy bring me?" I didn't let my eyes stray to Peter's window. Instead, I set my eyes on the man who'd summoned me.

McAlister turned and looked at me, eyes blank for a brief second, then they cleared. "Ah, Jonah Moby. Thanks. We've got an issue, and I think you're the only person who can clear this up without bloodshed."

That comment made me feel better, but the whimpering from the apartment building and a woman's cries of labor made me cringe.

"What's the issue?" I asked, looking at the building again. Surely they didn't think I could fix *this*. The back of the building was against the ground, while the sides of it held nothing but small bathroom windows. The front was up in the air, as were the majority of the access points. Even if the bathroom windows were easily accessible, the idea of getting a pregnant woman through them was laughable. The torn-up foundation gaped out at the world like the underskirts of a fallen southern belle.

"I'm sure you can see the building," he said dryly.

I just nodded. Mouthing off to the sheriff would do nothing but get me into hot water.

He continued, "We need to climb up the foundation and get in the front door. We know there's a couple in there—she's in labor—and we have one other, a teen with a broken arm. But we can't get in." Here his voice changed, and he sounded frustrated and sad.

"Why?" I knew he wanted me to ask.

"Because we have a barghest blocking the way and threatening anyone who gets close to the building."

Enlightenment and worry struck at the same time. He had a problem. Barghests were huge, dog-like creatures that had jaws with a crocodile's biting power, what looked like flame in their eyes, and they could open passages to the Hell realms. Normally they didn't bother humans, but when they did, killing wouldn't be difficult for them. They could be killed with mundane weapons—no silver or blessed steel needed—but it took basically cutting off their head. They healed fast, were strong and very intelligent, not to mention about the size of a small pony. They also didn't particularly like humans.

He paused long enough for the clue to sink into my head, and I nodded, showing that I saw the problem. "The creatures are protected, and while I could kill it, I don't want the Magical Animal Protection Agency sticking their noses in."

I didn't bother to repress my snort. MAPA was a pain in everyone's ass, especially mine. They felt that because I could talk to the animals, I should volunteer my time, and do nothing but translate for them. I avoided that like crazy, as none of the idiot bleeding hearts could handle what most of the magical beasts thought of them.

"Would you go talk to it and get it to let us in to get those people out of there?"

I glanced up at the building, my eyes locking on the window Peter had stuck his head out of. Was the woman his wife, or someone else? Did I have a grandchild on the way? I swallowed and focused on the sheriff.

"That's what I do," I said, pretending it was another day on the job. It wasn't, but men have to keep up appearances.

McAlister seemed to sag a bit. "Good. The beast keeps circling the building and whining. If it was a trained dog, I'd think it was trying to tell us something, but hell if I know." He rubbed his long face and sighed. "Go. We'll talk money later."

I nodded. I wasn't really planning on charging, no matter how tight money was. Granted, that was *why* money was tight. I didn't push for money enough. At this rate, I might need to use my CPA degree and become a bookkeeper. At least my bills were organized.

Walking toward the house, I stared at it more, trying to figure out why there'd be a barghest here. The hill above had been nicely forested until the house slid down it. Obviously, the foundation of the house had only been on dirt. The responders and gawkers stayed back at the road edge, and I moved deeper in. The lights from the vehicles made weird shadows, and I couldn't see anything.

Go way. Me kill.

The words galvanized me, and I spun to see a black shape disengage from the shadows. Everyone else probably heard growls and a woof, but I heard the meaning behind the words. Animals don't just talk with sound, but with their body and scent, as well. With my human nose, not even magic could help me with most of those, besides the ones that shouted, like skunks, but my magic could take care of the rest.

I crouched, though that put the barghest's head above mine, and spoke. While my words sound like English to anyone who might be listening, or at least bad American, magic lets it and my body communicate, hence me crouching. I didn't have ears that could move, or a tail, but I could look submissive and watch my eye contact. By this point in my life, it was almost automatic. Barghests are canines, and they tend to respond to similar language.

"No harm. Rescue our people." I pointed up. "Bitch whelping." Okay, English, but it needed to match the animal's world view, which made talking to dolphins very frustrating.

Hurt mine. Make suffer. Pay.

I stood there trying to translate, then frowned, looking around. "Your pups, hurt?"

Trapped, must get out!

The voice had panic and anger in it, and everything snapped into place for me. The apartment building must have come down on the den with her pups in there. I reached down to tug on my pants leg and looked closely at her belly. Sure enough, I could see swollen teats on her.

"We can rescue. Where?" I looked around, trying to see the opening to a den.

At least I could try, if they weren't already dead. This could end badly for everyone, including my son and soon to be grandchild. Tension made my back tight, and the barghest stalked forward a bit, ears perked up.

Help? You! Now!

She growled. Nothing that I needed my magic to understand.

"One minute." I turned and moved back a bit. "Sheriff McAlister?"

He stepped out of the crowd. "Get it to leave?"

"Her, and no. Her pups are trapped, I suspect, under the house. I said I'd try to rescue them."

He cussed and kicked the ground. "I don't have any equipment to do that, and she's freaking out most everyone. How the hell are we going to rescue pups when we can't talk and have no idea where to go?"

"I'll go. The ground is soft enough, and I should be able to get in. They build large dens. Can you get me some oxygen, gloves, and a small shovel?"

All in all, it was a good thing I wasn't claustrophobic. They provided the requested equipment in a few minutes. I headed back to the female, hoping I wouldn't get killed trying to do this.

"Take me. I help."

The barghest stood there for a long time, looking at me. Then she turned and spun toward the other side of the house. I followed, turning the corner as another barghest came at me. I flinched back, lifting my arms for the attack, but the male raced past me, growling. A mated pair, one protecting that side of the house, the other this side. That made sense. I swallowed my terror and followed her. There was a tunnel leading under the fallen building.

I've never been a big man. Wiry was the term most people used when describing me. Well, my ex-wife used "loser" a lot, but I topped out at five foot five and barely made 120. The barghest weighed more than I did by probably a hundred pounds.

"Why haven't you dug them out?" I looked at the female as she whined, staring at the hole.

Hard. Not stone. Blocking. Pup hurt.

That could mean one or all, and it could also mean dead. And "not stone" didn't mean much to me. I really wanted a second person here, but they were already trembling on a razor wire of stress and fear. If they lost control, they could kill too many people before someone managed to kill them. Barghests are tough, and the knowledge of the amount of pain MAPA would bring made me shudder.

I was wearing my normal attire; jeans, hiking books, a t-shirt, and a flannel shirt. The gloves they gave me would help, but I wondered if I'd need more than the shovel. No way to know except to go in.

"I'm going to go in. Try to get your pups."

Go. Rescue. Or I Kill. Kill them all until mate and I die.

Canines, always so direct. I inched my way through the tunnel. The barghest had dug it well, and normally the soil here was thick and strong, but a month of rain had made everything soft. Mud covered me in the first five minutes. The air tank on my back scraped as I wiggled on through, but at least I'd have a little time if the tunnel collapsed. There were days I wondered about my sanity, but the idea of pups down here dying in the darkness would've made me do this, and had made me do even crazier things. I could still get free drinks off the story involving Roc eggs.

I'd crawled about seven feet down, the lamp on the breathing apparatus letting me see the way, when I found the "not stone." It took me a minute to figure out what I was seeing. Best guess was that concrete steps from the building above had been shoved down and blocked the tunnel, making it so they couldn't get in. There was a tree to one side, and if I dug under it, mud just flowed down. There were deep gouges in the cement, and I could see traces of blood where the barghests' claws had torn.

I lay there and thought for a minute. I could hear the growls behind me, but I didn't talk to her. I keyed the radio McAlister had handed me.

"Sheriff, it's Jonah. Anyone got dry or rot magic up there?" Sometimes people had little magics that made life easier, but weren't enough to do anything with. The big magics got you power and impressive jobs. Little magics like mine had niches, but others were too small to even worry about except when you wanted to dry off after the rain.

"*One minute.*" His voice was distracted. I heard more screaming. "*Got a decay, not much range though,*" he said. "*What do you need?*"

"There's a tree the building has mostly knocked down. I've got a root ball next to me that I need to get through. Can they decay it so I can hack?"

"Need to get the dogs to let them get that close," the sheriff said. "But yeah, they're nodding their head."

"One minute." I wiggled backward. "Human come. Move tree. Let me get to pups."

I could hear a low growl but then, *Yes. Tree block. Move tree.*

The radio crackled a minute later. *"Okay, they let us near. Now if they'd let us into the damn building."* I didn't ask questions. Details as to what was going on wouldn't help. *"Wood is decayed, try now."*

I didn't have much room to move, but I thrust the shovel at the tree blocking my way, and it started to crumble. It took ten frustrating minutes with the barghest threatening to kill everyone behind me, plus the muffled whine of puppies, and sweat pooling down my back. Finally, I got the tree out of the way and continued to wiggle my way in.

My elbows were scraped raw, and I was pretty sure this flannel shirt would be in the rag pile when I got out, but I made it into the den and saw the pups. They were young, barely had their eyes open, and weren't at the walking stage, more at the cute tumble stage. Another two weeks, and they could have crawled out. They were all crying, high-pitched yelps that got more frantic when they realized a human was in their midst.

A warning growl echoed down the tunnel, along with her words. *Hurt them, I kill all humans. Kill whelping bitch.*

"No hurt I. I help." Working with an upset mother was never the easiest thing, but right now I needed to focus on getting them out. It was a largish litter, five pups, but the one that had me worried was the one trapped by a pipe that had speared down through the mud. From the cries, it was badly hurt and getting weaker.

Even though I'd dragged the shovel in here, there wasn't enough room for me to do anything to get under the pup to get it free. I racked my brain. I could try to dig, but she'd used claws to get down this far. A round hole got my attention.

"Anyone down there?" I called, using my animal call. It was the only thing I could think of. While I waited, I checked on the other pups. They were all healthy, if hungry, according to their cries. They enjoyed me rubbing their ears, and I kept them occupied while I tried to think what else I could do if no one responded to my call.

Two minutes later, a brown head cautiously poked out of the hole, and I smiled in relief. A gopher. They weren't the brightest creatures, but where there was one, there were four or more. They could help, if I could convince them.

"Help, rescue pup. Dig out?" I pointed under the whimpering pup.

It looked at me, nose twitching. *Why? What get?*

I swallowed a sigh. Rodents are the most mercenary of all the creatures. I got on the radio. "Sheriff?"

"*Yeah.*" He sounded abrupt and stressed. I didn't ask.

"Got any nuts or fruit or bread up there?"

A pause, then a grunt. "*Got some honey roasted peanuts. Why?*"

"Nuts. Spread when pup free."

The gopher jerked its head back in, chittering going on in the depths of that hole, and then a head poked back out. You didn't lie, ever, to animals. I'd heard of one whisperer who did, and no animal would touch or work with him after that. Even pets would have nothing to do with him. You kept your word, always.

Five of them squirmed out of the hole and started to dig under the hurt one. While they did that, I wiggled out of my shirt. That involved getting the oxygen tank off first, then the shirt. I tied it into a bag and carefully picked up the pups and put them in it. They tumbled around, yipping, but there was no fear or pain. Now if I could get the last one in and get out of here.

I ducked and pulled the pups close to me as the ground rumbled, and mud and dirt fell, bouncing off my back. I was sure the ceiling had gotten lower, and there was a small whine of pain from the injured pup as the pipe moved.

"What's going on?" I barked out on the radio.

"*Better get out of there soon, the house is shifting again, these damn dogs are about to get shot, and I don't want to do that much paperwork,*" McAlister snarled back. "*They're going crazy. They keep diving into the hole and back, and the one staying out here circles and lunges at anyone who gets close to the house. I really don't want to kill them.*"

"I've almost got them out. Just give me another ten." I shoved the radio back down, ignoring whatever else he said over the radio.

Chitter, chitter got my attention, and I turned.

Free. Nuts?

The gophers had done exactly what I needed, their small bodies much more suited to digging out a small pup than my hands.

"Nuts, up ground, when out."

Another chitter of agreement, and they dove back down the holes. I'd have to tell the barghest about their help. I managed to turn around again, already exhausted. If I got exhausted this easily, it meant age was creeping up on me. Maybe I'd have to put some of that aerobics stuff on my list to try.

I gently lifted the pup, cringing at the cries of pain. "It's okay, little one. Let's get you out of here." It looked like it had a nasty gash on its flank, and possibly a broken bone, but nothing obvious. That was good. Hopefully it would heal.

I kill you! The momma had her body mostly in the hole, snarling at me.

"He's fine. You knew he was hurt. Back up so I can get them out. All of them."

She growled once more, glaring at me, but scooted back, and I put the whimpering pup in my shirt. The others huddled around it, and they quit crying.

"Hush. Safe. Momma soon." I said the words softly as I got the air tank back on and turned so I could get all of us back out of the hole. With a heave, I managed to push and pull my squirming bundle ahead as I worked my way back out. I'd gotten the pups out past the concrete corner of the building when a rumble hit. I threw my body over the pups, arching up as more clumps of dirt fell down on us, some of them hitting like a baseball. A long, low groan vibrated the surrounding ground, and the building shifted.

The scream that ripped out of my throat as my leg snapped terrified the pups. The momma was back down there in seconds, fear making her froth.

Hurt?

I swallowed down the scream, but I couldn't stop the tears from flowing out as I tried not to sob. "Me. They not hurt." I rolled back a bit, uncovering them, and they were all there. Wiggling and whining, but not even a lump of mud had hit them.

She darted in, her teeth sinking into the collar of my shirt. With a glare at me, she backed out of the tunnel, dragging the pups along. When I thought I could talk without crying, I keyed the radio.

"She's out with the pups. You should be able to go in. I'm going to be a bit."

"*Roger. They're backing off.*" I didn't know if I should be glad he didn't ask where I was. I craned my neck around to check out my leg and immediately wished I hadn't. The bone was jutting out through my jeans. I sucked in air, trying not to throw up. How in the world could I crawl like this? The immediate answer of *carefully* ricocheted through my mind, and I choked out a laugh.

"You around?" I called out to the groundhogs. A minute later, there was a chitter by my leg. "Dig out please? Will provide more nuts weekly." At this rate I'd owe them food for a year, but better than being dead.

Chittering filled my ears, then warm bodies pressed against my leg, and I bit my lip trying not to scream. Time disappeared as I focused on breathing and not being sick. Then my legs and hips gave, the jarring of my leg startling me into a groan of pain.

I looked up to see a gopher staring at me and it chittered. *Got it. Move now. Okay.*

Setting raw elbows into the dirt, I heaved my body forward and sobbed out a scream of agony. This was going to suck. Each heave had me gagging in pain, but I was moving. The light at the end of the tunnel seemed forever away, and I had to lift up the breathing mask twice to let out the sweat that had accumulated in it.

"*Jonah, where the hell are you?*" McAlister's voice crackled over the radio.

"Coming," I choked out as I lay there, panting. I figured I still had twenty feet to go. It seemed like twenty miles.

"*They say the ground is giving. Get out of there now.*"

I tried to move a bit faster, but I was getting cold. The ground was leeching heat out of my body, and I suspected I'd lost more than a bit of blood. This would be a stupid way to die.

The light I'd been crawling toward disappeared, and I looked up to see a barghest come back in. This time it was the male, and if anything, he was bigger than his mate.

He growled at me.

Hands. Out.

I was already laying down flat, mostly because I hurt so bad that it was all I could do to lift my head up. Maybe I'd be lucky, and he'd kill me. I thrust my hands out in front of me and barely reacted as he opened his mouth and bit. It hurt, but I didn't think he broke the skin, and compared to my shredded elbows and my leg, it didn't rate as worth complaining about.

And then he *pulled*.

I screamed as my leg snagged, but he kept pulling, and I just concentrated on trying to lift my leg up so nothing else snagged on it or my foot. Each bump and jerk dug into my leg, through my t-shirt, and my arm. By now, his teeth had pierced my skin as he tried to keep a grip on me, but I didn't have the energy to cry or scream. I just breathed.

"We got him. You can let go now." Human voices sounded, and I lifted my head. The barghest dropped my arm, backing away, growling.

Don't hurt, we kill.

I didn't translate, as I wasn't sure if he meant me or them. I looked around for the mom and the pups. As hands lifted me up, I saw she was curled around them on the side.

A woman crouched next to her, a med bag in her hands. Her eyes darted to me. "Jonah, can you tell her I want to look at the injured one?"

I had to process that for a minute as they were pulling me onto a stretcher. "Help pup. Healer." Canines didn't really have a word for doctor, but most species could understand healer.

Heal? Safe?

"Yes," I replied.

Heal.

"You can look at it now," I said. "Try hard not to hurt it. Mom is a bit protective."

The ambulance guys had me on the stretcher and were cutting open my jeans. At the rate they were cutting, I'd be lucky to salvage shorts out of them. I looked at my white, hairy legs and decided that rags were a much better option. The bone sticking out of my leg looked like something from a horror movie.

Turning away, looking at anything but the gaping wound in my leg, I watched the vet gently tape the pup's leg, then hold the squirming critter for a while, a look of concentration on her face. That meant she probably was a healer, not just a vet. Interesting, as most of them went into human medicine, not animal. Before I could see more, McAlister stepped into my line of sight.

"You sure managed to screw up your leg. What happened?" he asked.

"Building slipped, snapped it," I muttered, still concentrating on not crying. That would go over well, guy laying there crying over a broken leg. I was still trying to decide between throwing up or crying. Which one made me look less like a wimp? I realized my thoughts were drifting and focused back on McAlister. "You get the people out?"

"Sure did. The barghest backed away from the building and pulled the puppies over here. After that, they ignored us. The woman is being loaded into the ambulance now, and we've called another one for you."

"They okay?" I meant mostly my son and daughter-in-law, but it was safer to ask about everyone.

"Yes. The teenager only has a minor break and a concussion. The woman will probably give birth in the next few hours." He looked up. "Someone wants to talk to you."

I sighed, wondering who wanted to yell at me. "Hey, those peanuts. Would you go spread them out over where the tree was? Payment for gophers." Even talking was getting harder. It felt like my leg was on fire, and I could feel tears leaking out of my eyes, but there was no way for me to stop them. I was a wreck.

"I can do that. I'll even get some extras for them." He nodded to someone behind me, and I didn't bother trying to crane my neck to see who it was. My attention was on the medic with a needle of pain meds. It couldn't come fast enough. "I'll be back before they take you away." He paused. "Good job, Jonah. I'll remember this."

I couldn't decide if that was meant as a threat or promise. A figure stepped into my view, and I felt my heart stutter, more scared than I'd been when I thought I might die.

"Peter?" I didn't really mean the quaver, but right then the medic put the needle in my arm. Needles weren't my favorite thing, but for this situation, it was welcome.

He looked at me, hands in his pockets. His hair was longer than in the picture, almost touching his shoulders. He looked exhausted.

"Jonah," he said, an odd look on his face.

"How's your wife and baby?"

A spark of joy flashed across his face. "They should be fine. They're taking her now, and one of the cops is going to take me there, but I wanted to talk to you first."

"Oh." I looked around and tried to smile. "Well, I'm obviously not walking away." I tried to make it a joke, but the drugs started to hit, and it came out as a sigh of relief.

"So I see." He shuffled his feet a moment, not looking at me. "They told me what you did. You could have just let them die, or shot them."

I snorted, enjoying the pain fading away. "You've never seen the paperwork MAPA requires. Besides, it's kind of my job, and they didn't do anything to deserve to be killed for."

"Why didn't you come to the wedding?" He blurted the question out.

I blinked up at him, surprised. "I wasn't invited. I got a notice you'd gotten married and some pics. There wasn't an address. I didn't even know you'd moved back to Washington."

Something in his expression changed, but I was too lightheaded to figure it out. "Just moved back here last month. Mom said your magic was useless."

I shrugged, enjoying the lack of pain. "It isn't as lucrative as hers, but I try to use it well."

"You saved lives. Stella's, and maybe the baby's. And the dogs'."

"They're barghests."

"Huh. So if you want, you can come see the baby after it's born." He didn't look at me as he said that. "Maybe you could come over some time?" Peter glanced back at the remains of his apartment building. "After, we uh, find a new place to live."

Words sprang to the tip of my tongue, but I bit them back. You have to go slow in building relationships with skittish animals, and Peter counted as very skittish.

"I'd like that. Let me know if you need help, or well, anything." I didn't have much money saved, but maybe I could help them move. I looked down at my broken leg. Or maybe not.

"I will. Thanks again, for you know—" he waved his hand around, encompassing everything, "—this."

The lightheadedness from the drugs was making my eyes water. "Any time."

He spun and headed away, and relief washed through me.

"You about ready, Mr. Moby?" the paramedic asked. "Your ride should be here any moment."

"Sure am." There was a surgery ahead of me, I knew, but all I could think about was that my son had invited me up to see the baby. I'd beg someone to wheel me up there if I had to.

A growl echoed around me, and I saw the paramedics backing up. I looked down to see the female barghest staring at me, about a foot away from the gurney they had me on.

Kept word. Pups safe. Healed.

I followed her head turn to see the male protecting the pups that all wobbled around, while the healer stood off to the side, a smile on her face.

"Good. I'm glad they're okay."

The bitch looked at me for a long moment, her eyes hard with flames in the depths, and I wondered if I was going to regret this.

Good human. Rare. Pack. Ours.

I blinked as she turned and walked away. Together they nosed all the pups into my shirt bag and then, each holding one end in their mouth, picked it up and walked away.

"What did she say?" the vet asked.

I blinked again—the pain drugs were great, they made me think pretty women were smiling at me. I shook my head, almost toppling over, and focused on the female vet. The pretty female vet.

"I think it was approval. And I'm a pack member now. Or lunch. Not sure which."

"Huh. Interesting magic there. I'm Kay Bigsby. I just took over Doctor Sol's vet practice. You interested in a retainer? Your help could be useful."

Did I just get offered a job?

"I want to say yes, but do you think maybe we can discuss this again when I'm not high as a kite?"

She had a nice laugh. "I think that can be arranged. I'll be in touch, Jonah Moby."

I closed my eyes as the ambulance backed up, and I tallied up the day. Broken leg, torn up elbows, more bruises and scrapes than I could count, a grandchild, an invitation to meet my son and his wife, and maybe a job. Even if I didn't know what the barghest meant, today had been a good day.

Even worth missing watching my movie. Who needed gods when you had magic all around you?

* * * * *

Mel Todd Biography

Mel Todd has over 27 titles out, her urban science fiction *Kaylid Chronicles*, the *Blood War* series, and the urban fantasy *Twisted Luck* series. With short stories in various anthologies and magazines, she hopes to keep writing tales that will capture your heart and imagination. With one co-author, and more books in the works, her stories can be found currently on Amazon.

You can sign up for her newsletter and follow her blog at https://www.badashpublishing.com. You can also follow her on Facebook at: https://www.facebook.com/badashbooks/.

* * * * *

The Problem with Garbage
by Michael Gants

The City, she has a feel all her own at three-thirty in the morning. In the city that never sleeps, this is the quietest time. My favorite time. She's a bit like the sea, dangerous and uncaring. The feel is even stronger in the winter. Black colors are deeper, somehow thicker. Solitary sodium lights cast their orange illumination, fighting to hold back the deep, still shadows that cross the streets and avenues, hiding more than they reveal. The darkness generates a danger all its own.

There's usually a slightly bitter tang to the air that blows off the Hudson and tickles the nose, the smell of diesel from the early deliveries coming across the bridges.

Enough wool-gathering, there's work to do. I shook my head, filled my cup with black coffee, chucked in a packet of creamer, and watched the whitish dust clump and disappear. I swirled it around, not wanting to find dough-like blobs at the end of my morning ritual.

Normally I could wait a few more minutes before grabbing Kelth and getting our truck. Not this morning, though. Today is Recruit Day, with all that entails. As soon as I got the concoction mixed, I popped the lid on my mug and cast my glamour. It's easier to do it before I give the morning briefing.

Mediterranean skin, thick curly black hair, and a prominent beak of a nose replaced my normal goblin appearance of greenish-yellow mottled skin, a sharp chin, and large, mobile ears. I glanced in the mirror over the sink. The glamour was impeccable, which it should be, since it was the same one I'd used for nearly thirty years. I pushed the door of the break room open and stepped into the garage.

The temperature change brought goosebumps to my skin. In here, the heaters struggled to keep the air warm against the routine opening of roll-up doors for the trucks. The new trainees were all clumped together, safety in numbers I supposed, or to share body heat.

There were only five of them, four men and a woman. Not that our garage could absorb more than that without bursting at the seams. I knew in my head Dispatch had spread the remainder across the seven boroughs, with each garage getting some newbies. We only did this once a year, right after the winter solstice. Best time to bring in new blood. Time of new beginnings.

I looked over the recruits, shaking my head. Each year, the group got younger. Of course, that was more than likely because I hadn't stopped aging and was moving away from my own birthdate at the same speed I always had. Still, they were so *young*.

The oldest hands stood near the assignments map, checking routes to see if anything had changed since their previous shift, making sure they knew about any construction or detours. Partially they checked to make sure their routes would be as efficient as possible. Part, I figured, was simply to keep from having to talk to the new blood. Other employees gathered in small groups, gossiping about the sports, the weather, traffic, or anything else to keep from talking to one of the recruits. Same problem every time. Even the people who only had a single year under their belt acted as if the newbies were below them.

I was the only one in human shape; the rest retained their true goblin forms. I stepped forward and whistled. All eyes turned toward me.

"Gather 'round. I got a few words to say before we mount up and head out. First off, 25DN-225 is repaired. Nothing anyone did, just a failed air blower motor. Keep that in mind. You have problems with your rig, mark it down during your end-of-shift paperwork so maintenance can get it checked out. If you don't and someone else finds it, you and your paycheck might be blamed." Loud boos sprang out of the crowd.

"Second, we're past Solstice and the holidays, which means everybody's dumping stuff from Christmas. Piles are going to get high if we don't keep on top of it. Finally, the elephant in the room." I shifted my gaze to the knot of uncomfortable trainees standing to one side. "New recruits have arrived. As normal, each recruit will spend a week with a crew, getting to know how the systems work, what the job is like, and how to keep safe.

"These recruits are here to learn the job, not to be slave labor so you can sit in the cab. Teach them and show them the right way to handle the job. *All* parts of the job." A few of the older workers grunted at that statement. I focused my gaze on the recruits for the next part.

"You've all managed to get through the training. Now you look around at where you've been stationed and think *What did I do to deserve this?* Well, what you did was join the force.

"Our job is to keep the City clean. That means we're here to keep the City safe. In return, the City protects us and gives us a place to live, unmolested. Our flesh, her steel and iron. It's a solemn pact between her and us. Your new job is keeping our part of that pact."

I glanced down at the clipboard in my right hand. "All right, assignments. Brono, you're on five-two-one with Githin and Turmno." A squat, dark-green-skinned recruit nodded and looked around. Githin raised his hand, and the newbie scooted over. "Next, Olcet…" I continued the callouts. Finally, I got to the last name. "Sheft, you're with Kelth and me on four-one-three. That's it, everybody. All ya have your orders, so mount up. Drive safe, watch out for people, and keep the city clean."

The group broke apart, the noise increasing as the crews talked among themselves, cast glamours, and engines coughed to life. I watched from the side of my truck as the shift filed out of the building and into the pre-dawn morning, making sure each one looked right. Can't have humans noticing that goblins are picking up the garbage.

Sheft wandered over to the truck. He quickly muttered a glamour spell, changing his appearance into a pimply-faced man with a thin, wispy-blond beard. The overall look reminded me of a twenty-year-old extra from *The Gangs of New York*, which might have been exactly what he was going for. He opened the door and slid in, moving to the center of the vehicle.

Kelth, my grabber, sat on the sidewalk side of the cab and shut the door. He'd cast his usual glamour, the visage of a slightly heavyset Latino with graying temples and a thick, push-broom mustache. "Mario of the Barrio," he'd joked after the video game had become popular. Sheft was wedged between the two of us and staring at the floor.

I started the truck. The vehicle shook itself awake and rumbled contentedly, the engine quickly warming up. I put the transmission into drive and pulled out of the garage and onto the narrow streets of Manhattan. Our headlights cut bright swaths through the muddied darkness.

I glanced skyward. Clouds had rolled in. We might see snow today.

Our route had us working on Roosevelt Island for starters, then back through the Upper East Side. That meant hitting Interstate 87 and driving for a bit, since the bridge to the island was out of Queens, not Manhattan proper. We needed to cross the East River and then swing west on I-278 till 36th Street. Traffic was steady but slow, moving us along at about forty-five miles an hour. Kind of silly on a road designed to move cars along at eighty. The radio played classic heavy metal in the background while we drove. Not my cup of tea, but I knew Kelth was a traditionalist about music.

I glanced over at Sheft. He was still staring at the floor of the truck. He wasn't even tapping his toes or mildly bobbing to the music. Just sitting there in some sort of funk.

"Spill it, Sheft. What's the matter?" I asked.

"Not what I wanted," he squeaked after a moment or two. "I was supposed to be working in Dispatch. Important work. Not stuck out here driving or grabbing."

Kelth broke in with a throaty laugh at that. "Not important. Whatcha think makes Dispatch more important than this?" Kelth had grown up in the deep Queens, and his thick city accent showed it.

Sheft gave him a slit-eyed stare.

"This is where it all happens. Friggin' Dispatch don't know nuthin', 'cept where things already gone wrong. We're out here preventin' where we can, saving what we can, and fightin' if we has to."

"Look kid," I said, "I know most folks think this job is at the bottom, but without us, the entire operation fails. Humans find themselves at the mercy of trolls. And why is that?" I asked, giving a pregnant pause, hoping some of the training had penetrated the kid's thick skull.

"Because anywhere trash builds up, trolls live. Where trolls live, trolls hunt," Sheft continued, "and when trolls hunt, humans die, since they usually don't even notice the trolls till it's too late."

I nodded. "How much history you got behind you?"

Sheft blinked at me, then gathered his thoughts. "I mean, I know the clans ran a racket for protection back in the old days, and the elves and us, we kinda had some big fights here in America back in the 1800s or so. That's about it."

I grunted. They're just not teaching history like they used to in school. "All right. Here's the quick down and dirty. You're right about us and the elves. We both came over here from Europe, each of us trying to carve out new territories. Elves, like always, hooked up with the humans. Us, well, we'd never been on great terms with either of them.

"Things got ugly, clans and gangs fighting. Then the city really started changing. Lots of steel and iron, plus the railroads were growing. That was bad news for the elves, since they have issues with the pure stuff. Makes their magic go all wonky. They decided to move out, and we slid in through the shadows, living on the sidelines.

"I mean, you know how much bad press those pointy-eared, hoity guys gave us. It's only been in the last seventy years or so that you could even mention us without someone immediately thinking we're evil."

"Or ask us if we've heard of the babe," Kelth muttered. "Hate that movie."

The recruit seemed to be interested. At least he was keeping an eye on me and nodding rather than staring at his feet. "Is that when the Pact was made?"

"Yep, back in '81—that's 1881 for you. The elves would keep the smaller towns and farms safe and quit badmouthing us. In return, we'd quit fighting them, and we'd provide protection inside the city, keep humans safe. After all, iron doesn't mess with us like it does with them. Surprised both sides when the City herself showed up at the ceremony and blessed the meeting."

"Things went okay right up until the Dark Forces in Europe got itchy." I paused and took the exit off I-87 toward I-278. "Next thing you know, war breaks out everywhere, and the gangs are pretty well gone. Then the trolls rolled in. Iron didn't affect them much either, plus the humans were tasty meals. Easy to catch, easier to kill. We had to figure out a way to stop them."

I paused in my talk as we rolled up the Roosevelt Bridge. Anytime we cross a bridge, everyone keeps their eyes open. The association of trolls and bridges is real, and you never know if one's going to decide that today your truck is a good target. Thankfully, we weren't the only traffic on the road, which meant less chance of attack.

Roosevelt Island is a bit of an odd duck, even in the five boroughs. Officially part of Manhattan, it's a two-mile-long sliver of land set in the middle of the East River between Manhattan and Queens. The island was used mostly for hospitals until after the mid-1970s, when several apartment buildings were built. Most of the island isn't exactly conducive to vehicular traffic, which makes getting the trash out more of a chore than in other places. Having Sheft along for the next week would make the job a bit easier with the extra set of hands.

I started us on the east side of Main Street, heading north. The first stop was the cans near the supermarket, then northward toward the park and the parking garage. When I stopped at the first can, Sheft and Kelth hopped out, their breath steaming in the frigid morning air. Kelth showed Sheft how to pop the can cover off, pull the can in a smooth motion, and toss the contents into the compactor. Then Kelth flipped the can back into the square red holder and hooked the cover back on. He grabbed the bar behind the compactor and climbed up on the street side. Sheft followed suit on the sidewalk side, clinging with both hands.

It's a bit dangerous riding the back. That's why we only do it for short sections where the cans are close together. The rest of the time the grabber sits up front. The biggest danger isn't the traffic, it's the problem of passing a dark alley or refuse pile and a troll or two swiping someone right off the back of the truck.

Things were going well. Sheft seemed to be getting the hang of tossing cans and understanding when to run the compactor. You don't run it after every load, or even every other load. You wait till either the tail is full, or you've reached the end of a section. Pause, make sure everyone's clear, then cycle the hydraulics and crush the trash up into the main box. The entire cycle takes time, which is why we only do it when it's needed.

We were thirty minutes on the island and headed toward one of the last sections, the south end near the Four Freedoms State Park. The state park relies on us to deal with the trash, so we always make it one of the last stops on this part of the route. Just before the park is the ruins of Smallpox Hospital. The area is fenced up, and there are *No Trespassing* signs everywhere. This time of year, though, some of the homeless drifters still find ways to get inside. The walls are high enough to keep out some of the wind, and the ground is safe for fires. The problem is, that means it's a prime hunting ground for trolls. There hasn't been an incident out this way for a couple of years, so I wasn't too concerned about taking the kid with us nearby.

I should've been.

Not every goblin has heat sight—only about one in eight. I have it; Kelth doesn't. It makes people and objects look a little fuzzy, but I can see afterimages of hot objects. I'd just stopped at the cans when I spotted a pool of something cooling in the grass just past the fence line to the ruins.

Kelth and Sheft jumped off and began dumping the cans. Whatever I saw was cooling rapidly, but it appeared to be a splatter, like when someone throws hot coffee onto the grass. I put the truck in neutral and hopped out. The pair was flinging the cans as I stepped around the front of the rumbling vehicle.

Kelth noticed me get out of the cab and put his can down, motioning Sheft to do the same. I pressed my face against the aluminum fence and muttered an enhancement spell under my breath. My vision changed, the color draining away as my mind focused on the heat signatures. A pattern jumped out of the spray in a sort of vee pattern. Probably arterial, based on how far it had gone, and how wide the top of the vee was. I could see a multitude of faint but thick heat trails on the grass where several people and trolls had run about. There wasn't enough detail for me to tell which ones were which. I could see the image of a small fire on the far side of the wall from where I stood.

"Blood," I stated coolly. "Looks recent, since I can still see heat. Less than ten minutes ago."

Kelth straightened and looked about, checking for danger.

I shook my head and pointed. "Whatever happened, they went north, taking their prey with them. I can just barely see the trail cutting through the ruins. Probably headed for one of the bridges."

Kelth cursed. "Any chance we can catch 'em?"

"Probably not. I think they planned it so they'd be on the opposite side of our approach. We gotta check out the hide before we go anywhere. Figure out how many were here."

Sheft started at my statement. "Shouldn't we call Dispatch, let them know what's going on? Maybe contact the cops?"

"Our job. Cops can't do anything against trolls except get hurt or killed. I'll let Dispatch know as soon as we have more of the story." I grabbed the upper section of the fence and pulled myself over, making sure not to stab myself on the pointed tops. Kelth climbed over behind me, leaving Sheft behind. He stared at us through the square black bars.

I paused and turned around. "Stay in the cab," I said, waving Sheft toward the truck. "Keep the doors closed in case they double back. Trust me, no troll is going to try to beat his way through that much cold iron."

I waited until the recruit had climbed in and shut the door before continuing, watching as he hunched down, trying to be as inconspicuous as possible. It was doubtful any trolls remained around here, but one could never be certain.

Dead leaves and grass crunched under our feet as Kelth and I made our way toward one of the fence-covered doorways dotting the ruins. We swung wide of the blood. It was supposed to rain or snow in a bit, but there was no sense in disturbing the evidence if we could prevent it. Kelth held open a sprung section of the fence, and I ducked through. Kelth followed, letting the chain-link fall back into place.

The remains of a small fire smoldered in a stone circle. It'd been set up using the corner of the walls as a heat reflector. Three crumpled, stained sleeping bags lay near the fire, as well as two backpacks. One of the sleeping bags was significantly smaller than the other two.

"Damn," Kelth whispered. "They got a kid. Bastards grabbed a *kid*." He drove one meaty fist into his left palm with a smack.

I nodded. "We don't have much chance of catching them. Doesn't mean we aren't gonna try, though." The two of us scrambled over the fence and ran to the truck. Once we piled into the cab, I shoved the transmission into reverse. Sheft clutched at his seatbelt, missing the buckle three times before the belt latched into place.

Kelth was significantly more sanguine. He calmly latched his belt and held onto the doorframe. "Any idea of how many?"

"No, but more than one, based on how fast they got away. Figure at least three humans, one of whom is probably dead, most likely the oldest man. I suspect a full family of trolls, three to five, though it might only be a mated pair. A sole male wouldn't hunt a group of humans. Take down a lone human, sure, but not a group."

Kelth nodded and picked up the radio's mic. He paused, then carefully enunciated, "Dispatch, two-five-henry four-one-eight. Probable troll attack at the Smallpox Hospital ruins on Roosevelt Island. Estimated size of the raid is two to five trolls. Victims are probably three humans, looks like a family unit with child."

"*25H-418, Dispatch copies. Situation?*"

"We're in pursuit. Probable death of one human prior to discovery. We're checking likely hiding spots. Request at least one additional unit." He released the key.

"*Roger, 25H-418. The closest unit is thirty-eight minutes out. Second is forty-six minutes out.*"

"Understood, Dispatch. 25H-418, out." Kelth put the mic back on its holder.

"Do we wait for backup?" Sheft asked, his voice a bit tight.

"No." My voice was flat. "The damn trolls took a kid. A *kid!* We don't have time to wait. We've got to find them fast before they go to ground for the day. The humans won't survive that. The trolls will kill them before the sun rises."

"Because the trolls will hibernate and can't keep an eye on them while the sun's up, right? Too big a chance the humans would escape. Kill them, and the food's guaranteed to still be there when the sun goes down."

"Righto," remarked Kelth. "Trolls'll turn to stone in direct sunlight 'less they already hibernatin'."

"How long till sunrise?" I asked.

"Not sure, lemme check." Kelth pulled out his phone and tapped the screen. "Seven twenty-three. That's a bit less than two and a half hours from now." He stuffed the phone in the glove box. "Not much time to find their hideout."

"I figure there are only three places they're likely to go to ground. One, the Queensboro Bridge, but that's unlikely, since the span is so high, and neither end is anchored on the island. Two, the Roosevelt Island Bridge. The west end anchors here on the island. Third possibility is that storage and trash area off West Loop Road. They still have a couple dumpsters left over from the New Year Gala they held on the green. One of the private companies has the contract on those, but I don't think they've picked up the units yet."

"That'd be the closest place for them ta get to," Kelth stated. He glanced at the route map. "Swing a left onto South Loop, then curve right onto West Loop. It's only about a third of a mile or so."

I killed the lights and coasted to a stop near some trees as we approached the storage area. No sense giving ourselves away if we could help it. Kelth checked his gloves, then grabbed two crowbars from behind the seat. Iron doesn't affect us as strongly as it does the elves, but it'll give us a nasty burn if we touch it with bare hands. He passed one to Sheft.

"When you swing at one of da trolls, make sure ya get it on the skin. That way they get both the hit and the burn. You stay in back and keep your eyes peeled."

I grabbed my shillelagh. I know, I know…I'm Italian. Why the wood instead of a knife or a gun? Because it works well. Plus, it lets me maintain more distance from the trolls than the knife would. Guns, well, trolls tend to shrug off the bullets, since lead is softer than their stone hides. I'd spent months carefully shaping a lightning-struck branch from a red oak in Central Park. It was about three feet long, and the knobbed end was blackened where the branch had originally been struck.

The lock was a simple key hasp, which Kelth opened before I could even get near it. He's handy that way. He opened the gate and slipped in, Sheft behind, and me guarding the rear. Tarp-covered stacks and storage boxes formed a tight maze inside the storage yard. I glanced around, searching for the pair of dumpsters. I finally spotted them at the back. Two industrial grade roll-off units painted fire-engine red. I signaled everyone to stop and listened.

The only noises were the tugs pushing cargo down the river and the soft sound of traffic passing over the island on the Queensboro Bridge. An early rising sparrow cheeped across the street in one of the trees lining the riverbank. Nothing else. I motioned Kelth to check the left dumpster and that I would check the right. He nodded and half-escorted, half-dragged Sheft with him.

I carefully climbed the side and peered in. Bags of trash and scrap lumber for building the gala stands met my gaze. I checked over the area with both my regular and heat sight as I used my shillelagh to sift through the top few layers of trash. It all moved freely and easily. Nothing I saw looked out of the ordinary. I dropped silently back to the ground and brushed the loose rust and dirt off my jumper with my free hand.

"Kelth, you find anything?" I hissed quietly.

"Nope. Don't see anything that makes me think they was ever here. Bridges next." Kelth pointed his crowbar toward the huge, flat arch of the Queensboro Bridge. "That one?"

"I think there's a better chance at the Roosevelt. I saw some piles of construction remainders as we swung down. It's a ways from the ruins, but the trolls have had time to get back there. I just can't figure out where they'd lair under the Queensboro."

We hurried back to the truck, Kelth locking the gate behind us. He stuffed the crowbars down by his feet after he climbed in the cab. "Might not be time to grab them out from behind the seats when we get there." I nodded in agreement.

I didn't dare push the truck much past 25 miles an hour on these roads, which were marked for 15 mph. We were passing Cornell Tech's campus, and even this early in the morning, a few people were out speed walking or jogging. I don't get freezing your rear end off for exercise. The campus had a perfectly good indoor gym.

A quick right onto West Main Street then a left onto Main itself. The traffic situation got worse as we got near the apartment buildings. A delivery van was parked crossways on the street just after we passed under the Queensboro Bridge, dropping off foodstuffs at a restaurant. I bounced our truck onto the sidewalk to avoid it, then back into the street, narrowly missing one of the multitudes of concrete flowerpots dotting the walkway. No cops spotted me.

We drove past the parkland on the right. I could see the lights on the bridge reflecting off the low-hanging clouds. Light snow began to fall, and I flicked on the wipers, streaking the flakes across the windshield. Another thing to worry about.

I turned just past the bridge's entrance, driving the truck under the upper portion that led off the island. The engine rumbled for a moment, then clunked to a stop as I shut off the motor. Each of us unbuckled and gathered our weapons.

"There are two refuse piles. One is against the side of the ramp directly across from us. There's another built up under the edge of the curve as it rises from the ground. The trolls could be in either or both. We'll check the nearer pile first. Sheft, your job is to keep a lookout at the other pile. I don't want to get jumped from behind."

The young recruit nodded, his arm muscles bulging slightly as he gripped his crowbar tightly.

"They'll have heard the truck, maybe even seen it. We aren't going to surprise them. That means they may be ready to ambush us. Keep your eyes peeled and your weapons ready."

Everybody nodded and we piled out of the cab as quietly as we could. I could see the flurrying snow past the concrete overhang of the bridge. An occasional flake blew in with the wind, but this area was clear. I gestured, and we hurried around across the ramp. Thankfully, no vehicles came down as we crossed. The wind hit us full force as we neared the edge of the meager shelter from the bridge's overhang.

A pile of construction waste, probably eight feet long and about three feet high, had been tossed against the concrete wall separating the road from the expanse of flat paving making up the bridge's foundation and anchor. The refuse looked like any other pile of construction waste.

That's what makes hunting trolls so difficult. They can camouflage their dens to look like garbage piles. You could walk right past and never know the danger lurking inside. We weren't going to walk by this one, though.

Kelth jerked his chin, and I nodded. We split apart, and Sheft hung back. I didn't want him right next to me. Different people act in different ways when confronted by danger. I hadn't seen Sheft in action yet and had no feel for which way he'd leap.

I sidled around toward the shore side of the pile, keeping my back to a Conex box where the construction company appeared to be storing tools and pilferable equipment. Kelth approached from the street side, his crowbar tucked back, ready for a solid swing.

Neither of us noticed the troll lying in wait atop the Conex box.

"Behind and above you!" Sheft shouted.

His yell gave me just enough time to turn around before several hundred pounds of stone-hided yuck landed on me. I curled into a ball, wrapping myself around the shillelagh to keep it from being torn out of my grasp. Fetid breath tinged with the scent of old blood washed over me.

"Gah. Ever hear of dental care, you mouth-breathing excuse for a mobile boulder?"

The troll roared and lifted one terrible, clawed hand to impale me. I caught a glimpse of Kelth's crowbar as it slammed into the upraised appendage. I heard, almost felt, the *crack* of the right arm bone. The troll howled in pain, rolling off me and staggering to its feet.

Kelth danced backward, narrowly avoiding the swipe from the troll's left hand. The force of the passing blow ruffled his overstuffed mustache. He Casey Jones'ed the crowbar at the troll's midsection. The troll leapt upward, the crowbar passing under his bulk. He landed on top of the refuse pile. I heard a stifled groan from under the broken boards and tattered garbage bags.

I risked looking over my shoulder. Sheft stood still, watching the fight, while also glancing around and checking for any other attackers. I hissed to get his attention. "There's something in this pile, probably one of the victims. I'll lure the troll away; you pull them out." He nodded, eyes wide with either excitement or fear. Probably both.

I turned back to the fight and poked my wooden club into the troll's ribcage. He roared in frustration and slapped the stick away. "Back up," I yelled to Kelth.

He stepped back about four paces. The troll, sensing weakness, followed, jumping lightly off the trash pile. Kelth and I stayed in front of the troll, drawing him away from the trash and into the open space near the bridge's support pillars.

The creature took a few tentative swipes, watching our reactions. He feigned an attack on Kelth, and I fell for it. The next moment he body-checked me into next week. The troll was nearly twice my height and mass, and I bounced and rolled all the way to the grass in the tiny green zone inside Roosevelt Bridge's ramp's circle.

I shook my head, attempting to clear my vision. I caught sight of Sheft throwing trash away as he dug through the pile and pulled out a thin human. From here, I couldn't tell whether the human was male or female. I rolled to my feet just in time to see the troll backhand Kelth, knocking my partner into the trash pile, overfilled plastic bags bursting under the assault.

This was getting out of hand. Backup was still at least fifteen minutes away. I could see a straight line burned into the troll's back hair where Kelth had landed a solid blow with his crowbar, but it didn't seem to be slowing it down any more than the broken arm was. I felt around, grabbing my club as soon as my fingers brushed against it. While the troll's back was to me, I rushed forward, lifting the shillelagh high over my head. With a word, I invoked the memory of the lightning in its scorched end. I brought the weapon down with all my might, the magic of that long-ago storm blasting the hairy monstrosity into the street. It flipped over the railing and landed in the middle of the ramp. The wound was mortal. Dark ichor leaked from the various spots where the lightning had pierced the body. The body folded in on itself, crumpling as the earth reclaimed the elements from the husk. Seconds passed, and only an oily brown stain remained.

There was a commotion behind us. Kelth and I turned, and Sheft looked up from where he was tending the wounds of the human he'd rescued. A second troll, female or young male based on its size, raced away from us, a tiny human bundle clutched in its oversized hands.

"Back to the truck," I shouted, "damn thing's got the kid!"

I raced over and grabbed Kelth. He grimaced as I hauled him out of the pile, his free arm wrapping around his midsection.

"You okay?" I asked.

He started walking toward the truck before answering me, then stumbled and had to catch himself on the cold metal railing. "Think that backhand might've busted a rib or two. Gonna need a bit to catch my breath."

"Hold here," I said and ran over to where Sheft had our rescue lying on the ground. It was a youngish female, bruised and battered. Sheft had bundled his jacket under her head. "How is she?" I asked.

The woman answered, "I hurt. Where's Tommy? They killed Roger, but I think Tommy's still alive. Where's my brother?" Then she mumbled something and waved one of her arms. I couldn't understand that part.

Sheft said, "She's hurt pretty bad. I think they hit her really hard. Might be internal bleeding, since she's coughed up some blood. Plus, I think she's got a concussion."

Kelth sat down hard by the woman and took one of her hands. "I've got my phone in the cab. Give it to me and go after the kid. I'll call 9-1-1 and stay until the ambulance arrives. That'll give me time to heal some and keep her safe."

Sheft ran to the truck. He was back with the cell before I'd made up my mind. He handed it over to Kelth.

"Go on, I'll be fine, but the kid's toast if you can't catch her."

"All right. I'll swing back by and pick you up after we do this." I patted his shoulder. "Come on," I said to Sheft. "We've got a rescue to do."

I pushed the accelerator and almost left tire marks pulling out from the bridge. I turned left onto Main and gunned the motor.

Pushing my speed past forty, I raced along the road. A single passerby offered me the New York City salute and gave an indignant shout as the front end of the truck nearly clipped them crossing the street.

By the time I got back to Firefighters Field, the delivery van had moved on. I breathed a sigh of relief at not needing to slow down. "Keep your eyes open. I've got no idea where the troll is taking Tommy." I slowed the truck as I rounded the traffic circle, coming out aimed at the ferry terminal.

The twin stacks of the old steam plant disappeared into the low-hanging clouds, and the snowfall was getting thicker. I kept an eye on the upper section of the Queensboro Bridge. *Where is it going? No good places under the bridge, no hidey-holes easily reachable. Maybe the uprights?* I thought as I turned toward the southern end of the island. Sheft's cry broke my train of thought.

"What?" I asked.

"The steam plant. I think I saw something going into the steam plant."

I hadn't even considered the steam plant. The power company had shut the plant down several years ago, but the building was still there. Residents on the island were pushing to put in a museum of technology in the remains, and a few movies had used the grimy industrial interior for settings. Perfect place for a troll to go to ground and enjoy its meal. I'm not even sure why the pair had gone as far as the Roosevelt Bridge. Trolls, not the brightest creatures to grace the planet.

Wrenching the wheel hard to the right, I bounced the truck into the old driveway. "I'm gonna have to request a paint job," I muttered under my breath as the front end hit the chain-link gate. The metal buckled and screamed in protest as the truck drove over it. I hit the brakes as soon as the truck's back end passed the fence line.

"Come on," I said as I threw my door open. I jumped down, club in hand. The snow was coming down in fat flakes, thick enough to obscure vision. Sheft followed, slamming his door behind him.

"Careful, that thing's city property. Show it some respect," I said as I raced toward the nearest entrance.

"I'm having trouble taking that seriously from the person who just rammed the same vehicle through a fence."

I yanked the building's door open. Thank the City it wasn't locked. "Different situation. This is an emergency."

"I'm here, too, so slamming the door falls under the same thing."

Arguing his logic would be pointless right now, especially since I didn't have a good rebuttal. I raised my finger to my lips and pointed down the hall. Sheft nodded and readied his crowbar. As one we slipped down the darkened hallway, past empty offices abandoned to the rats, mice, and spiders. I figured the troll would be deeper in the building, where the chance of sunlight was less, and there were more hiding areas.

It took the pair of us several minutes to work our way through the office section and into the vast interior of the plant. The scents of mildew, dust, rodents, and dampness tickled our noses unpleasantly. Rising ten stories to a glass and steel roof, the center section displayed a mixture of open and crowded spaces. Light from outside streamed in through a multitude of windows on the walls. Yellow painted pipes and tanks dominated the upper stories, while banks of incomprehensible instrumentation and switches lined the bottom floor. The upper decks reached out toward the middle of the building, forming a murky labyrinth of pumps, piping, and other machinery. Shadows tricked the eye into thinking they were solid and real, while hiding true openings.

I stopped and cast my sight enhancement spell again. Sharp edges blurred as the heat vision became my primary method of seeing. A series of faint lines crisscrossed the floor, the trails of the rodents that made this place their home. There were no obvious spots the troll had moved across.

"Let's head toward the back area," I whispered to Sheft.

We slowly made our way down the center aisle. I checked each opening we passed, attempting to catch some glimpse of the troll's trail. About halfway down, I finally saw what I'd been searching for: cooling footsteps leading up a set of concrete stairs. I stopped Sheft with my hand and pointed. He nodded in understanding.

As we stepped out onto the second level of the generating plant, I suddenly realized why the trolls hadn't used this as a primary lair. All the railings, the pipes, and several sections of the floor were iron. I saw reddish-orange rust peeking through flaking black paint in a multitude of spots. Even the walls were streaked with rust stains where condensation had dripped. Without coverings, the trolls risked burning themselves just moving about.

The trail became more pronounced in my sight. "Looks like the troll is just ahead, around that group of steam tanks. Be ready."

"I am," Sheft said, his voice trembling a little.

I couldn't blame the guy. They talk about the things we deal with out here during training, but it's a completely different situation to come face-to-face with evil on your first day on the job. He was doing well, though.

The trail suddenly stopped in the middle of an intersection. I held up my hand to stop Sheft while I attempted to figure out where the trail had gone. To my left, there was a section of metal grating spanning the center opening to allow workers to go to the opposite side without taking stairs. Ahead of me, the tile corridor continued past another yellow steam tank. *Where could the troll—*

Sheft screamed as the troll landed on his back, shoving him to the floor. The crowbar flew out of his grasp, clattering loudly as it bounced off the wall and fell. His voice cut off with sickening suddenness as the troll grabbed the back of his head and slammed his face into the floor. I swung around and charged, screaming at the top of my lungs. The troll rolled off Sheft and rose to meet my assault. I caught sight of blood pooling around Sheft's head. There was no time to see if he was alive, though.

For the first time, I got a good look at the beast as I ran toward it. It had been a mated pair of trolls we were dealing with. The female was ugly in a way only another troll could genuinely appreciate.

The troll dodged my charge by leaping upward and landing on the top of the steam tank behind her. I suddenly understood how she'd tricked me. She'd jumped backward from the intersection to the tank's top, causing the trail to disappear, and giving herself a perfect ambush spot. It's easy to forget that trolls aren't stupid, just evil. I swung at her legs, trying to knock her off balance. She leapt over the piece of wood, then dropped out of my sight at the end of the tank. I gave chase, hoping to catch a glimpse of her before she could hide.

She was running all out when I cleared the tank. I continued after her, dodging equipment and parts she knocked into the path. At the end of the floor, she turned right and crossed another gangway. I could see smoke curling from her bare feet as she raced over the metal grating. I caught the faint sound of sirens from outside, but couldn't tell if they were passing by or stopping. It didn't matter right now.

At the end of the crossover, I lost sight of her as she turned around a bank of instruments.

I kept running, the need to catch the troll overriding my normally good sense of self-preservation and tactics. Rounding the corner, I stared down a straight and empty stretch of floor. This side was like the other, filled with yellow painted steam tanks, instrument banks, and piping. "A veritable cornucopia of places to hide in," to quote my over-educated cousin.

The blow struck me before I even registered her shape crouched between a set of pumps and a pipe rising to the ceiling. Her arm scythed my legs out from under me, and I tumbled to the floor, momentarily knocking the wind from my lungs. I gasped and wheezed, fighting for breath, while rolling away from her next strike. Her talons left scored lines in the tiles. Scrambling, I gathered myself into a crouch, my back against the open railing. Another blow, and my shillelagh flew from my grasp, striking the concrete floor below a second later.

With one foot she kicked me, sending me sprawling, my arms outstretched. The same foot slammed down, impacting my chest and pinning me to the floor. She gave a guttural laugh, dark and throaty, reminding me of the sound of rocks grinding together. Her toes pressed inward, tiny pinpoints of needle-like pain where the sharp ends of her nails dug into my flesh. Bending down, she clasped her hands together above her head in preparation to crush my skull.

"Hey, ugly!" a voice cried. "I think I have something you want."

The weight on my chest lessened as the troll snapped upright and shifted her weight. I craned my head backward and caught sight of

Sheft, his face a mask of blood from cuts and a broken nose. He held a young boy by the hand and kept the other arm up as a small form of protection.

There was no quaver in Sheft's voice now. "This boy is not yours to have." He took a deep breath. "By the City and the Pact, by the blood that sings in my veins, he is protected by me and mine. He *shall not* be yours."

It surprised me that Sheft had remembered the proper wording of the protection creed at a time like this. What surprised me even more was the flash of light between Sheft and the troll. I closed my eyes at the intensity. When I reopened them, a woman the color of burnished copper in a flowing gown of the same hue and with a crown on her head stood carrying a torch in one hand and a tablet in the other. She was no taller than five and a half feet, yet dominated the room as if she were a giant.

Her voice was both powerful and melodious as she spoke. "Evil lives in the city; even I may not remove all of it. In this time, though, with the call of protection so clear, I may act." She raised the torch higher, and sunlight burst forth from it, bathing the entire room. Every shadow was driven from hiding, and not a single place was left unlit. The troll screamed, turned to stone, then crumbled to dust. Moments passed until even the dust had dwindled from view.

The light faded, leaving only the peace of its memory. Her torch and tablet disappeared, and she held out her hands toward Tommy. He walked to her as in a daze, a beautiful smile splitting his face in joy. Lady Liberty drew him to her breast, her arms wrapping about him in an embrace of both love and comfort.

She glanced down at the top of the boy's head. "I will ensure Tommy and his sister are reunited and find a good home. A home with people who will love and protect them, as you have chosen to. I wish I could extend this to all those who need it." She bowed her head away from the boy. Tears sparkled in her eyes. "Unfortunately, the power only works when invoked by others."

Sheft walked over and reached out to help me get back on my feet. I rose with his assistance, keeping my gaze on the City's spirit the entire time. I was in awe. No one I knew had ever seen the Lady before. The stories hadn't done her justice.

Still clasping Tommy in her arms, Lady Liberty looked over at us and gave us a small bow with only her head. "For keeping the Pact and for rescuing these forgotten ones, I thank you." In a shower of welding sparks, she and Tommy disappeared without a trace. I waited a few seconds in awe, then shook myself.

I pointed over my shoulder. "Come on, we need to pick up Kelth before someone cites him for vagrancy. It's not like he looks completely reputable." Sheft laughed and followed me out of the building. I was surprised when we returned to the truck. Both the gate I had smashed on our way in and the truck's grill had been repaired. I chuckled. I guess the City felt that was part of putting things right. I wasn't going to complain. That meant no insurance paperwork or claims. I slid open the intact chain-link gate, then backed the truck out, and Sheft locked the gate behind us. We drove back to the Roosevelt Bridge and found Kelth talking with a police officer, answering her last few questions.

The officer handed Kelth a card. "If anything else comes up or you think of anything else, give me a call. Thanks for helping her out. That kind of wound, she might have died before anyone else noticed her. You probably saved her life." The officer waved at us and got into her cruiser. Kelth climbed into the cab.

"You're a hero," Sheft said and clapped Kelth on the shoulder. Kelth grunted in reply.

I grabbed the mic. "Dispatch, 25H-418. Cancel the backup. Two survivors in good hands. I'll give the full report when we finish the route."

"*25H-418, Dispatch. Roger on that. Boss says he wants to have a verbal brief as well as a written report. Finish the route, then stop here prior to drop-off.*"

I rolled my eyes. "Dispatch, 25H-418. Roger on the verbal. Out." I put the mic back in the holder.

"We're just gonna go back to picking up the trash? Drive around and dump garbage into the truck?" Sheft looked first at me, and then at Kelth.

"Yep. That's the job."

"Even after something like this?"

"That's why we've gotta debrief afterward. Trash ain't gonna pick itself up, and you've now seen firsthand what happens if it ain't."

I put the truck in gear and pulled back out onto Main Street. We were a solid hour behind, and still hadn't finished here on the island. The engine rumbled, the wipers cleared the snow off the windshield, and we rolled toward our next pickup. I kept one eye on the road and the other on the falling snow. It promised to be a good snowfall, draping the City in a fresh blanket of white.

We're the goblins of the Department of Sanitation, New York City. This is what we do, protecting the City and everyone living here by taking out the trash. It doesn't matter if it's refuse someone created, or refuse that crawled into the city on its own.

Our job is to keep the City clean.

* * * * *

Michael Gants Biography

Michael Gants is a Nuclear Inservice quality inspector currently working with TVA. He is a proud retired USN submariner, trained in the maintenance and upkeep of nuclear power plants. During his time in the military, he visited 25 countries on five of the seven continents, has been around the world, and through every ocean.

Michael's previous jobs include being an insurance salesman, computer programmer, journalist, air conditioner mechanic, small business owner, small craft boarding specialist, a Navy anti-terrorism trainer, and an aquarium maintenance technician for Ripley's Aquarium of Myrtle Beach.

He and his amazing family now reside in Chattanooga, Tennessee with several fur babies.

* * * * *

Magic Chooses
by C.A. Farrell

My sister Emily lacked any instinct for self-preservation. Apparently, that was my job. She was too cute for her own good, with a slender figure and blonde curls, and she'd never met a stranger she didn't like. That's why I bartended at the same Denver pub where she waited tables, to keep her safe.

One night in June, it all fell apart. Pulling Emily out of a party wasn't easy. That night, I liked my chances. After last call, Chuck the bouncer was doing a decent job of easing drunks out the door without pissing them off, and the place was quiet. The roads looked reassuringly empty, with only two hulking figures leaning on a wall across the street. From their matching hunchbacked profiles, I suspected they probably weren't human, but I didn't care as long as they didn't try to get inside. I stood over the sink, washing glasses at top speed so we could get home on time for a change. Emily was supposed to be wiping down tables.

Instead, she bounced up to the bar, dragging a tipsy customer who stumbled over his big work boots. "Hey, Melanie, let's drive by the Ritz Carlton on the way home. There's all kinds of excitement outside. The Maker's there, and you can see the fireballs a block away."

I didn't even try to hide my eye roll. Damon Erickson, the Maker. Obviously, that loose cannon was a good reason to steer clear of the Ritz, but Emily couldn't see it. Neither could the customer, a dumb, dark-haired guy in a mechanic's shirt. He nodded and smiled like getting caught up in one of Erickson's crazy battles would be fun. *Who's the Maker fighting this time? Governor Richter? One of the mutant motorcycle gangs?* It didn't matter. My feet ached, and I wanted to go home, roll down the blast shields over the windows, and get some sleep.

"Don't get anywhere near Erickson. You know what happens if you get caught in the blowback from his magic," I said.

"What, you might turn into a monster, or maybe a supah-sexy vigilante? That's an urban myth," Emily scoffed.

"It's true," the mechanic argued. "Why do you think they call him the Maker?"

"I'd make a great vigilante. Can't you see me as a superhero?" Emily stood on tiptoe and raised both fists. The hem of her short, white dress hiked up, making her look more 1950s pinup than warrior woman.

I had to laugh. My little sister could be annoying, but she was adorable. "Oh, yeah. You're terrifying."

The mechanic tore his eyes from Emily and turned his bleary attention to me. He stuck out his hand for me to shake, even though mine were elbow deep in dishwater. "Hey, Mel, remember me?"

I ignored the offered hand and snuck a peek at the name on his shirt, where only a rumpled letter B was visible. "Yeah...uh, Brian?"

His sad puppy face told me I was wrong. I tried to care and failed. Emily fell in and out of love in a matter of days, and I couldn't keep up. It was always the same. At first, he was the one. In a week, they'd take a trip together. She'd come home complaining that he was too clingy, and then she moved on. I didn't have the patience for it.

"Melanie, this is Braden," Emily said with an edge to her voice that told me we'd been introduced before.

"Whatever. If he's still around in two weeks, then I'll remember his name." I pursed my lips and blew at a strand of damp, red hair that had escaped from my waist-length braid and stuck annoyingly to my cheek.

"Melanie," Emily hissed.

"It's okay," Braden said evenly. He rested a skinny arm on the bar and leaned in. "So, me and Em were thinking it might be fun to take a ride over there and watch the battle—from a safe distance, of course."

"Take a ride. Like, in *my* car?" I grabbed a towel and started wiping down the bar, ramming his elbow with the damp cloth once or twice, like he wasn't even there. He didn't get the message.

"Come on, Mel," Emily begged. "Just this once. Braden's gonna get his license back soon. Then we'll have his Mustang."

"Once I get it running," Braden added.

"Sure," I said sarcastically as I turned away. I meant it snarky, but at quitting time, they both piled into my Subaru like they owned it, with Braden in the passenger seat. I didn't kick him out.

"We're not going to the Ritz Carlton. The place is crawling with monsters," I said. "But I'll drop you off wherever you want to go."

"Your place is fine." Braden arched an eyebrow at my sister while she giggled.

"Ugh." I pulled onto 20th Street and glanced toward the hotel as we crossed Arapahoe. The traffic light was out, along with almost all the streetlights, but that hardly mattered since we were the only car on the road. Red and blue police lights flashed in front of the hotel. Erickson's fault, no doubt.

This town had been fine until he came along. Now almost everyone had died, changed, or fled. If I'd had the money, I'd be gone, too, but nobody was buying houses in Denver anymore, not since the weirdness began. Without the money from the house Mom left us, Emily and I would have a hard time starting over someplace else. Besides, with monsters spreading, other cities might not be any better, and we already had this house fortified.

A red streak jetted across the sky above us, followed by an explosion. I slammed on the brakes. For a few seconds, orange firelight lit the dark street. Braden and Emily had their windows down, and he hung halfway out of his, howling drunkenly at the sky. "Look at that! The Fae Army's fightin'…I dunno—somebody."

I slapped his knee. "Quiet. Don't attract attention." He ignored me, so I zoomed down 20th past the bus station.

Mutant bikers caught us at the next intersection. They'd probably heard Braden yelling and showed up for the free meal. Dozens of motorcycles swarmed around my car and blocked our way. The pair of soldiers stationed at the corner refused to get involved. They didn't want to die any more than we did. My headlights caught the riders' apelike profiles and glinted off their piggy eyes. One pulled his bike up next to my window and peered in, showing yellow tusks in a leer. My heart raced, and I gripped the steering wheel hard. I'd heard of those guys, of course, but I'd never seen one up close. The sheer size of him was intimidating as hell. He had to be seven or eight feet tall.

"Get inside," I cried, and for once, Braden and my sister obeyed. They rolled up their windows and I hit the automatic lock button on the doors. I threw the car into reverse, but more bikes roared up behind me and blocked us in. When I laid on the horn, the riders laughed.

We stared, wide eyed, as a motorcycle with a sidecar rumbled slowly toward us. The passenger had a long, white beard that half obscured his apelike face. Beads dangled from his matted hair, and his gnarled hands gripped a thick tube. He pointed it at Emily and waved the tube at her, drawing complex patterns in the air. Silver mist wafted toward our car, melting through glass and steel to cling to my sister's head like the halo of an angel.

"What's he doing?" Emily breathed.

"Drawing sigils," Braden said in a rush. "The clans use young women in their rituals. Some religious thing. Melanie, we can't let 'em take her."

"They want to *sacrifice* me?" Emily squealed.

"No, they won't kill you. They catch women and…uh, change them," Braden muttered.

"Into what?" I asked. He wouldn't answer.

Emily pointed at a neon-blue glow in the sky, a block to the west. "Look!"

"What the hell is that?" Braden asked.

"Magic," I said shortly. Even I knew that much.

Rogue magic rolled toward us like iridescent fog, floating over the ground and sending tendrils questing between buildings. The faint blue light illuminated a fast-moving animal, one of those new human-coyote hybrids that ran around Denver in homemade armor. Barely ahead of the wave, the coyote raced between motorcycles and leaped over the hood of my car. Our headlights glinted off the fine silver metalwork on the segmented leather armor he wore. The coyote's front paws hit the windshield and spread, leaving clear dirt prints of five prehensile toes. He vaulted the car and was gone.

We gasped as tentacles of light whipped over the two soldiers at the corner. Their backlit silhouettes raised their arms against the crackling cloud, and the men disappeared, gone like they'd never existed. Baboon-faced bikers gunned the engines of their Harleys as they roared away. A gap opened in front of our car.

Emily leaned forward, clutching the back of my seat with both hands. "Go, Melanie, go! Don't let it touch us."

I stomped on the gas, and the engine of the gutless little Impreza whined. Most of the motorcycles outdistanced us and disappeared, but four of them held their positions around our car. The shaman in the sidecar pulled up on our left and pointed his wand at Emily. I cut the wheel hard and slammed into him.

Braden whooped in victory as the motorcycle and sidecar crashed in a shower of sparks. The three surviving bikes roared away.

In the rearview mirror, I saw the shaman lift his head from the wreckage and point a pale arm at us. A blazing projectile flew from his hand. A streak of fire skimmed the pavement and erupted beneath my car with an ear-shattering boom.

My sister screamed as we rolled. My car came to a stop upside down. My body hung painfully from my seatbelt as blood ran from cuts on my face. Nauseating gas fumes stung my throat. I coughed and felt a stabbing pain on my left side. Intense blue light filled the car, so bright it hurt my eyes through closed eyelids. Neon-blue flames licked up my body and set the cuts on my face ablaze. In seconds, the magic faded.

Braden was gone, crushed or thrown clear, I couldn't tell. My sister hadn't had her seatbelt on, and I couldn't see her, either.

My voice rose high in panic. "Emily? Em! Are you okay?"

Something smashed into the driver side window. I screamed. A man loomed outside in the shadows, swinging a tire iron. *Is that the shaman?* I could barely see through the spiderweb cracks that spread across the glass. Dim blue sparks glinted from his eyes.

I recognized Braden when he shouted my name. His button-down work shirt was torn open, revealing six-pack abs, broad shoulders, and a chiseled physique. No way he'd looked like that before. I would have noticed, even if he was a loser.

My head ached, and my chaotic thoughts turned back to Emily. I still couldn't see her.

With a groan of bending metal, the car door opened. Braden reached in over my head and slashed at my seat belt with a knife. When it parted, I fell painfully to the ceiling, which was now below me. My sister lay still, her white dress crumpled against the rear window. Ignoring the searing pain in my side, I crawled into the back of the car. Emily was breathing, thank God. Gently, I rolled her toward me. The crash had destroyed her jaw, so it protruded into a point, like the long muzzle of an alligator.

How can a jaw break like that? The sight made me sick.

"Lie still. You're going to be okay," I said softly.

My sister shuddered and opened dull, red eyes. Her lips parted, revealing a jagged mouthful of fangs. I recoiled.

"Oh, Jesus. Come on, Melanie, come on." Rough hands tugged at my shoulder. Braden dragged me bodily from the overturned car, ignoring my shrieks of pain. My knees buckled, and I collapsed on the ground. He hoisted me over his shoulder and ran.

The shattered edges of my broken ribs grated together, and I thought I might vomit. "Put me down."

"Quiet," Braden ordered. "Someone's following us. Oh, shit. It's Emily." He eased me off his shoulder and set me on my feet, facing back the way we'd come.

That was when I saw my sister squatting in the street. Long, thin legs bent sharply, so her bony knees were even with the top of her head. By starlight, her skin looked rough and gray. She tipped her muzzle up and locked her gaze on me. In the moments since we'd gotten out of the car, those bulging, red eyes had migrated around to the sides of her head. Except for the white dress, she was completely unrecognizable. Blood dripped down her animal face.

"Em? You're hurt," I whispered. "I can...uh, find a bandage someplace."

Braden grabbed me by the hand. "Don't be stupid. Stay away from her."

My sister fixated on the trickle of blood dripping from my chin and licked her lips. A thin stream of drool hung from her jowls. The hump on her back rippled and swelled until a spiky ridge of bone tore through the flimsy fabric of her dress.

A pathetic mewling sound escaped my throat as Braden and I backed away. Emily dropped to all fours and stalked us on splayed legs. With each step, her head swept from side to side, nostril slits skimming the pavement. My palm felt damp against Braden's.

"Emily, stop it, it's me!" I cried.

Emily halted. She pressed her thin lips together and moaned. The sounds were almost words, almost my name. Her red eyes gleamed with what I imagined were tears. *Is she still conscious, trapped in a monster's body? Can I cure her somehow?*

She sprang at us, jaws gaping. White fangs reflected moonlight. Braden dropped my hand and ran. In a blur, the thing that had been my sister passed me and pounced on him. He never even had time to scream.

I stumbled away, numb with shock. Every breath hurt, and a heavy, painful weight sank into my left lung. If I didn't find a place to hide soon, something worse than Emily would find me.

I pushed through a squeaky gate in a chain link fence, entered an abandoned yard, and climbed the low branches of a big cottonwood. From there, I wiggled onto the nearly flat roof of a garage. Overhead, leaves whispered in the breeze. I stretched out on my back. The ache in my ribs subsided and let me focus on the agonizing fact that Emily was gone, and she was never coming back.

An electric tingling sensation tickled my scalp and soothed my broken rib. I sat up and almost groaned out loud. That weird blue fog orbited my hiding place, clearly marking my location for any observer, human or monster. I doubted the shaman had sent it. His men had scattered when it rolled in. *Does someone control it, or is it just a side effect of one of Damon Erickson's insane magical explosions?*

I plastered myself flat as a dented Jeep Cherokee came down the road, headlights off. It stopped, and two dark figures emerged. Moving inhumanly fast, they split up and ran around opposite sides of the house.

I was in trouble. Keeping low, I retreated from the garage roof onto the higher, steeper roof of the house. Light, fast footfalls followed me up there, and I made out the silhouette of a woman carrying a rifle. She was pale skinned, long and lean, and a lot taller than me. She could probably kick my ass without the gun.

"Hold it right there," she said. "You're coming with us."

Without thinking, I whirled and leaped off the two-story roof. I hit the grass hard, rolled, and came up on my feet. Somebody tackled me from behind so hard I tasted dirt. Panic threatened to overwhelm me as a man's giant hand wrapped the back of my head and held me down.

"Easy. Nobody's gonna hurt you. Please don't scream and call in the monsters," he said in a soft, deep voice with the hint of a Southern accent. "If you're quiet, I'll let you go."

The pressure on the back of my head eased, and I nodded. My captor released me. I stood, spitting turf, and looked over the young black man who stood over me. He didn't seem mean or angry, just cautious.

"Nice jump," he said, glancing up at the roofline. "You always been able to do stuff like that?"

"No. She scared me." I gestured at the tall woman, who was now striding across the yard toward us. Up close, she was younger than I thought, in her early twenties, like me.

"Scared don't let you jump like that," the man said.

The tall, pale woman stopped a few paces away, folded her arms, and stared me down. "What were you doing out here all alone?"

"I had a car," I said defensively. "We got caught by one of those mutant motorcycle gangs. They tried to grab my sister, and I ran 'em off the road."

"You ran the Orcs off the road?" The black guy gave a low, impressed whistle. "Dang. I like her already."

The woman nodded at me, like that had earned me a measure of respect. "Go on."

"Their shaman blasted us and wrecked my car. Rogue magic caught us, and my sister turned. She's lost. Gone." Tears welled up in my eyes. Saying it somehow made it more real.

"You're lucky she didn't attack you," the woman said. She shifted her grip on the rifle and swept it around the dark yard.

"She, uh, killed Braden instead. Emily wouldn't hurt me," I said.

The woman snorted. "Don't count on it."

"Pink, we gotta get moving," the man said. "We don't have the manpower to be out here like this, and this one's obviously a freak. We ought to—"

"Freak? Who you callin' freak?" I interrupted.

Pink ignored me. "You're right. Let's get her back to the house."

"I can't just leave my sister," I protested. "She's lost and probably hurt. We need to find her and bring her, too."

The man shook his head. "We don't bring monsters to the house. We're pushing our luck bringing you."

Monsters. That shut me up.

"It's okay," Pink said to her companion. "We're always short on freaks. If she works out, she can stay."

The pair moved around toward the front. I tagged along until I reached the Jeep, then dug in my heels. "I don't need to stay with you. I have a house and a job."

"Within walking distance?" Pink asked.

I shifted my feet. "Um, maybe. If nothing bothers me on the way."

Honestly, I wasn't too eager to go home. Without Mom, me and Emily were barely hanging on. With my sister gone, too, I might lose my mind. The old house held too many memories. Besides, how was I supposed to get to work without a car? At the bar, Chuck bartered liquor for food, ammo, guns, sometimes clothes. Things you could trade. Our paychecks were mostly crates of canned food. Money wasn't worth much anymore, at least not in Denver.

The man opened the back door of the Jeep, stood aside, and gestured me in.

I looked up at the stranger and took a step back. "I don't even know you."

"Nobody's kidnapping you, Princess," Pink said tiredly. "Do what you want. We're going back to the safehouse."

I got into the Jeep. "My name is Melanie. Don't call me Princess."

Her lips quirked at that, but she didn't answer. Nobody talked much as we got underway. I scanned the sidewalks, guiltily searching for Emily. I couldn't just leave her, but I was too scared to stay there alone.

The guy in the passenger seat turned and gave me a reassuring smile. "I'm Jamal. Glad you decided to come along. Nobody lasts long alone, not even freaks."

"Freaks?" I repeated.

"Yep. Freaks like us. You might've noticed you're faster and stronger than you were before, and that's just the start. You'll get better as you train. Pink's one of our best, since she got turned in the first wave. By now, she's got about a ten-foot vertical leap."

"More like eight most of the time. Unless I'm being chased," Pink said without taking her eyes off the road.

As she took us northeast on Speer, my mind replayed my crazy leap off the roof. A couple of hours ago, I'd have broken a leg trying that. I had no idea what possessed me to do it. Some part of me must have known.

We arrived at the vigilante safe house, a big, dark, brick building without a glimmer of light anywhere. Black plastic covered the windows, same as my house. That much was normal. Everyone knew light attracted monsters. We waded across the front yard through knee-high weeds. Above us, tall trees blocked out the sky. The fire-scarred front door was boarded up, so Pink and Jamal veered right and led me around the side of the house. A big steel cage filled the side yard. The cell door swung open as we approached. I hesitated.

Pink sighed. "We aren't planning on keeping you in a cage, Melanie. It's part of our security system. We lock it behind us before we open the door into the house, so nothing forces its way in on our heels."

From her dark tone, I figured that must have happened before, and I didn't want to know. I'd had all the trauma I could take for one day.

"Makes sense," I grunted.

The wide, dark wings of a queen harpy soared overhead, briefly blotting out the moon, and from the scrabbling of claws on the roof, I was pretty sure she landed up there. The unmistakable, rotten-meat stench of harpy filled the air, meaning there had to be a whole flock around. That made up my mind, so I followed Jamal into the cage without another word.

The safehouse had once been someone's trophy home. Young adults crowded the spacious kitchen, along with one older guy, a short, muscular Latino with a two-toned silver and black ponytail. I blinked in mute surprise at his black roots. Was he really aging in reverse? I heard Damon Erickson could do that to a person, but I was too numb to ask if it was true. So much had happened. Emily was out on the streets, hurt and terrified. I'd run off with strangers and left her. Some sister I was.

In the safety of the home, the reality of it all hit me. Braden was dead. Emily, worse than dead. I'd been changed into some kind of freak. I huddled in a kitchen chair, shaking, and let the tears roll down my face. When a pretty brunette with golden, bioluminescent skin pressed a cup of tea into my hands, I barely nodded.

A black puppy clung to her shoulder, as balanced as a kitten, and it took me a second to realize that it wasn't a dog at all, but a human-coyote hybrid. His brown-striped feet had stubby fingers instead of dog toes, and the eyes had the same hint of neon blue as all Erickson's creatures.

I was one of his creatures now. That hit me hard. Conversation droned around me, and I only half listened. About half the vigilantes were freaks, judging by their Olympian physiques and near-universal beauty. I couldn't be one of them. It wasn't real. This wasn't happening.

"Come on, don't be shy," the sparkly brunette told me encouragingly.

I tuned in with a start. I'd missed something. "Huh?"

Pink got in my face. "I said, what's your story? Who are you? What's the most important thing about you? Why should you get to live when so many others have to die?"

God, she's relentless. My gaze swept the kitchen. All eyes were on me. I didn't know what to say, so I settled on the truth.

I took a deep breath. "My name's Melanie. They tell me I'm a freak now. The thing about me is, well, I...I let my sister down tonight. We got hit by rogue magic, and she changed. I didn't go after her. We just left her on the street alone, lost and bleeding, and turning into a monster with alligator jaws and big jumping legs like a cricket. Why should I get to live? I don't know. Maybe I shouldn't."

Out of nowhere, Pink delivered a powerful slap across my face that almost knocked me off my chair. Everyone gasped. Furious, I jumped up and started swinging. The taller girl easily blocked my punches. After a dozen shots were brushed aside without a single touch, I stepped back and lowered my fists, breathing hard. Pink had humiliated me without even trying.

She turned her back on me and spoke to her crew in a calm, even voice. "Listen up, people. This is the kind of shit that gets our fighters *killed*."

The vigilante chief paced the silent kitchen, looking into each face in turn as she talked. The only person she ignored was me. "What do you think's gonna happen if you go into battle feeling special because your sins are *sooo* much worse than everyone else's?"

After a moment of silence, the Latino spoke up. "You die." His silver and black ponytail swung as he turned dark, piercing eyes on me. "And you'll probably take your friends with you."

"That's right," Pink snapped. "Leave your guilt at the door, Melanie. It's bratty and self-indulgent, and we can't afford that. We're living way too close to the bone as it is."

"You don't even—" I began. She cut me off.

"Face it. Your sister isn't human anymore. Those things with alligator jaws and big jumping legs—we know the type. There's more like her, lots more. They find each other and pack up. They're smart, hard to kill, and absolutely fucking ruthless. If you ever see her again, those jaws will be at your throat. You know how many people we lost in the last two weeks? Nine. We're down to forty people, and only nineteen freaks, not counting you."

Not counting me. That sounds like they're about to kick me out. What'll I do? Search for Emily? Try to survive the long walk back home?

Pink turned away dismissively. "Isabelle, you have your first apprentice," she said to the girl with the puppy. "She has three days."

"Three days?" Isabelle echoed. "I thought new freaks always got a week."

Pink closed her eyes for a second and let out a slow breath. "That's all I'm willing to invest here. If she fails her hunt, she's done."

When Isabelle jumped off the kitchen counter, the weird puppy stayed right with her, clutching her shoulder with four tiny monkey hands. "Yes, ma'am. I won't let you down."

Pink shrugged. "It's a long shot, so don't feel bad if she doesn't make it." The chief strode from the room, the pink-dyed tips of her dirty-blonde hair sweeping down her back.

Up close, my new coach looked about sixteen. I couldn't believe they'd put a kid in charge of me. That's what I got for losing control, for crying and striking back at Pink. I'd never show weakness in front of the vigilantes again, not for one second.

If I hadn't needed them to survive, I'd have walked out. Truth was my odds of making it home on foot were slim. And if I made it, what then? I couldn't walk to work every night without becoming monster chow. I'd have to hide in the house until the food ran out, then hit the streets with the other scavengers. Alone, I'd be easy prey. My test, whatever that entailed, would happen in only three days. I had to pass it and earn a spot with the vigilantes. That was the only way to survive, at least until I figured out how to get out of there.

Instead of training me, my teenage coach bustled around the kitchen, frying up a pan of mystery meat. Judging by the leathery wings, it was a young harpy, but when it hit my plate, I ate the meat down to the bones. Then she led me upstairs, where I hoped we'd learn something useful. Instead, Isabelle pushed me into a darkened bedroom with no furniture and a floor covered with sleeping bags. A few girls snoozed there.

"Sleep," she whispered. "I'll wake you when it's time to go."

I let out a frustrated groan. "I'm not sleepy. We should get to work, we only have—"

Angry fireflies zipped across Isabelle's face. "Do as I say, or I'll fail you right now."

"What happens if you do?" I blurted.

She put her hands on her hips. "You leave. Alone, with baby harpy on your breath. Why do you think there's a queen sitting on our roof?"

"Oh." I gulped. "Okay."

Isabelle supervised annoyingly as I took off my shoes and stretched out. Then she slipped from the room. A tear in the black plastic over the window let in a slit of morning light. I'd been up all night.

My thoughts churned. *I lost Emily. How can I be worrying about some stupid test?* I fell into an exhausted sleep and woke alone at twilight. I swore. My teacher had forgotten me. A whole day of training was gone, wasted. Without Emily, without a car, these people were my only chance at survival. I couldn't fail out. I sat up and shoved my feet into my tennis shoes.

Isabella came in quietly. By the light from the hallway, I saw she wore fighting gear—an armored vest of harpy leather that protected her vital organs, black jeans, and a pair of lightweight boots. Dark makeup hid the light from her skin.

"Hey, Melanie, I brought you a present," she said.

That quashed whatever bitchy thing I might have said. Isabelle sat down cross legged on the foot of my sleeping bag and pulled out a foil-wrapped square of chocolate.

I leaned forward. "Real chocolate? I haven't seen that since the Change."

"Hard to believe it's only been six months. Seems like forever," Isabelle said. She turned over the candy in her hands. "I've been saving this for a special occasion. We used to celebrate whenever we got a new freak, but with Damon missing, and so many dead, nobody has the heart for it anymore. I still thought it was important." Bright tears filled Isabelle's eyes. She reached out and dropped the chocolate into my hand. "Congratulations, Melanie."

"Damon Erickson disappeared?" I blurted, and then put a hand over my mouth, embarrassed. I should've offered condolences about the dead people, or at least thanked her. To hide my discomfort, I broke the chocolate in half and shared it. We took tiny bites, making it last.

"Damon went to war alone. None of his friends went with him. Well, not exactly alone, because he's allied with the Fae, but Pink and Jamal didn't support him," Isabelle whispered with a nervous glance through the open door.

I raised an eyebrow. "Why not?"

Isabelle leaned close and whispered. "Because friends of Damon Erickson tend to die young."

I wasn't one bit surprised. "Oh. Who's he fighting?"

"Governor Richter. Richter took Damon's girlfriend hostage, and he mobilized the Fae to take her back. That's why we're taking care of his puppy. But don't worry, we won't get involved in that tonight."

"What are we doing?" Excitement tingled through me. I stood and stretched, feeling limber and strong.

"Reconnaissance mission. We need to find the pack of monsters that has your sister. Come on, let's choose our weapons." Isabelle led me downstairs and through a living room with a corkboard wall, where fistfuls of throwing knives bristled from colorful targets.

A left turn through an open archway took us into the former great room, a gymnasium now, with blue mats on the floor and weapons on the walls. Planks covered the floor-to-ceiling window on the far end, leaving the room dark except for a shrine where candles flickered beside pictures of the dead. Photos crowded the table, dead heroes grinning with friends or posing with the carcasses of monsters. Their ghosts drew me in and forced me to stare.

"So many," I murmured.

"Yeah. That's why you can't fuck this up," Isabelle said.

I swallowed hard and followed her to a barrel of spears, where I hefted each one until I found one that felt right. Hope bloomed in my heart. "We're gonna find the monsters that have my sister, and I'll take her back. Magic made Emily into a monster. Magic has to turn her human again! Damon Erickson will know. I'll find him, too, and I'll make him tell."

Isabelle busied herself sorting through a rack of armored vests. She didn't meet my eyes as she laced me into one that stank of boy sweat and old blood. "Yeah. We'll have to talk about that." Gripping her spear, she headed for the door.

I didn't follow. "Hey, wait up. Shouldn't we practice first?"

She shook her head. "Stationary targets give you bad habits. They don't fight back. Besides, we don't have time. You have one night to locate the pack, and one night to hunt."

"I had three nights before you wasted one," I griped.

"You were an emotional wreck. It would've been suicide to take you out last night."

I shrugged. "Fair enough. Say we find the pack. How many of them do I need to kill to pass this test?"

Isabelle took too long to answer. Her words came haltingly, a few at a time, like each one hurt to squeeze out. "Only one. Just…your sister."

"What?" My stomach twisted like I might hurl right there on the mat. "*That's* the test?"

Isabelle sighed. "I'm sorry. There's no easy way to tell you, but yes. That's the test."

"That's deliberately cruel. Evil. Whoever designed this test must be a psychopath!" My voice rose higher with every word until I was screaming. Concerned faces peered in through the archway. "Pink made this up just for me, didn't she? Didn't she?"

She winced. "No, she didn't make up anything just for you. You're not that special, Melanie. This is our tradition. This is the most painful thing we do, and the most honorable. If our friends turn, we end them ourselves. Who else would you have do it? Some stranger?"

I fell silent, staring at nothing.

Isabelle put a sympathetic hand on my arm. "Have you ever had a pet that needed to be put down?"

I nodded. "A golden retriever. His name was Griffin. He...got cancer." My eyes stung. I couldn't think about him, not now, on top of everything else.

She squeezed my arm. "When Griffin went on that last trip, who went with him?"

I took a shuddering breath. "Our whole family. Me, my mom, and Emily. She was ten."

"You went because you loved him. Because it was your responsibility. Because we don't let our friends go on like that." She twitched her chin at the photos of the monsters, and for the first time, I saw that they weren't trophies. The shrine was for them, too.

Tears threatened, but I wouldn't let myself cry. Isabelle was right. I had to do this for my sister's sake. I told myself that Emily would have done the same for me, even though I knew it wasn't true. Clutching our spears, we slipped out into the night. The sentries in the cage unlocked the gate, and we were on our own.

Isabelle led the way down the middle of the dark street. The back of my neck tingled as if unseen eyes watched me. The eerie feeling intensified as we entered a decaying commercial zone.

She halted. "Hear that?"

What I had taken for the rustling of leaves came closer. A huge, snakelike form longer than a car emerged from the shadows and scuttled toward us on a thousand tiny legs. On the blunt, almost eyeless head snapped a pair of hooked, bone-white mandibles.

"That's a good one to practice on," Isabelle said, talking fast. "Both ends are venomous, but you can stab it in the middle if you're quick. Watch out for the stinger on the hind end. See it?"

"Yes." I hesitated, eyeing the foot-long spike at the end of the tail. "You aren't going to help me?"

"No! Get in there."

"Oh my God." I danced forward, brandishing my spear, and stabbed at the monster's head.

The stinger arced over its back and snapped down, mousetrap fast. I barely twisted out of the way in time, and the knife edge of my spear caught the tip of the tail. The thrill of victory surged through me as I slashed sideways to sever the poisonous barb. The muscular tail cracked like a whip, tearing my spear from my hands and flinging it away to clatter against a wall. Panic took me. Screaming, I dove on the monster, seized the cylindrical base of its stinger, and wrenched at it with all my strength.

The monster dragged me along the asphalt, ripping my jeans and grinding off patches of my skin. I fought the powerful tail as it lifted me into the air and slammed me down again. Buggy ichor soaked my hands.

With a guttural cry, I wrenched the base of the stinger, and it snapped off in my hands.

I fell. The back of my head struck pavement as the beast came over the top of me, mouth open and mandibles snapping. A million tiny legs tickled revoltingly up my body and over my face.

I slammed an elbow into its toothy mouth, wiggled backwards, and freed my upper body. With an overhand strike, I drove the stinger deep into the top of its head. The monster shivered and thrashed.

With a sudden lunge, it seized my left elbow in its mouth. I screamed, yanked the stinger out, and stabbed it again and again. Finally, the monster lay still.

I rolled out from under it and lay in the street, shaking. My torn left arm burned, and stinking bug blood soaked my clothes. I hoped it wasn't poison.

My coach gave me a hand up. I expected congratulations, but instead she said, "Melanie, look at your hands."

I held them up. They glowed with a magical, neon-blue light that faded as we watched. I shrugged. "Cool. They're lit like yours."

"No, better." On hands and knees, Isabelle rooted around the carcass and came up with the severed stinger, holding it by the smooth, chitinous base. Even by moonlight, blackened burn scars clearly outlined the shape of my hand.

I gulped. "What the—"

From somewhere in the dark came hissing sounds and the drumroll of countless tiny feet. A wave of giant centipedes rolled toward us, enough to pack the street for a block.

"Oh, shit." Isabelle grabbed my arm. "Run!"

We sprinted down the street. I lost my bearings, but that didn't matter, not with thousands of monsters on my ass. That familiar, neon-blue fog hung in the sky not a block away.

I pointed. "Look, rogue magic. Does it always mean freaks?"

"That, or Damon himself is there," Isabelle said.

With new hope, we ran toward the light. My legs ached, and my lungs burned, but the prospect of rescue pushed me on. We rounded a corner and abruptly stopped.

An enormous wall blocked the street, concrete blocks stacked thirty feet tall, like they had around the secure compounds Emily and I used to wish we lived in. A slow tornado of magic spun in the center. I raced up to the wall, slapping it with open hands and screaming, "Help us! Let us in."

Nobody answered.

We followed the wall to the nearest guard tower and pounded on the door. "Hey. Open up."

A sliding metal panel slid sideways, and a man's anguished face appeared, visible by the light of two torches that burned from sconces on the wall. "We called hours ago, and two girls is all we get?"

"Look behind us!" Isabelle shouted.

A spotlight on the wall illuminated the monsters. They'd be on us in seconds. I raised my hands in mute appeal, and their glow about scared the piss out of the guard.

"All right, all right!" His face disappeared from the portal. Uneven footfalls came from the stairs, a step and a thud, a step and a thud.

My impatience built to the breaking point. Isabelle and I stood with our backs to the closed door. She held her spear ready, for all the good it would do.

Forty feet away, the first wave of giant centipedes paused and raised their front ends as if they smelled the dead bug juices on my clothes. All at once, they flopped forward and charged.

I screamed.

The door opened behind us, and a haggard, bloody man appeared. He yanked us inside and slammed the door. Crashes shook the wall as monsters threw themselves against it. We crowded together in the small, dark space, breathing hard.

"You're hurt. What happened?" Isabelle asked our rescuer.

"We can't talk here; it's not safe. Quick. Up the stairs." Leaning hard on the handrail, the wounded man led the way up a staircase and into a small, windowed room at the top of the guard tower. He closed the door behind us and rammed a bolt into place. The room held one stool and a small, round table, where a single beeswax candle burned beside a CB radio. A second closed and barred door stood opposite the one we'd come in.

The guard looked about thirty, with thin, wiry limbs, a soft belly, and an unkempt brown beard. Triple claw marks scored his tanned face. Judging by his physique, he was no freak.

"Thank God you're here," he said. "There are survivors, but I can't get to them."

"What's your name?" I asked.

"Scott. Scotty to my friends."

"I'm Melanie, and this is Isabelle. Do you want us to see to that leg?" I asked.

"No time. We've got women and children trapped on the other side. They can't hold out much longer." Scotty lifted a rifle from the wall and slung the strap over his shoulder before he unbarred the second door.

Behind his back, Isabelle and I made eye contact. This was bad. The poor guy thought we'd been sent to save him. I swore to myself I'd try. I had to. He didn't know I wasn't trained. He didn't need to know. Better to give him what hope I could.

We stepped outside onto a caged walkway that overlooked a courtyard below. I heard scuffling and the faraway hum of a generator, and it smelled like death. Hooded spotlights lit each end of the yard, leaving the center, where we were, in shadow except for the nebulous glow of magic. Faint blueish tendrils swirled through the air and hung down from above me like the tentacles of jellyfish, at turns becoming unbearably bright and then disappearing.

"What do you have for weapons, Scotty?" I asked softly.

"There's an arsenal of edged weapons on the other side, if we can get to it. I got the AR-15 here, but I'm down to my last magazine. Shooting just draws them in, anyway. You can pump these things full of bullets, but it takes a lot to kill 'em. The others had pistols, but, but—" Scotty's voice broke. He pinched the bridge of his nose and closed his eyes for a moment. "It wasn't enough. We don't have magic like you."

Jesus. Scotty thought I'd shown up empty handed because I was the weapon. I winced. To hide my expression, I wrapped my fingers around the wire mesh barrier and looked down into the courtyard. The carnage was indescribable, but the monsters disturbed me more. They were tailless, with long, folding hind legs, splayed forelegs armed with three long claws, and the muzzles of alligators—exactly like Emily. Some wore the tattered remains of clothes. There had to be two hundred of them, chasing and leaping and fighting over corpses. I turned my face away.

Scotty grabbed my vest and jerked me backward. "Don't put your fingers through—"

With a high, nearly human shriek, a monster hit the mesh in front of my face. A shot went off next to my head, and the thing fell. My ears rang.

Scotty lowered the rifle. "See that? That's about the only sure way to kill 'em. Right between the eyes."

I stepped back from the barrier, shaken. Monsters gathered below us, clawing at the wooden walls, trying to get to us. Scotty was right. Guns didn't help. They made the problem worse.

"We better move." He led us along the catwalk, following the perimeter counterclockwise around the compound. Low buildings lined the wall. We saw no other people, and no lights but the two spot-lights.

Isabelle matched steps with me as we walked. "Let me see that arm."

I flexed my fingers at her. "I'm okay. It didn't get me."

"I mean this." Isabelle lifted my left arm to inspect the elbow. "Where the centipede bit you—it's healed."

She was right. Over the fang wounds, hypersensitive new skin tingled under her touch. When it had quit hurting, I'd forgotten it. "Whoa. Is that part of being a freak?"

Isabelle shook her head. "Only for you."

We fell silent as Scotty pointed. "Careful. This is as far as we go."

We rounded a corner and stopped. A section of walkway was torn off the wall, so the free end hung in a twisted mess of wood and metal that nearly reached the ground. Scattered carcasses lay below it. While we watched, a huge male leaped onto the hanging wire mesh and began to climb. Scotty fired a shot and swore as the creature dropped to the ground and ran off.

From the other side of the gap, a baby cried. The sound electri-fied the monsters. They massed outside one of the buildings and clawed at the door. The doorknob rattled as they turned it with their three-toed paws. The baby wailed on. I pictured the frantic mother trying to soothe it.

"Scotty, where's that arsenal? I'll grab some weapons and jump down onto the roof of the house. See the wall where the catwalk used to be? There're cracks between planks for handholds. I bet I can get the survivors to safety that way."

It was insane. What new mother could climb a three-story verti-cal wall, carrying a baby? I fully expected him to say no.

Scotty considered the idea for all of two seconds and then nodded. "Okay. I need to run back to the radio in the guard shack and tell 'em you're coming. The arsenal's the second door on the right. Um, after the gap." He grimaced. "Sorry."

Isabelle and I backed into the shadows and waited. We tracked Scotty's progress by the moans of the monsters following him. Occasional shots rang out.

"That was brave," Isabelle whispered.

"I had to. They are *babies* there." My voice broke. "When's the last time you saw a baby?"

Rogue magic swirled toward me. Violet tendrils drifted across my face and stroked my cheek, feeling surprisingly cool and solid. Somehow, they strengthened me.

Uneven footfalls came down the catwalk. Scotty limped rapidly toward us, his face tight with pain. Monsters followed him along the ground. In unison, dozens of them leaped and hung from the walkway by jaws and claws, swinging, working together to bring it down. Scotty shouted in alarm as a huge steel bolt tore from the wall beside his head. Adrenaline jolted my system.

"Go!" Scotty slapped a key into my hand. Another bolt popped loose, and the whole catwalk jerked.

Isabelle squealed. Scotty grabbed for the wall and hung on. I shoved the key in my pocket and sprinted toward the gap. My heart raced as I neared the abyss. It had to be twenty feet wide. Arms and legs pumping hard, I leaped. The ground below writhed with monsters. I pulled my knees high and hit the shattered planks of the far side two feet past the edge.

My triumphant whoop became a scream as the broken walkway tipped and spilled me off. I seized a fistful of metal mesh and swung by one arm, legs kicking. Sharp wires cut into the skin between my fingers. I yanked my feet up as monsters leaped for me. Jaws bumped my shoe. Hand over hand, I worked my way upward and climbed back aboard the catwalk, gasping.

The key got me into an armory full of swords, axes, and spears. I chose a long sword and a short one, and peered outside. Rogue magic waited for me like an idiot friend, feeding me power and advertising my location to my enemies. It followed me down the easy drop to the rooftops, where I crouched, smelling smoke. A bonfire burned on the far side of the compound. Monsters swarmed toward it. Silently thanking Scotty for the diversion, I dropped to the ground and ran for the door.

"Vigilantes," a brunette woman exclaimed, pulling me inside. A little girl of about five clutched her hand. Behind them, a second woman cradled a newborn in a cloth sling.

"Hurry. We've got to move," I hissed.

I dragged a table outside, and from there managed to boost the women and children onto the roof. Isabelle met us up there, bleeding badly from three deep gashes across her face.

She stumbled. I caught her by the arm, and blue light erupted from my hand. Wonder filled me as a wave of magic spread up her body and cascaded over her face. When the light faded, Isabelle was healed.

The women let out breathy, awestruck noises. After that, when I told them to climb, nobody argued. The five-year-old led the way. She climbed like a champ, her tiny fingers and toes fitting securely into the cracks between boards. Her mom went next, jaw clenched in a determined line. The mother of the newborn bundled her baby tightly on her back and followed them up.

I caught a flash of white in my peripheral vision as a pack of monsters ran past and, with horrifying certainty, I knew. Emily was there.

Isabelle hesitated, looking at me. "You okay?"

I passed her the short sword. "Take care of the survivors. I have to find my sister."

"Be strong." Isabelle tucked the blade into her belt and began to climb.

I was alone. My stomach churned, and my damp palm slipped on the hilt of the sword. Tendrils of magic drifted past. I opened my free hand to them and felt their soft, cool strands bunch into my fist. Arms spread, I jumped off the roof.

My sword swung wide as I landed. Out of the dark, three monsters lunged at me, jaws gaping. I whipped magic at them and brandished the sword. They ran.

Magic lit my way across the nightmare courtyard to its center, where I pivoted, searching for a telltale flash of white. "Emily! Get over here!" My shouts drew monsters, but not the one I wanted. Cracking tendrils of energy at them like a fistful of whips, I forced them back.

Fifty feet away, monsters hemmed me in. My sister materialized at the edge of the crowd, appearing and disappearing as she wove between her larger packmates. Drifting magic lit her scales in an eerie violet glow. Black blood stained her muzzle and the torn remains of that white dress, and I knew she'd been feeding.

"Emily, this is wrong. It has to stop," I said softly.

My sister raised her chin at me like a defiant child. She wasn't sorry. With a last, disdainful glance, she disappeared into the crowd.

"Get back here!" I shouted. She was gone.

A knot of monsters approached me, but she wasn't among them. Hissing, they leaped. I swung the sword, missed, and staggered sideways, thrown off balance by its weight. Something heavy slammed into my back. Talons ripped the nape of my neck and yanked on my armored vest. I bellowed with pain.

Pivoting left, I came eye to jaw with Emily. My dear, deceitful sister had sent her packmates as a distraction while she snuck up on me, and now she had a claw stuck in my harpy leather vest. She thrashed to free herself, and her weight threatened to pull me over backward. I grunted and fought to stay upright. If I went down, I'd die. The sword was too long, and in close quarters, nearly useless.

She changed tactics, pushing forward, jaws snapping. With my free hand, I gripped Emily's leathery throat and squeezed. Heat blazed from my palm, and my sister shrieked, a purely human sound.

My heart broke. "I love you. I'm sorry. Please forgive me."

I turned up the heat, and Emily threw herself backward. I steeled myself, spun, and drove the sword deep into her chest. She slumped to the ground. Magic whipped around us in a crackling whirlwind that scoured the tears from my face. As my sister's lifeblood ran out, the lights faded. Emily lay in the dirt, still kicking weakly. Scotty was right about them being hard to kill. When the pack rushed me, I ran away and left her there.

A red streak jetted overhead. Fire split the courtyard with a river of flame. Monsters scattered. A fire fairy flew past, wearing glowing armor of molten metal. Something hung on a rope below her. The fairy banked, her burden swinging wide, and came back to hover above me. Powerful wings drove blasts of superheated air that stung my eyes and parched my lips. The fairy's slender, dark-skinned form looked almost human, except for her wings and pointed ears, and a pair of clawed feet that gripped the ropes of a cargo net. In the net lay a still human form.

Fifteen feet above the ground, the net opened, and a man tumbled into the dirt with a grunt. It had to be Damon Erickson. The Maker had landed.

He rolled over and bellowed, "Naomi, light 'em up."

"With pleasure." The fairy's twenty-foot wings buzzed like chainsaws as she roared off after the monsters.

The Maker stood stiffly and limped toward me. Up close, Damon looked younger than I'd expected, eighteen or nineteen, too thin for his six feet, with unruly blond curls that spilled over his shoulders. Dirt caked the cuts on his bare legs, and dark circles shadowed his eyes.

When he saw me, his face lit with something like pride. "You're one of mine."

I was a freak. Time to own it. "Yes. I'm Melanie."

The Maker took my hand. "Rough day?"

I gave him a shaky nod. "Worst day of my life. I came out looking for you. My sister turned because of you. I found her, and I had to—" My throat tightened.

Anguish twisted Damon's handsome face. "I understand. I know that saying I'm sorry doesn't begin to touch it, but I am sorry."

"Then fix it," I snapped, dropping his hand. "Turn the monsters back."

"I can't." Damon pressed his lips together as if the admission hurt. He shifted and winced when his knee popped.

I stepped in to support his elbow, and violet light beamed from my hands. Magic crackled over the Maker's body, and where it touched him, he healed. His muscles went loose.

"Sit down," I said, helping him to the ground.

A wave of dizziness left me exhausted, and I sagged to the dirt beside him. Sitting was stupid with monsters around, but if I stood, I'd pass out. Magic had a price.

The Maker rubbed his knees with both hands. "You're a healer."

"It's nothing you can't do. I just don't understand why you won't. You wrecked the world, you ought to fix it." I looked away to avoid his weird, reflective eyes.

"Don't you think I tried?" Damon demanded. "I can't cure monsters. I'm not a healer like you."

"Are you saying I might—" A faint exhalation came from behind us.

We jumped up. "Oh my God, Emily." I snatched up my sword and ran to her. She writhed on the ground, alive and in agony. The sword strike must have missed her heart. She'd been suffering all this time. I never meant to torture her.

"Hold on. I can bring you back." I dug deep for my strength.

Magic played over her. As the wound in my sister's chest closed, I watched intently, eager to see her pretty face return. I couldn't wait to hug Emily again. We'd go to work, tell the story over drinks, and laugh.

Healed, the monster rolled to her feet and lunged for my throat.

I blocked with the sword, cursing myself for being a fool. Emily was gone. Extending my empty left hand, I took back my gift. Magic flowed into my body. The monster stumbled. My sister's round, red eyes held all the hurt and betrayal she couldn't voice.

"I'm sorry, Em," I whispered as the wound in her chest reappeared. This time, when she fell, it was me who screamed.

Emily's packmates converged on us. Naomi incinerated them until her petroleum-scented breath choked the air, but more came. Spheres of golden light blasted from Damon's hands, bright enough to light the whole compound, but even he couldn't hold them off forever. I wielded my sword and screamed as talons tore deep into my arm. Naomi arrived in a blast of superheated air, and the cargo net hit the ground beside us. We dove onto it. The net tightened around us as Naomi lifted off. Damon and I lay on our bellies, gripping the net, flying like superheroes as we swooped over the wall.

Outside the compound, vehicles evacuated Isabelle and the survivors, while tanks rolled in to mop up. Damon and I returned home at sunrise, dropping from the sky like angels. The loud buzz of Naomi's wings brought everyone outside to see us. When the net dropped open, I landed on my feet and was swept into a celebration. Isabelle hugged me. Pink shook my hand and welcomed me into the tribe. Later, sated with food and drink, I found a quiet spot in the backyard to grieve. Damon was there with his hybrid coyote pup. We sat in silence for a while before I spoke.

"Emily was always the nice one. I hate to admit it, but sometimes I'm not. Why did she become the monster?"

Damon petted the puppy as it settled onto his lap. "Magic chooses, Melanie. It has an intelligence of its own. Maybe you're a better person than you think."

* * * * *

C.A. Farrell Biography

C.A. Farrell is a biologist and the author of 24 published books, including the urban fantasy *Bait,* which became a finalist in the Indie Book Awards. When she's away from the keyboard, C.A. enjoys hiking and horseback riding in the Colorado mountains. She lives in Colorado Springs.

* * * * *

Choices
by C.M. DeMott

"It's fading, you know," Berl said. His long, pale hair rode the breeze, parting now and then to reveal his elegantly pointed ears.

I stared off over the green. "I do. Yet still, it remains."

He shook his head. "Ah, poor Ferli, ever the optimist. Is that what your pets tell you?"

An old, familiar argument. "They aren't pets. They're people. Just like you and I."

"If you can call something that breeds like prey and lasts but a moment 'people.'"

I gave him a stern look. "Hardly fair."

He affected a sigh, blue eyes crinkling with silent laughter. "True enough. The right ones can be most entertaining."

"And you've been well and truly *entertained*."

"I have." He turned away from the view to face me. "But that doesn't answer my question. King Huon is planning to close all but the Merlin gate. If you want to keep access to the Fair Lands, you'll need to leave soon."

"I'll think on it."

"Don't take too long." He opened a Folde with a gesture. "See you later."

He slipped through the glowing circle and vanished. The Folde sealed behind him. I looked back down on the forest. Broceliande, also known as the Paimpont Forest from its closeness to a village of that name. I'd been born in the Royal Forest on the Isle of the Mighty, but I'd lived here most of my life. In spite of the tourists, it was still a wilder place than where I'd grown up. As much as I liked my visits to the Fair Lands, this was my home. The thought of leaving was painful. So was watching it die.

An evening breeze came up from the forest, bringing the scent of ancient trees and fresh growth. I started down the hill, taking care to walk into the breeze where possible, and keeping aware of the life around me. There shouldn't be any humans at this time of day, but that didn't always mean there weren't any.

I wandered through the familiar trees, nibbling when something caught my fancy. No particular destination, just a desire to be in the forest, feeling its ancient rhythms. Thought of slipping back to a more peaceful time, but didn't. Here and now was what concerned me. This was what I'd be leaving. If I decided to go.

I stopped for a drink at a stream, then continued on, breaking into a run. The trees sped past, my hooves making scarcely a whisper as they struck the ground. Some time after, I crossed out of the park and into a private estate. Seeing a flicker of light through the trees, I slowed to a walk. The trees pulled back a little, giving way to a low stone wall partially covered in vines. Ignoring the gate, I leaped the wall, landing on the path of a neatly laid out garden next to the rosemary.

"Greetings, Ferli." A small woman straightened from two beds over. "You're out a little early."

"Felt the need for a run."

"And your feet led you here, just in time for fresh bread and honey."

I whickered softly. "Ah, baking day. Fortunate me."

She laughed, tucking a strand of hair nearly as white as mine back over one ear. "You've been coming here long enough. Come in."

I followed her to the stoop, ducking my head to enter. Moira was an excellent cook, and her bread truly delicious, even without the honey. She sliced a piece, spread butter and honey, and passed the plate over, then cut a piece for herself. I took a taste.

"Apple blossom honey?" I asked.

She laughed. "Yes, it is. Can't fool you." She took her own bite. "Is there any honey you haven't tasted?"

"Not that's found here or on the Isle. And more than a few from the Fair Lands."

Her eyes took a faraway look. "Ah. I remember the blue amber one you brought me that time. Evening starflower?"

I nodded.

"The best I've ever tasted. I dream about it sometimes."

I swallowed. "Not too much, I hope."

She looked at me with merry eyes. "I'm not pining for the Fair Lands, if that's what you mean." She took another bite. "Though I wouldn't mind seeing them again. And…" The humor fled, leaving her serious. "That's not likely to happen if it doesn't happen soon, is it? Assuming the king would allow it."

"What have you heard?"

She set her plate down. "Enough to know the Good Folk aren't pleased with how things are going this side of the gates, and they're planning to close them."

"That's true enough." I sighed. "With what humans have done to this world, can you blame them? All of nature besieged by those wanting things of the moment, and not caring what it costs?"

"We're not all like that. There's a push to make our footprint lighter. To be more in harmony with the land."

I dropped my head, nibbling more of the bread and its sweet burden. That knowledge was one of the reasons I had hope for the forest. "I know. That's one reason I'm still here, but it's one thing to stay knowing I can leave any time I want, and another to know I might be stuck here when I need a place to hide."

She finished her bread. "True. That's one reason I'm amazed to see you at all." She took my plate and put it with hers in the sink. "When will you be leaving?"

"I haven't decided yet."

She ran a little water on the dishes and came back to join me. "When to leave, or if?"

"Both, actually."

"I was hoping you'd stay a bit longer. Long enough to meet my great niece, anyway. She's coming over from the States and should be here in a few days." She paused, meeting my eyes. "She's had a rough time. Needs to see there's more to life than what that wretch of a boyfriend showed her."

"I'll be around."

Moira smiled. "I think you'll be pleasantly surprised. Anne paints. She's coming here to see if she can make a living at it."

"We'll see. No promises."

"I know. Want any more bread?"

I shook my head reluctantly. "It is good, but I need to see a few more things tonight. I'll keep an eye out for your niece."

"That's all I can ask." She walked me to the door and out to the garden gate. "Take care, Ferli. Do what you have to do. I'll miss you if you leave, but I'll understand."

I leaped the gate and trotted into the forest. Visited a few of my favorite trees, then turned toward the Vale of No Return. The crescent moon was high over the trees when I reached the lake at its entrance.

A feminine laugh rang out, followed by splashing. I slowed to a walk. Giggles, and more splashing. "Ooo, that's cold." I saw a flash of pale skin through the trees. As I stepped into view, a woman, clad only in long, yellow hair, turned in my direction.

The come-hither smile on her face quickly became a pout when she recognized me. "Oh, it's you, Ferli." She dropped back down in the water. The two other ladies with her, equally beautiful and similarly clad, sighed and did the same. "And you never bring anyone interesting with you."

"Why would I? What I like and what you like are two different things entirely."

"Still." The first lady moved closer. "You could let yourself be chased. I'm sure there are still some ardent young huntsmen about."

I moved over and took a drink. "Hunting's not allowed in the park, and those on private lands know better."

"What about those would-be druids?"

"Most of them mean no harm." I sighed. "But if, and I say *if* I run into any who do, I'll consider it."

"Good." They moved further out into the water. "We'll be waiting!"

"I said IF!"

Too late. All I heard was one final giggle and a splash. I sighed again. *Korrigans.* It would have to be someone more than stupid I gave to them, given their prey's chances of escaping with their sanity. Assuming they escaped at all.

I spent the rest of the night walking through the deep forest, visiting favorite places and trees. Toward dawn, I reached the Tomb of Merlin. No illicit visitors were at it tonight, which suited my mood. Contrary to legend, Merlin's body wasn't there, though it was the final place he'd been in this world. Instead, tired of watching the failure of what he'd worked for slowly grind to its end, he'd made a bargain with Nimue to gain a permanent place in the Fair Lands. I closed my eyes, feeling for the Gate.

I opened a Folde and stepped through.

* * *

A cool breeze was blowing. I took a deep breath. Here, the air was clean, more alive, with no taint of machines or other traces of 'modern' man. A pair of sylphs chased each other in what could have been a dance. The trees, taller, older, and more regal than their Mortal Realm counterparts, rustled as I passed. I answered their whispered greetings, and continued down the path, the soft green moss pleasant underfoot.

A short walk, and I was approaching a covered area that gave a good view of the garden around it. Berl looked up from the table where he sat with an older lady playing Fox and Hounds. "Ah, Ferli. So you did decide to come."

"For a while." I turned to his companion and nodded. "Greetings, Lady Evnial."

"Greetings, Ferli, and a pleasant evening to you." She took a small bowl and poured me some wine. I sipped, enjoying the flowery sweetness of it. She waited until I'd had a few more sips, then asked, "So you've finally given up on the mortal forest? Thought I'd never see the day."

"You still haven't."

"Truly? Even an optimist like yourself must have limits."

Berl laughed. "And he hasn't found them yet. I've been after him for years to admit the place is doomed, but he still says there's hope."

Evnial shook her head. "Even when the rulers of the Fair Lands have given up?"

"Even so." Berl looked at me. "Though you need to reconsider, and soon. The final decision will be on Midsummer Eve. I'd hate to see you trapped on the mortal side."

"So would I," I answered. "If he's leaving the Merlin Gate open, there should be magic enough to open a Folde. And there are always other whens to be if my current one isn't working out."

"Why even risk it?" Evnial asked. "The Mortal Realm is amusing, but there are plenty of other things more so here."

"There are, but I think the Fair Lands will lose more than they know if we lose our connection to it."

She laughed. "You're joking. The Mortal Realm is a pale shadow of ours. We'll never even notice."

I sighed. "Perhaps you're right, and I'm simply blinded by what was."

"But you don't think so," Berl said.

"No. Before I give up on the forest, I have to be sure."

"Suit yourself." Evnial moved a piece. "Your turn, Berl."

"Do what you need to be sure, my friend, but I'd hate to lose you over a broken dream." Berl turned back to the board. I finished my wine, nodded to them both, and left.

I'd come for more than a mere visit. Every unicorn here belongs to one of the seven herds. Mine was Efstanorien, the Starry Night herd. Given what I was considering, I needed to talk with my herd leader. That was Misliarinil, lead mare since well before I'd been a twinkle in my dam's eye. I knew where she was likely to be and headed in that direction, opening a Folde to avoid the city.

I came out on the grassy bank of a clear stream. The white snow-shine flowers leaned over the water at one place, complemented by the various greens of the moss growing on a fallen tree. The scent was cold and reminded me of raspberries. I brushed past the flowers and took a drink as the water flowed over the stones. Nibbled a flower, and a bit of moss to balance the flavor. Walking slowly, I let the sights and sounds of wood and water soothe the tension I always felt when going to such a meeting. Misliarinil had a prickly disposition, and it wouldn't do to intrude when she wasn't feeling like visitors.

I slowed down a little more. She'd been more than prickly the last time we'd met. Granted, I really shouldn't have slipped bittervine in with her violets, even though I thought it improved the flavor, or at least made it more interesting. She hadn't been at all amused. It didn't taken long for her to find out I'd done it, and the scolding I'd received still stung. "Idiot donkey" had been one of the nicer things she'd called me. Still, she hadn't banished me from her presence, and this was a serious matter. One that required her counsel, as well as her permission.

I continued forward, my pace getting slower as I did. Almost, I turned around. *Maybe she'll be in a better mood later. Much later. Maybe late enough that I can ask for forgiveness instead.* I stopped. *Maybe—*

"Get your sorry white hide over here, Ferli! Lurking in the bushes isn't making things any better."

Raising my head, I took a deep breath and picked up my pace. I stepped into the clearing. Misliarinil was standing by the spring. Her eyes narrowed when she saw me. So much for waiting until she was in a better mood. I suppressed a sigh, stopped three strides away from her, and bowed my head.

She looked me up and down. "Well?"

"Most of the gates into the Mortal Realm will be closed on Midsummer Eve. I haven't decided which side I want to be on when they do."

"And?"

I met her eyes. "I'd like permission to wait and decide on that day."

"The choice should be obvious. Do you really want to stay in a world being slowly poisoned by humans without regard for any other species sharing it?"

Did I? "They aren't all like that. Some—"

She cut me off with a snort. "Are in the minority. Most think saving it is a lovely idea, and might throw money at those actively trying to do so, if only to make themselves feel better. Some are bent on stripping it for their own gain. "

"It's still worth saving." When she didn't say anything, I went on, "And we need to try. If only because of what we stand to lose if it falls."

Another snort. "What? Greedy, blind beings who fear anything they can't control? Who have no use for anything they can't profit from? That doesn't stare at them as if they were the most wonderful things to ever grace a Realm?"

"Dreamers. Poets. Singers. Those who create beauty and joy from their very being."

"We have those here, and better."

"Do we?"

The soft mutter of the water as it flowed on its way filled the silence between us. There was nothing further I could say to make my case. I could only harm it. As the silence stretched out, I began to hope. Maybe she'd decide in my favor. Maybe she might even offer advice. At the very least, she might not forbid what I wished to do.

"You do have a point. But—" she gave me a stern look, "—so do King Huon and the other rulers of the Fair Lands. Granted, some of them have scant patience with mortals. He's not one of those. If anything, he's been beyond patient. For him to make this choice…" A sigh, and the slightest relaxation of her look. "As much as you annoy me by merely existing, you're still a member of this herd, and bring some value to it."

"Why, thank you, Herd Lead—"

"Don't flatter yourself. Every member of this herd has worth."

When she paused, I said, "So you'll grant my request?"

"Perhaps. What sign are you waiting for?"

"Sign?"

"Yes, sign. Or dream, prophecy, whatever. On what will you base your choice?"

I paused.

She snorted. "Thought so. You have no idea. Have you thought any of this through?" Another snort. "Obviously, you haven't. So, were you just going to visit your favorite places, stare at the tourists tramping around in the park, and get advice from your human friend?"

"Something like that. The trees—"

"The trees are afraid. Of course they'll ask you to stay. You give them power and hope by merely existing, but can they help you? Without a tie to the Fair Lands? No. They'll slide slowly into sleep. Merciful for them. Not so much for you, when the last one falls and you have no place to hide."

"There are other whens."

"And how long do you think your ability to go there will last, with access to the Fair Lands closed?"

"People still believe in unicorns. That provides some power."

"Hah! I've seen what they believe in. Little candy-colored, glittery cute rainbow horsies that dance with tiny butterfly winged people in amusing stories made for children. Found on all sorts of merchandise to fill the pockets of those who wouldn't recognize a true unicorn if one came up and bit them in the ass!"

"There are others who take us more seriously."

"Ah, yes. Those fantasy and science fiction authors. Poets, Artists. Some of them, anyway. Precious few, compared to the rainbow-glitter crowd."

"How are the others going to learn if their Realm loses access to the truth?"

Silence again. She closed her eyes. When she looked at me once more, they held sorrow. "You're truly set on this, aren't you?"

"Yes, Herd Leader."

"In spite of what happened to your brother Shindarial?"

"Things have changed—"

"So they won't trap you with lies and slaughter you like a stag. They'll just study every part of you and put what's left in a zoo when they're done. Answer the question."

"Yes. In spite of what happened to my brother."

"Then you have my permission to go."

I bowed my head. "Thank you, Herd Leader."

"You may regret this later. For now…" She straightened up, looking every inch the leader she was. "Remember the Mortal Realm as it is, not as you wish it to be. And remember that there will be others watching you and waiting to make their own decisions based on yours, Ferliurial. Choose wisely when the time comes."

I bowed again. "I will do my best, Herd Leader."

"Then go with my blessing. And pray we're not both making a grave mistake."

"My thanks." I bowed a third time. "You won't regret this." I flicked my tail and turned to go.

"I hope not. I truly do."

* * *

The memories she'd summoned by naming my brother wouldn't let me alone. At last I yielded to temptation and called up a Folde to that when, just as she'd probably intended. Such things would let you see what had been, but allowed no change of important events. You couldn't talk to or otherwise influence your younger self, or anyone close enough to know you in that time. Most used the skill to relieve triumphs. Mine was bittersweet. I'd chosen the exact time with care, because there was only so much I could face right now. I moved forward slowly, staying silent and hidden.

"You should see her, Ferli," Shindarial said. "Golden hair. Shines like real gold. And her scent. Cream and roses."

The younger me gazed adoringly at his big brother. "Gold will look great with your trophy band! It'll really stand out in all that brown."

Shindarial laughed. "That it will. And she's as sweet as her scent."

My younger self sighed. "When do you think I can start my trophy band?"

He nuzzled my neck with affection. "Not for a while, Ferli-burli. Leave that to the young stallions. At your age, you should be chasing butterflies, not maidens."

"But…"

"But, nothing. There's no filly for you to impress with your skill and daring in dealing with humans, so you don't need one." At the sadness in my eyes, he laughed again gently. "Tell you what, brother. When I go to win that hair, you can watch. I'll even give you the flower garland afterward, if she makes one."

"Really?" I saw the shine in my eyes, remembering. Remembered what came after, and turned away as silently as I'd come.

I walked until I reached a grove of willows and went into them, finding the nest I knew was there. Trophy bands. Something young stallions made to show their grace and skill in charming young human females. They'd pick out a likely girl, one young enough not to be concerned overmuch with boys, and let themselves be courted into coming close enough to be petted. They'd get a tasty treat or two, flowers woven into their manes, or an entire garland, and collect a few hairs from her head while nuzzling their quarry. Then they'd go gracefully, leaving the girl starry-eyed and hoping to see them again. Depending on how choosy the stallion's chosen filly was, he might have to collect a varied number of strands in all sorts of colors. The older the girl and the closer she lived to a city, the more daring the trophy. If older humans, especially the men, found out, the stallion would have to run for his life instead of spending a quiet moment with an adoring young maiden.

I shivered and dropped the thought. Too much pain. I'd never gotten that garland. Never started a band of my own. If Misliarinil wanted to steer my choice toward the Fair Lands, she could invoke no better memory. I stayed in the willows, breathing the old, familiar scents a little longer. Then I moved on, listening to the soft songs of trees, wind, and small creatures unconcerned with what I thought. Only when the moon began its descent did I open a Folde and come back to the present time in the Mortal Realm.

* * *

Evening, in my own time and the present world. Three days had passed while I'd been away. If I wanted that weekend back, I could get it, but one weekend was much like another this time of year. Lots of people tramping along the paths, staring at guide maps in one form or another. Most knew only the most modern tales of Arthur. More didn't care. It wasn't worth the effort for me to do it when the next weekend would be the same.

I thought of going to Moira's cottage. My feet decided that was a good idea and brought me there. Moving slowly through the trees, I stopped as the wind brought a strange scent. A few steps let me see into the garden.

Moira sat on a stone bench near the porch with a younger woman. "Think you'll be able to find something to paint?"

A laugh. "Too much. The forest is beautiful in its own right. And the ties to King Arthur and the rest? It's hard to know where to start."

Moira chuckled. "You'll find a place. If you don't like it, try again. There's always more than meets the eye."

"Now you sound like that old man at the coffee shop in Paimpont. He said there was more to see than just traps for tourists." She shivered. "He said I looked like one of the few who had an eye fit to see it. Any idea what he meant?"

"That sounds like a compliment of sorts. That you have the wit to look beyond the shine and see the forest as the natives see it."

"Like you do?"

"Yes."

The young woman sipped her drink. "Do you like what you see?"

Moira laughed. "Most of the time. Regardless, it's never boring."

I slipped away into the forest, leaving them to stare at the garden. I sought out a little grove of oaks, eating as I went. Found a soft bed in some fallen leaves, and went to sleep.

* * *

Over the next few days, I kept moving. There were still a few weeks before Midsummer's Eve, but I wanted to visit as many places in the forest as I could before that night. Some brought back good memories. Some didn't. The antics of the tourists provided amusement when things got too serious.

During that time, I came across Moira's grandniece painting more than once. I didn't show myself, but I did enjoy watching. She had a good eye and an excellent sense of color. From what I saw, she seemed someone I might be able to talk to, but I'd only seen her at peace, focused on her work. How she'd act under stress I didn't know. Not yet. Not enough to be sure it was worth the risk. Past experience said however much most humans liked to imagine a world with magic, few would welcome the reality. Too much they couldn't control.

I was watching her sketch the Hindre's oak when a man came striding up the path. He was tall, blonde, and walked with the confidence of the self-important. Anne saw him, stiffened, and increased her focus on sketching.

He saw her and smiled. It wasn't a pleasant smile. "Hello, Anne. The keeper of your bed and breakfast said you were probably out here."

She stopped sketching. "Hello, Don. Thought you'd be in Paris."

"Thought you'd be coming with me." He moved to look at her sketch. "Still wasting time on those scribbles?"

She shifted to face him. I'd seen hunted does less tense. "It seemed a better way to spend the time than being your arm ornament when you could certainly find better." She closed the book, tucking the pencil into it. "I was about finished, anyway. My aunt's expecting me. Good bye."

He moved to block her. "I'm certain she won't begrudge you time with me."

"It's over, Don. I thought I made that clear."

He stepped closer. "And I thought I'd made it clearer that it wasn't over until *I* said so."

She turned and ran. He moved to follow, clearly in no hurry to end the chase. A chase it was plain he'd win. I caught a glimpse of her face as she passed. It was full of desperate fear and determination to go down fighting. That decided me. I leaped out in time to knock her pursuer down. He yelled. She kept going. I followed. When we were out of his sight, I opened a Folde and took us through.

* * *

I brought her to a quiet forest clearing in the Fair Lands that looked much like the place we'd left. Once she realized she wasn't being chased, she stopped, leaning against a tree and trying to catch her breath. Head down, she said, "Don't know where you came from, pony, but it was lucky for me you did."

I didn't answer. When she raised her head and turned to face me, the look on her face was priceless.

"You're...not a pony," she said.

"Certainly not." I inclined my head to her briefly. "I am Ferliurial Efstanorien. Ferli to my friends. You seemed to need one."

"You're...that Ferli? The one my aunt mentioned?"

"The same."

She stared, taking in all the differences between me and the stray pony she'd thought I was. Her eyes finally focused on my horn. "You're a unicorn." I stayed silent.

She stepped back. "I'm not a virgin."

I snorted. "I know."

"Then why—"

"Why did I bother to save you?" I snorted again. "Let's just say I've come to value purity of spirit over that of the body. It's a lot harder to find, and worth infinitely more."

She looked at my face. "You sound bitter."

"With cause. It isn't anything you did." I sighed. "Let's find a more comfortable place to talk."

I started walking. She fell into step with me. "Shouldn't we be moving faster? He's bound to find us."

That earned her another snort. "Not unless he can cross into the Fair Lands. Which I sincerely doubt he can."

"The Fair Lands?" She took a good look at our surroundings. "So, that flash of light?"

"Was a Folde. It was the quickest way I could get you out of there."

We came to a mossy bank overlooking a small pool. I folded my legs and lay down. She sat beside me, fidgeting with her sketchbook and staring at the water. "My aunt will be worried. I need to go back, but I don't want to lead him there."

"I can get you back. As for him, she has some protections, and her neighbors like her."

"He knows where I'm staying."

"If you need your things, they can be secured, and I believe you have ways to pay your bill there without actually going."

She clutched her sketchbook tighter. "Yes. I still have a couple credit cards he doesn't know about. Yet." She placed the book down carefully, then let her shoulders slump. A tear slid down her face. "It was going so well. Why did he have to follow me here?"

"I'd say it's because he's not through with you yet." My tone grew harsh. "Not through 'playing.' And that kind is the type that breaks their toys." I sighed and softened my voice. "How did you come to meet him?"

"I was younger, and stupid. He can be nice when he wants. That's all I saw. And then..." She went on to weave a tale of how she'd met him at a party. She was flattered that someone who appeared like a gracious fairytale prince would show any interest in her. His demands had started small, just inconveniences in a schedule that could easily be rearranged to accommodate them. Until they weren't. Cosmetics could hide the bruises on her body, but not those on her heart as the fairytale she'd thought she was living in turned dark. When her great aunt suggested a visit, she'd taken the opportunity to cut ties and run. She'd truly hoped she was free. Now she knew she wasn't.

We sat silently when she finished, listening to the sounds of leaves in the breeze, of small creatures going about their own business.

"Why do you care?" she asked at last. "I appreciate your listening, but why?"

"Because I know his kind. I've seen what they can do, and I swore I'd do what I could to stop them." Memories of my brother rose. "I can show you why, if you're willing. To do so means travelling to the past." She nodded, standing when I did. I reached for the memory and brought us through the Folde.

* * *

We stood hidden in a grove of young oaks. "Be silent," I told her. "We can't be easily seen, but noise could be heard. What I'll show you is past, and can't be changed." She nodded.

There was a faint rustling, and I saw Shindarial and my younger self walking toward us. I waited for a few moments after they passed, then slipped out to follow. We walked until we could see them standing at the edge of a clearing. A pretty place, with a young maiden of fourteen years braiding a flower garland as she sat on a mossy rock.

"Wait here," Shindarial whispered.

We watched as he left my younger self, stepping gracefully from the wood to approach her. She looked up, eyes wide, then smiled. A stray bit of sun turned her hair to gold. "Oooh. You did come."

My brother lowered his head graciously. "Of course. Such beauty and kindness as yours are too sweet to deny." He stepped up to her. She held out some bits of apple, which he nibbled daintily from her fingers, making her laugh. Further treats and nibbling. She ran her fingers through his long, silken mane, exclaiming at the texture. He blew gently, ruffling her hair, and slipping a few strands loose as he did. "Yours is also beautiful. Bright as spun gold."

She sat on the grass next to the rock, patting a spot beside her. Their backs were to thicker growth. She put a few more flowers in her garland, then slipped it over his neck, giving him a gentle kiss on his nose as she did. Taking out a comb, she ran it through his mane and began to sing.

I tensed. Anne looked from the idyllic scene to me. Almost spoke, then remembered what I'd told her. I listened to the singing, then forced my will beyond. Caught the stealthy rustle in the growth behind them. The wind brought no scent other than that of my brother and the maiden. It hadn't then, and it didn't now. Shindarial bent his head so she could comb behind his ears. She laid one hand on the garland, then brought the other up with long, soothing strokes. He closed his eyes and sighed.

Sharp crackling as five men on horseback broke through the bushes. Shindarial's eyes flashed open, and he moved to leap away, only to feel a sudden jerk from the garland. A garland woven with a cord strong enough to hold a bull. He pulled it loose from her hands, but not soon enough. The spear took him in the ribs behind his shoulder. He finished his leap on his knees, thrashing as he tried to get his legs under him, and failed. Bloody froth sprayed from his nostrils with breaths gone ragged with pain. He looked past the one who'd speared him to meet the maiden's eyes. "Why?"

She ignored him, intent on the young lord. "Did you bring it?"

A smile. "Of course, my darling." With one eye on my brother, he slipped a necklace of garnets and silver over her head, then gave her a lingering kiss that promised much more. Letting her go, he stepped toward my brother. "Why? Because she doesn't have time for some silly horse with a horn. Whereas I have the prince coming as guest and need something fancy for the table."

Shindarial ignored him, continuing to stare at the maiden. She ran her fingers along her new necklace while glancing coyly at the lord. No longer roses and cream, she smelled more like a doe in heat. The lord paid her no attention. He saw the pain in my brother's eyes and stepped forward to twist the spear. Shindarial screamed, scrambling again to rise and strike at his foe. He missed and fell back. His tormentor laughed and gave the spear another twist.

This time Shindarial made it up enough to lunge forward. One of the huntsmen in the group blocked his horn thrust with the haft of his spear. "My lord, let me slay the beast so we may prepare it to go back to the castle."

The lord considered my brother, bloodstained and smeared with dirt and grass from his struggles. "No, John. He's weak enough. Bind him to a pole and bring him along. The meat will taste the better for it."

The huntsman bowed his head. "As you wish, my lord."

The lord took one last look at my poor brother, then mounted his horse as another huntsman held it for him. He offered a hand to the maiden. She took it and was boosted onto his mount's back behind him. She put her arms around his waist, holding him close as they cantered out of the clearing, followed by two of his men.

Those remaining stared at Shindarial. One cut and brought a pole, while another readied the ties. "Have to have that spear out of him to do this proper," said the one called John.

The one with the ropes shook his head. "Do that and you'll likely kill him. Then m'lord'll serve you on the platter next to him."

"He'll do the same if we break the spear. It's his favorite."

With a quick toss, the one with the ropes caught a back foot and tied it to the other. The process was repeated for the front feet. Through it all, Shindarial lay gasping bloody foam. His eyes searched the woods and came to rest on where my younger self was hidden. A younger self too frozen with horror and shock to move. Shindarial shook his head slightly, then closed his eyes. The men slipped the carrying pole through his legs and tied them to it. John gently took hold of the spear and slid it out enough to lay more parallel my brother's body. Aside from a quiver, he didn't move.

John shook his head. "Poor way to treat any beast, much less one like this."

The one holding the horses gave a harsh laugh. "Better him than us. Besides, he doesn't have too much longer." They hoisted the pole up, tied it so it was held between two horses in single file, and left the clearing.

All was silent when young Ferli moved out of hiding. He walked over to where the torn earth was still soaking up his brother's blood. The treacherous garland lay where it had fallen. Young Ferli saw it and screamed, a cry of pain torn from his heart. He leaped on it, shredding the cord and sending torn bits of wilted flowers flying. Then he ran into the forest, headed for the willow grove.

I stood, waiting until I knew he'd reached his goal. My goal, so many years ago. Anne laid a tentative hand on my shoulder, using the other to wipe tears from her eyes. "That…" she began.

"Is why I don't think much of physical virginity." I sighed and turned to go back the way we'd come. We walked for a while.

"What happened to her?"

"He kept her as long as it amused him and got her pregnant. Had her turned out in a heavy snow about a month before she'd have borne the child. I found her frozen body in some bushes the next day, her child still unborn. Looked like she'd been trying to go home."

We walked a little further. "And him?"

I bared my teeth slightly. "A few years after, he got separated from his men while hunting, and was thrown from his horse. I found him before they did."

"And?"

"They thought a boar got him." I remembered that day, and the satisfaction of it, then sighed. "It still didn't bring my brother back."

We continued to walk until we reached the spot we'd entered. I thought of a quiet spot near Moira's cottage and opened a Folde. "Let's go."

* * *

It was evening when we came out. I scented the wind and found only the scents of the garden and the forest. Heard nothing beyond what I expected. I led Anne to the back gate. She opened it enough to slip in with only a slight squeak. I nudged it shut and leaped over to join her. No sense in making any more noise than needed.

I led the way to the back door. "Wait here." Moving quietly, I walked around to the front. Moira sat on the porch, watching the gate intently. I let one hoof chime on a stepping-stone. She turned quickly, rising and coming to me. "Have you seen Anne? There was a man here looking for her. I told him I thought she'd gone back to her lodgings."

"I left her at the back door."

Moira went past me, going back the way I'd come. Anne ran to her when she saw us. She hugged her aunt and started crying. Moira hugged her back. "Come in, dear, and tell me all about it." They went in. I followed.

Half an hour later, Anne relaxed with her aunt and her second cup of tea. "And that's when your friend found me and got me away from him."

"To the Fair Lands?"

"Yes."

Moira looked at me. "Thank you, Ferli. He's not the sort I want around my niece."

"Nor I in the forest."

She turned back to Anne. "What now?"

"I'll need a safe place to stay, and to get my things from where I was staying. "

"Which he'll be watching for. Ferli?"

I smiled. "I have friends who'd be willing to get them. Give me a few hours, and call the place. Say something came up, and you had to leave suddenly, then pay."

"I can do that," Anne said.

I left them discussing details and went outside. The last of the sunset was fading as I left the garden, and went to one of the prettier and more secluded clearings I knew. There I sought out an older beech tree and tapped three times on the trunk. A sharp-eyed little man stuck his head out of a hole above me. "What's up, Ferli?"

"A damsel in distress, Pathhider. I need someone clever to get her things out of her lodgings in the village. There's fresh bread and milk in it."

He laughed and jumped down. Standing, he came up to my knees. "That would be Dame Moira's niece?"

"The same."

"Saw the pompous bastard who was looking for her at Moira's earlier." His face darkened. "Heard what he tried to do." He laughed and brightened. "My brother gave him a rough time getting out of the trees. Made him fall twice."

"Good. He's bothering her, and she needs her things from the Duchess' Whim brought to Moira's."

"How much?"

"A duffle of clothes and a small pack. She left the art supplies at her aunt's earlier."

"Need them tonight?"

"If you can. They at least need to be gone in a few hours."

"No problem. One of my cousins knows their Lutin, and the folk there have always done right by us. You'll get them."

"My thanks. I'll let Moira know. She'll have something nice waiting."

He slipped away into the forest. I turned to go back the way I'd come. What a Pixie wants, they generally get. I'd no doubt Anne's things would be back in her possession by morning.

On the way back, I crossed the trail Don had left leaving Moira's. On a whim, I backtracked it. Pathhider's cousin had indeed given him a rough time getting back to his motorcycle. There was blood where he'd first fallen, and more at the second. Not to mention the scraps of cloth left along the way. I memorized his scent and that of his vehicle, and went back to Moira's.

When I got there, she let me in. "Anne's asleep. The room's taken care of. I'm guessing your friends got her things out?"

"Should have by now. I took the liberty of promising them some of your baking."

"Pixies?" I nodded. "Then I'd best bake something special. It'll be worth it to keep her from meeting that brute again."

She set about making the promised payment, a couple loaves of white bread with some honey and nut rolls to go with them. I sighed as the smell reached me. "Wouldn't mind if there were a few extra."

She laughed softly. "There will be." She fixed us some mint tea and sat down. "She said she told you about him after you saved her, and that you showed her what happened to your brother."

"It seemed the thing to do. Besides, she was having trouble with the 'unicorns only like virgins' thing."

She sipped her tea. "Thank you, Ferli." Another sip. "You know he won't let this be."

I took a drink, savoring the mint. "His kind never do."

"And?"

"I'll keep watch for him. If he tries anything again, he'll be dealt with."

"Be careful, Ferli. He's dangerous."

I enjoyed more tea. "He's not the only one. Plus the forest doesn't like him."

Anything else she was going to say was interrupted by a tapping at the door. Moira rose and opened it. "Come in, please. You can put Anne's things over there."

Three Pixies entered. Pathhider was carrying the smaller bag, the others the larger. They placed them where she'd indicated. When they turned, Moira held four small baskets out to them. "My thanks for what you've done. The fourth is for your friend at the Duchess' Whim. You're welcome to stay for more bread and milk. Or cream, if you prefer."

Pathhider nodded. He and his kin accepted plates with nut and honey rolls and cups of milk rich with cream. They finished quickly, picked up the baskets, and turned to go. Pathhider paused at the door. "Good fortune and fair going on this house and those who dwell here."

"And good fortune also to those who have given such aid," Moira said. She closed the door after they'd gone.

"Well done," I said. I finished my tea. "I'll be keeping an eye out for your niece. Tell her there are interesting things to see at the Valley of No Return. The lake's especially beautiful at sunset."

"I will. Good night, Ferli."

"Good night, Moira." I slipped out the door and was gone.

* * *

I spent the next week going to my favorite places in the forest, talking with others from the Fair Lands I met, and watching over Anne while she looked for places to sketch and paint. Pathhider and his clan were busy keeping Don from returning to Moira's. They enjoyed every moment, but his anger was growing, which didn't bode well for Anne when he found her. And Midsummer's Eve was coming fast. I still hadn't decided where I'd be when it did.

Three days later I was watching Anne sketch a view of the Rock of False Lovers when I heard the soft crunch of footsteps coming up the path. Don's scent was on the breeze, rank with anger. I stomped gently, caught Anne's eye when she turned, and nodded toward the path. Then I slid further into hiding. She secured her pencil, then closed her sketchbook, tucking it in her satchel.

Don came out into the clearing, saw her, and narrowed his eyes. "You've led me a pretty chase." He spared a glance toward the valley and the Rock. "How fitting for you to come here. A place dedicated to the imprisonment of false lovers."

"One could say the same for you." Anne took a step back toward me, still facing her ex.

"You won't get away so easily this time, even with that pony of yours."

Anne raised her head and met his eyes. "There are park wardens making the rounds."

A laugh. "Amazing how little pay they get. It didn't take much to ensure the one patrolling here would go elsewhere." Another laugh as she took two more steps away from him. "Not so fast, Anne. We're going to settle this right now."

I leaped forward, stopping only long enough for her to grab my mane and drag herself onto my back. Even so, his fingers slid from her leg as I leaped again. "No you don't!" I heard running steps moving back down the path as I ran. A motorcycle engine roared to life.

"Hold on!" I turned away from the valley at a gallop. Behind, I could hear the motorcycle gaining. I increased my speed, dodging down another, narrower path before he could close. He overshot, turned, and continued to follow. This close to sunset, it was dark under the trees. Still, he didn't slow as much as I'd thought he would. I needed to be farther ahead before we reached my goal. I stretched out and really began to run.

Smooth as my gaits were, Anne was losing her grip when we reached the lake. I stopped. "Ladies?"

A chorus of giggles, and one of the Korrigans stood up in the water at the shore's edge. She stared at Anne for a moment. Her form wavered. When she was done, she looked like Anne, but with her clothing shredded by her flight. "Did you bring him?"

I gave a gracious nod. "Right behind me, ladies. He's all yours."

I moved Anne quickly into cover, leaving the false one standing there. Mere breaths after I'd done so, the motorcycle came out of the forest. Don stopped. He took in the shivering woman with a smile of satisfaction. "Pony throw you? How sad." He cut the engine off. Dismounting, he moved toward his prey.

The false Anne cowered. "Leave me alone!"

"Oh, no. You've disobeyed me for the last time." He stopped a stride away. His quarry took a step further into the water, then another. Don laughed. "If you think a little water's going to stop me, you're wrong. I like water sports." He took two quick strides into the lake and grabbed her arm.

There was a shimmer as the Korrigan returned to her usual form. "Wonderful! I like them, too!" She got a grip on him, pulling him further into the lake. He stumbled as the water rose to mid-thigh. His eyes widened as he saw the lovely hair-clad woman clinging to him.

"Who are you?"

"A friend of Anne's. It's *so* good to meet you at last." She drew him further into the water. Her two sisters rose up silently between him and the shore. "Let's play!"

She dragged him forward, pulling him under. Her sisters dove after them. The water rippled as we watched. Something light blue floated to the surface, Don's shirt, followed a moment later by a splash as Don himself came up, gasping. The Korrigan followed. She let him take a few more breaths before planting her lips on his and dragging him down again. It was longer before he surfaced further out in the lake. The Korrigan rose next to him. "Oh, you are good!"

He tried to move back toward the shallows. "I'm better...when...I can stand." A few more gasps. "Let's...go back...into...the shallows."

"That's no fun." The Korrigan pouted. "Besides, you haven't met my sisters yet."

"Your...sisters?"

The other Korrigans emerged, one on either side of him. The one to his left smiled, revealing sharp teeth. "Yes. And we *all* want to play." She bit his shoulder. His scream cut off as they dragged him back under the water.

Anne shivered and buried her head in my mane. I turned away from the lake, taking a different path into the forest. Behind us, there was more splashing, followed by another scream and assorted giggles. "Thanks, Ferli!" The sounds faded as I cantered into the trees.

* * *

It took three cups of Moira's best calming herbal tea blend to get Anne over her initial reaction to the evening's excitement. I wasn't sure if it was knowing what Don had planned for her, or seeing the

Korrigans in action. Moira listened to her retelling of the tale, nodding at the appropriate points, and being a supportive ear. By the fourth cup, Anne had talked herself out and was yawning. Moira steered her into the spare room.

When she came back, she poured us both more tea. I helped myself to another seedcake.

"Why the Korrigans, Ferli?" she asked.

I finished chewing and swallowed. "Because his kind don't give up until they've ruined what they touch. He was planning rape, and worse. This way, they'll find his bike parked by the lake, and his clothes piled on the shore. They'll drag the water, find nothing, and write him off as another fool who went swimming alone and drowned in the process. Case closed." I ate another cake.

She ate her own cake slowly, then nodded. "Better than having him fall off a cliff, or you trampling him. The one's not certain, and I don't think there are any wild boar left to blame it on."

We drank in silence. When I finished my tea, I sighed. "I'd better make sure they put his clothes back."

As I got up, Moira asked, "Have you decided what you're going to do on Midsummer Eve?" When I didn't answer, she gave me a sad smile. "I'll miss you if you go. So will Anne. She gave me this for you." She held out three strands of auburn hair. When I didn't take them, she set them on the table. Then she reached up and pulled three of her own gray ones. "I know you aren't making a courting band. We thought you might like these to start one to remember us."

"A friendship band?"

"That's a good name for it. "

I stared at the hair, then picked it up. "Thank you. I'll do that."

"Good luck, Ferli. If you do decide to go, come back one last time if you can."

"I will." I turned and left, not trusting myself to say more.

* * *

Midsummer Eve. I crossed into the Fair Lands at Merlin's Tomb an hour before sunset. A pavilion of green and gold had been set up along the opposite edge of the clearing. All manner of folk, from Pixies to Korrigans, Elves, and more crowded the space before it. I saw my mother standing near Misliarinil with representatives of all the herds. Beneath the pavilion, thrones had been set up, awaiting the arrival of King Huon and his queen, Claramonde.

I moved over to join my mother.

She fixed me with a stern eye. "Well?"

"I've made my decision."

"That's good. You won't look like an idiot when King Huon calls you up to tell him."

"He's going to do that?"

She snorted. "For a matter this important? What did you think he'd do? Discuss it over tea and biscuits?"

I was spared a response as the king and his retinue arrived. We bowed as he passed. Once he'd seen his lady seated, he sat. A herald called us to order. King Huon looked over the crowd. "You're all aware of the state of things in the Mortal Realm. After much deliberation, the rulers of the Fair Lands have decided to further restrict access. There will be only three gates left open in Our lands: the Great Stone Circle on the Isle of the Mighty, the Rock of the Serpent at Loch Ness, and the Merlin Gate here in Broceliande forest. All others will close at dawn tomorrow. Each gate will have a guardian to watch over it and regulate its use. Those for the Great Stone Circle and the Rock of the Serpent have already been chosen. For the last…" He nodded to the herald.

"Ferliurial Efstanorien. You are summoned into court."

I raised my head and stepped forward, walking gracefully up the aisle to stand before King Huon and his queen. I bowed. "I am here, Your Majesties."

"Ferliurial Efstanorien, you asked to be given time to decide on which side of the gate you would remain after this night. Have you made your decision?"

I stood a little straighter. "I have, Your Majesty."

"And?"

"I choose to stay in the Mortal Realm."

The king's eyes met mine. "And your reasons?"

"As those of the Mortal Realm benefit from the dreams and possibilities of the Fair Lands, so we benefit from their questing for new things and new ways to use old things. Separated, we would both suffer. If I stay there, I can work through my friends for the good of the forest and keep a little more light and magic in a Realm that sorely needs it."

He nodded. "Then, I ask: Do you accept the Guardianship of the Merlin Gate?"

I hesitated. *Can I? It's more responsibility than I've ever had. As much, maybe more, than being herd leader. It would be easier to decline.* Yet. I thought of Moira and Anne, and their response. Thought of the band of auburn and gray I'd started. Saw how Queen Claramonde was watching me, one hand on her lord's arm. Both she and her lord had been born in that Realm. She saw me looking and smiled.

I bowed. "I accept, Your Majesty. It is a great honor."

He smiled. "Then I name you, Ferliurial, Guardian of the Merlin Gate." He beckoned, and an attendant handed him a gold chain with a round medallion depicting a great tree and the tomb. He took it and placed it over my bowed head, to lie with the medallion on my chest. "Serve well, Guardian."

I bowed, lowering my nose to the ground as I went to one knee, then rose again. "I shall do my best, Your Majesty." I backed up three steps, bowed my head to them again, and turned to go back as the crowd cheered.

The rest of the court was a bright haze. I spent it next to my mother. After it was over, others came with congratulations, and at least three invitations to various parties. When things settled, Mislia-rinil turned to me. "Well done."

"My thanks, Herd Leader."

"You're welcome." She looked me over and said with a laugh, "Don't screw it up."

* * * * *

C.M DeMott Biography

C. M. DeMott is a small animal veterinarian living in southwest Virginia. Since discovering the Society for Creative Anachronism in 1976, she has been writing and performing original ballads based on legend, faery tales, and myths under the name Morgan Wolfsinger. She currently has seven CDs out and is working on an eighth. "Choices" is her first published story. You can find her music at morganwolfsinger.bandcamp.com.

* * * * *

The Name of the Moon
by Rich Hailey

It was still dark as I walked up to my office. The garish neon from the massage parlor next door illuminated the sign on my door: "Calder Sharpe, Investigations."

What a joke. The only investigations lately had involved finding new ways to dodge bill collectors. I hadn't had a good case in weeks.

Unless you count scotch.

I stepped over the scattered bills, hung up my coat and hat, and slumped into the chair behind my desk. I pulled my flask from the top drawer and scowled. It was too early to be drinking, but technically, it was still yesterday. I took a healthy slug and followed it with an unhealthy one.

It had been a long week, and it was only Tuesday.

I knocked back one more swallow, put the flask away, and tried to come up with a reason to leave it there.

My only active case was a nasty divorce. The wife suspected her hubby was cheating. He was, and having dealt with her, I couldn't blame him.

She wanted me to find proof, and I did. All it cost me was a night's sleep and a sliver of my soul.

Back in the day, I'd believed I made a difference, changed things. Now, I know the only thing changing is me, and not for the better. Freya, the Viking bartender two shops down, says I'm going through a mid-life crisis brought on by the Rending, but you have to have a life for that, so that can't be it.

Booze and exhaustion had made me maudlin, so I stretched out on the cot I kept in the file room and hoped to sleep a few hours. There was no point in going to the apartment upstairs; the booze up there was the same as the booze here, and here was closer.

The noon sun in my eyes woke me. My mouth tasted like the ashes of dreams torched by dragon fire, but my head didn't hurt, and I take small wins where I can get them. I went into the tiny bathroom in the back and splashed tepid water over my face. The face in the mirror was closer to fifty than forty, and looked it, washed out blue eyes rimmed in red and surrounded by bags. Two days' beard with more gray than brown. Nothing remarkable. You look at me and your eyes slide right off.

As I dried my face, the bell over the front door jingled, telling me two things. I had a customer, and I'd forgotten to lock the door before crashing. It was just good luck that monsters hadn't come through while I was sleeping. Or worse, my landlord.

I walked up front to find a damsel in distress coming through the door.

Yeah, things like that happen since the Rending, short for Rending of the Veil. Ten years ago, for reasons we still don't understand, our world and the Otherworld of the Tuatha de Danann merged completely. Monsters, damsels, and strip malls, all jumbled into one chaotic mess.

Technically, she might not have been a damsel, but she had the look, and was certainly distressed. Her auburn hair was disheveled, the wrinkles in her dress said she'd worn it yesterday, and her jade eyes were as red-rimmed as mine. Her figure was enough to make men want her and women hate her, but she was trembling with exhaustion, and unless I missed my guess, fear. I couldn't tell her age. Women purchased glamour spells and appeared whatever age they wanted, but something about her told me she was young. Maybe in her twenties.

"Can I help you, Miss…?"

"I doubt it very much," she said, "but you're the only choice I've got." The quaver in her voice took some of the sting out of her appraisal, but not all of it.

She wasn't wrong. After the Rending, we'd learned our new world held to a caste system. Sidhe, Fae, or fairy, whatever you called them, ruled the roost; the rest of us scrambled for what was left. With the coming of magic, the need for a human investigator had dried up. The only work I could get lately came from those who couldn't get help anywhere else.

Or couldn't afford anyone else.

"Since I'm your only choice, why don't you tell me your troubles, and we'll see what I can or can't do, Miss…?"

"Oh, sorry! My name is Lucia Parson. And you're Mr. Sharpe?"

"At your service, ma'am. Is it Miss or Mrs.?"

"Miss," she said, "but Lucia is fine."

"Nice to meet you, Lucia. You can call me Calder," I replied. "Can I get you some coffee or tea? You look like you could use it."

"No, thanks. But some milk would be wonderful, if you have it."

I didn't. Come to think of it, I didn't have coffee or tea, either. And my belly told me to put something zero proof into it, or it'd go on strike.

"I'm sorry, I don't. But look, I haven't eaten yet, and its lunchtime. Let's grab a bite at the diner across the street. The food is good, and you can get milk or whatever you want. My treat."

I wasn't being generous. If she hired me, it would go on her bill.

"I don't know," she said. Her voice trailed off, and I knew what she was worried about. Her innocence surrounded her. She really was a damsel, and that made her vulnerable.

"I'm no wolf," I said. "I'll tell you what. I'm going to get some lunch. You can join me or wait here. Your choice."

I grabbed my hat and opened the door, looking back at her. She hesitated for a moment, then, eyes a little wary, body held tense and ready to bolt, she went through the door and followed me across the parking lot to Davos' Place.

It was a throwback to the diners of the 50s. Built to look like a railroad car, it was all brushed metal and red leatherette booths, with seating at the bar, and a window to the kitchen. Tina, Davos' eldest, worked the counter and the register, yelling orders back to Davos and her two brothers in the kitchen, while watching over her twins as they did schoolwork. Francine, Davos' wife, covered the booths, managed the front of the house, and kept the books in the black, but not too much so. No sense in giving the tax man more than you had to.

Yeah. Magic in the world, and we still paid taxes.

Francine noticed the girl with me, grinned, and came to meet us at my usual spot at the bar.

"Calder, good to see you!" she said, covering me with a hug. Francine Davos stood 5 feet tall, and was built like a Greek grandma should be—sturdy, stout, and comfortable. Her hugs are one of the true miracles in this new world. No matter what worries you, you feel better.

"And who is your date?" she asked, hugging Lucia before she could back away.

Lucia blushed when Francine's words registered.

"Oh, no!" she stammered. "He's not…I mean, I'm not, er, we're not…"

"This isn't a date, Francine. Lucia's a client." That wasn't precisely true, but close enough.

"Nonsense!" Francine laughed. "It might not be a date, but then again, it might be. Yayas know things. We see things!" She laughed again and showed us to a table in the corner where we could talk.

"Don't mind her," I told Lucia. "This is a family place, and Yaya treats her favored customers like family. Which means she gets to say what she wants, but she doesn't mean anything by it."

"Oh, I don't mind that at all. Her heart is clean, one of the cleanest I've ever…" she trailed off, looking embarrassed.

So not human. Or human and gifted.

"Food first. Then business. I think better when I'm not hungry. Davos makes traditional diner food, and there's none better in the city, but if you want his best, go with the special."

Davos knew more about Greek food than anybody I've ever met. His family brought recipes over from the old country before the Rending. In fact, I'm pretty sure his family wrote most of those recipes. Whatever the reason, eating at Davos' was always worth every penny.

"You decide," Lucia said.

Yaya came over to take our order.

"Two specials," I said. "Coffee for me, and milk for the lady."

"Coming right up," Yaya said as she bustled away.

In less than a minute, Tina came to the booth with my coffee and Lucia's milk, and a few moments later, Yaya came to the table with two steaming plates.

"Spanakopita for the lady and moussaka for Calder!" She set the plates before us with a flourish. "Dig in! Eat!" she said.

We did. The next few minutes were quiet, as we both demolished the food in front of us. Yaya remained in the front of the diner, coming over only to refill our glasses as we ate. Lucia chased the last bite of the spinach pie across the plate, finished it, and set her fork down with a contented sigh.

"You've proven yourself to be trustworthy, sir," she said with mock dignity. "I believe you may be the right choice after all!"

"I aim to please, milady." I matched her formality, and she smiled, and I found to my surprise that I wanted to make her smile again. There's something about sharing a good meal with someone; we hadn't said more than ten words while we were eating, but she ate with a cheerful gusto you rarely see in a beautiful woman, and I realized I was enjoying her presence.

That was a problem. Investigators can't afford to care about their clients. If things go sideways, it's one more reason to dive into a bottle.

I had plenty of reasons already.

"So, what is this quest?" I said briskly, putting a clamp on my emotions.

"A werewolf stole my unicorn."

Things went sideways.

A werewolf. A 300-pound monster with the intelligence of a man and the strength and savagery of a wolf, complete with teeth that could rend marble and claws that could shred a battleship. And they're rabidly contagious as well.

Great.

There was no way I could take on a werewolf. It wasn't even a contest. I should have gotten up and walked away right then.

But I knew she had nowhere else to go. If I didn't help, there would *be* no help. I couldn't just walk out on her, not and keep whatever shreds remained of my soul.

I needed to know more. Maybe there was an angle to work, a way to retrieve the unicorn without confronting the wolf.

"First," I said, "beating a werewolf is impossible. Werewolves are at the top of the food chain. Nobody messes with them, not even the Aes Sidhe, unless they absolutely must. And they bring the heavy artillery when they do. What exactly do you expect me to do for you?"

"I don't know," she said, tears welling in her eyes. "I just know that my unicorn is gone, and I must get it back! I must!"

"All right then, start with the unicorn. How do you know it's still alive? Why is it so important to get this one back?"

A few years ago, I hadn't believed unicorns were real. I still didn't know anything about them, but I wasn't surprised to find out they existed. It even fit with the whole damsel thing. If the legends were true, of course. The Rending had showed us that legends weren't always accurate.

"Unicorns aren't real, Calder. At least," she said, "I don't think they are. I've certainly never seen one, and I don't know of anybody who has. But I guess they could be real, just very rare. They could live in a remote area, or have strong camouflage spells that hide them from humans, or…"

I interrupted her.

"Stay with me, Lucia. So it's not a real unicorn. Check. What is it, and why is it important?"

"Sorry," she said. "I get carried away sometimes. The unicorn is a talisman of purity. It's a jeweled figure about 12 inches tall. As a talisman of purity, it wards things from evil. Like the unicorns of legend, only the innocent can find anything within its ambiance. Our village uses it to protect us from disease, monsters, and other evil things. I was its keeper, and I lost it!"

She began to sob quietly. I handed her a napkin and tried awkwardly to comfort her, patting her on the shoulder.

"So, how did the werewolf find the unicorn? Couldn't it hide itself?"

"No," she said. "The magic of the unicorn doesn't protect itself, only the things around it. For it to remain hidden, it must be kept by a person who is pure. I was that person, and I failed!"

I rushed in to try to keep her from crying again. "Hold on a minute. None of us are pure. We're human, and we're defined by our flaws, but we aren't limited by them. You made a mistake, and the wolf got the unicorn. But you only fail if you don't try to get it back!" I sighed, having a feeling I knew the answer, but I asked anyway. "Now, what did you do to make the unicorn vulnerable? A boy?"

"A…a man," she answered. "A peddler. Flint Lugar. He came to our village every few months. He was friendly with all the children, but seemed to take a special interest in me over the last two seasons. I was flattered by the attention. He was so much more interesting than the village boys."

"Go on," I said.

"When he came to the village a week ago, he asked me to walk with him along the greenway one evening. It's a path that starts in the village square, then wanders around the edges, always close enough to hear what's going on, but far enough out to steal a kiss or two. I went with him, and during the walk, he kissed me."

"And that's all it took to lose your purity? A kiss?"

"Oh, no!" she said. "The kiss was fine. Love is the purest emotion of them all, and the physical part of it can be pure as well. But Flint kissed me as we were approaching the square, and Elder James came by. I was startled and ashamed to be caught kissing the peddler, and I lied to cover it up. I slapped Flint and acted like he was forcing me. And that's when it happened. The unicorn disappeared from my ken; I wasn't pure enough to sense it anymore."

"Okay. Now what about the werewolf?" I asked.

"Flint smiled the most awful smile, filled with hunger and too many teeth. He became a large black wolf, then bounded from the path to rip Elder James' head off with one swing of his claw. He crossed the square to the inn where the unicorn was kept. I heard the screams, and then he was out, carrying the statue in a bloody claw."

"Then what?"

"He crossed the square at a dash to where I stood, frozen with terror and guilt. I knew I was about to die. I felt his hot, foul breath on my face. 'Soon,' he said, then left. He was gone before Elder James' body stopped twitching. I could still feel the warmth of his lips on mine, and I knew it was all my fault."

I was silent for a moment. The entire diner was. I looked up and noticed that other than Davos' family, the diner was deserted. Davos and his sons had left the kitchen and were seated on the counter stools. Yaya gestured me to turn back to Lucia.

She was quiet, beyond tears. The confession had drained her. Having said it out loud, she couldn't hide from her guilt, the horror, or the shame. That kind of load can crush a fully grown man, much less a young girl.

"Lucia," I said gently, "I'm not going to lie. This is bad, and yes, you are responsible. I know what you're feeling right now, and you have reason to do so, but I'm telling you this story is not over. Not unless you give up."

"But you said it yourself," she said. "This is impossible. There's no way to win!"

"True," Yaya said, "but you have assets he didn't know about when he said that."

"You were listening?" I asked.

"Of course I was," she said, answering me first. "Not only does Yaya get to say what she wants, she gets to hear what she wants as well! As for you, young lady, first, we must consider the unicorn itself. It's a talisman of purity, and it can't be happy being held by a werewolf! Talismans aren't sentient, but they do have rudimentary feelings. That's how they sense what to protect and what to protect *from*. It'll resist the wolf as much as it can, which means Flint will be distracted trying to control it. It won't be much, but it'll help."

She turned to Lucia. "Second, there's more to you than you're telling, girl. How old are you?"

"Older than I look," she said quietly.

Yaya looked at Lucia with a firm glint in her eye. "Now's not the time to be bashful, child. He needs to know everything if he is to survive."

I was confused. In listening to her story, I'd revised my estimate of her age downward to seventeen, eighteen tops.

"I'm forty-nine years old," Lucia said quietly.

I was getting tired of being wrong all the time.

"What!" I exclaimed. "That's some glamour you have. I thought you were, well, not forty-nine , that's for sure."

"It's not a glamour, Calder." Lucia looked at me with eyes pleading for acceptance. "I'm forty-nine and will look like this for at least another thirty years. My mother is fae, and my father was human. I'm a mongrel," she spat out, self-loathing on her tongue.

The word hung in the air.

Davos spoke. "We don't use that language here, child. Ever. Purity is not of the flesh, but the spirit," he rumbled. "Only pompous fools look down on others for their blood. My wife is part fae, as are my children and grandchildren. Are they to be despised? Or do we cherish each for their unique combination of gifts?"

That was the most I'd ever heard Davos say in over five years of eating in the diner.

"I'm so sorry," Lucia said, jumping up. "I didn't know. I meant no insult. All the people in my village are of mixed blood. We were called mongrels for so long in the Otherworld that we call ourselves that now in this one."

"Not in this diner you won't," Yaya said. "Not ever, not where I can hear it. And you know what kind of hearing I have! Now, sit back down. We have more to talk about."

"Not yet," Lucia said. "I have something I must do first."

With that, she went to each member of the family, even the twins, formally introduced herself, then begged their pardon. Only after receiving it, along with hugs from all of them, did she return to the booth.

Yaya was beaming. "A proper apology done in the old way!" she said. "Any being who knows when and how to apologize can and will be forgiven in this house. Davos! Get this girl a slice of baklava!"

She continued as Davos went to get the treat, "Lucia, you're not the dainty little damsel Calder thought. You're fae, and that gives you power. I knew that the instant you said you'd read my heart. You're forty-nine, and unless I miss my guess, Calder is as well. That's another advantage. Both of you are seven sevens, which is a powerful number. You're both at the peak of your power, and that may be enough to tip the balance."

"Wait a minute," I said. "I'm fully human. I don't have magic."

"Oh, really?" Yaya said. "How do you explain your success as an investigator? How many human detectives are left? A dozen? Fewer? And you're one of them. How often do you get a hunch and follow it? How often does it turn out right? Calder, you have a bit of fae blood in you. The Veil was never impervious; beings leaked through from each side over centuries. Think about it; how else would we have legends about all the creatures from the Otherworld? How do you think I have fae blood? Do you think I got it 10 years ago?"

She laughed at the look on my face.

"Yaya, I didn't know you had fae blood until five minutes ago. Give me a few minutes to process all this, okay? So, I'm part fae? How much?"

"Not much," she said, "but maybe just enough. You weren't wrong; going toe to toe with a werewolf is suicide. But outwitting one, that's a different story. It's still risky, but there's a chance you can pull it off."

Not much of a chance, as I saw it, but when it's the only chance you have, you take it.

I turned to Lucia. "It looks like I'm on the job."

She smiled at me, and just for a moment, I knew why some men were fool enough to tackle a werewolf with just a pocketknife and good intentions.

Some men, but not me. I needed to know more.

I shook myself, told everyone we had a lot of planning to do, and we agreed to meet for breakfast early, before the diner opened. Lucia stayed at Davos', and I went to the library to learn everything I could about werewolves.

What I learned gave me little hope and a lot of nightmares.

I walked into the diner the next morning, bleary-eyed after being torn to shreds by razor sharp claws fourteen times. Keeping count was easy because each time was excruciating in a completely different and appallingly memorable way.

Tina was at the register, took one look at my face and a few minutes after seating me at a long table, brought over a tiny, long handled pot of coffee and a demitasse cup, along with two amygdalota cookies.

"Thanks, Tina, but I need the real stuff, a couple quarts worth. It was *not* a good night."

"Just try it, Calder. Give it a second to steep and settle, then try it. If you don't like it, I'll bring you all the coffee you can swill."

The Davos family had never steered me wrong, and I didn't expect Tina would. I tried it. Picture pureed coffee beans, lightly roasted and liquified with the barest amount of water possible. Then add honey. A lot of it. Then add some more. The honey powered through the bitterness of the coffee, and the foam on top gave it a fuller feeling than cream usually did. Everything rounded together in my mouth, making the perfect coffee experience. I wanted to get down on one knee and ask Tina to marry me, but Yaya would probably kill me. I took a bite of the cookie instead, then another sip of the coffee. I drank two cups, all that was in the pot, and when Tina returned to the table, she didn't even need to ask if I wanted more. I vowed that lesser brews would never touch my lips again.

A few minutes later, Yaya and Lucia appeared from upstairs. Lucia was plainly dressed in blue jeans and a blouse that might have been Tina's at one time or another. Her face was clean of makeup, her eyes bright, and her hair washed, brushed, and arranged in waves over one shoulder.

She was gorgeous.

"Try not to drool, son," Davos said as he brought breakfast out of the kitchen.

Moments after the food hit the table, the rest of the family stormed in and sat down to eat, Lucia sitting directly across from me. Scrambled eggs, fried green tomatoes, pancakes, cat head biscuits and sawmill gravy, grapes, sliced apples, fresh pineapple, and more loaded down the table, all washed down with juice, Greek coffee, and milk for Lucia. I noticed she ate mostly fruit and the tomatoes, along with pancakes.

"Are you a vegetarian?" I asked her.

"Yes," she answered. "Most of the people in my village are. The Sidhe like their blood sport, and hunt often. The taste of flesh appeals to our darker nature, so most of us avoid it."

After the meal, the twins went off to school, while Tina, Davos, and the boys headed into the kitchen to get the diner ready to open. Yaya, Lucia, and I went into the study upstairs to plan.

"It would be best to do this tomorrow," Yaya said. "The new moon begins, and Flint's power will be at its ebb. He's still plenty powerful, but he won't be able to transform, except through tremendous effort, and his power of regeneration will be weak."

"But how do we find him?" I asked. "He could be far away from here by now."

"He isn't," Yaya said flatly. "Lucia and I traced him last night. He's still close by, waiting."

"How'd you trace him?" I asked.

"We traced the unicorn," Yaya said. "Despite her lapse, there's still a link between it and her. Each time Flint tries to use it, it resists, and that sends a pulse to her. With a bit of quiet and patience, we were able to use those pulses to get a direction on it. If it were more than a few miles away, we wouldn't have been able to get even that. Now that she's aware of it, Lucia can follow that link without me, and the closer she gets, the better she'll be able to pinpoint the location."

"So now all we need," I said, "is a plan that will allow us to get close enough to steal a unicorn from a werewolf without getting us all killed in the process. Anybody got any ideas?"

We had lots of ideas, just no good ones.

After an hour, I asked, "What did Flint mean when he said 'Soon' to Lucia? And does that have anything to do with why he's still here?"

"Maybe," Yaya pondered. "If the unicorn is still linked to Lucia, maybe Flint needs something more from her to break it to his control. If he marked her, we might be able to use that."

"Marked me? How?" asked Lucia.

"Tell me, girl, you were drawn to Flint before you knew him to be a werewolf. Do you still feel that attraction?"

"Of course not!" she cried. "He's horrible! A monster! I could never..."

"Oh, hush, child!" Yaya snapped. "A wolf is powerful and virile, and an alpha wolf like Flint even more so. It doesn't matter that he's evil and dangerous; in fact, that can add to his magnetism. There're very few women who can honestly say they feel no attraction to the dangerous animal locked inside a werewolf. I need you to be honest with me. If he tried to kiss you again, would you let him?"

I watched Lucia's face work and knew her answer, probably before she did.

"No. I wouldn't let him kiss me," she said with a conviction her earlier protest lacked. "But I would want him to," she added in a still voice.

You don't always get the answers you want in this world. Sometimes you get lies, other times the truth. You can never tell which will hurt the worst.

"Good," Yaya said. "That's our way in. He needs something from you to break the talisman to his control, and he's marked you to make sure he gets it. He's waiting for his power to rise to draw you in, but we're going to get there before he's ready. You'll go to him, the nervous maiden, and he'll believe you were drawn like a moth to the flame. You'll distract him while Calder kills him."

As plans go, it wasn't much of one, but sometimes simplicity is a virtue.

The next morning, Yaya prepared us for the fight. She handed me a rifle and a sword. "The stock is mountain ash," she said, "and the bullets are lead clad with silver. They'll fly true. The sword is steel, and the edge is coated in monkshood. Be careful with it; it's a deadly poison for humans and werewolves. The poison will make even a non-fatal cut a problem for Flint. Once Lucia has his attention, shoot fast and true. Get the blade in him and take his head off, then get the unicorn and get out of there."

The plan required putting Lucia at risk. I didn't like it, but this job often means doing things I don't like.

Davos fed us breakfast, Yaya said a prayer in Greek and another in Fae, and we left. New moon or not, I wanted this over before it got dark. Werewolves are active at night; maybe Flint would be asleep when we got there. Given the chance, Flint would happily rip out my throat in my sleep; I had no compunction about doing the same to him if I could.

Fair fights are for morons who don't know any better.

We walked outside, and Lucia paused, closed her eyes, and turned in a circle.

"That way," she said, pointing down the road north out of town.

"Walk or drive?" I asked.

"Drive," she said after a moment's thought. "It's a few miles at least."

That made sense. We were already on the north side of town. A few miles down the road put us into the Barrens, hundreds of acres of forest that had literally appeared overnight after the Rending, overlapping farm country. It was the perfect place for a werewolf's lair.

I held the door for Lucia as she took shotgun, then got in and drove slowly down the road.

"Our second date," I quipped.

Lucia kept her eyes closed, slowly scanning back and forth as I drove.

No sense of humor.

Three miles out of town, she had me slow down.

"He's off to the right," she said, "about two miles from here."

"Johnston's Farm Road is just up ahead," I said. "We'll take that, get a little bit closer, then walk in the rest of the way."

Lucia just nodded, her eyes still closed.

About three or four minutes later, she said, "We're about a mile away now, I think."

I pulled the car off the road and shut off the engine.

I looked over at Lucia. She was breathing fast and shallow, anxiety mixed with fear, but just a little eagerness on her face. "Are you sure you want to do this?" I asked.

"I'm sure I don't want to!" she answered. "But I have to. If I don't get the unicorn back, my village will suffer even more than it already has."

The eagerness hurt, and suddenly, I wanted to hurt back.

"Admit it, Lucia," I snapped. "Part of you *wants* to. You said it last night. You want him to kiss you again. Even after everything he did. You want to feel those bloody lips…"

The slap echoed off my cheek.

"Don't you dare, Calder!" she cried. "Don't you dare hold that against me! What I want and what I do are different things! I'm accountable to no one but myself for how I feel! And I feel bad enough about that without you piling on! Are you jealous? Is that it? Do you want to kiss me? Are you mad because the big bad wolf got there first? When we first met, you said you weren't a wolf. What does that make you? A little puppy dog?"

Kissing an angry woman is dangerous. Ninety-nine times out of a hundred, it'll get you slapped, beaten, kneed in the groin, and probably arrested.

This wasn't one of those times.

I pulled her to me, trapping her arms against my chest, and kissed her hard. She beat at my chest for a moment, fighting to free her arms, but she never bit me. She finally got her arms free enough to shove me backward, breaking the kiss. Her eyes locked on mine, blazing with fury and passion, looking for something, some answer to a question I didn't know. Whatever she was looking for, she must have found it, because her arms locked around my neck and pulled me in to her lips, and this time, *she* kissed *me*.

Being kissed by an angry woman is amazing.

A few moments later, we both pulled back, aware that now was not the time, but that the time would come.

"If it makes you feel any better," she said softly, "I have no interest in kissing him anymore."

"If it makes you feel any better," I said, "neither do I."

I sat back, cleared my throat, and got my head back in the game.

"He's holed up at what's left of the Johnston farm," I said. "The road leads straight to it. I'm going to come up to the house from the woods on the south side. It'll take me about 45 minutes to get into position. Wait here, then walk to the farm. Get him onto the porch, and I'll shoot him."

The plan still sounded thin, but for some reason, I felt better about it now.

I shouldn't have.

I got into position with the rifle sighted on the porch. Lucia came down the road, stopped just shy of the porch, and called for Flint, as planned.

The plan went to hell at that moment.

Flint erupted from the house, moving faster than I could track, crossing the porch and wrapping an arm around Lucia, holding a dagger to her throat. He turned and looked right at me.

"Come on out, boyfriend!" he called. "Or do you think you can shoot me without hitting her? I promise if you try, I'll rip out her throat before the bullet hits me."

I knew he could do it. Hell, a human could.

"You won't kill her," I yelled back. "You could have killed her in the village. You need her for something."

"True," he said, "but I don't have to kill her. I can just cut up her face, scar her so badly that no man would ever think to look at her again."

"Maybe I should kill her," I said. "If she's dead, you can't get what you want. That's a win in my book!"

Flint laughed. "As if you could. I can smell you on her! And her on you. That's how I knew where you were, by the way. Next time you try to sneak up on a werewolf, make sure you're downwind. Of course, there won't be a next time! Now, drop the rifle and come here, or I'll see just how many screams it'll take to break you."

I went over my options, which didn't take long, because I didn't have any. I stood up, threw down the rifle, and walked toward them.

"That's a good puppy," Flint mocked. "Now we can have a civilized conversation without all that yelling."

That puppy crack burned.

As I came closer, I looked at Lucia. Her eyes were wide, her nostrils flared, on the edge of panic.

"It'll be okay," I started, but Flint laughed again.

"No, Lucia, it won't. You started this path with a lie, and I won't let you be comforted by another one. Nothing is going to be okay.

I'll break you and use you to break the unicorn. Using its power, I'll pass undetected through every ward and every barrier spell. I'll walk the earth, unhindered and unstoppable. And the best part is, I'm going to have so much fun breaking you!" He motioned to a spot about two paces from himself and Lucia. "Now, for the first. Boyfriend, stand here."

"I have a name," I said.

"Not for much longer," Flint said. "You do have your sword, though, and that's more important than a name. Here's my wager. I'm going to release Lucia. When I do, you're going to attack me. If you're fast enough to pierce me with your blade, you win, and I die. If you're not fast enough…well, I'm sure you can guess the rest. On three then?" His grin widened, showing more teeth than a human mouth should hold. "One."

He doesn't know about the poison, I thought.

"Two."

I have a ghost of a chance.

"Three!"

As his lips moved, I drew as quickly as I could. My training with a sword was basic, but it wouldn't have mattered if I were a master swordsman from Heidelberg. In a blur of motion, Flint hurled Lucia away and turned toward me. Before my sword cleared leather, his left hand punched into my shoulder, and my right arm went limp. I had a moment of regret that Lucia and I had only shared that one kiss before his right hand crashed against my head, and all went dark.

I never had a chance.

I came to several hours later, lying in the dirt of the Johnston farm, with my head pillowed on something soft and warm. My head ached, and my thoughts fuzzed in and out as I tried to recall where I was and how I'd gotten there. I'd start to drift, and drops of water would fall on my face, keeping me awake.

Eventually, my head began to clear, and I realized that my head was pillowed in Lucia's lap, and the drops of water were her tears. She was silently weeping, like her heart was broken, but she was alive.

I tried to speak, to let her know she didn't need to cry, that I wasn't dead, but she seemed to cry even harder as I grunted. I cleared my throat and finally managed to put two words together.

"Wha...hapnd?"

Lucia continued to cry, but I thought there was some relief in her tears.

"Let's just go home," she said, still sobbing. "Let's just go."

It took a while, but I was finally able to stand up. We slowly walked the mile or so to the car. As Lucia drove back to town, I asked her again what had happened. She wouldn't answer. Just repeated that we should go home.

Apparently, home wasn't my place, but Davos'. Davos and Yaya met us at the door of the diner, and Yaya ushered us both upstairs. I was put to bed. Yaya rubbed something on my head that first hurt, then took the pain away, then had me drink something that brought the fuzzies back. I drifted, half awake and half unconscious.

The next thing I remember, my head was clearer. It hurt, but not as bad as I thought it should, and I take small wins where I can get them. I felt something warm beside me and looked over to see Lucia, sleeping peacefully next to me, her head on my shoulder, and her arm across my chest. I knew I was safe and fell into a dreamless sleep.

I awakened to find Lucia no longer beside me in bed. She was sitting in a chair, watching me sleep.

"Why are we alive?" I asked. "You were crying like your heart was broken. What happened?"

"Can we not talk about it yet?" she asked. "Please? Let's eat breakfast first, okay? Let's have a few minutes more before we have to deal with…things."

"One question," I said, "and then you can decide what to say. Okay?"

Lucia nodded.

"Were you in bed with me last night?"

Lucia grinned and blushed. "Yes," she admitted. "You were lying there, moaning and whispering, and Yaya told me not to disturb you, but I thought I might be able to calm you down. I came over to the bed to hold your hand, but you pulled me closer. So I got onto the bed with you, but only for a few minutes, so you'd sleep. I guess I was tired, because the next thing I knew, it was morning. But you did sleep well, didn't you? It worked, right?"

"Yes, it did, and thank you!" I said. "And I'll thank you again to stretch out beside me for a few minutes before we go to breakfast."

She was still blushing as she came over and snuggled into my arms. I could smell her hair, her scent, and a part of me relaxed. I knew she had things to tell me, terrible things, but right now, in this instant, I had a loving woman in my arms, and that meant the world was not entirely awful.

I should know better by now.

"Lucia," I said, "we should be dead. We're not. That means you made a deal with the wolf, and I can guess what kind of deal. So tell me now, tell me later, it won't change anything. I know everything but the details. So let's put it all on the table, figure out the worst of it, then try to figure out how to make it better."

She was silent for a few minutes while I stroked her hair and waited.

"You're right," she said in a tiny voice. "He made me vow, on my soul, my honor, and the unicorn, to return to him at the full moon. He said if I made the vow, he would spare your life. Now, if I break the vow, the unicorn's protection will be corrupted. If I let him break me, it's the same result. Either way, he's won, and it's my fault."

She was silent; the tears had already been shed.

"He hasn't won. Not yet. It looks bad, but we have time. We'll figure out something. The important thing is that we both know the truth; no more secrets."

"We couldn't beat him at his ebb," she said. "How are we going to do it at his peak?"

"I don't know, and right now, I don't care," I said. "That's a problem for later. Right now, the problem is food, as in I need some. Problem number two is pants. I need them, too! Now scat, or I'll get out of this bed and make you blush even more!"

"Oh, poo!" she said. "Who do you think took your pants off in the first place? Yaya?"

It was my turn to blush, but as I started to get out of bed, Lucia dashed out of the room, not quite as bold as she let on. It felt good to finally have things out in the open with her. The dance had more steps, but we both knew where it would lead.

Breakfast that morning was a merry affair. We ate, talked, laughed, and just enjoyed being alive. Yes, the future held danger and darkness, but it always does. This day was a day for being happy, and that was a precious thing. That night, Lucia and I went to the room I'd awakened in, which had somehow become our room, and we made love for the first time.

The next morning, we tried to play it off as if nothing had happened, but it seemed only the twins were oblivious. Tina had a gleam in her eye as she brought me coffee, then told Lucia it was to be her job from then on. Yaya just looked on with approval, but I thought I caught an echo of something else as well. I ignored it.

That night was our only honeymoon, because the next morning, we began searching for a way to beat Flint. As the first week passed, our optimism became tinged with desperation. We had only two options, both of which resulted in the breaking of the unicorn's protection.

There didn't seem to be a way out.

Our lovemaking changed as our desperation built. Lucia became more aggressive, more demanding, as if she wanted to milk every bit of pleasure out of the time she had left. Her appetite changed as well. She began to eat meat, no longer worried about its effect on her fae blood. A strip of bacon with breakfast one morning became a full steak at dinner the next night.

Yaya watched, and the 'something else' in her gaze became more evident.

Pity.

The day before Lucia was to return to Flint, Yaya pulled me aside while Lucia was cleaning up and presented a third option.

"You've been strong for Lucia," she said, "but now you need to be stronger still. There are truths you need to know."

"What are you talking about, Yaya?" I asked. "No matter what she does, Flint will break the unicorn. There's no way out."

"There *is* a way out," she said, "but it's hard. So hard. I don't even want to tell you of it. But I must. The unicorn cannot be allowed to be broken."

I felt sick. If Yaya had a way, she'd have told us a week ago, unless that way was too horrific to think of. I didn't want to ask. I knew the answer could destroy me.

But damn me forever, I asked.

"How do we save her?"

"We don't save her. We save it. The unicorn."

"What do you mean?" I spoke the words as if in a dream. There was a rushing in my ears, trying not to hear the words coming next.

Yaya whispered, but it was as loud as the Trumps of Doom. "She can't break the unicorn if she's dead." She went on, relentless and implacable, "She was bitten by Flint. She's changing. Tomorrow night, if she's not killed, she *will* become a wolf, and with her first kill, she'll corrupt the talisman forever."

"Stop it," I said. "Just stop it!"

She didn't. "She must die, and it would be best if it were by the hand of one who loves her, one she loves. Love has tremendous power. Your love can free her and save the unicorn."

She handed me a small dagger; I could smell the monkshood on it.

"Like hell," I said. "Like HELL! I will not do this. There's another way, and I *will* find it!"

"There is no other way," Yaya said. "We've looked, but you've known it from the beginning. You've had two weeks of joy with her, but that was all you were allotted. The time has run out, and to save her, you must kill her."

"I won't," I said and discovered I was on my knees, sobbing. "I can't."

"You can," she said. "You must. And you will."

She took my head into her hands and held me to her skirts like I was a small child. I was raging, crying, and swearing as sobs racked my body. I fought against the weight of a cruel fate, denying the impossibility of the burden Yaya had placed on me. I left before Lucia came down, not ready to face her, walking the town for hours, looking for an answer I knew wouldn't come. I raged and denied.

But I kept the dagger.

That night in our room, Lucia looked me in the eyes.

"You know?" she asked.

"Yeah."

"Are you mad that I kept it a secret?"

"Probably, but what good would it do except spoil what time we have left?"

"Are you going to do it? Put me down like a dog?"

"NO! Hell no!"

"What if I begged you to?" Lucia asked.

I looked into her eyes.

Save me, her eyes said. *Free me.*

Her words were different but said the same thing. "Don't let me become the monster."

That night, we made love for the last time. It was wild, animalistic, and passionate, then tender and loving as the mood swept us. Our final round found us finishing face to face, mouth to mouth, kissing deeply. She bit my lip, and I tasted blood, biting her back as we finished together, crashing back to earth in a tangle of limbs and sweaty sheets.

You should never know that it's the last time you'll make love to your mate.

The next afternoon, we left the diner for the last time, heading for the Johnston farm. Yaya frowned at me but kept her peace. Davos crushed us both with huge hugs, and Tina hugged Lucia, then fled, crying. The twins weren't sure what was going on, but picked up on the somber mood, and were quiet.

I opened the door for Lucia.

"Third time's the charm?" I asked.

It was a weak jest, but she smiled faintly.

As we left town, Lucia asked me to pull over.

"Calder, I can feel the wolf," she said. "There's no way I can control it. If I change, I'll kill you. Don't let that happen to me."

"I won't let that happen," I said. "I'll…"

She interrupted, "If you don't kill me now, you'll let it happen! You won't be able to stop it. I'm begging you." Her voice broke. "Kill me now so I don't have to live with killing you!"

I pulled out the dagger. It seemed so small and inconsequential compared to the sword I'd held two weeks ago, but a cut with it would end this. It would kill her.

And destroy the last vestiges of my soul.

I put the knife down.

"Lucia, I love you, and I'll never hurt you or let you hurt me."

She was crying. "You don't understand! When I change, I won't be *me*. I'll be the wolf! I'll tear you apart without a second thought! And I'll remember when I change back. I'll remember forever. Only you can save me from that!"

I had to find the right words to convince her of what I knew.

"It's you that doesn't understand!" I roared. "It's not up to you! I claim you as my wife and my mate. You *are* part of me, and you *will not* hurt me!"

Lucia was stunned for a moment as the echoes of my shouts died out.

"All right, then," she said. "Let's do this."

We stopped short of the farm, and this time, I made sure to go downwind. I don't like to make the same mistake twice.

Flint was on the porch, waiting for Lucia. I was much closer this time, but Flint didn't seem to notice, or care if he did. He didn't care to bathe, either, because I could smell his musk from a quarter mile away.

It was dusk when Lucia came up the road. The change hadn't hit yet, but the wolf was coming to the surface. Her gate was a slow, sinuous stalking. Her body was coiled taut, ready to pounce, but seemed at the same time to be relaxed. In the twilight, her pupils dilated, and her eyes gleamed golden with the last light of day.

Flint gloated. He made no move, forcing her to come to him. He pulled the unicorn from his pocket. "You've come as agreed," he said. "Good. I'll enjoy breaking you."

She stared at the ground.

"Look at me!" he commanded.

Lucia's eyes snapped to his crimson gaze. Moonrise was only moments away, and I could see their breathing, hear their hearts beating as the change came closer.

"I told you I would spare Calder, and I did. But he has one final part to play."

"Calder!" he called. "I know you're out there. Come closer so you can see what a pretty bitch I've made of your girlfriend!"

I started to rise, a low growl in my throat, but I'd dealt with my anger and hatred for far too long to let it take control. I remained hidden, waiting.

Stalking my prey.

"You don't think she'll kill you because she loves you? I turned Lucia, and she must obey me! I'm her alpha. Lucia, I want you to find Calder, kill him, and eat his heart!"

At that moment, the first rays of the moon burst over the horizon. Lucia's keening whine became a full-throated howl as the change took her. It happened so quickly, it was hard to take in. In a few moments, an auburn wolf stood, snarling and raising her muzzle to the moon to howl.

"Now!" Flint cried in a guttural voice as he was mid change. "KILL HIM!"

Lucia howled again, and my heart broke, for in the howl I heard loss and pain, rage and hunger.

But there was nothing human, and no love.

She cast about, looking for a scent to follow as I readied the blade. My plan, if you could call it a plan, was to evade her long enough to cut Flint. Even if Lucia killed me, or Flint gutted me, if I killed him, the unicorn would be safe.

A thin plan, but all I had.

As usual, I was wrong.

Lucia picked up my scent, looked directly at me, and then howled again.

Again there was nothing human, but this time, there was love.

She turned and charged at Flint, who'd finished his transformation into a giant black wolf. He was twice her size, but she fought like a bull terrier, and he wasn't prepared for the attack. She hit him at full speed, knocking him off his paws, then darting in and out, slashing at his hamstrings, going for the tendons, trying to bring him down with a thousand cuts. She was running with the moon, and that made her strong.

I stood and cheered my girl as she ran Flint ragged, but size and experience count for more than heart in a fight, and both were on his side. He caught her foreleg on one of her darting attacks and crushed it in his jaws.

A screaming wolf sounds a lot like a screaming woman.

I roared out of my hiding place, determined to protect my mate. Lucia intercepted an attack from Flint that would have cost me my life, but his claws scored deep gashes in her belly, and she fell bonelessly to the ground and lay still. But I scored a deep gash in Flint's left fore-shoulder. It would heal, but it would slow him down.

Flint whirled on me, and his claws just missed gutting me as I skipped backward. I saw his next swing coming and stepped inside it, scoring a hit on his left hind leg and spinning away out of range.

I was doing much better this time; fury and adrenaline are a wonderful combination.

His next attack landed, gouging my left forearm to the bone. I continued to step back, forcing him to move toward me and away from Lucia, who lay panting on the ground.

Flint shook his head as the monkshood took effect. He favored his left side, and I took advantage, diving in and plunging the dagger deep into his chest. The knife hung up on his ribs, and that kept me in range a fraction of a second too long. Flint lunged down to rip out my throat with his jaws, and I had to let go of the knife and grab his muzzle with both hands, holding him away from my throat with every muscle I had.

I shouldn't have been able to, but somehow, I did. We were locked together, Flint trying to rip out my throat, and me trying to keep him from it. It seemed like forever we held that pose, but it could only have been a couple of seconds. My grip was slipping, and it was just a matter of time before my life ended.

Then Lucia hit him from behind, burying her jaws in his neck and shaking until something snapped. Flint's limbs spasmed out of control, scrabbling on the ground, gashing me, and throwing Lucia from him. I grabbed the knife and stabbed until the giant black wolf lay still.

To be sure, I sawed off the head, then urinated on the corpse. I'm not sure what made me do that last, but Yaya had said to go with my hunches.

I turned to Lucia. She was human again. And dying.

I dropped down into the dirt and pulled her into my lap, babbling, "No, no, no, no."

Her breathing was faint, her words even fainter.

"Yes," she said. "This is best. I didn't fail. I didn't kill you, and I saved the unicorn."

"Please," I whispered. "Stay with me!"

"I'll always be with you," she whispered. "You're my alpha."

She died in my arms.

I don't remember much about the next few hours. Yaya told me the police found me in the dirt next to a dead wolf with Lucia on my lap, the unicorn in her hand. They brought me in and questioned me. They didn't like the answers I gave them, so they made up their own story about a picnicking couple attacked by a wolf.

Davos and Yaya picked me up at the station and brought me back to their place. I stayed for one night, then went back to my apartment over the office. I couldn't sleep in the bed we'd shared.

I didn't reopen the agency right away. I wasn't ready to deal with other people's busted lives when I wasn't sure I could deal with my own. Freya, the Viking bartender two shops down, suggested I was suffering from a broken heart. But you have to have a heart for that to be true.

She could be right.

But I was worried about something else.

Lucia said I was her alpha, but could werewolves *have* a human alpha?

I finally went to Yaya and told her everything.

"What am I?" I asked.

"I don't know," she said finally. "The wolf sits lightly on you. You were bitten, but the bite was given in love. I told you, love is powerful and can change many things. But the important question is not what you are, but *who* you are, and that one I can answer. You're Calder Sharpe, and you're always welcome in our home."

Sometimes the answers you get aren't the ones you're looking for, but they're exactly the ones you need.

The next full moon, I was deep in the Barrens.

Just in case.

I looked up at the moon and felt the pull of the wolf, but I didn't change, not much. The night came alive with rich smells and sounds. Foxes, mice, moles, raccoons, and other night creatures moved in the darkness, hunting and being hunted in turn. I was aware of them all, but saw nothing; the moon held my gaze, glowing with sadness and loss…and love.

A low moan began deep in my chest, building and rising in pitch until it became a full-throated howl. I howled my sorrow and pain at the moon, and the moon welcomed and accepted it and knew it for love.

And the name of the moon was Lucia.

* * * * *

Rich Hailey Biography

Born and raised in Tennessee, Rich Hailey has been reading science fiction and fantasy since grade school, when a nun introduced him to Robert Heinlein via *Tunnel in the Sky*. From there, he found Bradbury, van Vogt, Clark, Del Ray, Asimov, and so many others.

His first job after dropping out of college was as a night manager of a Mini-Mart. His second job was operating nuclear reactors for the US Navy. Since then, he's worked in a variety of fields, learning something new in every one of them. Now he's a technical writer and compliance management consultant.

Over the years, he's written a few stories, but never submitted any of them, although his mother said they were very good. When he's not reading or writing, he can be found engaged in one of his many hobbies: astrophotography, 3D printing, HAM radio (KO4LNC), hiking, making awesome barbecue, or just sitting poolside with his wife, 8 kids, and 17 grandkids.

* * * * *

Electrum
by Marie Whittaker

An Eldros Legacy Story

1708 MG

Village of Montbracken, Silvanon, Continent of Pyranon

Mekaid Rem finished the embellishments on the fine electrum torc he'd been commissioned to design by High Queen Ariana for one of her consorts. Wearing insulated, protective gloves, he expertly tooled the metal with a Mavric iron stylus, then finished up the last of the scrolling design before the iron's poison could affect his system. He shook off the gloves and unclamped the gleaming neckcuff, holding it up to the light, where the reflection danced silver and white against the dark skin of his hand.

"Not bad," he told himself. The workmanship was easily some of his finest. Montbracken was home to the largest electrum mine for miles, and the naturally occurring alloy was the purest on the continent of Pyranon. Although electrum was the currency of Pyranon, using it as a medium to create made for quite expensive treasures. Jewelry, utensils, and the statuary he created were highly sought after. Payment for this torc would be a welcome lining to his coin pouch.

Keena, his son, busily loaded and secured the wagon to transport the cuff and other tooled electrum pieces to Pyraeya. The paid guardsmen assisted in securing crates and checking the horses' gear, awaiting the last of the goods to haul through the forest surrounding Montbracken to the Seat of Queens. The lead guard, Iaku, was a solid man in both integrity and his bulky, imposing form. He was a longtime friend, and Mekaid wouldn't trust another with the safety of his son or his finished goods.

Keena laughed, slapping Iaku on a thick shoulder. Mekaid wondered at their jokes. Keena had known Iaku since he was a toddler, and the two were just as close as old friends.

Mekaid leaned in the doorway, watching the jest. A deep frown tensed his face and jaw. He didn't like the idea of sending Keena to the palace alone. At seventeen, Keena was the same age as Princess Mahaela. The two had been fast friends since Keena was old enough to ride along the first time for deliveries to the palace.

Mekaid huffed a laugh of disbelief. Had it really been a dozen years that he'd been taking Keena on deliveries? Keena had outgrown him during his fourteenth year in both height and weight. Slightly lighter skinned than Mekaid, he bore his mother's deep blue eyes, although all their only child's remaining features mirrored his own deep brown skin and wavy black hair.

He laughed again. *Poor youngster.*

And now, here he was about to send his only kin off to the palace without him. He quietly cursed his luck with the Citizen's Lottery. The village of Montbracken called on townsfolk to pay taxes in the way of services. He and nineteen others would spend the next three days at the village hall, working off their yearly tax. The queen wouldn't wait for her commissioned piece, and there was no postponing the lottery. Queen Ariana Bellagrave was the queen of the entire Empire of Pyranon, not just Silvanon, and an old "acquaintance" from his youth. It was best to serve her well and timely.

Keena had stepped up immediately to help. His son had insisted all would be fine, that he could handle delivering the orders to the capital city without his father for once. Keena was intent on proving himself to his father. Mekaid knew, though, one reason Keena was so adamant about making the delivery himself was so he could see the princess.

"Do I need to come get that last order, or are you going to bring it over here so it can be packed up with the rest?" Keena called, a teasing smile on his face.

Iaku slapped the back of the boy's head and playfully shoved him toward his father. "You go," the guard said in his broken version of the common tongue.

"I'm going!" Keena held up his hands in mock defense. The rest of the swordsmen chuckled.

Mekaid handed over the wrapped bundle that contained the special order. "Give this only to Banu, the queen's advisor, understand? The rest will be sorted out at the citadel when the guard takes it in."

Keena tucked the bundle in a pouch at his hip. "I won't make mistakes, Father. I've watched you make your deliveries for as long as I can remember."

Mekaid embraced his son, then held him by the shoulders to look at him sternly. "Listen to what Iaku tells you. Steer clear of the lava canals. Keep your eyes open on the road. Don't run the horses in the heat."

Keena gave his father a bland look. "All will be well. I mean it." He patted the pouch and smiled reassuringly. "We'll be back before you know it." He turned quickly and ran back to the head of the small caravan of two wagons escorted by a dozen mounted swordsmen and archers. He swung gracefully astride his mare, who pranced in place, as anxious to go as Keena.

"Goodbye, Father," Keena said.

Iaku nudged his mount into stride next to Keena's. "Do not worry, my friend. I will protect him with my life."

Mekaid nodded. "Thank you, my friend." But again, he cursed the lottery and Queen Ariana's impatience to dote upon her consort.

* * *

"If we had bats, we'd be there by now, wouldn't we?" Keena slid to the grass, unfastened his pack, and set it aside. When he removed the saddle and bit, his mare scrubbed her forehead lovingly along his shoulder. He scratched behind her ears and kissed her muzzle.

"Riding bats don't love you the way your horse does," Iaku answered.

"You've had bats before? Are they fast?"

"I was a stableboy in Ignatia, back home. Not my bats." Iaku grinned and nodded. "Yes, they are very fast."

"If we had bats, we wouldn't have to stop for the night." Keena handed over the mare's lead to one of the guards, who took her to the temporary rope pen with the other horses.

"Your father doesn't wish to keep bats. You know this," said Iaku.

"It doesn't hurt to let him know the benefits."

Iaku kept smiling, but shook his head as he shouldered his pack to join two guards around a fledgling fire. The others fanned out in teams of two to set up the watch for the night.

Keena followed him and dropped onto an old fallen log. Although the caravan made it a point not to camp in the same place as the last few trips, the spot seemed familiar. Usually his father sat where he did now, with Keena beside him. It felt good to fill that seat.

He sat tall, reminding himself to act as an adult would. To act as *Father* would. The fire grew, red orange glinting off the thick forest canopy over their camp.

The day's ride had put them close to the Great Gates. Just a few hours after the sun came up tomorrow, he'd be able to see Mahaela. Princess Mahaela. He had to remember to address her properly now that the two were growing up and taking on the roles that awaited them in adulthood. His childhood friend would go on to rule as High Queen someday. As for Keena, his training as a smithy and jeweler was complete. Father said now that he had the knowledge, it was time to hone the craft. His fate was set, and it was far from the destiny of his "friend," whom everyone travelling knew was much more than that.

He hadn't realized he'd sighed out loud until he noticed Iaku watching him.

"Thinking about your princess?" the old guard teased.

"No," Keena lied. "Just wish the trip was over, and we were at the citadel in the capital, enjoying ale and a good meal."

"Aye," Iaku agreed with a nod.

The horses snorted and stamped their hooves, suddenly restless when they should be exhausted from travel. Keena squinted into the night but couldn't make out the entire herd. Iaku waved to get his attention and held a finger over his mouth for silence. He came to his feet, listening. Keena withdrew a flare arrow and kept it nocked and ready to light the tip quickly and send the beacon into the midnight sky. They were close enough, just a few hours' ride, that the queen's guard would see the flare and raise the alarm for help.

Brush parted, revealing a triangle of darkness where light from the meager fire couldn't reach. An Arachlan drone stepped into the circle of light. Keena's gut knotted, and his heart hammered in his chest. The Arachlan were an eight-limbed race that were half man and half spider, intelligent, fast on four legs, and nearly uncatchable on all eight, and about a foot taller than Keena's six feet two inches when standing upright on only their back legs. This one not only towered over him, but was much taller than even Iaku. The Arachlan looked from Iaku to Keena, eyes narrowed.

"What business have you here, Drone? Aren't you too far north for the comfort of your kind?" Iaku hadn't lowered his sword, and Keena wished he wasn't holding a flaming arrow rather than his own blade.

Arachlan dwellings were in the south, where the climate was more suitable for their hives. This one didn't look like he'd been home in a while. His hair hung in greasy clumps, sticking to the gray skin of his collarbone and chest. He smelled of sweat and filth. Certainly, a proper drone wouldn't be spotted in such a state, but nothing about the beastly Arachlan seemed proper at all.

"I could ask you the same, Human. Your guard raided our camp." He snarled, showing vampiric fangs.

"Nonsense," Iaku growled. "Be on your way." Iaku moved to put himself between Keena and the rogue Arachlan.

"Nonsense, indeed," the beast growled. One of his four arms flung something large at their feet.

"No!" Keena yelled. The head of one of the guards rolled to a stop beside his boot. He jumped away, but adrenaline burned through his veins. He dipped the arrow into the flames, but instead of shooting into the sky, he shot the flaming tip at the murderous Arachlan. From such short range, the shot drove into the thick muscle of the rogue's shoulder.

Iaku lunged at the Arachlan as it hissed and ripped the arrow from its flesh. "Run, Keena!" he bellowed and swung his sword mightily.

The sounds of men screaming in pain seemed to come from all around him in the night. Keena sprinted toward the road to the palace because it was closer than running toward home and his father. He leapt low branches, keeping an eye out for anyone who might help. His boot slid along a tree root, and he lost his balance.

When he hit the ground, his hip and back erupted with pain, but he couldn't stop. He must get help.

With one knee beneath him, he managed to sit upright just as another Arachlan plunged from the canopy above. Keena got to his feet, but something hit him in the back, hard enough to send him sprawling back into the dirt and leaves.

He rolled over and reached for his ribs where cold pain erupted. The cold spread through his body quickly. His arms dropped as if made of sacks of wet sand. He fell forward onto his chest, a tremor running the length of his spine as poison coursed through his system. The last thing he saw was a meaty hand grasp his forearm as he was yanked from the ground.

* * *

Mekaid opened his door the next morning and stepped into the yard to see to the animals. He had much to do before he went back to pay his third day of taxes. He rounded the side of the house to the lean-to where the horses were penned and stopped short when he saw Keena's mare across the fence from the other horses. A deep gouge gaped in her neck, and she held one hoof off the ground, resting it gently on the toe of her other hoof.

"Easy," Mekaid said. The wound on her neck wasn't as deep as it had first appeared. The blood was dried and dark in the horse's soft coat. He looked across the pen at the rolling hills where he'd last seen his son and the band of men setting off to make the delivery. There was no way Keena was already back from the trip, which meant the mare had escaped and run back through the night.

The thought of Keena in danger tumbled with his thoughts as he hurried to saddle his gelding. Without even a flask to carry water, Mekaid gave the horse his head so the steed could sprint into the gleaming sunrise. He tried to control his worry as he guided the gelding along the trail to the main road, but a father's thoughts always went to the worst.

He let his horse continue to race for a while longer, then reined him in so he wouldn't exhaust himself. One horse always made better time than a caravan with a wagon, but slowing the horse for its own safety was the hardest thing Mekaid had ever done. Once the horse's breath slowed and he fell into an easy trot, Mekaid allowed him to pick up speed again, carefully cutting through switchbacks in the forest. Hours went by, and the sun hung low, brushing the tops of dark pines before he came to the site where Iaku had planned to camp for the night.

He slid from the saddle and landed quietly, wrapping the reins around a tree to secure his horse. A body lay face down beside the blackened, cold firepit. As he approached, he recognized one of the paid guards, pale and chilled. He left the body undisturbed and continued searching for Keena.

"Keena!" Mekaid called. He wandered through the trees surrounding the camp, finding no evidence that the same fate had befallen the rest of the guard. One of the horses had been killed. The wagon had been tossed and was empty of cargo. He searched the surrounding woods, leading his horse, until the sun had set beyond the horizon. The band of rogues was nowhere in sight.

Neither was his son.

Mekaid was nearly back to the main road when his horse stopped behind him, shying away from something in the path, and pulling on the reins.

"Runa have mercy," Mekaid whispered. Two bodies lay before him, the twilight barely enough to make out any features. He put a hand on the first man's shoulder and turned him over, quickly coming to his feet once he saw the condition of Iaku's body. His friend had always been a robust man, thick in the chest, and a bit round at the belly, but the frame of his body was scarce more than a husk. The front of his armor and tunic had been torn away to reveal bite marks riddling his skin and torn out bits of flesh. The wounds hadn't bled.

Arachlan.

Vampiric rogues. Civilized Arachlan would never feed on Humans. The Arachlan were amicable, quiet people that tended to keep to themselves. Mekaid didn't think he'd seen more than a handful of them north of Mystmoor.

Rogue Arachlan hadn't been heard of since he was a child. His village outside of Montbracken had been set upon by a band of the blood-crazed beasts. Two families had been taken apart before the rogues were driven off and later hunted down. He'd seen the aftermath of an attack before, and never thought he would again.

At least he'd always hoped.

There wasn't time to wonder why they'd turned rogue. He had to find his son. He braced himself before turning every body or clearing their faces—what was left of them—hating the way he was relieved each time to find none of the bodies were Keena's. When he'd checked them all, he stood amid the camp with his stomach in knots and his soul broken, as thoughts of the deadly worst about his lost son wound through his mind like vipers in a pit.

Cracking branches broke the eerie silence. Sword drawn and at the ready, Mekaid turned with the single, daring hope that it might be Keena returning after hiding during the raid. But he saw nothing but darkness beneath the canopy of branches and squinting eyes on gossamer tree trunks.

"Keena?" His voice shook with fear for his son.

Silence answered until the snapping came again. One boot at a time, he stepped into the dimly lit grove, tracking the sounds. He walked in darkness only a moment before coming into a clearing where an Arachlan man was tangled in a stand of trees with trunks as big around as a Human man's head.

Mekaid padded forward silently. The Arachlan's exoskeletal plating beat against wood as it attempted to free its enormous body. A trickle of black blood pooled beneath the thorax. Mekaid toed forward, becoming more and more certain of his safety as the puddle of blood grew.

"Come, Human. Finish me." The Arachlan stilled.

Mekaid came to face him cautiously. The beast was unkempt. Crimson Human blood coated his lower jaw from where he'd fed. Brown eyes were drawn to slits from intense pain.

That's when Mekaid saw the fletching of an arrow protruding from a thin gap between two bands of arachnid plating. It was one of Keena's. Mekaid had helped the boy make it himself. The precision of the shot indicated Keena had been at close range. He searched the underbrush frantically, eyes glancing over rocks, dry leaves, and finally his son, lying rigid on his back.

Mekaid hit his knees beside his son, searching for signs the boy drew breath. He lowered his head close to Keena's deathly pale face, biting back tears, until he felt the slightest bit of breath against his cheek.

"Thank the gods," he said. He gripped Keena's shoulders, but his body was too rigid to bend at the waist to sit him up. "Son? Can you hear me?" He pried the bow from the boy's frigid, locked fist. He placed a palm against Keena's face. The skin was so cold, as if ice filled the veins beneath. Mekaid searched for an injury, finding a deep bite on his son's shoulder where fangs had pierced the leather armor and torn skin to ragged strips. The wound stank of venom and poisoned blood.

"He put up a good fight," the Arachlan said.

Mekaid shot to his feet and lunged at the beast. He knew good and well how to craft a blade sharp enough to impale or otherwise carve into flesh nearly by its own will. He steadied the tip of the blade atop the Arachlan's collar plate and soft, humanoid throat below his chin.

"By the Giants, you piece of filth, tell me how to help my son, or your next breath will be your last," he growled. The tip of the blade dug into the Arachlan's skin, where dark blood oozed over the armored collar and down its chest and abdomen.

The Arachlan sneered, despite the sting of the blade. He tilted his head to one side and then the other, leering down at Mekaid like a wolf that was curious about its prey. "He is lost," he said. The sneer broke into a sinister smile of jagged teeth and protruding incisors. "See for yourself, Human. Venom has claimed him. Such a waste."

"There has to be a way!" Mekaid shouted.

"None exists. I've killed your son. Best use that blade to take your price."

Mekaid lowered his sword and stepped back. "It won't be that easy for you." He gestured to the arrow. "My son has already killed you, but it'll be slow, and very painful. I have a deal for you. Tell me how to save my son, and I'll make sure you suffer no longer."

"Unacceptable." The Arachlan grinned.

"There's more. If you choose not to, I'll tie each of your arms and legs, one at a time, to my horse's saddle and pull you apart like the insect you are. Good and slow."

The beast laughed. "Either way, you lose, Human."

Mekaid's heart dropped. The Arachlan wasn't about to help, and he was also correct about the possibility of losing Keena. He backed away and sheathed his sword as he went. The only thing to do was to get his son to the palace. Someone there had to know how to help.

He dragged Keena's failing body back to the camp and his gelding, then hefted the board-straight boy across the saddle. Sensing the venom, the horse danced in place until Mekaid swung up behind Keena. He urged the horse forward through the trees until they were back on the main road. Darkness had nearly claimed the day, but he spurred the gelding into a run.

Keena's body slowly relaxed and hung over the horse's withers with the horse's galloping pace. Mekaid locked a burly hand through the strap securing the quiver to his son's back.

"I am so sorry, my son. I should never have sent you out alone."

* * *

The ride to the towering gates of Pyraeya was a jolting trek through the terrifying night that seemed to take days rather than hours. Once he'd convinced the guards of who he was, being the chosen jeweler and smithy of High Queen Ariana bought him access to the palace.

"He was attacked by a rogue Arachlan," Mekaid said. "The venom is taking him."

The drawbridge was lowered over the flowing lava moat deep in the ravine surrounding the great walls. The inner guard seemed overly attentive and concerned about Keena, although Mekaid thought it was merely his fear for his son's life making it so. They whisked him from the horse's back and carried him gently through the palace doorway.

Mekaid gripped Keena's freezing hand in his. "Hold on, son," he whispered.

The inner guardsmen sped through the great room. One of the men who lifted Keena by the arm opposite to Mekaid called out, "Alert Banu. The smithy's son has been bitten by the Arachlan!"

"Rogue Arachlan, not *the* Arachlan," Mekaid yelled. "There's a band who've turned vampiric. They attacked in the forest just beyond the main road."

The guards exchanged a glance that Mekaid didn't understand.

"Why must we seek the Banu?" He didn't want the vile sorcerer anywhere close to his son. "We seek an antidote to the bite, not an audience with the queen's advisor."

"Who?" a shrill, female voice called from a balcony above the hall. "Did you say the smithy's son?" Princess Mahaela kicked the shoes from her feet, gathered the length of her gown in fists of luxurious silk, and sprinted to the stairs. "Keena!" she called.

"Princess, please," the lead guard said. "Stay back."

But Mahaela shoved one guard aside and was at Keena's side that moment. She was out of breath, but kept pace as the guards surged forward, intent on getting to the Banu's quarters.

"He's so cold!" she wailed, pulling her hand from Keena's cheek. Tears welled in her eyes, mirroring the desperation that matched Mekaid's.

"Banu!" the princess screamed. "Get your wretched bones out here!"

"I am here, Your Grace," Banu said. He'd appeared behind them, having been somewhere else in the palace rather than his quarters when they'd arrived.

"What's the excitement?" High Queen Ariana asked. She appeared in a doorway off the main passage. The guards who weren't burdened by Keena's weight dropped to a knee. Mekaid gripped Keena's hand as if his own life might somehow keep his son alive just a moment longer.

"Oh, my," she said, peering past the guard, then gazing at Mekaid.

"Your Highness, please allow your men to help. He's been bitten by an Arachlan rogue."

The High Queen locked eyes with Banu and jerked her head in the direction of his quarters. The men lurched forward, carrying Keena after him, the princess sidestepping along with them. She then turned her gaze to the guards who remained on their knees with their faces bowed to the polished jade floor.

"Rise. Now," she commanded. The men came to their feet and straightened before her. She paced to the one closest. "I trust you've already sent out a hunting party to bring in the rogues?"

The guard's eyes shot sidelong at another man, who didn't break stance. "No, High Queen."

Ariana sighed loudly, then pursed her lips. The guard said nothing more as she approached within a few inches of his chest. "Then go," she hissed.

She turned to Mekaid as the guards scattered to set off on the hunt. "Come," she said, pulling him by the wrist toward Banu's quarters.

"Thank you, Ariana," he said. "Please make that monster help my son."

"I will. On his life." She pushed the door open, and they went inside.

The guards laid Keena on a long table underneath a bank of light-reflecting glass that cast light the length of the table. Keena's pallor was sickly beneath the gold illumination.

"Leave us," Ariana said, much gentler than Mekaid expected. The guards bowed quickly and were gone.

Banu leaned over Keena, holding one of the boy's eyes open for examination.

Mekaid stiffened when the sorcerer put his hands on Keena. Ariana squeezed his wrist, then patted the top of his hand. He took a long breath to remain calm. Be what he may, awful, ugly, and evil, Banu was Keena's only hope at this point.

"We need to remove his clothes," Banu said. He looked meaningfully between the high queen and the princess.

Princess Mahaela tore her eyes away from Keena. "I am *not* leaving him."

"Mahaela—" the queen began.

"Please Mother! Don't make me go," the princess pleaded.

Mekaid stepped aside to make way for her to get to the door. He hated to appear to gang up on the poor girl, but it wouldn't be proper to strip Keena bare with her present. "I'll give you a full report as soon as I can." He gave her a reassuring smile.

The princess began to cry. She bent and placed a kiss on Keena's hand. Scrubbing tears from her cheeks, she turned to go, then appeared to change her mind. She gave the Banu a scathing glare. "If he doesn't make a full recovery, I'll never forgive you. Keep that in mind as you cure him. And you *will* cure him. Think of how awkward and sad your future will be with me hating the sight of you for the rest of my life."

The Banu didn't respond, but he bowed his head as she left the room and slammed the door behind her. When she was gone, he looked up at the queen.

The two appeared to exchange a silent conversation, which made the last of Mekaid's patience raw. "Will you please stop staring at one another and help my son?" he growled.

"I'll be just outside." Ariana locked eyes with Mekaid. He saw something there, some unspoken fear or anxiety that was uncommon for the high queen. She stepped away and gently closed the door.

Mekaid found himself alone with the Banu; the one "person" who could help him. Without words between them, he began taking off Keena's boots. He noticed the sorcerer hadn't begun treating his son.

"What are you waiting for?" he hissed.

"We must discuss terms," the Banu said.

"What terms? Your high queen ordered you to save my boy. Now, get to it before you no longer have the time."

"There is time for what I need to do."

Mekaid smashed a fist down on the table. "What are these terms?"

The Banu considered Mekaid carefully for a brief moment. "By the High Queen's decree, your Keena must wed the princess."

Mekaid huffed. "Ariana would never agree to that! Our children are close. She knows what that would do to them. It means a slow death for my son, thanks to your twisted, never-ending curse upon the high kings of Pyraeya!" He turned to reach for the door. Ariana would want to know what her "advisor" had suggested.

The Banu stilled his grip on the door latch by locking an icy fist over Mekaid's. "Your High Queen is aware of the terms for my saving your son."

Mekaid jerked free and shoved the larger man back. "Liar! She would never do this."

The Banu threw his hands up and backed away. "Keep wasting precious time then. Go and talk with the queen. Be my guest." He sat on a bench beside the wall and leaned his head back, closing his eyes.

Mekaid ripped the door open. "Ariana!" He hadn't realized she was waiting just outside before he shouted into the corridor.

"I'm right here," she snapped.

"I have to tell you of these terms your sorcerer demands of me before—"

The queen silenced him by holding up a hand. She sighed and dropped onto a cushioned bench. "Tell him to continue, then we shall talk."

All the air left Mekaid's lungs in a gust. He shook his head. "Tell me you didn't agree to this. Please."

She nodded toward the door. "I'll be right here."

He turned away from her, hate boiling in his heart. The woman he used to know—the girl she was before she was the high queen, and before the Banu got his hooks in her—would never set Keena up to die a death of insanity. Disagreeing with the person she was now would do him no good. He had to deal with saving his son now. Then he'd look for a way to end the Banu's curse on the boy.

He jerked the door open and stalked toward the Banu as he got to his feet. "We are in agreement," he growled. "Take my warning to heart, demon. Do nothing to harm my son. No dark magic. For if you do—" he rapped his finger against the sorcerer's sternum, "—I will kill you and take joy in watching as the souls trapped inside you creep back into the underworld where you all belong."

"Harm him? Oh, no, I won't do that. Now leave us." The Banu turned his back, pulling bottles from a cabinet with sure speed. Mekaid wondered if he might slam one into shards.

Mekaid bent to place a kiss on Keena's cheek. "I'm so sorry, dear one," he whispered. "I sent you into the midst of an attack, and now I must give you over to the will of the queen. I love you, son." Without a glance at the Banu, he left his son to the mercy of the queen's monster.

Ariana scooted over on the bench to make room for him to sit without them touching. Mekaid dropped onto the cushion and didn't say anything. He was too busy praying for Keena's recovery to see the expression on her face. She sighed loudly to get his attention.

"Ariana, I shall never forgive you for this." He couldn't bear to look at her.

"We're all fond of the boy."

"I think the only one who truly adores my son is your daughter. For you, he's apparently just a tool to sate the needs of that bastard advisor of yours." He kicked at an imaginary bit of dust on the polished floor.

"Well, that's not fair," she began.

"Then send him away!" Mekaid turned to face her and grasped both of her tender hands in his. "Better yet, have him arrested for crimes against the crown. He controls you. Be the ruler Pyranon needs. Be…you," he pleaded.

"It's not that easy." She jerked away from him. "Don't you think I've wanted to? It's not possible, and you know that. Denying him means death for my family line. I can't do that to my children."

Mekaid gave her a scathing look. "But you'll sentence Keena to death with the terms of this deal, or you'll let him die."

"The legacy that's held my family for eons wills it so. My daughter will deliver an heir by Keena. My family line will be stronger than it ever has been."

"This is madness," he growled and got to his feet. The moon frowned through a layer of clouds, beckoning him to a window across the hall. Ariana's life was bound to the Banu. If he wanted to save Keena by killing the Banu to release his grip on Pyraeya, it

220 | KENNEDY & HOWELL

would mean Ariana's life, too. If only he'd bided his first instinct to keep his son at home.

Mekaid turned when the door creaked open, and Ariana shot to her feet. To his dismay, only the Banu stepped into the corridor.

"Where's my son?" Mekaid asked, peering around the mage's dark robes. The room was empty, the table bare. He shoved the Banu into the wall. "What have you done with Keena?" he growled.

"Mekaid, release him," the queen said. She put a hand on his forearm and pulled him away.

Mekaid released the sorcerer, who straightened his robes and scowled.

"See for yourself." The Banu gestured out the window with his staff.

Mekaid didn't see anything at first, until just below them, the dark figure of an Arachlan did his best to break free of a chain that bound him to a ring set in a stone wall. "What is that thing doing here?" he asked.

"It's one of the rogue band that set upon your son's party," the Banu supplied.

Before Mekaid could react to that odd news, Keena appeared on the walkway, too close to the insectoid for his own safety.

"You bastard. I knew I shouldn't have trusted you with his safety." He turned back to the window. "Keena! Get back!" He had to get down to help his son before he was bitten again, or worse. He sprinted toward the end of the corridor.

"Stop!" the queen shouted.

Mekaid barely heard her above the pounding of his boots on stone.

"Mekaid, I am your high queen, and I order you to stop and return here to me!" she yelled.

He heard her and slowed, astonished that she would order him so with Keena in obvious danger.

"Don't think I won't use my *monster* to bring you to heel."

He came to a defeated stop and glanced at his one-time friend. The Banu had stepped next to her, grinning and ready to do her bidding.

Mekaid shook his head. "No matter the outcome, I'll never forgive you for this."

"Regardless of what you think of me, I would never consent to sending your son to certain death." She jerked her head toward the window. "Come. See what we've done for him."

Mekaid didn't like the sound of that one bit. He stomped over to the window, shoving the Banu out of the way as he went.

The sorcerer stepped behind them, easily tall enough to look into the courtyard over their heads. "Keena must fight. The rogue will prevail if it is the will of the gods."

Keena was below, sword in hand, circling with the Arachlan. The chain dropped away from where it had bound the arachnid's hind legs. The boy wielded a sword that gleamed with each of his strikes. The slight oil-on-water tint of the metal was that of a blade crafted from Mavric iron, which was so toxic that it was deadly if contact was prolonged. Keena knew that, so why was his son using such a weapon? The boy held his own against the Arachlan, however. The beast towered over Keena, but Keena was fast, and seemed to have gained more knowledge of swordsmanship. He dodged strikes and continued hacking away, drawing more blood as he went.

"What's all the shouting about?" Princess Mahaela appeared at the end of the corridor, wearing boys breeches, having shed the grand gown. Mekaid was much more accustomed to seeing her dressed this way. He'd been shocked earlier to see her in finery meant for a princess of her stature.

She stalked toward them. "You said you'd let me know when Keena was healed. Thanks for nothing." She wedged herself between Mekaid and her mother, stiffening when she saw Keena battling the Arachlan. "What are you doing?" She slapped at the Banu's face but was unsuccessful at landing a blow across his cheek.

Her small hand smacked into the mage's as he blocked her strike. Mekaid took note of how practiced the exchange seemed. This wasn't the first time the princess had tried to hit the Banu. He'd give a lot to see little Mahaela Bellagrave blacken the monster's eye.

"Save him!" she shrieked.

"Young lady," the queen said, "collect yourself this instant."

The princess burst into tears. "Keena, stop!" she called, but her friend was too busy engaging his foe to respond, if he'd heard her at all.

Just when Mekaid thought Keena wouldn't react to the princess's plea for his own safety, Keena stepped back and glanced up toward them. He smiled at Mahaela, who wailed even louder.

"Watch out!" Mekaid yelled at the lovestruck boy. The Arachlan sprang forward on his back legs, taking Keena to the ground. The beast bit down on Keena's thigh.

"No!" Mekaid and the princess yelled in unison. They fell silent, watching Keena skitter away from the beast. The Arachlan howled with laughter. He turned toward the window, gazing up at them, and clacked the exoskeletal plating of his lower forearm against the plating that spanned from his collarbone and separated in two over his humanlike pectoral muscles. It was a sign of victory.

Mekaid's blood chilled. He shook his head, vision clouded by grief.

"Wait, my friend," Ariana whispered beside him.

The princess slumped to the floor. "Crelei, Goddess be with him," she prayed. She glared at the Banu. "I hate you," she said through gritted teeth. He didn't act as though he heard her, but that was unlikely.

Through tears, Mekaid watched his son roll onto his back. Keena's chest heaved. The boy's limbs would go rigid any moment as the venom from the bite set in. A sob caught in his throat, and he leaned away from the warmth of the queen's arm next to his.

Keena's face was a mask of pain, pale and tortured. He continued to writhe, but his limbs grew sluggish. The boy stilled, his body locked, straight as a board, as poison settled throughout his body.

"Wait," Mekaid said through tears. He turned on Ariana. "Wait for your demon to kill my son. Is that what you meant for me to do?"

The queen peered up at the Banu. "I don't understand. Why isn't he getting up?"

The Banu looked as shocked as she did. He opened his mouth to speak but, as if he didn't know how to answer, he simply shook his head, staring down at the body of Keena Rem.

"Have him killed, Mother, please," the princess wailed. "He's always been a murderer."

Queen Ariana bowed her head, closed her eyes, and pinched the bridge of her nose.

Mekaid observed his old friend the queen's reaction to what she'd allowed to happen to his son. Keena's body hadn't moved, the life surely washed from his young body by the Arachlan's strike. The princess cried and cried. Her words tumbled on the sea of emotions inside him. *Have him killed...*

Silently, Mekaid slid an electrum blade free of the protective scabbard. He gripped the handle with fierce determination. With a roar of vengeance that came from the depths of his soul, Mekaid lunged at the Banu and struck at the monster's heart.

The Banu reacted quickly and caught Mekaid's arm, wrestling for control of the blade.

"Die poisoned," Mekaid yelled, "the same way as my son!" He yanked the blade free of the Banu's grip and sliced back and forth, attempting to draw blood from anywhere he could. He succeeded, but barely. The dagger caught the edge of the Banu's jaw as the demon tried to turn his face away. Mekaid drew back to strike again, loving the sight of crimson slathering the Banu's jaw and throat.

"Stop!" Ariana commanded.

Surprised, Mekaid tried to look at her and keep a hold of the Banu's twisted up cowl, but he lost his balance and stumbled back. In a blur of red and black robes, the Banu plucked the dagger from his grasp so fast Mekaid didn't see him move.

Mekaid rolled to his feet and peered at Ariana, and the princess, who was on her feet and hanging out the window. He staggered forward to see what they watched.

Keena's body twitched wildly, bucking so hard that his back came up from the ground. A growl rumbled from deep in his chest. His body stilled again, then turned on his side so his flushed, olive face could be seen beneath a tangle of dark hair.

Keena opened his eyes.

"Keena!" Mekaid bellowed. His feet were stone blocks welded to the floor by shock and grief, but he managed to lean closer to the edge of the window.

The boy's gaze seemed to glance past him. Mekaid squinted. Something was different in his son's eyes. The deep blue color of his irises seemed to flicker somehow. Mekaid clenched his jaw. It had to be the darkness the Banu had left within his son.

Keena rolled forward onto his hands and knees, then clamored to his feet. Body trembling and chest heaving, the boy seemed to fight for each breath. Seeming as shocked as Mekaid was, the boy glanced down at his chest and legs with wonder. He looked at his hands, curiosity furrowing his young brow.

Mekaid felt the soft fabric of the queen's sleeve, realizing he'd gripped her arm as he watched Keena's recovery. She patted his hand, smiling, with tears of her own threatening to pour down her fair cheeks.

As fast as Mekaid had ever seen anyone move, Keena burst into motion. He dipped to snatch his sword from where it had fallen and lunged at the surprised Arachlan. Keena leapt high, bringing the blade above his head. With blinding speed, the boy jammed the sword into the minute gap between the Arachlan's protective exoskeleton, piercing the beast's neck. The rogue flailed all four of his arms, jerking the blade free with the two hands closest to his throat. The damage was done, however. Dark blood gushed forth from the wound.

To the astonishment of both Mekaid and his son, Keena had dealt a deathblow with stunning speed, strength, and accuracy after being viciously bitten by the venomous Arachlan.

"He's immune," the queen breathed. The princess came to her feet.

Mekaid noted the way the queen had ignored her daughter's grief. He shook his head, heart surging with relief that his son still drew breath. His emotions swirled, gratitude battling with rage at what the Banu had done to transform Keena.

No matter how grand the boy's powers were, they were borne of dark magic. No good would come of such strange sorcery.

Mekaid turned from the spectacle and raced the course until he was outside. It wasn't until he found himself lost in the maze of passageways that he found the princess keeping stride with him.

She grabbed him by the tunic sleeve. "Come on!"

Mekaid sprinted to keep up with the lithe girl, catching the courtyard door before it smacked him in the chest after she'd gone through.

She didn't stop to see if he was behind her as she ran toward Keena, skirting the fallen, bleeding Arachlan. Keena dropped his sword and caught her as she leapt toward him, wrapping her arms around his neck. The teens laughed as they embraced in the lavender pre-dawn light.

With familiar blue eyes that lacked the odd flicker of light, Keena looked over the princess's shoulder. "Father!" He released Mahaela and ran forward.

Mekaid caught his son and held him tight to his chest. Tears threatened anew. "My boy. Oh, my son," he whispered. "I'm so sorry."

"I don't want to know what for," Keena said with a laugh. He stepped back and looked at Mekaid. The boy's eyes danced with lively excitement.

Mekaid beheld his transformed child, who was more a young man than a child at all. The boy's voice seemed deeper, and when they'd embraced, strength had radiated from Keena's arms and chest as he'd gripped his father close.

The princess's eyes were wide with wonder, but she wasn't smiling. Her mood matched Mekaid's apparently.

"What?" Keena said. "I'm fine. Great, really." He grinned and looked from Mekaid to Mahaela.

"I'm glad you…recovered well," the princess stammered.

"Recovered?" Keena shook his head questioningly.

"Let's go home, son. We can talk on the way."

Keena looked at the princess, who smiled wistfully. "I'll send a message today to see how you're feeling." She looked at Mekaid. "Safe travel home to you."

Mekaid nodded his gratitude at her well-wishes as she turned for the doorway inside.

"I'm fine," Keena said, watching her go.

Mekaid guided his confused son toward the gates. The Giants give him strength, he'd never set foot in this cursed palace again.

* * * * *

Marie Whittaker Biography

Marie Whittaker enjoys teaching about publishing, writing craft, and project management for writers. She works as Associate Publisher at WordFire Press and is Director of Superstars Writing Seminars, a world-class writing conference concentrating on the business of writing. She also puts in time as the personal assistant to *New York Times* bestselling author Kevin J. Anderson. Marie is a proud member of the Horror Writers Association and keeps steady attendance at local writer's groups.

When not at work in publishing, Marie is an award-winning essayist and author of horror, urban fantasy, children's books, and supernatural thrillers. Her supernatural thriller, *The Witcher Chime*, was a finalist for the Indie Book Awards in 2017. She's the creator of *The Adventures of Lola Hopscotch*, which is a children's book series concentrating on getting sensitive childhood issues out in the open between children and adults. Many of her short stories appear in numerous anthologies and publications, including *Weird Tales*. She's currently working on a new paranormal mystery, titled (working) *Little Boy Lost*. Marie is a founder of *Eldros Legacy*, where she writes epic (and a little Gothic!) fantasy novels. Find out more about her at www.mariewhittaker.com.

* * * * *

Dawn of the Lightbringer
by Mark Stallings

An Eldros Legacy Story

Drounid

The large gold medallion of command landed heavily on the maps covering the table. Dried blood and hair matted the chain attached to it. Chairs were pushed back noisily from the table in surprise.

"Prima Centura is gone," Ora growled at the assembled group, his face stern.

First to recover, Jeffic stood and made for Ora. "You arrogant ass, this is a closed session." Jeffic was the commander of the Fourth Cohort. While Ora's equal, everyone considered him a bootlicker, more concerned with his career than the safety of his men.

"Get out." Jeffic grabbed Ora's left arm and pushed him toward the door.

Green energy flared over Ora, enshrouding his arm. He unleashed a lightning fast punch straight into Jeffic's chest, hitting the pristine twin of the blood-soaked medallion on the table. The two-hundred pound man, armor and all, flew back four paces into a column, then slid to the floor.

"Commander Ora." General Marcello pointedly ignored the altercation. He moved around the table with a smile and grabbed Ora up in a vigorous embrace. He looked deep into Ora's eyes, and his smile faded. "Are you—"

Prince Gervase moved closer. "Prima Centura is *gone*? The pride of the Legion? Gone?" The Prima Centura was the unit every soldier aspired to join.

"Yes, Your Highness."

Marcello waved at the maps on the table. They showed the Kingdom of Drounid, and the surrounding kingdoms of Reosha to the east, Voutia to the north, and Chatera to the west. Marcello pulled a chair over. "Tell us what you found, and show us where."

Ora pointed at the confluence of the Brimar and Cobalt Rivers. "We found the remnants of the century here. Every man, Wlewoi, Delver, and all the animals had been killed, and the bodies mutilated." Ora shuddered and stared blankly at the wall. "There were no bodies of the enemy. Not a one."

Marcello poured a cup of wine and handed it to Ora.

Ora downed the entire cup in one go. He looked at the two men. "What could tear a hundred men apart like that?" His eyes burned with unshed tears. *Commander Albrico and I entered the Legion together. What they did to him*, Ora thought. He shuddered at the images that wouldn't leave his mind.

Marcello refilled his cup and encouraged him to drink.

Gervase poured his own cup of wine. "Your cohort will have to take up the call."

That got Ora's attention. "What call?"

"You're going to send *his* cohort?" Jeffic sneered. "The Fourth—"

Marcello cut him off, "—is going to stay right here." He turned to Ora. "The League of Kingdoms put forth a call for aid to all the kingdoms in Drakanon. A vile force led by a demon calling itself Wrok has invaded Gardshom."

"A demon?" Ora was horrified at the thought. "I thought that was myth. Like the Giants or the Gods."

"They exist, and it is here. Conveniently, another evil has been felt in many of the kingdoms at the same time." He pointed at the maps. "That evil is probably what wiped out Prima Centura."

Gervase shrugged. "We need to send forces, and—" he pointed at Ora, "—you're it. Your Life Magic just might be the edge we need."

"I serve at your pleasure, Your Highness. Where do we go?" Ora asked.

Marcello tapped the maps. "Take your entire cohort north of Braizolux, along the Auldur River, past the Great Forest."

"My entire cohort?" Ora leaned toward the maps and tried to picture the terrain. "Logistics?"

"I've made arrangements," Marcello said. "They were for the Prima Centura, but will still be sufficient."

Ora tilted his head in confusion. "Why are we meeting at this location if Gardshom was invaded?" The Kingdom of Gardshom was in the extreme northwest of the continent up by the Dragon's Reach, the mountains that ran along the northmost edge of the land.

"You're going there to protect a special group," Marcello said. "Five groups of beings that will combine their magic to create weapons for each kingdom's forces. These weapons will be used to counter the Demon's powers." He sipped his wine.

"What kind of weapons?" Ora asked.

"You'll find out more when you reach them," Gervase assured him. "They're keeping the specifics quiet until people get there."

"When do I need to be there?"

"In a fortnight," Marcello replied.

Ora snorted. "Impossible. It'll take six days of hard riding just to cross Voutia. Braizolux will be double that."

"I said I've made arrangements." Marcello smiled. "You just need to make the river Auldur. We'll have a boat waiting for you."

"A boat? For five hundred?" Ora narrowed his eyes in suspicion. "What kind of boat?"

"Don't worry about it," Marcello replied with a grin, which didn't reassure Ora in the least.

Gervase got up and went to the door. One of the two guards came back in with him. "I'm going to allocate a squad of the Royal Guard to your cohort," Gervase said gravely. "This is Captain Rowlga. Use them well."

Ora nodded. "Thank you, Your Highness."

The Wlewoi on the guard were worth any ten human soldiers. A full squad of ten was like having an extra century, and Ora could think of several scenarios where swinging a hammer like that in combat could turn the tide.

"Is there anything else I need to know?" Ora asked, mind already awhirl with planning and logistics.

Marcello shook his hand. "Get to that meeting. The fate of the kingdoms rests with you."

* * *

Voutia

The scout pulled his horse in sharply. "The river is beyond the next ridge, Commander," he said, pointing to a saddle break eight thousand yards ahead.

Ora turned and waved at the centurions. Once they gathered, he relayed the information. "Atticus, I want First Century to lead the way." Atticus peeled off from the group and rode back to his unit. The sounds of orders being shouted preceded the movement of the troops.

As the hundred men filed past, Ora addressed the other centurions. "Move forward and keep your eyes open." They each gave assent and returned to their men. He addressed the Wlewoi. "The river is on the other side of the ridge. Do you have an indication of where we're supposed to meet the boat?"

Captain Rowlga shook his head, black fur rippling in the breeze. "On the ridge, we should be able to see the vessel."

Ora squinted toward the ridge. "I certainly hope so. We're running out of time." He leaned forward, shading his eyes. "What's that on the ridge?" Black shapes moved around.

Rowlga turned to look and snarled. "We are attacked."

"Sound the defense!" Ora commanded.

The bugler whipped up his horn and blared three long notes.

Instantly, the century in the lead slowed and compacted as they moved into a defensive formation. The other four centuries moved in double time to get into position to support First Century.

Like kicking an anthill, a mass of black figures flowed over the ridge and onto the grassy slope, rapidly moving toward the cohort.

Ora watched their progress. "Sound magics."

The bugler sounded, and there was a perceptible shifting of the troops. Ora knew from experience, they were letting the Magi forward.

As the enemy reached a thousand yards from the front line, elemental fury flew from the century, and raked into the running creatures with devastating effect. Lightning, fire, ice bolts, and a fierce dust devil savaged the front ranks of the enemy. Ora could hear piercing, animalistic screams from them as they died.

Ora and his guard advanced toward the rear of First Century. The other centuries settled into place, with Second Century on the left, Third Century on the right, and Fourth and Fifth directly behind them to protect the flank or bolster any breaks in the line of battle.

The enemy passed the five hundred yard mark.

"Sound archers," Ora commanded.

Each century had fifteen archers, and they let loose a stream of steel-tipped arrows. The creatures were so densely packed, almost every arrow found a target. In less than a minute, magic and arrows had reduced the enemy forces by half.

"Sound engage."

As the bugle's call rang out, the front line across three centuries stepped forward in unison. At a hundred yards, elemental fury once again savaged the front ranks of the enemy. Something in the enemy line detonated violently, instantly shredding everything near that point.

The blast washed over the cohort. "What was that?" Ora asked in amazement.

"It was a Zhurgur," Captain Rowlga declared.

Ora just stared at him for a moment.

Rowlga just shrugged. "They have them where I am from. Not pretty when you kill them."

Ora turned back just as the remaining enemy slammed into the front.

A slight eddy in the enemy forces gave Ora insight to their plans. "They're going to push to their right. Tell Fourth to cover left."

The bugler sounded the command, and Fourth Century jogged into position just as the black creatures reached the end of Second's line.

The clash of steel and the screams of creatures mingled with the yells from the men. In minutes, it was over. Those few of the enemy who'd survived ran off.

"Scouts out," Ora commanded and nudged his horse forward. Once he reached First Century, he dismounted and handed the reins to the bugler. He made his way to the front line.

The bodies of the creatures were hideous, twisted beings. Ora started when he began to make out what they might have been originally. One had a tiger face, but used to be human. Another had spider features and a Delver's body. Yet another looked like it had been assembled of parts from multiple Elves. He peered closer. Everywhere talons, fangs, and horns had been mutated onto the creatures. *What horror could do this?*

He pulled his gaze away and focused on the soldiers around him. "Who's hurt?" he asked.

"Here, Commander." Ora made his way to the sound. A soldier's arm was cut and bent at an unnatural angle. "Curtis, Third of the First," he told Ora, indicating that he was in the third squad of the first century.

Ora called for bandages and water. Once he'd cleaned the wound, he pulled on Shimmershield, and by weaving the flows of energy, knitted the bones back together. Not everyone could master Shimmershield. The soldiers knew the drill. They moved the wounded into a line, cleaned the wounds, and made ready for Ora to work his magic. Each century had their own Magus, but only one other was Life Magic trained, and Ora had converted him to Shimmershield, the philosophy to only use Life Magic to help others or for defense.

When the last soldier had been healed, Atticus came forward.

"Commander, we lost two in that exchange," he reported.

Ora grunted. "Considering that we just slew twice our numbers, we got off lightly, indeed. These can't be the same things that took out Prima Century." He looked up the hill. "Get the soldiers' bodies wrapped and on the pack mules. Once that's done, let's get out of this cursed land."

"What do we do with the creatures?" Atticus asked.

"Leave them." Ora pointed skyward, where buzzards had already gathered. "Our feathered friends will clean up."

Within minutes, the troops were moving. Once again, First Century took the lead. As soon as they crested the ridge and started down, Ora rode to the crest for a look.

Ora just stared at what he saw on the river. "Are you kidding me?"

On the riverbank sat two grain barges, empty, with a giant box behind them. A floating cube. He'd never seen the like and just stared at it as the cohort passed around him.

"I guess we better see what this is." Ora spurred his horse forward.

When he reached the barges, a man in blue work clothes was speaking with Atticus and some of the other soldiers. "Commander Ora, this is Captain Therin of Vill, owner of *Aaliyah's Hope*," Atticus said.

"How fast can you get us loaded?" Ora asked.

"We have the horse ramps already in place on the second barge." Captain Therin squinted up at the sun. "If your men do as instructed, we should be ready within the hour."

"Atticus, make it happen." Ora couldn't help but ask, "How does the box move?" He pointed at the strange vessel. There were no apparent oars or sail.

The captain grinned. "Magic. It uses the energy of the water and somehow converts it into movement. We can go upriver as well as down. The current doesn't impede us much. As to how it works, that's a secret of the riverwrights of Stuitor. This particular vessel is almost a thousand years old."

Ora stared at the vessel in amazement. "A thousand years? It looks brand new."

The captain laughed. "The wood on the outside is less than five years old. We refit down in Reosha, and they know their woodworking. The core of the ship is the old part. Made by Magi of old, though I heard the riverwrights still have the ability to make smaller versions today."

Ora was impressed and eager to see the vessel move. "How long will it take us to get to the meeting place, Captain?" Ora asked.

"If your Wlewoi will spot for trouble, we can travel overnight. My people can't see in the dark like they do," Therin replied. "With their help, we can be at the meeting spot in two days."

"Two days?" Ora said with astonishment. That would put them three days ahead of schedule.

"Speed costs money, and you hired the best. She may not be the prettiest river crawler, but *Aaliyah* will get you there as fast as she can."

* * *

Braizolux

After two full days on the barges, they pulled into a segment of the river with a short dock and a large camp.

A group led by a man in Reader's robes met Ora when he stepped off *Aaliyah's Hope*. The Reader was thin and bald, with vibrant green eyes. "Greetings, Commander. I'm Reader Aken. With me are Commanders Havard of Gardshom and Silvije of Grules. May I ask who you are?"

Ora bowed. "I'm Ora Earl, commander of the Second Cohort, Third Legion of Drounid."

The Reader and two commanders watched as the troops unloaded from the barges. After the second block of troops assembled and moved past them, the commanders murmured quietly.

"Commander, how many soldiers did you bring?" Commander Havard asked.

"I have a full cohort plus one squad," Ora replied.

Silvije uttered something and, wide-eyed, involuntarily took a step back as Rowlga and his squad of Wlewoi came off the barges and arrayed themselves behind Ora. Each stood six feet tall and rippled with muscle. They wore black leather cuirasses and greaves, and carried small round shields with several short throwing spears in their left hands. At their waist they wore spatha, long swords favored by cavalry. Of the ten, only Rowlga looked at the group. The rest had their eyes out, looking for threats.

"Have you never seen the Royal Guard of Drounid?" Ora asked mildly.

Silvije recovered himself and stepped forward. "My apologies. I've never seen…"

"Wlewoi," Ora offered. He gestured. "This is Captain Rowlga of the Royal Guard. My prince sent him and his squad to supplement the cohort."

Rowlga bowed and flashed Silvije a wide, toothy smile. Ora could see he was amused by Silvije's initial reaction.

Havard nodded appreciatively. "I've heard they're formidable." He smiled at the captain. "Welcome."

"You said one cohort. How many men is that?" Silvije asked.

"A cohort is five hundred troops. With staff and the guard, I brought five hundred eighteen," Ora said. "Though we lost two in a skirmish just before we boarded the barges."

"You were attacked?" the Reader, Aken, asked. "By who?"

"Some warped combination of Human, Elf, and Delver mishmashed together. I've never seen their like. However, we were able to overwhelm them."

"It must be because you brought all these soldiers," Havard stated.

"I was told to bring the full cohort after the first troops we sent to you were slaughtered within our own borders," Ora said. "Besides, I've been campaigning against all kinds of invaders, Human and not, for seven fighting seasons. They weren't organized, and relied more on ferocity than skill. My cohort is mostly veterans."

"Ora," Aken said, "of the seventeen kingdoms to receive the call to send a company, only eight have made it unscathed. We're glad you're here."

The other two murmured their agreement.

"If I may ask, what *are* we doing here?" Ora asked, looking around at the encampment.

Aken stepped closer to Ora. "We've invoked the Pentad," he said softly, and in a way that seemed like it was significant.

"What is a Pentad?" Ora asked.

"It's a group made up of Elves, Delvers, Shagar, and Humans."

"I'm not sure what Shagar are, but that's four. A Pentad is a group of five, right?" Ora pointed out.

Aken looked around to see if anyone was near, then leaned even closer and whispered, "The fifth is a dragon." He met Ora's eyes and nodded.

Ora laughed. When no one else laughed, he sobered. "Are you serious? I've seen dragons. We had to kill one that had been eating cows in western Drounid. They're mighty beasts, but just that."

"This one is different. You'll see when it arrives," Aken assured him.

Ora shook his head. They were crazy, but his orders were to help them. "When do the others in the Pentad get here?"

"The Elves are in camp, and Aken represents the Human faction. The others should have already been here," Silvije said. "We're worried they might have been attacked, as you were."

Ora stared off into the distance. "Do you know from where they're coming? We could send out patrols."

Aken shook his head. "We can't risk the troops."

"He brought five hundred men," Havard pointed out. "I think it would be prudent." He looked at Ora. "Would you be willing to hold one of your centuries back? That might make Aken more comfortable."

Ora considered for a moment before answering, "I'll rotate them through. That way one will be here in camp for rest and refit at all times. Will that be acceptable?"

Silvije eyed Rowlga. "What about them?"

"They were assigned to me by my prince. As such, they go where I direct them," Ora stated. "Do you have maps? I'd like to get patrols out as soon as possible."

Aken nodded. "At the campaign tent."

"Then I suggest we get the routes set up." Ora turned to one of his staff members. "Send runners and have the centurions report to the campaign tent. Get the troops setting up camp, as we will be staying here and patrolling in force." The man headed to the team of runners. Ora turned back to the party. "Good sirs, shall we?"

As they walked, Ora asked, "What are Shagar?"

"They're the shepherds of the WaterWird," Aken said.

Ora groaned silently. He'd almost forgotten he was dealing with a Reader. He disliked how they assumed that everyone knew as much as they did. Outwardly, he smiled. "And what is a water word?"

"Wird, WaterWird. It's the way of the water, but more than that. It's a philosophy as much as it's a specific kind of magic."

"Much like Shimmershield?" Ora asked. His school of Life Magic was more than technique. It incorporated a blend of moral codes to guide the practitioner.

Aken nodded. "Yes, exactly. WaterWird guides their culture."

"Where are they coming from?"

"This group is coming from the island nation of Brouhan. We never heard from the Shagar in the 'Nid Islands." Aken frowned. "To think of it, we never heard from the Kingdom of Chacoton, either." He looked at Havard, who shook his head. "We'll have to look into that. Anyway, I'm not sure how they would arrive. My guess is, they'd come up the river like you did. However, I'm unsure whether they'd come up the Auldur from the sea or from Lake Eho-ta."

They reached the tent and gathered around a table with a large map on it. Aken pointed at the lake and traced the Ehota River from its source in the lake to the confluence with the Auldur.

"We can ask Captain Therin, the master of the river crawler that brought us here," Ora offered. "It should be easy enough to get him to head back down the Auldur toward the sea." Ora looked at the map. "What about the Delvers?"

Aken tapped a mountain range on the eastern edge of Eshita. "They're coming from here."

Ora traced their path across the map. "Maybe they made it to Lake Ehota and got a boat to come here? Maybe they met up with the Shagar?"

Havard laughed. "Delvers on water?"

"Well, if not by river, they would have to cross Ehota, a very long trek." Ora considered. "What about Ehota? Did they send troops?"

"Yes," Aken replied. "They were among the first to arrive."

"Excellent. Let's send a runner for their leader. I'd love to get his perspective on this," Ora asked.

Silvije shook his head. "Her perspective. Their leader is a wom-an."

Ora stared. "I take it you don't let women fight?"

"Oh, no, not that at all," Silvije said soberly. "Our women are fierce warriors and great stewards of our kingdom. They're too pre-cious to go to war since they are the only ones who can continue our people. Men are the only ones our society can afford to lose." He grinned suddenly. "Besides, my wife likes it when I'm away."

"That's interesting. I hadn't thought of it like that."

Atticus and the other centurions arrived. "Commander, we may have an issue."

* * *

The Dragon

The group exited the command tent and before them, a battered squad of eleven men stood protectively around a makeshift stretcher. The standard bearer held on to a staff with a tattered banner.

"Which of you is the leader?" Aken asked as they approached. The soldiers glanced at the man on the litter.

Ora stepped forward. "Is he still alive?" He moved toward the man and knelt next to the litter. The man's scaled armor had been pierced in several places. Blood-soaked bandages were evident through the holes. Ora placed his hand on the man's chest, closed his eyes, and reached out with his magic. His hand glowed green, and tendrils of energy spread over the prone man. "Let's see, three ribs are broken, stomach is punctured, right arm is dislocated, and his brain is swelling." Ora opened his eyes. "Atticus, get Jerund and his assistants here to the command tent."

After ten minutes, Jerund—Second Century's Magus—and his assistants arrived, carrying water and their satchels of medical gear. Ora set them to work removing the man's armor, the soiled bandages, and cleaning the wounds.

When everything was ready, Ora and Jerund knelt on either side of the still unconscious man. "I need four of you to hold him down," Ora said.

"But he's been out for almost a day," one of the soldiers said.

244 | KENNEDY & HOWELL

Jerund chuckled. "When the magic starts on him, he'll be awake like you've poured cold water on him." They moved into position.

Ora bowed his head and invoked Shimmershield. The verdant energy flowed up and through the unconscious man. Jerund held his hands out, and his chartreuse energy intertwined with Ora's. The man shook gently at first, then with increasing violence. The men holding him down strained with the effort. Then everything was suddenly quiet. Ora and Jerund put their right hand on their hearts and held left hands palm to palm. The surrounding soldiers stared as Ora stood up.

"He'll be very hungry when he wakes. Feed him." Ora walked to the tent and sat heavily in a chair. Aken handed him a cup.

"It's water," Aken reassured him. Ora drank deeply. "That was impressive, Commander."

"We were able to fix the damage to his body. It's up to him to want to live." Ora shrugged and eyed a plate, selected a couple of slices of apple, and paired them with some yellow cheese. The tang of the cheese contrasted with the sweet of the apple.

A soldier from the company approached the tent. Ora waved him to enter. He fell to his knees in front of Ora and Aken.

"Thank you, my lord. We had given up hope Thegn Tilman would survive. We smelled his stomach as we carried him."

"Tell us your name and where you're from," Aken said with interest.

"I'm Theabul, a carpenter of our fyrd. We're from Eshita."

"What happened to you?" Aken asked.

"We crossed the river at Chalon, well east of Lake Ehota. Once out of view of the town, we were set upon. Initially, it was a light, harassing force. They came at us at night. Once we crossed the

Auldur, they hit us hard." He paused for a moment. Havard handed him a mug, and Theabul took a drink and continued. "Half of the remaining fyrd bought us time to get Tilman to you." His eyes shone with unshed tears.

The Reader helped Theabul up. "See to your countrymen. You'll be made comfortable. Your thegn's in good hands. Once you're cleaned up and fed, you can come back here to stand watch over him."

"Thank you, my lords." The guards led him away.

The planning session broke up well after the sun had set. Ora dismissed his centurions and walked over to the river to listen to the sounds of the river frogs croaking and crickets chirping. Rowlga and the other Wlewoi gave him some space. He looked into the night sky. This far north, the constellations he was used to were lower in the sky. He located the five stars that made up the Sword and followed the blade to the constellation of the Lady. It represented the goddess Ishtar.

The frogs and crickets fell silent, breaking Ora out of his reverie. He turned to see a man standing next to him, also looking up at the sky. This man had dark skin and robes that blended with the night. He spoke in a slow, deep voice.

"I love looking up at the stars. Figuring out the different shapes. That one is the Bear. That is the Serpent."

The man's arrival surprised the Wlewoi as much as Ora, though he'd have guessed not even a fly could have gotten past their vigilance. They started for the stranger, hands on hilts.

Ora raised up a hand to stop them. The man glanced at Ora. "I didn't mean to startle you."

"Who are you?" Ora asked.

"A participant in the activities, like you." He looked back at the sky. "That one is the Hunter." He pointed out a cluster of stars.

Ora followed his finger. "Ah, we call that one the Archer."

"Can I ask you a question, Ora Earl of Drounid?"

"You may." Ora watched him from the corner of his eye.

"Why are you here?"

That surprised him. "My prince ordered me here."

"But why are *you* here, Ora?"

Ora turned to the stranger. "I was the one selected." Ora really didn't understand why this was so important to the man.

He met Ora's gaze. "But why *you?*"

"I'm here to do my duty," Ora said firmly. "Why do you care?"

The man's eyes flashed orange for a moment. "I too am here for my duty." He looked back into the sky and said softly so that Ora barely heard him, "For what I have started." Ora watched him in confusion.

The man sighed, then turned back to the camp. "Good night, Ora Earl of Drounid."

"Wait, you never told me your name."

The man paused, then grinned at Ora. "You may call me Mushussu." Then he flickered into a huge creature and sprang into the sky.

* * *

Delver

Ora moved his horse closer to Atticus. He held out the map depicting the area from the southeast of the camp to the border of the dead zone. The local tales said two gods had fought, and the battle was so violent, it ripped a hole in Drakanon, allowing the sea to rise in the middle of the mountains. Legend also said their hatred for each other kills anyone who enters the area, even after two thousand years.

"Scout approaches in a hurry," Rowlga said and pointed.

The command staff turned. Orders went out, and First Century came to a stop. It took several minutes before they heard the thud of a horse at a gallop. Atticus turned to Rowlga.

"Are you looking for a position in my century? Your hearing is amazing. I could definitely use you," he said, admiration in his eyes.

Rowlga chuffed. "I like my position fine, but if I get bored, I'll come find you."

The scout arrived and saluted. "Commander, we found a party that's engaged with more of those twisted creatures. They're defending a wagon and fighting a withdrawal."

"Water for this man," Ora said to his orderly. Then addressing the scout, he said, "Show me on this map." Ora held it out.

The scout pointed to a position on the map that was less than a mile away. Ora put a finger on it and turned to Atticus.

"Get the century moving to this spot. Send riders to the Third and Fourth Centuries. They should be in their sectors to either side of us. Get them moving with all speed to the same point." He indicated a position closer to the camp than where the scout had shown. "I expect we'll meet them in flight." Ora looked around. "Questions? No? Then let's take it to them!"

A flurry of orders, and the century was in motion. Soon enough, they advanced at a ground-eating pace. In ten minutes, they'd moved far enough they could see a wagon in the distance. Ora squinted but couldn't make out the details.

"Rowlga, can I borrow your eyes?" Ora asked him. Ora moved his foot out of the stirrup and held out a hand. Rowlga grabbed it and stepped into the stirrup. Ora leaned to the other side to compensate for the added weight. Rowlga stood up straight and watched for a couple seconds, then stepped back down.

"There are archers in the wagon shooting at the creatures following. There is a mounted guard of six harassing the creatures and trying to draw them away from the wagon." Rowlga flashed a toothy grin. "They are headed right for us."

Atticus called orders to tighten up and let the wagon pass the line.

"Atticus, send a scout to guide them right down the middle," Ora said.

The centurion gave the order.

After a few minutes, Atticus gave the order to shift formation into a V with the mouth toward the wagon. Two scouts returned.

"The centuries approach, Commander."

Ora stood in his saddle and could just make out Third Century on their left side. He didn't see Fourth, but there was a slight rise between First and where Fourth should be.

Another five minutes, and Ora could hear the wagon on the grass, the rumble of the wheels through the long blades. Ora could also hear the keening cries of the creatures, just like the ones that had attacked them as they'd approached the river.

"Ready archers!" came the cry.

"Ready Magi!" Atticus bellowed. The order was relayed.

Ora could see the wagon clearly now, the driver hunkered down in his seat. A Delver sat in the seat next to him with a bladed pole-arm. It looked like a cross between a Rhomphaia pole weapon and a sword on a stick. In the back, he saw archers popping up and firing on the creatures chasing them. The horde that chased didn't falter under the constant onslaught of arrows.

"Ready!" Atticus bellowed. The order rippled through the century.

The wagon rocketed into the mouth of the V, the bottom of which flowed apart to allow the wagon to pass, then merged back together to form the base of the kill pocket.

"Fire!" came the order, and arrows flew, and magics blazed into the horde. With a fantastic crash, the two groups collided.

An ear-piercing cry went out from the horde, and sickly yellow light shone from a creature at the back. A huge monster easily head and shoulders above the others strode forward. One of the Magi let loose a bolt of lightning and, to Ora's amazement, the creature deflected it into the crowd behind, where it blew a giant furrow through the twisted monsters. Purple light blazed from its eyes. It raised a staff and turned a beam of that sickly yellow light on the Magus. He frantically tried a deflection of his own, but wasn't powerful enough, and was melted on the spot like butter dropped on a hot skillet. The soldiers near him flinched as they were spattered with bits of their teammate.

Ora pointed. "We need to take that one down now." He spurred his horse and drew his sword. He pulled his Shimmershield to strengthen his sword arm. *I can't repel a strike like that, but we can get there quickly.* He wound the green energy through his horse, which bolted forward with a burst of speed.

Another bolt of the putrid energy flashed past Ora, narrowly missing him. "Drounid!" Ora yelled. His sword bit into the creature. Unfortunately, it was like swinging a sword into a tree, where it stuck and yanked Ora from the saddle. The ground knocked the wind out of him, and he stared at the creature as it contemplated the sword sticking out of it as if it were an unwanted insect. It appeared to be a fantastically large Delver, only with purple flames for eyes.

It looked down at Ora and raised its gnarled ebony staff, the head glowing with yellow light.

A spear slammed home in the middle of its chest, barely a finger from Ora's sword. Then another struck. A third hit it in the shoulder, rocking it back. It swung forward, violet eyes blazing, just in time to meet a leaping Rowlga, spear thrust forward, whose blade stabbed right into the creature's throat. The creature slid back off the spear, sickly yellow light leaking from the wounds as it crashed into the ground.

With the death of their apparent leader, the other creatures in the horde lost all will to attack and fled. The century surged forward after them.

Rowlga's spear smoked, the metal pitting as it melted. He threw it on top of the body, which was bubbling as it dissolved.

Ora rolled to get up. Rowlga and another Wlewoi helped Ora regain his feet and moved him away from the noxious smelling corpse.

"What was that?" Ora gasped, trying to regain his breath, and wincing from the pain lancing his ribs.

"A Dreadlord," Rowlga said. "Creatures of twist. You must stab them through the throat."

A scout brought Ora his horse, and Rowlga helped him to mount.

Ora wreathed himself in the healing energy of Shimmershield. He would deal with the consequences of a rapid heal later. "Let's go see what's so important about the wagon."

* * *

The Baleforge

The wagon had stopped not too far from the back edge of the century. The Delver had dismounted from the wagon. He was broad shouldered and built like a blacksmith with a thick chest. He wore a jerkin sewn with dark steel scales. He had bright eyes that watched Ora with interest as he approached.

Ora bowed slightly. "I'm Ora, commander of the Second Cohort, Third Legion of Drounid."

The Delver spoke in a deep, rumbling voice. "Well met, Ora. I am Zak Mik of the Rise, member of the Pentad. Thank you for the timely intervention." In the distance, they heard bugles and the sounds of combat. Zak Mik looked in that direction.

"That's the other two units engaging the twisted from either flank," Ora reassured him. At Zak Mik's curious look, he said, "We use the bugles to communicate and relay status." Zak Mik nodded. "May I ask where you're from and what's in the wagon?" Ora peered into the bed. A large metal box occupied the space in the center.

"I am from the Rise. They are mountains in what you call Eshita." Zak Mik bobbed his head as he talked.

Ora was confused. "But Eshita is to the west. You approached from the east."

Zak Mik looked around warily, leaned in closer to Ora, and in a whisper that carried to everyone, he said, "I traveled the Halls." He said it in such a way that it seemed Ora should know what he was talking about. Ora decided to ask Aken later. "It was fortunate I ran into these fine folks when I emerged. With all the excitement, I am unsure where they are from." He glanced at the six horsemen standing to the side.

"We're from Poseria," one said. "I'm Commandant E'shar of the King's Own Dragoons. We were set upon by those…things. There were eighteen of us when we came across the Delver and his wagon." Ora nodded with sympathy.

He turned back to Zak Mik. "And the box?" Ora asked politely.

"Mavric iron," Zak Mik stated proudly. Everyone stepped away from the wagon. The archers from Poseria made ready to jump out when Zak Mik held up his hand. "Wait! It is safe in the box." Everyone relaxed a bit, but they were still uncomfortable. Mavric iron was well known for its magical properties that killed humans. Zak Mik continued, "It is the primary component of what we are doing here." Ora didn't have a good feeling about this.

Ora turned. "Sound the recall. Let's get Master Zak Mik back to the encampment," he told the bugler. The bugler turned toward the centuries and sounded the reform. Ora's knees sagged for a moment, but Rowlga caught him under the arm. The bill for the rapid healing had arrived. "Help me into the wagon. I'll ride with Master Zak Mik. I have some questions for him."

Soon enough, they were in the camp. Aken, Havard, Silvije, and Tilman met them, and introductions were made. While they were excited to see Zak Mik and the Mavric iron, they weren't happy that the Poserian unit had been so ground down.

"Now that the last of the Pentad is here—" Aken indicated Zak Mik, "—we can start crafting the weapons." That surprised Ora.

"The Shagar are here?" Ora asked.

Aken nodded. "They arrived while you were finding Master Zak Mik."

Zak Mik brightened at that. "Can you lead me to the forge? I would like to get set up."

"It's this way," Aken said and moved toward the forest. Curious, Ora followed. A path barely wide enough could be seen in the grass, heading for the thickest section of trees. Aken wasn't stopping and headed straight for a tree, then he disappeared. The wagon proceeded to the same spot and disappeared. Ora looked at Rowlga.

"It is Elf magic," Rowlga said and waited for Ora to step through the glamor.

Ora inched forward to the tree, and the view before him shifted abruptly. The trees melted away to reveal a short cliff with a waterfall pouring into a deep blue pool. A bright white forge sat at the edge of the water. A myriad of diverse people mingled around the forge. A group of Elves stood talking with Mushussu in his Human form. The Dragon locked gazes with Ora, and it was as if they were connected, then Mushussu turned back to the Elves. On either side of them, two large pavilions stood. Tables and chairs had been set up inside each. Seated in the pavilion close to the water was a small group dressed all in black. Ora assumed they were the Shagar, the water mages. Ora was impressed. From the outside, none of this was visible.

Zak Mik drove the wagon directly to the forge. As he jumped off the wagon, the other members of the Pentad came to greet him, Aken amongst them. Ora just watched. Rowlga touched his arm and pointed to one of the pavilions, where they were setting out platters of food.

"Can you let Atticus know where we are?" Ora asked. Rowlga sent one of the guard off and followed Ora to find a vantage to observe the activity of the Pentad.

Zak Mik spent the day arranging molds for various weapons, thirteen in total. One for each of the commanders who'd made it to the assembly point.

As the sun set, Mushussu changed into his Dragon form and blew into the forge. An azure flame glowed in the center of the forge. Soon enough, Zak Mik set a crucible in the flames and pulled ingots out of the box from the wagon. Ora watched intently as Zak Mik used tongs to pour the molten metal into the molds. He repeated the process time and again until all thirteen glowed.

That was when the Shagar stepped forward and performed their dance, weaving their water magic with the sinuous flow of their bodies. Ora sat entranced as wispy tendrils of blue and white magic surrounded each of the molds.

One by one, the Shagar finished their dance, and the molds were dark. Zak Mik pulled the pins holding the first mold tight and struck the side with a sledge hammer, splitting the mold apart with a bell-like ring. The first was a spear, which he set back in the flames. Aken motioned for another Reader, who stepped up next to Zak Mik as he worked the weapon on the anvil. Red energy flowed out from the Reader and into the metal as the Delver worked to finish the spear.

Back into the fire, and the Dragon blew his flame into the forge. This time Zak Mik withdrew the glowing metal and held it out. The Shagar once again sheathed the weapon in their water magic in a flash quench to harden the blade. Zak Mik skated a file along the edge of the spear and nodded. He then turned to a wheel stone and pushed on the pedal to get it moving.

An Elf stepped up and bathed the blade of the spear in a white energy as Zak Mik removed any imperfections and sharpened the blade. He dropped a flimsy piece of cloth on the blade of the spear, which cut it neatly in two. He set the spear on a table and turned to the next mold.

They worked through the night, and across the next two days, until all thirteen weapons were complete. The Pentad had the thirteen commanders come forward to receive a weapon. The Reader raised his hands, and the combined powers of all five groups that made up the Pentad washed over the warriors.

"You're the Baleforge Commanders. Go with our blessings and defeat Wrok," Aken intoned. The powers faded, and the commanders dispersed. Aken moved over to where Ora was admiring the craftsmanship of the sword he'd been given.

"It's a beautiful sword," Aken said.

"As this was made from Mavric iron, how will it not kill us?" Ora sheathed the Baleforged Blade.

"This is the gift of the Pentad. We combined our powers to bind the weapon to you. You alone can use it safely." Aken gave a fatherly smile that slowly faded into seriousness. "The road ahead is perilous, and Wrok's forces are moving. We've set things in motion to get you to the plains of Ar Leen." He looked Ora dead in the eyes. "Are you ready?"

* * *

The Demon

As Aken had promised, the journey to Gardshom was fraught with turmoil, as if the very elements were against them. Thankfully, at least one Shagar stationed themselves on each of the ships, and they fought the worst of the weather.

The combined forces of the kingdoms met the enemy host on the plains of Ar Leen. Each of the Baleforge Commanders led a section of troops. Ora had put Tilman and his squad with the Fourth Drounid Century, and E'shar and his remaining troops with the Fifth Drounid Century. The last soldiers from Gardshom, along with forces from Eshita, Voutia, and distant Ikriledian formed the body of troops with the fifteen hundred led by the other Baleforge Commanders to form the spine.

The sky above them turned green with the approaching horde. Black clouds flashed ugly orange lightning. A fetid wind blew in the army's face. Up and down the line, unit leaders barked orders and gave words of encouragement.

Ora turned to the bugler. "Sound ready." The bugler blew a clear note, and the different units responded in their own way, with horns and drums. "Sound the advance." The forces moved forward. In response, the creatures across the plains voiced an incredible howl and surged forward to meet the armies.

Ora had arrayed Second and Third Centuries under Atticus to form the wedge that would breach the center of the enemy formation and allow the thirteen units stacked behind them through to hunt and kill the demon.

Every elemental form of destruction leapt from the allied armies and erupted with fury in the enemy's front ranks. Lightning blazed from several Magi, igniting the twisted enemy in droves. Flame fountains blossomed in the enemy's ranks, flash-frying scores with each blast. Subtler magic made plants grow razor-thorn patches or tripweed to slow the foe.

Ora gave the order to launch arrows. The steady stream of missiles savaged the creatures running at them, all the more effective because of the plant magic that slowed them.

Ora yelled, "Advance!" and First Century moved forward to follow the main body.

Second and Third Centuries punched the center hard, then turned to either side to widen the gap in the enemy lines. Ora's unit exited the rear of the lines to run full on into a sleet storm. Ora fought through the ice and wind to the front of the line and drew his Baleforged Blade. A bubble of calm sprang up around him, blunting the storm's effect, and his unit pushed through. The terrible storm ceased. Ahead of them, a tight knot of twisted were arrayed in front of seven Dreadlords. In the middle stood the massively tall form of the Demon Wrok.

The thirteen units surged forward as one. Their goal was to punch through the line and get the commanders beyond to deal with the Dreadlords and Wrok.

With a horrendous crash, the forces collided. Screams of creatures and men were almost overwhelming in volume. Ora pushed his horse through the line, swinging his sword to either side. Where the blade touched twisted flesh, it ignited the creature in an all-consuming white flame. He didn't cleave, but cremated his foes on the spot. A sickly yellow bolt burst through his horse's head. Ora jumped from the saddle as his horse's corpse crashed to the ground. He rolled to his feet and laid about him to clear a path to the Dreadlord, who followed his movements with flaming violet eyes. It raised a blackened stick that resembled a crow's foot and unleashed a bolt of putrescent light directly at Ora.

Ora brought his Baleforged Blade up and winced as the bolt died out in a flash of white and yellow sparks.

That surprised the Dreadlord, who took a step backward, but Ora was on it in a flash, sweeping across the creature's belly and whipping the sword around and down into the top of the Dread-lord's head, cleaving it in two. The edges of the wounds blazed white and consumed the falling corpse.

Ora glanced around. For the first time in the battle, there wasn't a creature within reach. He took stock. Most of the Dreadlords had fallen.

A detonation behind him caused Ora to whirl. Commander Tilman had sacrificed himself to kill the Dreadlord he'd faced.

Ora turned back toward Wrok. The demon stood there, watching the carnage and grinning in delight. Ora pulled his Shimmershield to give him speed and ran at the demon.

Wrok met Ora's blade with a spear of blackest metal. Eight blades made up the glowing tip, and heat waves shimmered around the weapon.

A wound from that would be hard to heal, indeed, thought Ora.

Wrok whirled the spear in an impossibly fast arc at Ora's head. Only years of fighting let him lean back just enough that the spear tip flashed an inch from his nose.

Ora added speed and strength to his attacks and parries with Shimmershield. Only combined with the power of the Baleforge Blade could Ora and his magic hold off Wrok, but Ora could only use Shimmershield for so long. Wrok, in all his demonic fury, didn't seem to be slowing down.

Ora stepped on a round river rock and staggered to the side to keep his balance. Wrok seized the advantage and stabbed Ora in the left chest with the glowing, multi-bladed spear. Ora screamed as the unholy spear tip entered his body. Fueled by Wrok's dark magic, Ora felt his soul shredding. With triumphant glee, Wrok held Ora off the ground to dangle.

The smell of burning flesh and melted metal permeated the air. Wrok inhaled deeply of it as if it were perfume. In a raspy, gloating voice, it spoke. "I will enjoy killing you, Hu-man. Then I will find your offspring and your mate and have them serve me." With that, Wrok yanked the spear out. The hole in Ora's armor glowed from the heat of the multi-bladed spear.

As Wrok drew back to finish Ora and claim victory, it failed to notice that through all the torture inflicted on Ora, despite his soul-wrenching screams of agony, he'd retained his grip on his Baleforged Blade.

Ora used his last shred of Life Magic to power his arm and drove the Baleforged Blade deep into Wrok's chest. For a bare moment, nothing happened. Then Wrok's eyes widened.

The white flame from the blade fountained into the demon's body. Wrok's skin bulged with internal pressure, and white lines, like cracks in marble, ran over his face, chest, and arms. He leaned his head back, white light pouring from his mouth and eyes, and screamed, "Brother!"

The resulting detonation knocked everyone on the Ar Leen plains flat, immolated the Twisted where they were, and threw Ora a quarter mile backward. The explosion shattered the sky above the battlefield, and for a moment, the only thing anyone alive on the field could see was a pure, searing light.

* * * * *

Mark Stallings Biography

Mark Stallings is an Amazon bestselling author, a member of Pikes Peak Writers, a speaker at international conferences on technology topics, a writer of wuxia, fantasy, thrillers, and military sci-fi. He's a competitive shooter, avid martial artist, drinker of craft beer, and motorcycle enthusiast. He became an Amazon bestselling author with his contribution to the military sci-fi anthology *Set the Terms*, part of the *Four Horsemen* Universe, was released through Chris Kennedy Publishing in the spring of 2020. Mark released the first book in the *Silver Coin Saga*, *The Elements*, through Shadow Alley Press in the summer of 2020. He continues to sling the ink with further stories in the *Silver Coin Saga* and the *Four Horsemen* Universe. You can find Mark at MarkStallings.com.

* * * * *

The Hunter
by Sam Witt

An Eldros Legacy Story

The grolkin refused to die.

No matter how many of its lashing limbs Kor removed, more rose to take their place. Hitting the creature's blubbery body was just as pointless. The flab absorbed the hunter's axe without leaving a mark.

If it had only been his life at stake, Kor would have left the damned thing to its own devices, but the villagers of Tama Kalai had sent for a hunter because the grolkin had stolen what was most precious to them.

Their children.

The seer from the Sainted Order of Hunters who'd dispatched Kor on this job had told him the children still lived. But they wouldn't last the night if he didn't kill the beast.

And that was how the grizzled slayer of monstrosities found himself staring down the gullet of a creature twice the size of a cow, its pebbled, iridescent skin stretched tight over rolls of curdled fat.

The grolkin fought by snaring its prey, dragging it in close with sucker-lined tentacles, then smashing it flat with its grotesque bulk. When its prey died, the monster slid a tentacle into the body from both ends to devour the innards.

The grolkin struck again, a pair of tentacles sweeping in toward the hunter's feet. Another rubbery appendage sliced through the air in a scything arc aimed at his head.

The hunter cursed, hopped above the first pair of tentacles, and swung his axe down to lop off the end of the limb directed at his head. His blow struck true, but the grolkin adjusted the attack mid-swing to catch Kor in the groin with the stump of its bisected tentacle.

The beast's impressive strength hurled the hunter through the air. His legs hit a tree, arresting his flight, and Kor tumbled back into the freezing sand encroaching on the Galasong Forest from the neighboring Lorikai Desert. The dual impacts, combined with his aching groin, left Kor dazed.

He lay there, ears ringing so loudly he could no longer hear the grolkin, and stared up through the skeletal tree limbs at the starry sky. The crucial words of his hunter's vow, "I am sworn to protect the people of this land from predators," rang in his ears.

Kor had killed his share of monsters over the years. Pananggalans along the sweltering southern coast of Drakanon. Ratfiends in damned near every farming village he'd ever stumbled across. Venoripedes in logging camps not far from this village. He'd killed too many monsters to count, including those so rare they had no names.

But the years hadn't been kind to the hunter, and he felt himself slowing down. Just a little, so far, but enough to land him in this bad spot.

If there hadn't been kids involved, the hunter would have lain there under the branches clawing at the sky and accepted his fate. Everyone in his profession met a violent end, eventually. Their vows didn't allow for peaceful retirements.

But to save those kids, Kor knew he'd have to pull on the arcane powers of his order. He could become stronger, faster, even harden his skin like armor, but there was a dark price to pay for using those abilities.

"Better than being dead," he muttered, drew on the vital Life Magic that lived within him, and activated the Hunter's Curse.

The calligraphic tattoos that encircled his body in a continuous spiral filled with magic. The power wormed its way through his body, hardening his flesh against all but the strongest blows. However, the curse's protection wouldn't last long. Kor had to finish the fight before he was vulnerable again.

"Come and get me, pigtopus!" he shouted. He dragged himself to his feet.

The thing was too stupid to be offended by the mocking name. It was not, however, any less enraged than if it had understood the insult. With a hellish bellow, the beast lowered its head and charged through the forest.

Its tentacles hammered small trees aside and uprooted saplings. Its massive shoulders cracked the boles of even full-grown trees, sending them toppling into their neighbors in a horrible, roaring storm of falling oaks. The ground shook with each footstep, and Kor had to steady himself against a tree to keep from stumbling.

Too late, he realized his axe wasn't in his hand.

The weapon was three yards beyond his reach, the blade half-buried in the frozen earth. Kor dove for the leather-wrapped handle, putting all his strength into the leap.

It wasn't enough.

Tentacles wrapped around the hunter's hips and ankles, hoisting him into the air. The grolkin dangled Kor twenty feet up, where he hung helpless as a newborn about to have its ass slapped by the midwife.

"Burn your eyes!" Kor shouted and dug his fingers into the thing's tentacles. Normally, that would have less effect than a butter knife. But the tips of his now iron-hard fingers were incredibly strong. Bit by bit, Kor's hands burrowed into the meaty tentacles.

The grolkin screamed as Kor ripped and tore. The hunter threw fistfuls of slimy fat and muscle into the monster's open, upturned mouth.

"How's that taste?" he shouted.

The grolkin responded by lowering Kor toward its toothy maw. The beast turned Kor head down. Its horrible, swampy breath washed over the hunter, making his eyes water and his stomach tighten into a rebellious knot. As awful as the situation was, though, that was exactly what Kor had hoped the thing would do.

He braced one hand against the beast's face, straightened the fingers of the other, then shoved his open hand directly up the grolkin's nose. Kor's arm disappeared up to the elbow. He pushed his hand deeper, searching for the thin wall of bone that separated the grolkin's nostril from the tiny morsel of tissue it called a brain.

"Don't like that?" Kor asked when the monster squeezed his legs in an attempt to crush them into paste. Despite the grolkin's immense power, the protective magic of the Hunter's Curse held strong.

Kor knew the price of his salvation would come due when this fight ended.

And it might be more than he could pay.

Just then, though, he was more concerned with the monster doing its damnedest to pull him apart like a sticky bun. New tentacles joined the fray, hooking around Kor's biceps and throat, pulling so hard the suckers ripped away patches of his skin.

Kor was tired. Not just of this fight, but all the fights like it. He was sick of the smell of monsters, always some revolting combination of brine and rot. He hated their endless rage and fathomless hunger for mortal flesh and blood.

The hunter was so tired that he wondered if this was his last battle. Maybe that would be for the best. Fighting a grolkin was an honorable exit from this life. He could accept his fate and then rest.

The fabled hunter might have met his end that way, one arm up a monster's nose, his body in agony, but a memory swam up through the red haze of impending doom.

When Kor had gathered the village elders to discuss the grolkin's rampage, they hadn't come alone. A young mother, her belly still round from pregnancy, her voice choked with fear and rage as she clutched her newborn, spoke up to be sure Kor heard her voice.

"Do something," she'd pleaded with such ferocity the babe had cried. "That bastard monster is stealing our *future*."

The plea reminded the hunter why he bothered with any of this.

"To hell with dying," Kor growled. He could do that another day. For that young woman, for the stolen children, he would live for at least a bit longer.

The hunter drove his fingers deeper into the grolkin's skull.

A wet *crack* sounded from within the thing's blubbery head. The tentacles around his waist and shoulders suddenly jerked in opposite directions. Kor's spine made an unpleasant rattling sound as it whipsawed back and forth.

But the hunter pushed through the pain.

He clawed his way into the grolkin's brain, fingers ripping and tearing the vital organ into sticky clumps.

The grolkin let out a strange, horrible scream and collapsed.

The monster's tentacles uncoiled into loose tubes of flaccid meat, and Kor fell to the ground. The magic that shielded the hunter faded away.

Kor braced himself for what he knew was coming. He closed his eyes against the Hunter's Curse and focused all his attention on the smooth cycle of his breathing. In. Out. In. Out. In—

Pain tore through him like a rusty saw.

Channeling magic damaged the hunter, and the price hit him like a knife to the gut. The pain knocked Kor senseless, and something important deep inside his body ruptured.

The hunter looked down on his twitching body and knew he'd begun the long, laborious process of dying. The price hadn't killed him outright, but the wound would be mortal in time. He was too far from the Sainted Order's healers for them to repair the damage.

That was all right. The grolkin was dead. The children would live. Kor's sacrifice would earn a place in the Books of Dark Memory. Other hunters would know his tale.

Finally, he could rest.

* * *

Tiny fingers that stank of suet dug at Kor's lips. The persistent digits found their way into his mouth, where their revolting, *gritty* surfaces raked against his gums.

"Get off!" the hunter shouted. His hands were clumsy and weak from the price he'd paid for his magic, which was the only thing that saved the life of the child who'd crawled onto his chest to pick at his face.

"You're okay, Binnie," a grandmother with a face like a hatchet chided the child. "No thanks to the corpse man, here."

Kor sat up on the stone floor of a room that smelled of death. Bars of pale silver light fell through the window, telling the hunter full night had come.

He'd never thought he'd see moon again and cursed it now that he had.

"Where am I?" Kor asked the old woman. His throat felt as dry as the desert's freezing sands.

"Gravewatch," she replied, then spat between forked fingers pressed to her lips. "You a shambler?"

Kor groaned and staggered to his feet, causing the woman to recoil in horror. "Shamblers don't talk," he informed her. "What time is it?"

"Nine bells," she said, pulling the boy closer and covering his eyes with her hand. "You swear you're not one of the risen dead?"

"If I was, I'd have eaten the kid and already be neck deep in your guts," Kor said. He raked his fingers through his hair and winced when they came away greasy and stained with the grolkin's blood. The stink of that stupid pigtopus would be on him for days. At least the villagers hadn't appropriated his gear. His axe, dagger, and supplies were piled on the stone floor next to where Kor had awoken. "Is there somewhere I can get a bath and a bed?"

She pursed her lips and hugged Binnie even tighter to her chest. "Marya's Inn is outside, to the right. Can't miss it."

"Thanks," Kor muttered, gathered his meager belongings, and left the stone tomb.

268 | KENNEDY & HOWELL

It annoyed him that a town that knew enough to post a gravewatch over the recently dead didn't have enough sense to make
sure he *was* dead before they laid him out on the stone. He'd saved
little Binnie and all the rest of the town's children, and they'd treated
him like a monster.

"Same as always," he grumbled.

The Order of Sainted Hunters was in high demand, but low desire. Monsters were no longer satisfied to haunt the wilderness. Now,
the foul beasts and devilish fiends sought juicier, meatier prey within
the bounds of civilization. That meant more villages, towns, and
cities in need of protection from the walking nightmares.

It also meant more people actually *saw* the hunters in action, and
when that happened, the common folk often worried they'd traded
one horror for another. That fear led to resentment, which led to
hunters being cheated and lied to, again and again.

By the Giants' black hearts, it was exhausting when the people he
tried to save turned their backs on him once the deed was done.

The village's inn was a ramshackle building, much like the others
Kor had seen in these parts. Gaps between walls and bald patches on
the sod roof made the place look more abandoned than welcoming.
But firelight gleamed through the building's windows, and the aroma
of roasting meat wafted to Kor on the smoke that drifted through
the patchy roof.

The hunter paused before the inn's threshold. For that one moment, he took in the smells and sounds of the patrons within. For
that sliver of time, Kor could pretend he was just another weary
traveler about to join the revels of others inside.

The instant he opened that door, though, the truth crashed down
on him.

A lute player's hand froze over her instrument's strings, the last echo of a note vibrating into silence. Villagers went stone still, drinks paused on the way to their mouths, and food steamed on forks an inch above their plates. Even the innkeeper, a sturdy woman with a shaggy mane of night-black hair, stared at him, dumbstruck, without so much as a word of welcome.

It was always like this. The hunter's colorless eyes and scarred face—not to mention his tattoos—marked him for all to see. Kor was a reminder of the dangers that lived beyond their village's pathetic walls.

"Bath and a room?" Kor asked, digging a silver coin from his belt pouch. At least the old woman hadn't looted his 'corpse.'

The innkeeper stared at the coin for a moment. It was more than she'd make in a month from this dump, but she was still reluctant to take it. Everyone knew hunters were cursed. Some of them believed that curse would spread to others like the boils of the plague.

It was all bullshit, of course. The curse hunters willingly took on gave them the power to save the world. You couldn't *catch* it from them like dropsy or the pox.

People were stupid, ignorant, and exhausting.

Kor was about to leave the inn when the dark-haired woman nodded and extended an open hand toward him. The hunter gratefully strode across the inn's common room, careful not to touch anyone or get too near the crowded tables, and dropped the coin into her cupped palm.

"No one else is staying here tonight," the innkeeper said. "You can have the last room at the end of the hall up those stairs. Don't have no bath, but there's a basin in the room, and you can get a bucket from the well out back to fill her up. I'll get you breakfast in the morning. Black bread, blood sausage, and potatoes is the best I can do."

"And that's the best feast I've had in a week," Kor said. "Thank you for your hospitality."

That was the end of their exchange. For the next ten minutes, Kor endured the stares of the villagers as he carried buckets of water up to his room. Then he splashed himself with cold water while doing his best not to disturb the gnawing injury at the center of his being, and settled in for a long, well-deserved rest.

* * *

Though his rented bed was home to a small army of bedbugs, Kor's breakfast made up for a night spent slapping at the biters. By the time he'd finished and pushed back the wooden plate, the village had come fully to life.

And the mayor stopped by Marya's place for a visit.

"Here," the stooped old man croaked as he shoved a ratty, jingling sack at Kor. "It's all there. Count it if you want."

"I do want," Kor replied. He licked the grease from his fingers and tugged the pouch's mouth open. Most of the coins he saw were copper, which he hated. The stuff was heavy and next to worthless. His battle with the grolkin had damaged his armor and his axe, and the repairs would eat up a mountain of copper coins.

"It's all here," the hunter agreed after he'd stacked the coins into neat columns of ten under the mayor's watchful eye. "Don't worry. I'll be moving on now."

"About that," the old man said. He sank down in the chair across from Kor, tugging at the wispy hairs of his beard. "A trader came through before you arrived. Claimed a dragon had slaughtered one of his horses and took his apprentice in the dead of night."

An involuntary grunt escaped Kor at the word "dragon." Most of the critters people called dragons were big, dumb, flying lizards. They favored the mountains and fed on cows and sheep, making them a nightmare for the alpine tribes. Killing them was a chore, though hardly worth a hunter's time.

But there was another type of dragon that was far smarter, and deadlier, than the flying butcher shop most considered when they heard the name. These other dragons were descended from the Giants. They wielded magic, breathed fire, and were far smarter than mortals.

They were a challenge worthy of a hunter.

"Which direction?" Kor asked. As tired as he was, as much as the curse's wound burned inside him like a torn stitch, his vow goaded him to ask the question. Even if he didn't want an answer.

"North," the mayor said.

Of course. It had to be north. Into the frozen desert.

Kor sighed and pushed back from the table. "Sounds like I've got a hike ahead of me. Best I get moving."

* * *

Kor followed the road north into the freezing desert. Though his vows to the Sainted Order of Hunters demanded he search for this supposed dragon, he had a more practical reason for finding a creature of such immense power.

His curse hungered for the dark ichor found only in the vilest of creatures. Their blood held a power hunters could use not only to heal the injuries caused by using their curse, but to enhance their control over the magic.

Finding and killing a dragon would do far more than simply rid the world of another monster. It would heal the hunter and give him the strength to resist future damage from his curse.

Tired as he was of the hunter's life, Kor couldn't pass up this opportunity—even if most of those he saved didn't deserve his help.

As Kor's first day's march ended, the dark peaks of the Dragon's Reach range loomed above him. They were tall and jagged as spears, their slopes streaked with patches of snow.

He camped at oases when he could find them and hunkered down among the desert's scattered boulders when he couldn't. He drank icy water and ate horned lizards he found sunning themselves on the desert road.

Finally, after five days of walking, he found where the dragon had attacked the merchant's caravan.

The spilled blood had frozen into gritty scabs on the stone road. The wind had taken most scraps of evidence away, but Kor found a handful of teeth stuck in the frozen blood.

What he didn't find were the scorch marks that a true dragon's attack would certainly have left behind.

Kor studied the scene for long moments, disappointment warring with relief. On the one hand, fighting a true dragon would have almost certainly ended his life. But if he'd somehow won, the beast's essence would have healed him.

He considered turning back.

And then he smelled it.

The bitter, gut-wrenching stench of dark ichor. His nose twitched, and the curse's hunger stirred inside him. Kor followed his nose up the stone road. A hundred yards farther north, he found a black stain on the stones.

A yawning gulf of hunger opened in Kor's belly. This beast might not be a dragon, but it held the foul power his curse craved.

The weary hunter nodded his head slowly, as if in answer to the benighted hunger within him.

He continued his march north, toward the mountains, the ache of his magical injuries competing with new hunger pangs.

* * *

After another week of slushy water and raw lizard meat, Kor reached the mountains. The merchant's road became a switchback scar across the dark faces of the challenging peaks, and Kor followed it for most of another day until the road became a wide, flat plateau in front of a heavy iron gate. Blazing bonfires raged on either side of the barrier, their heat so intense Kor felt it from ten paces. By the time he'd reached the gate, he was warmed from the top of his head down to the bottom of his aching feet.

"Hey," he shouted, his voice a dry rasp from days of disuse, "open up!"

To Kor's surprise, someone *did* just that. The sound of heavy gears turning and chains clanking echoed from the stone walls that flanked the gate, and the heavy halves of the barrier swung outward to reveal a trio of guards. They wore ragged chain shirts and carried pikes with rust-speckled blades.

"What brings you to the gates of Alura Kenai?" one guard asked, leaning on his weapon's haft. "Come on, come on. Gates lock at sundown, and you don't want to spend the night out there. Cold as a Giant's tit, sleeping on stone."

"I'm a hunter," Kor began.

"Well, that's something," the same guard said. "Can't say we've seen many of your kind. Let's get you to the inn."

The guard left his two comrades behind and led Kor through the strange town.

Alura Kenai was nestled in the throat of a mountain pass. Past the twin rows of structures that lined the main road through the pass, homes and businesses were stacked like a child's blocks up the mountains' sides. Catwalks crisscrossed from one edge of the pass to the other, allowing the villagers to travel from building to building without ever touching the ground. Chimneys jutted from the top of most buildings, emitting dense clouds of wood smoke that formed dark banks above the pass.

The buildings closest to the road were filled with life. Bright light spilled from their windows, and voices rumbled within their cozy walls. But the farther up the slopes his eyes traveled, the more shuttered windows and closed doors the hunter saw.

"And here we are," the guard said, interrupting Kor's thoughts. "The inn."

"Thank you," Kor said, grateful for the courtesy. In their short walk together, the guard had shown the hunter more kindness than the people of the last five villages he'd saved.

The guard turned on one heel and left, and Kor cursed to himself. He'd forgotten to ask if the man had seen any strange flying creatures. Over the days of marching, Kor had caught scent of the monster's dark ichor spoor, so he knew it had come this way. Surely if it had nested up here, though, the guards would have mentioned it to the hunter.

With a shrug, Kor entered the inn. The patrons welcomed the hunter, and the middle-aged barmaid slinging drinks bobbed her head and shot him a wink.

Kor took that as an invitation and made his way through the common room toward the bar. To Kor's surprise, the locals weren't repulsed by his scars or tattoos. Instead, they reached out to shake his hand as he passed their tables and thanked him for his service.

The unexpected camaraderie and polite greetings rattled Kor. He was used to being feared and shunned, but these people greeted him like a long-lost friend returned from a journey to a distant land.

For one all-too-brief moment, Kor felt like he'd found a place he belonged.

Until the smell hit him.

Thick as the smoke from a dung fire, the stench of dark ichor clawed at his nostrils.

The hunter did his best not to react to the stench. If the monster was hidden in this room, Kor didn't want it to know he'd sensed its presence. Judging by the intensity of the smell, this creature was powerful. Kor would need every advantage he could get to defeat it.

"Looking for a room, stranger?" the barmaid asked, her wide smile telling Kor she couldn't detect even a whiff of the gruesome stink.

"And a meal if I can get it," Kor said.

The barmaid turned out to be the innkeeper, and she haggled with Kor until they arrived at a price of five silver for a room for the night, dinner, breakfast, and a complimentary sipping glass of whiskey. The price was far steeper than his last room, but this place was also much nicer. After so many days in the frozen desert, Kor would have paid double that for a warm room.

"Best booze you'll find," the innkeeper said with a smile. "Don't tell anyone, but the secret is, I only use snowmelt for water. Can't get any cleaner taste than that. How long do you think you'll stay?"

"I'll be here a bit," Kor admitted. "I don't suppose you've heard of any work for a man in my line of business?"

The barmaid wiped her hands on the towel dangling from her thick leather belt. "And what business would that be?"

"Hunting," Kor responded. He tugged the chain around his neck to reveal the iron disc stamped with the Sainted Order of Hunters' sigil.

"Well, now," she said. "Pleased to meet you, Hunter. I'm Tallis. You'll be sad to know we don't get many monsters around these parts. Though I will say there's a cavern or two nearby you might want to explore this evening."

"Is that right?" Kor asked. A grin to match Tallis's stretched across his face.

It had been a long time.

"Let me get a bowl of stew for you," Tallis said. "We'll see about your other hunger after dinner."

* * *

"Where are you going?" Tallis asked as Kor slipped out of bed in the dead of night

"Need some fresh air," the hunter lied. "Go back to sleep."

The woman sighed and flopped back onto the pillow. "You'll freeze out there. Come back to bed and let me breathe some life back into you, old man."

"Such a sweet talker," Kor said, "but after so long on the road, I'm not used to sleeping indoors. A quick walk and I'll be able to rest."

"Your loss." Tallis pulled the blankets up to her chin. "Don't get lost."

The barmaid faked snoring, which drew a chuckle from the hunter. He felt bad about lying to her, but telling her the truth would be dangerous for both of them.

Because Kor smelled dark ichor almost *everywhere* in Alura Kenai. The hunter had no idea what that meant, but he was determined to find out.

The hunter strapped on his damaged axe and armor, then paused at the doorway. He looked back over his shoulder at Tallis, and the sight of the barmaid's tousled hair and pale face hit him like a hornet sting to the heart.

He was no foolish romantic to think he loved the woman. They'd just met, even if they had enjoyed one another's company.

And Kor hadn't smelled the dark ichor on Tallis.

That made him happy.

He really did *not* want to kill the woman.

* * *

Alura Kenai was a different city at night. Those shuttered windows Kor had seen high up on the walls of the mountain pass when he'd arrived were now thrown wide. Ruddy light jumped and guttered within the buildings, making the openings look like baleful, blinking eyes.

It was almost impossible for Kor to see through the thick layer of smoke trapped above the city, but looking out toward the horizon showed him several hours remained until dawn. That gave him time to poke around. With any luck, he'd find the monster soon.

Alura Kenai had one main street that ran from its southern gate to its twin in the north. The thoroughfare was wide and well-lit by lanterns fueled by something that burned the pale blue of an early winter's morning. Buildings were clustered shoulder-to-shoulder along this main thoroughfare, with occasional gaps that allowed pedestrians to move off the street to find other businesses and homes that ran all the way back to the mountain slopes, where they climbed up to the clouds of smoke hanging in the pass.

Kor moved quickly down one of these alleyways to reach the buildings farthest from the main street along the face of the mountain. Though there were no blue lights to illuminate his path, the hunter could make out some strange details.

The stones used to construct these buildings were mostly white and gray, but those that touched the mountain's surface seemed much older. The hunter tested one of them with his knife and found the blade's tip couldn't make a divot or even leave a scratch on the stone.

They were metal, he realized, but not like any he'd ever seen. He rubbed his fingertips across another dark, exposed piece and felt the slightest of indentations in its surface. It was too dark to make out any details, but the hunter would have sworn he felt neat, even rows of symbols.

A man's snoring just beyond the wall he'd examined goaded Kor into moving. He wouldn't find monsters in the homes of sleeping families.

He hoped.

Switchback staircases climbed up the face of the mountain and provided access to more buildings and homes embedded in the stone. Kor moved with all the stealth his years of practice had burned into his muscle memory.

The internal injuries he'd received from overextending his magic made it hard to climb the stairs, and Kor had to stop every so often to catch his breath and let the pain subside. However, if push came to shove, he could fight; there was no doubt in his mind. But there was also no doubt that the fighting would *hurt*, and he wouldn't be at his best.

And yet I'm still chasing a dragon, he thought to himself, and shook his head. *Or something worse.*

The stink grew more intense as he followed his nose, higher and higher. As Kor climbed, he was able to piece together a better understanding of the city. He'd originally thought the buildings clinging to the mountains were a haphazard collection of structures held together by dubious support beams and interconnecting ladders.

Now, though, he saw that the city was arranged in tiers, and the very highest levels weren't attached to the mountains at all. Those buildings climbed iron and wood scaffoldings that arched out over the main street, like the strange claws of a grasping giant.

While the rest of the city slept, the highest reaches were quite lively. Music, raucous and strident, fell from the open windows along with the strange crimson light. Kor felt drawn to those places. There was something wrong with them.

Something that snared his attention and demanded he investigate.

Years of hunting monsters had taught Kor not to ignore those feelings. He dragged himself up the stairs and ladders until he found himself blocked by a wide trough that jutted out from the mountainside. The sound of rushing water rumbled through the trough. It piqued Kor's curiosity, and he pulled himself onto a nearby support strut to look down into the rumbling structure.

The water left a cave in the mountainside and flowed down the trough. Past Kor's vantage point, the trough directed the water into a wide-mouthed metal barrel nearly ten yards across and twice as high. The barrel sat atop a manifold, which directed the water down into a maze of thinner and thinner pipes.

"Amazing," the hunter whispered. This mountaintop village had created a system that delivered water into the homes of its people. No more trips to the well or river, no more worry about tainted water because something shat upstream or died deep below ground.

But as impressive an engineering feat as the water system was, the fluid *reeked* of dark ichor.

Kor's nose twitched at the stench. It was stronger up here. He climbed down from the support toward the trough, careful to maintain his footing and handholds as he transitioned to a new scaffold. Rough wood drove splinters into his palms, and the freezing wind that blew through the gap between the mountainous peaks made his eyes water. He hung between his former perch and the trough for a moment, blinded and unsteady.

Not to mention exposed.

The longer the hunter remained where he was, the greater the risk someone would see him.

The weight of Kor's body aggravated his internal injuries. A stitch in his side unraveled into a grinding ache that made his teeth chatter and wrenched an involuntary groan from deep within his chest.

He couldn't see. Moving would be the death of him.

But he couldn't stay where he was, either. His strength was fading, and the pain would soon get the best of him.

"Shit," he groaned.

Kor blinked furiously to clear the tears from his eyes, but the wind kept kicking stinging flecks of ice and snow into his face. The cold set off shivers that racked his arms and threatened to loosen his grip.

The hunter only had one choice.

Closing his eyes and grinding his teeth against the pain he knew was coming, Kor activated his magic to strengthen his body.

He hoped it wouldn't kill him.

* * *

Power rippled out from the center of Kor's being. It flowed through his flesh and bones, then stitched itself into his muscles.

Kor forced his eyes open and blinked furiously to clear them. The best he could manage was a temporary, blurry image of the trough beneath him before the wind blinded him again.

It would have to be enough.

The hunter used his enhanced strength to swing his feet toward the trough. At the height of his arc, he let go of the struts that had supported him and sailed out into the empty air.

At the same moment, someone shouted from below the hunter. Their words were torn away by the whipping wind, but the hunter didn't need to hear them to understand their angry tone.

Kor's feet hit the wide lip of the trough. The rough soles found purchase, but the sudden addition of his weight set the whole structure swaying. A rivet gave way with a shrill ping, and water exploded through the open hole. A split second later, one of the support trusses beneath the trough cracked, and the whole thing shifted under Kor's feet.

The hunter twisted toward the higher edge of the trough, thrusting one leg out to balance his weight across the width of the water. That stopped the dangerous tilt, but the structure hadn't been built to hold the weight of rushing water *and* a full-grown, armored man.

Kor had a choice. He could run down the half-pipe to the more stable structures of Alura Kenai, or he could run *up* the trough to the cavern. The second option was by far the more dangerous, but the hunter knew it was his only real choice.

The stream was filled with dark ichor flowing out of that dark hole in the mountainside.

Caves are a natural habitat for monsters.

Kor put his supernatural strength to use and ran up the trough. It was a tricky stunt that required him to step from side to side to keep from unbalancing it, but his curse's hunger goaded the hunter to move faster.

The dark ichor called to him.

Kor was halfway up the trough when a crossbow bolt missed his shoulder by a hand-span. The missile plunged into the rushing water and hit the metal trough with a loud *clang* before the current carried it away.

With a start, Kor realized the bolt had come from *above* him.

A risky glance over his shoulder showed the hunter his enemies. A group of hulking men clad in black armor had emerged from one of the top tier buildings. They stood on the edge of a platform that jutted from the back of the structure and calmly took aim with crossbows.

The hunter had no room to dodge. Even the most rudimentary of evasive maneuvers would dangerously unbalance the trough.

He ran, head hunched low, arms and legs pumping for all they were worth. His only chance of surviving this was to reach the cave's mouth before his enemies turned him into a pincushion.

Which would have been a hell of a lot easier if the trough didn't bounce up and down with every step he took. All it would take was one moment of inattention to send him plummeting to the rocky mountainside below.

More crossbow bolts whipped through the air, but the icy wind gusted their attacks off course.

A hundred yards was all that remained between Kor and the cavern entrance. A handful of heartbeats, and he'd be safe.

Well, at least *safer*.

The hunter put on a final burst of speed, pushing himself harder than he'd ever thought possible. Lightning jolts of pain stabbed through his legs with every step, a warning of the price he'd pay when this was all said and done.

The cavern loomed before him, a gaping mouth lined with stalactite fangs. The stench of dark ichor flooded out of it, clogging his nose and clawing at his throat.

Whatever darkness had spread through this town, its origin was not far ahead.

The wind suddenly kicked up around Kor, conflicting currents sweeping in every direction. A sound like sails cracking in a tempest emerged from the storm, and Kor raised one hand to shield his eyes as he ran.

He couldn't afford to stop. The crossbow bolts were getting nearer their mark, and the trough bucked and groaned beneath him.

A shadow stretched out from the cavern, unfurled wings hammering at the air as it rose before Kor. Red eyes burned with hatred above a grotesque, suckered mouth, and the creature plunged toward the hunter.

Kor knew he was dead if he stayed on the trough. The magic of his curse still glowed from his tattoos, but the light was fading. He had a few seconds at best to use it before the power faded entirely.

The hunter charged at the beast as it fell from the sky. He unslung his axe from his back with his right hand and drew his dagger with the left. Kor tracked the beast's dive, his mind ticking off the hair-fine slices of time before they collided.

He ignored the crossbow bolts that slammed into the trough or ripped through the air inches away from him as he ran. There wasn't enough space left in his thoughts to worry about those lesser dangers when a flying monster was nearly on top of him.

Long hind legs stretched out from the beast's furry body as the bat-like creature's wings arced around Kor. Ropy strands of pink saliva dangled from the thing's jaws, and its eyes blazed with unholy light.

The stink of dark ichor flooded Kor's nostrils. This was the creature that had attacked the caravan. All he had to do to heal himself was kill it and devour its dark ichor.

At the last possible second, Kor jumped up to meet the creature's dive. The beast plunged into the trough where the hunter had been standing a second before. The aqueduct collapsed at the point of impact, shattering into two halves.

The bat monster fell through the gap in the structure, its wings flailing for purchase in the freezing air. It hadn't anticipated this turn of events.

The hunter slammed his dagger into the horror like a climber driving a piton into a cliff face. His axe bit into the creature's outstretched wing, hewing through the hollow bone and leather flesh to open a horrible tear. The crippled appendage flopped uselessly in the stiff mountain winds, twisting the monster to one side.

The creature lashed out at Kor with its sucker-like mouth, but the hunter was still on the move. The attack missed Kor as he pulled himself up and over the creature, using the dagger as leverage.

A flurry of crossbow bolts meant for Kor punctured the giant bat instead. The wooden missiles shredded the creature's other wing. Its claws scrabbled at the trough's supports, but without wings, the creature couldn't support itself.

The monstrosity fell, broken wings fluttering behind it like two halves of a torn cape. Droplets of dark ichor trailed through the air as it plummeted away.

Kor jumped free of the beast as it fell. His arms pinwheeled as he sailed through the air. Crossbow bolts narrowly missed the hunter, but none found their mark. For once, luck was on his side.

He landed on the remaining section of the trough. The wet metal offered no traction, though, and Kor's feet shot out from under him. He landed hard, his chin hitting the bottom of the channel.

Water pouring down the trough shot up his nose. Sputtering and shaking from the cold water that had invaded his sinuses, the hunter scrambled forward, hands grabbing the edges of the trough. The aqueduct tilted dangerously, and he struggled to climb it before the whole thing plunged a hundred feet to the rocky mountainside below.

The next seconds were the longest of Kor's life. The light had faded from his tattoos, leaving him in pain and without the strength of his curse. He felt like he slid back three feet for every foot he moved forward. Crossbow bolts slammed into the metal trough and kicked up splinters into Kor's face when their shafts shattered. And beneath him, the trusses and supports shook and trembled.

All while cold water splashed into his face and made it difficult to catch his breath, much less make any progress.

The trough beneath Kor's legs suddenly vanished in a roar of tearing metal and breaking wood. His fingers caught hold of the trough's edge, but the weight of his lower body coming down on his grip caused his arms and shoulders to scream in pain. Water blinded him. The freezing wind made him shiver uncontrollably.

Kor wanted to give up. It would be easier to just let go and fall. A moment of weightlessness, crushing pain, then…

Rest.

But even as his thoughts turned to the blackness, an image snapped into focus.

Tallis.

She'd shown him compassion and offered comfort. If Kor fell to his death, whatever was in that cavern would eventually come for her.

The innkeeper deserved a better end.

The hunter dragged himself inch by painful inch up the tilting trough. The last supports collapsed under the hunter's weight. Water arced down into the darkness as metal and wood tumbled into the snow.

For a moment, Kor was sure he'd join the falling debris, but a final lunge carried him up onto the stony floor of a cavern.

He was alive.

For the moment.

"What is this?" a strange voice asked. The syllables were sticky, making it hard to tell where one ended and the other began.

Kor dragged himself up to his feet and glared into the darkness. He could only make out vague outlines from the starlight that fell into the cavern, but he didn't need to see to know the truth.

He could smell it.

This was the source of the dark ichor.

Kor's knuckles crackled as he clenched his fists and answered the question. "Your death," he said.

Kor's injuries ached like nuggets of broken glass buried deep in his guts, but Tallis needed him to keep going. And for the first time in a very, very long time, Kor believed someone deserved his help.

He could survive this. He would grow stronger, but only if he killed the source of the dark ichor.

"Have you brought my meal?" the alien voice asked.

The sound brought chills to Kor's skin. The way the words clung together made his head hurt. It was as if a frog had learned to talk.

There was a strength in that voice that mirrored the power of the dark ichor stench that surrounded Kor. Whatever lay ahead of him was stronger than any beast he'd ever faced.

And there he was, with only a boot knife for a weapon. His axe and dagger were long gone, lost to the snow and ice far below on the mountainside.

"This'll be fun," he whispered and crept forward.

The cavern wasn't as dark as he'd expected. Shadows from the entrance had lengthened, but as Kor rounded a corner, a new light grew ahead of him. Faint pulses of green light emanated from the mouths of other tunnels that led off the main cavern. Purple radiance gleamed from spheres embedded in the roof.

"You are not one of mine," the voice came again. It sounded more curious than hostile, and somehow that worried Kor more than any threat.

The walls of the cavern became smoother, and signs of ancient craftsmanship emerged. Complex mazes of glyphs and runes covered every surface, and tinges of pure white light raced through the dense network of patterns. The lights drew Kor's eyes more surely than a flame gathered moths, and he had to force himself to look away again and again.

Kor wondered what kind of creature would live in the freezing waters of a mountaintop cave. It was too cold for krakens, and he doubted there'd be space for one in this place, anyway. A dread tortoise could survive in this climate, but he'd never heard of one growing as powerful as the thing lurking here. Naiad terrors might fit the bill, but he'd never heard one of them speak.

Kor was still pondering what enemy lay hidden in this ancient place when he heard angry voices. Shouts echoed from the smaller tunnels attached to the main corridor. The people of Alura Kenai must have another way to reach this cavern than the treacherous path Kor had followed.

"Fantastic," he grumbled.

The pieces of this dark picture fell into place for Kor. Whatever creature lay ahead of him, the dark ichor it leaked into the water had infected the town, thanks to their advanced plumbing.

Except for Tallis. She only drank snowmelt.

To save her and the rest of the town, Kor had to kill whatever lay ahead.

His body ached from the curse and the injuries he'd suffered, which made the going hard. The tunnel he followed became steeper and slipperier as water from the channel sprayed into a mist and settled onto the floor as ice. Kor pressed on until he found himself standing on the stony shores of a lake of crystal-clear water.

Chiseled strings of runes surrounded the body of water. Woven Life and Land Magic filled the runes with power that weighed against Kor's skin. Whoever had created this place didn't want intruders.

Something stirred in the water as the hunter pushed ahead. A dark form unfurled from the depths, revealing a tall, gangly figure that burst from the lake and towered above its surface.

The thing was humanoid, but its arms and legs were far too long for the proportions of its body. The water had worn away patches of the thing's skin to reveal slick, oily muscles and pale bones. The monstrosity threw back its elongated head to reveal a face robbed of any humanity by the places where meat had sloughed from its skull. The thing's lips were long gone, revealing a dark gash that held four enormous fangs and a wide line of gleaming, chisel-tipped teeth.

"What have we here?" the creature asked, its voice hammering against Kor's mind with every syllable.

Kor's heart thudded irregularly. His eyes ached from looking at the thing, and he knew he'd stumbled upon something ancient and awful. The size of the creature before him dredged up memories from his history lessons.

This was a Giant. One of the most ancient and dreadful of all the horrors this world held.

And it was hungry.

"You can't escape, Hunter." The man's voice drew Kor's attention back over his shoulder. "The master demands your life."

"And he thinks you pups can take it from me?" Kor asked.

Nine guards occupied the tunnel that led to the "master's" chamber. Three of the men held crossbows trained on the hunter's chest, while the other six had halberds at the ready.

"You're unarmed," the leader of the guards said. "You can't beat us."

"Poor choice to hunt a hunter, lads," Kor said and rushed the men.

The hunter's injuries slowed him, but he was still stronger and faster than these fools. His skills and experience were his biggest edges, though, and he knew he'd need them against ten foes.

Crossbow strings thwapped as the guards unleashed their bolts. One of the barbed missiles snared in the chain mail under Kor's left arm. Another razored open a deep gash on his left cheek. The third went far wide and bounced off the cavern's walls with a metallic *twang*.

The man who'd fired the last bolt had eyes the size of saucers. He'd realized Kor was headed in his direction, and fear had clenched his trigger finger before he could aim. The crossbow fell from his hands, and his nerveless fingers scrabbled to grab the short sword from the sheath dangling from his belt.

Kor was too fast for that.

The hunter grabbed the guard's wrist with his left hand and twisted it inward until the bones snapped like dry twigs. With his right hand, Kor grabbed the blade's handle and wrenched it free. The hunter dragged the weapon across the guard's throat, unleashing a thick spray of blood.

And the stench of dark ichor.

The intense, grotesque odor repulsed and fascinated Kor. The hunger welled up inside him, and for a moment he imagined himself drinking the tainted blood straight from the guard's throat.

Disgusted, the hunter hurled the dying guard's body away. The spraying corpse slammed into two of the halberdiers.

"Kill him!" the Giant howled. "I crave his blood!"

The master's exclamations had a physical weight that hit Kor like gut punches, robbing him of air, and staggering him so badly he nearly fell prey to a clumsy thrust from a halberd.

After deflecting the blade with a crude parry, Kor whipped his short sword up and around. The tip missed the man's neck by a handful of inches.

Instead of neatly slicing the guard's throat, Kor ripped the man's jaw clean off his face. The agonizing wound dropped the man to his knees, and he released his halberd to clutch at his mutilated face.

Kor expected the guards to hesitate after that deadly display. It was hard for men with little training to accept the sudden and brutal ends of their comrades.

But these men didn't spare a glance for the fallen. They drove forward, pushed by an invisible hand built of hate and ancient power. The halberds dove at the hunter's guts, while the crossbowmen smoothly and efficiently reloaded their weapons.

Even in the hands of someone with Kor's skill, a short sword was no match for five polearms.

Kor braced himself for the brutal impact of four blades hitting his guts.

The blows never landed.

Kor's magic flared to life. The curse refused to let him die.

Power lit up the tattooed runes on his legs and burned his eyes from within. The world slowed to a crawl. Kor snatched a halberd from a guard and used it to slap aside two more attacks. A nimble leap carried him away from a fourth strike.

Kor had escaped his attackers.

The cost, though, was terrible. Lightning bolts of pain zigzagged up from his legs and clawed at the wound within him. He choked and tasted blood on his tongue.

His blood.

The superhuman speed was already fading. If he had to use his magic again, Kor knew he would die.

There was only one chance left.

Kor turned from the guards and ran at their master.

The guards screamed at Kor to stop. The men and women of Alura Kenai were bound to the master from generations of drinking its blood and dissolved flesh. The insidious creature controlled them through this dark tradition. As long as it lived, these people would defend it.

But Kor also knew the villagers hadn't bound the thing here. As he ran for all he was worth, his memories churned until an ancient, dreadful word bubbled to the surface. This place was not merely the home of the bound Giant.

Alura Kenai hid the presence of a *nuraghi*, one of the ancient and horrifying complexes created by the Giants to pursue their sorcerous arts.

The dark ichor in the water wasn't the real threat here. The Giant's plan had unfurled over countless years. Left unchecked, the horrors of Alura Kenai would spread like a plague across Drakanon.

Kor leaped into the air, his wounded muscles propelling him out over the water. He let the short sword fall from his grip and clasped the halberd with both hands. He raised the weapon over his head, arching his back to give himself the maximum strength for his strike.

The Giant had other ideas.

One lanky arm shot out, and an enormous fist closed around Kor's waist. The beast opened its mouth wide and pulled the hunter in for a fatal bite.

The hunter almost welcomed the death he saw before him. He'd fought longer and harder than any man he'd known.

His sacrifice would end this monstrosity.

That would be enough.

The stink of dark ichor, rotten and laden with ancient power, flooded Kor's nostrils when he was a yard from the master's gaping mouth. The stench was everything he'd fought against.

Kor cried out against the crushing pain of the master's grip. His injuries roared to tortured life as he twisted his body to drive the halberd up into the roof of the Giant's mouth. Eight feet of wood tipped with polished iron wedged into the creature's maw, holding it open.

Blood poured from Kor's open mouth as he gasped for air. He choked on his own lifeblood, a pink foam coating his lips as the beast squeezed him tighter and crushed his lungs.

Confused and furious, the monster thrust Kor into its mouth. It tried to bite him, but the halberd held its mouth open.

The pressure of the attempted bite pushed the weapon deeper into the Giant's head. Thick, sticky blood poured from the wound.

Kor threw his head back and drank from the gory fountain. His curse ignited as the dark ichor flowed into him. The hellish fluid transformed the hunter's body, and death became life.

The hunter's hands found the haft of the halberd. Kor braced himself against the master's twisted tongue. His body burned with ferocious energy, every muscle popping and creaking as their fibers swelled to accommodate this monstrous strength.

With a furious roar, Kor drove the weapon up into the bony vault holding the Giant's brain. Or at least he tried.

The combination of his strength and the skull's durability were too much for the halberd. It shattered in his grip, and the Giant's jaws slammed closed.

The creature swallowed.

The hunter thrust his legs out ahead of him. He was partway down the thing's gullet when his heels dug into the meat of its throat. Kor still had half of the broken halberd in his grip, but he was lost in darkness and drowning in dark ichor. His only hope was to find something vital to stab. Even that was a long shot.

The creature swallowed again, and its tongue slammed him into the back of its throat. Bony ridges ground into the hunter's face. There was something familiar, but also alien, about those structures.

Kor knew what he had to do.

He drove the jagged, broken end of the halberd's haft between two of the ridges. He threw his weight against it, and the makeshift weapon sank between the chunks of bone.

Into the Giant's spinal cord.

The monstrous fiend tried to swallow, but the working of its tongue only pushed the halberd in deeper. The Giant fell.

Darkness swallowed the hunter.

* * *

Kor woke from dark dreams of bitter blood and icy water. He bolted upright, but strong hands pushed him back down.

"Stay there," a familiar voice commanded.

"Where the hell am I?" Kor asked, slapping away the hands that held him down.

He remembered drowning in dark ichor, his curse struggling to absorb the power, even as it stitched his wounds together. He remembered using the broken halberd to hack his way out of the Giant.

Then water, so much water...

"Ouch," Tallis yelped. "You're at my inn, but you won't be for long if you do that again."

"The inn?" Kor shook his head. A vague memory of cautious voices and careful hands emerged from the shadows of time he'd lost since fighting the master. "You brought me all the way here from the mountain?"

"No, the guards brought you down."

That made no sense. "The guards tried to kill me."

"The *master* tried to kill you," Tallis corrected him. "It controlled the others. When it died..."

Kor's hand rose to Tallis' chin. He cupped her face and looked deep into her eyes. "You never drank the water."

"Lucky me," she said. "I always felt like there was something wrong here. Until you came, though, I was the only one."

"And the others?" Kor asked.

Tallis shrugged. "The ones most closely tied to the thing died along with it. Others have died since. They were dependent on its blood. I'm afraid Alura Kenai is breathing its last."

"What about you?" Kor asked.

"I can't stay here," she said. "I was hoping I might leave with you."

The hunter considered that. A few weeks ago, he'd been ready to lay down his weapons and let the grave take him. He'd grown weary of saving the undeserving, of being cheated and spat upon by the people who needed him the most.

But Tallis had shown him the world wasn't *all* bad, and it would be easier to remember that with her beside him.

"I'd like that," he said, stroking her cheek with the back of his hand.

Together, they watched the sun's rays find their way into Alura Kenai, lighting the path to a new day.

* * * * *

Sam Witt Biography

Sam Witt is an avid gamer, RPG designer, and author of horror and fantasy. When not adding tales to the *Eldros Legacy*, he spends way too much time attempting to smoke the perfect brisket.

* * * * *

A Rhakha for the Tokonn
by Quincy J. Allen

An Eldros Legacy Story

Ty Kotha placed his hands on either side of the large stone pestle his father had fashioned for him when his majea—his gift from the goddess Amarassa—had manifested after his twelfth birthday.

He also had an exceptional ability to work with metal. With it, he'd already surpassed his father and the rest of the Sakari people in weapon smithing.

The autumn mid-day sun made it hot, even where he stood beneath the smithing shed's overhang. He worked alone today on something he hoped would be strong enough to complete his Tokonn—his rite of passage into manhood—and do so in a manner none other had before him.

Drawing in a deep breath, he focused his will upon the ingot of iron and two chunks of ore laying in the pestle. He spent a good deal of time just feeling his way through the different metals. He could see them—not with his eyes, but with his mind. Iron he knew well. One of the new ores was crystalline, hard, with sharp edges that Ty suspected would force the iron into stronger lattices. The other was hard but dense, smooth, and malleable. He'd never felt anything like them before and was excited to see what they became.

It had all begun at the River Market. Ty had started up a conversation with a Delver smith and merchant that was passing through the area. One thing led to another, and Ty had shown the Delver one of his very special daggers, claiming it was stronger than any regular steel. The metal of the blade was like none other the Delver had seen before, with fine patterns of dark and light gray flowing through it. Everyone knew Delvers—the short people from beneath the mountains—were masters of smithing, so when the smith had asked, it had meant a great deal to Ty. Ty, however, was unwilling to just give his secrets away.

A deal was struck. Ty handed over his dagger and described his method of folding metal over and over again with a mixture of iron filings and powdered charcoal layered into each fold. In exchange, the Delver gave Ty two ingots of ores that, once blended with iron in the right proportions, would make for an incredibly strong steel that resisted rusting. Ty hoped the new ores would result in something truly remarkable. What he planned for his Tokonn would take a very special weapon that could cut through thick scales, assuming he mustered up the courage to try.

Ty closed his eyes and tapped deeper into his majea. He let it flow from within him into the iron and ores. He could feel them, every part of them, as if they'd somehow become an extension of his self. He pressed harder and harder, pushing energy into them from without and within. Warmth radiated along his hands, through his arms, and all the way up to his face. There was no longer a separation between himself and the now glowing objects in the bottom of the pestle. He opened his eyes, still pouring his *majea* into the metal and ores…and lost track of time. They were red hot, the edges softening and smoothing. He picked up a gourd from beside the pestle and carefully shook out a small measure of pulverized charcoal onto the glowing ores.

First, the shape of the iron gave way to his majea, turning molten and melting like churned butter in a hot pot. The small, shiny ore gave way next, and finally the crystallized ore softened and flowed into the molten pool within the pestle. Ty shook out more of the charcoal, and as he did, he felt the three elements within the pestle begin to lose their distinction from each other. He sensed they wanted to blend together, and a surge of excitement filled him. He could always tell when the metal was working with him rather than against him.

It's time, he thought.

He focused his majea again and set the molten mixture into motion, gently stirring and blending, until there was no longer a sense of different elements, only one mass that felt like nothing he'd ever worked with before. This was new, and deep inside, he knew it was special. However, his work had only just begun.

Ty let out a long, slow breath and grabbed the lever attached to the stone pestle. As he pulled it back, the pestle pivoted in its cradle, and the molten metal, coaxed by Ty's majea, flowed completely out into a waiting clay mold. The metal filled the mold almost to the top. Once again, Ty's measurements had been precise. He now had a long ingot of the new metal, perfect for forging a wide-bladed hunting spear with which to complete his Tokonn.

He stepped back and let out a long, weary breath. Melting the ores had taken a great deal out of him. It would take several days to complete the new weapon, and much of it would be with hammer and anvil, but something told him it would be worth it.

Leaving the ingot to cool, he stepped out into the pale evening light and stretched his arms over his head. It had taken all afternoon to complete his work, but he was happy with what he'd wrought. He reached out tentatively to the cooling ingot, probing deeply with his *majea*. He could sense the strength within, the potential. It was just as the Delver had said. This new metal was stronger and more resilient than regular steel, and once folded, it would be like nothing anyone had ever seen.

* * *

"I made a new metal today, Father," Ty said as he spooned up some of his mother's koodoo buck stew. His father had killed the buck the previous day, and they would be able to feed themselves for a month or two with it.

Ty's family was fortunate. Both his parents had been granted majea by Amarassa, and Ty had inherited the gift in spades. His father was an earthshaper like Ty, but his mother was a lifebender. It was because of her majea that they ate so well and why their family always had more jerked meats, hearty vegetables, and pungent spices than the other Sakari villagers.

Hence, Ty's family was considered wealthy by many standards, blessed by Amarassa in the extreme. Ty didn't care about such things. He was grateful, of course, but his gift had always been a means to an end—namely, becoming the finest smith ever known so he could one day create a smithy of his own. For now, however, he just wanted to finish his new weapon and pass the Tokonn in a way none other ever had.

"Did you lace up that canoe for Master Koola?" Ty's father asked quietly. His father always spoke in soft tones, even when he was angry.

"Yes, Father," Ty replied.

"Did you pull those new hides out of the mash and lace them to the stretching racks?"

"Yes, Father."

"Did you tighten the older hides?"

"Yes, Father. The oldest can be pulled down in two days and brought to the River Market for sale. I'll deliver them to Salla when I return again to the market. The other three batches of hides are coming along, and none of them have torn, despite the heat of these past weeks."

"Good. Then I am pleased you made a new metal today." His father cast a sidelong glance in Ty's direction. "What will you do with this new metal?"

Does Father suspect? Ty thought. He kept his face calm.

"I'm making a hunting spear for the Tokonn."

His father stiffened slightly, and his mother's spoon hesitated for just a moment before she put it in her mouth.

Now that he'd turned seventeen, it was time to undertake the rite of passage. For years, Ty and his father had discussed the sort of beast Ty might hunt for his rite. A koodoo buck would be sufficient, of course, or even one of the large wild pigs that inhabited the forests surrounding their village. It was Sakari custom that none learned of what a young hunter took for his Tokonn. The belief was that the rite was to test the man against himself, not test him against another. Ty didn't even know what his father had taken for his Tokonn, although he'd always wanted to ask.

The Tokonn required little more than proof that a Sakari male could provide food, and therefore everything derived from an animal's death, both to his family and the village. It also proved he could, at least in a limited fashion, handle some sort of weapon to dispatch not only beasts, but enemies of the Sakari. The Sakari had few of those, but there was a tribe of Bhirtas'Vuoda—amphibious water goblins—that lived in the river well upstream of their village.

None of that mattered to Ty. He knew he could bring home a koodoo anytime he wanted. He was after something more. He wanted a trophy none other had taken as part of his Tokonn, and not just because none other had done it, but to test his own abilities to their utmost limit.

"Have you decided upon a beast?" his father asked carefully. They both knew Ty's questions about the Nil'Saur forest over the years had left his father uneasy.

"Not quite," Ty replied as easily as he could, hoping his father wouldn't press the matter. It wasn't quite a lie, but part of the truth would fetch him a beating before he ever set out on his Tokonn. It would all depend on if he could truly muster enough courage to cross the river into the forbidden Nil'Saur. "I thought I might travel into the forest and let Amarassa guide my hand...and my spear...to whatever suitable beast crossed my path."

"Our faith leads us to our destiny," his father intoned, his eyes closed.

"Faith and Destiny," Ty and his mother repeated in the way of their people.

His father reached out and gripped Ty's wrist. The grip tightened. And tightened. Ty's eyes widened as his father's grip bordered on painful. Their eyes met, and there was iron in his father's eyes.

"If you go to the Nil'Saur and return, you will be beaten. If you do not return, you will be dead."

"I am aware of these truths, Father," Ty said.

His father nodded once, his eyes narrowing, then drew his hand back.

"Will you finish the weapon tomorrow?"

"I believe it will take two or perhaps three more days," Ty replied. "I will fold it one hundred times, and this new metal is hard. Once I quench it, I will test the temper, and if it passes, I would like your leave to undertake my Tokonn."

His father stiffened once again. They both knew Ty preferred to take the harder path, the one more dangerous but with greater reward. He'd always been that way.

"Do you swear before Amarassa to remember all I have passed on to you?"

"I do, Father."

"Do you swear to honor your mother and I with courage, honor, and strength?"

"I do, Father."

"Do you swear to uphold the laws passed down to our people?"

"I do, Father."

His father met his gaze once again, and there was a gentleness there, hidden deep within the mettle father had passed on to son.

"Then you have my leave to undertake the Tokonn. You must return two days after you set out, or not return at all. Do you swear to abide by the Law of the Tokonn?"

"I swear, Father."

"Amarassa go with you, then."

Ty bowed his head in thanks and tried to keep the satisfied smile off his face. He glanced at his mother and saw the worry there. It seemed both of them knew him well—they just didn't know he was contemplating going after a rhakha.

* * *

Ty paddled up the narrow stream, his hand-carved oar silent as the cured skin of his canoe cut through a gentle current. He was many miles from home, on the wrong side of the river, and deep in the forbidden wetlands of the Nil'Saur Forest.

A canopy of trees cut off most of the late-morning light, leaving the thick forest a gloomy pattern of mottled shadows and pale streaks of sunshine. As he slipped beneath the canopy, he scanned the nearby banks for the telltale signs of a rhakha, preferably an adolescent. He'd picked a narrow stream for just that reason. If he encountered an adult, he'd have no chance. Adult rhakha were far too large to navigate the rivulet beneath him.

He pressed himself into the bottom of his canoe and slid beneath a thick, overhanging branch, ever watchful for any one of a dozen creatures that could kill him with their deadly venom. The Nil'Saur was forbidden for good reason. As he rose up again, he spied what he'd been looking for. Off to his right, a few yards ahead, the tall grasses along the riverbank had been pushed aside and crushed. It was the telltale passage of a rhakha, a large adolescent by the width of the trail it had left as it pulled itself out of the stream.

Ty gave a short backpaddle and brought the canoe to a stop, scanning both banks. Rhakha were territorial, slipping in and out of the water throughout their hunting grounds in search of prey. Their sinuous green bodies were eel-like, with thick, armored scales covering them from nose to tail tip. They had four powerful arms ending in long, bony fingers with fearsome claws. Their heads were truly horrific, with wide, gaping mouths full of long, sharp teeth, powerful jaws, and eyes set atop long, retractable stalks that they drew in when they attacked. Their hearing was exceptional, and they could see in both daylight and the murky darkness of river bottoms. Their keen sense of smell allowed them to track wounded prey at great distances, as well. They were the deadliest of predators in the forest. Fortunately, they weren't that common and rarely traveled beyond the borders of the Nil'Saur.

Ty carefully stood up in his canoe and scanned the knee-high sway grass beyond the banks along both sides of the river. There was only one rhakha trail cutting through the grass, and it disappeared off to the right. He would begin his hunt there. Glancing above him, he spied what he needed. He pulled himself along the overhanging branch and reached the edge of the river. It took him mere moments to toss his bow, quiver, and the newly fashioned hunting spear onto shore. He grabbed a coil of rope from the bottom of the canoe, stepped onto the riverbank, and threw the rope over a branch well above his head. Catching it as it came down, he stepped around the wide bole of the tree and hoisted the canoe out of the water until it dangled several feet above the surface. Tying it off, he slipped the strap of his quiver over his shoulder, checked the dagger at his waist, and picked up both his bow and the new hunting spear.

He was immeasurably proud of his latest creation and considered it easily the finest weapon he'd ever forged. The long, broad tip gleamed in a sliver of light shining down through the trees. The close-set lines of gray and black set into the silver metal revealed the care he'd taken in folding it over and over again. At the base of the blade, he'd shaped an edged crosspiece with sharp, dagger-like points angling forward. This would prevent the shaft from sinking in too far and give him purchase on his prey when he impaled it. He'd also used his *majea* to shape the haft into a long, conical receiver for the ironwood shaft he'd fashioned. Few blacksmiths were capable of manipulating the metal in such a fashion, but as his father had told him many times, he was destined to become one of the finest bladesmiths ever known.

The forest around him was silent save for a smattering of birds calling out, as well as a large insect in the tree directly above him, chittering with all the vigor of one looking to mate. He wished it the best of luck and then, hefting his spear, set off along the trail the rhakha had left. He threaded his way through the tall grass and dense foliage of the forest, doing his best to leave little or no sign of his passage.

The rhakha, on the other hand, hadn't been at all careful. Its long tail—Ty estimated it was at least ten feet long for what he guessed was no more than a six-foot-long body—had cut a deep, swishing swath through the underbrush. As he tracked the beast, he realized its passage wasn't in a straight line. It drifted left and right, sometimes turning sharply. At each turn, Ty found a yallaho bush that had been picked clean of its berries.

At the third such harvested bush, Ty paused for a moment, scratching his head. He examined the ground around the bush closely. The rhakha had definitely stopped there briefly. Ty kneeled down, inspecting the ground for any other sort of track. Its body had settled into the grass, and it had even turned around once before moving on.

That didn't make sense. Rhakha were carnivorous. They didn't eat berries. They ate meat and preferred live prey, although they weren't above eating carrion if they were hungry enough. Yet, the bush had been picked clean of berries that were useless to a rhakha and poisonous to humans.

There was only one answer. The rhakha was hunting something that was picking the berries. *But what?* As far as he knew, no humans lived in the Nil'Saur, and the rhakha kept the various races of water goblins out of the area. It had to be something else. A buck of some kind? He knew yallaho was poisonous to them as well. In fact, the berries were poisonous to just about everything.

Ty let out a long breath. Something else was going on here, and he wasn't sure if he wanted to know what. All he wanted to do was kill the rhakha, take its head, and go home. He would take as much meat as he could, but only so much would fit in his canoe. He considered turning around and finding the trail of another rhakha, but he'd come this far already.

A roaring hiss echoed through the forest, followed by the sound of something tearing into a tree trunk. It was the unmistakable sound of an enraged rhakha, and it sounded like it was only a few hundred yards off.

Ty rose. It was coming from roughly the direction the rhakha's trail had been going. The beast roared again, and the sounds of splintering wood increased.

It must have cornered whatever it was stalking, he thought.

Ty closed his eyes and prayed.

Great Amarassa, as you have always looked over my people, I ask that you look over me now as I seek to complete the Tokonn. I vow to remember all my father has taught me. I vow to keep my strength and not waver from my task. I vow, should I succeed, to serve my people and keep my faith above all.

Ty opened his eyes, tightened his grip on the spear, and headed straight for the enraged rhakha.

* * *

Ty exited the dense forest into an open field of sway grass dotted with thick tree trunks and low shrubs. On the far side rose a thick copse of massive trees, looking almost like an island amidst the grass. The sun and wind made shadows flow across the area like water.

Ty raced through tall grass, shifting nimbly around the occasional tree trunk shrub. He kept an eye out for patches of the shorter, dark green kella grass that ringed bogs throughout most of the river country, especially the Nil'Saur. The ground was soft beneath his feet, but firm enough he didn't fear sinking in. He no longer cared if he left tracks. As territorial as rhakha were, the one roaring and tearing into timber ahead of him would be the only one for at least a half-mile.

If it's focused on its prey, it won't sense me coming.

A second, deeper roar echoed through the forest. It could only be the angry challenge of an adult rhakha. He couldn't believe it. An adult had apparently challenged the smaller one for dominance over the territory. The sound of the larger beast shook the leaves, and he felt it in his bones. The terrifying roar was followed by the pained shriek of a lesser rhakha that quickly cut off.

Again, the sound of timber getting ripped to pieces echoed through the forest, but it was louder now, as if the grandfather of all rhakhas was tearing the grandfather of all trees asunder. It was very close now, and its roaring pressed in on his ears.

Ty spotted a patch of kella grass and leapt over the six-foot swath at a dead run. The sound was coming from within the dense grove of trees ahead. He ran another hundred yards and entered the thick copse of trees.

As the interior of the grove finally came into view, he came to a skidding halt.

As he'd feared, there was not one but two rhakha inside what appeared to be an unnaturally round grove of immense trees. It was an almost perfect circle, and within was a thick carpet of moss that covered the entire area. He'd never seen anything like it, but that wasn't what had forced him to stop and hide behind a tree trunk.

On the far side were the rhakhas. The smaller lay on its side, lifeless, with a massive bite taken out of its back, just above its shoulders. It looked as if it had been cast aside by the largest rhakha Ty had ever even heard of. Its tail, nearly twenty-five feet long, thrashed back and forth, digging great furrows into the moss and soil beneath. Its body was almost twelve feet long, and its four clawed arms were longer than Ty's body. Its gaping maw held dagger-like teeth six inches long and looked large enough to swallow Ty whole.

Its powerful upper arms had latched onto the thick roots of a giant tree, while its lower arms ripped and tore into the ground beneath. Splinters, branches, and roots lay scattered everywhere, and its lashing tail had dug a furrow through the soggy turf of the forest. It reared its head back and roared in what sounded like frustration. Whatever it was hunting had taken refuge beneath the tree, somehow, and it was desperate to tear its way down to its meal.

There's no way I can kill this beast, Ty thought.

He was about to turn and run for his life, when the massive rhakha jammed one of its muscled arms into the hole it had dug.

There was a sound of splintering wood, and then it yanked its arm out and threw something behind it into the grove. Ty's eyes went wide when he realized what it was. There was no mistaking the wreckage of what had once been an intricately carved wooden chair, with colored stones set into it and a finely woven mesh of hide strips.

The rhakha reached into the hole again and seemed to root around for a moment before there was another crunch of splintering wood. It yanked out another chair, similar to the first, and tossed the remains behind it.

Ty couldn't imagine a human living in a hole beneath a tree, but there were many tribes of the Bhirtas'Vuoda who might live in such a place. They came in many shapes and sizes, some possessed of legs and webbed feet, while others had tails like fish, or even eels like the tail of the rhakha. Some were friendly, and some were not. Some spent their entire lives in water, and some didn't.

Regardless, Ty's duty was clear. It was just as his father had taught him…and Amarassa required of him: one does not leave the helpless to die. Such dishonor was not a thing to be tolerated by the Sakari.

The rhakha reared back, roaring out its fury and frustration, then it tore into the base of the tree once again. If there was someone in there—and Ty believed there had to be—he needed a plan. If he simply stepped out into the grove and challenged the rhakha, he'd be torn to pieces and eaten. His bow would have no effect on the thick, armored scales of the monster, and his spear, which he was mostly certain could pierce its armor, would do him little good if he was merely snatched off the ground and eaten.

So how can I kill it?

His eyes traced along the bole of the tree beside him, up into the lower branches, and out across a long, overhanging branch that spanned two thirds of the grove and ended above the rhakha. Rhakha had small brains set far back inside their thick skulls, just above the top ridge of spines that ran down their backs. It would be a long way, and his timing would have to be perfect, but it was the only way he would have any chance at all. Everything or nothing in a single stroke. That was how one completed the Tokonn...with courage, honor, and strength.

With the rhakha raging only a short distance away, Ty slipped his quiver up over his head and dropped it and the bow to the ground. He then slid the shaft of his spear down his back, hooking the cross piece into the collar of his tunic, and pulled himself up the tree along several branches as quietly as he could. When he was high enough, he scrambled around the trunk, stepped quickly out onto the branch he wanted, and pulled the spear out.

The rhakha tore away one of the thick roots it had been clutching, widening the hole it was ripping into the earth beneath the tree, and then jammed its large, tooth-filled maw into the hole. It was the perfect opportunity.

Ty hesitated for only a moment, knowing if he missed his mark, he would certainly die. He stepped away from the trunk and put on a burst of speed, running along the thick branch as he reversed the grip on his spear.

Ty planted a foot on the branch, felt it sink beneath him, and then heaved, letting his momentum and the force of the branch springing back lift him forward and up as he raised the spear above his head. Time slowed. He eyed his mark as he sailed through the air, tensing his muscles for what would have to be a perfect strike. At the last instant, he planted his feet on the rhakha's broad shoulders, and the impact shoved the rhakha's head deeper into the hole. Ty thrust down with the spear, aiming for the base of its skull.

The rhakha grunted as its toothy face hit bottom.

The blade of the spear disappeared into the back of the rhakha's neck with a jarring jolt as it cut through flesh and bone. The spiked flanges sank into the crosspiece, jarring the weapon sharply up along Ty's arms. The rhakha gave out a piercing shriek of agony. Its body convulsed from tail-tip to head and flung Ty skyward.

He managed to keep hold of the spear shaft and landed hard on the rhakha's back, straddling it like a horse. Lancing pain shot through his groin at the impact as one of its spines jammed through the meaty part of his inner thigh.

Ty screamed but grabbed on tighter, wrapping his legs around the monster's thick neck as it lurched beneath him again and again. Its body twisted mid-air, flailing wildly, as its upper arms swung back over its head to get at whatever had impaled it.

Ty ducked beneath its grasp and gave his spear a vicious twist. The rhakha's body convulsed again with a shriek of pain. As Ty tried to ride the wave passing along the monster's body, he was slammed into an upper branch. The world flickered black. He vaguely felt himself flying through the air, followed by a distant thud as his body crashed into a tree trunk and dropped onto a patch of thick moss.

He opened his eyes, his vision blurry, and saw only the green canopy above. High up in the trees, amidst the branches and leaves, he though he saw a pair of strange golden-green eyes staring down at him. The eyes blinked slowly once as the rhakha's thrashing seemed to draw closer to him. The beast wasn't dead. He knew he would be the rhakha's next meal. He'd failed in his Tokonn, and he was about to die. As consciousness faded, he sent both his thanks to Amarassa for his life and an apology to his father for such a dreadful failure.

The world went black.

* * *

Consciousness came to Ty slowly.

First, his head felt like it was going to come apart, and he let out a groan. Through that pain, he slowly became aware of his situation. The air was moist and cool. It must be night, which meant he'd been unconscious for hours. There was a strange scent upon the air, that of cooking meat, and it made his mouth water. His shoulders ached, and as he shifted, he winced as a sharp pain lanced up his arm. He realized the ground beneath him was neither grass nor soil. It felt more like the lightly furred hide of a koodoo buck. That notion confused him. He'd brought no such hide with him, and he hadn't been conscious enough to even stand, let alone lie down upon a hide he didn't possess. He slowly opened his eyes to the deep darkness of the Nil'Saur at night, but with a pale, shifting light illuminating a ring of thick tree trunks and a thick canopy above him. Was he still in the grove?

Amidst the trees, he saw the glint of eyes, like those he'd seen before he'd passed out, but there were many pairs above him, not just one, and they were hidden amongst the greenery, as if the trees had somehow grown eyes that peered down at him.

"*It wakes.*"

Ty blinked several times. He'd heard the words, but not with his ears, and the words weren't his. Was he going mad?

"*We should kill it, ShakTi,*" a different voice filtered into his mind. "*Meat should not be wasted.*"

Ty's eyes went wide in shocked fear.

"Not yet, KroSoon," the first voice said with a hint of impatience, *"if at all. We must learn. ChulaKai breathes because of this one. There is a Debt."*

"The Law is paramount. The Outside must never know." KroSoon's words carried with them both anger and fear.

"I know the Law," ShakTi replied with iron. *"I am its teller. The Debt can take precedence. We must learn, as it is written, and letting this one live would not be the first time."*

Ty turned his head to the side and gasped in fear.

A small fire burned only a few feet away, and over it a large chunk of meat sat on a spit made of tree branches. Beyond that, staring straight at him, were two creatures the likes of which he'd never seen. They crouched on the other side of the fire, staring at him intently. One of them was about five feet tall if it rose to its full height, and the one beside it, nearly identical in appearance, was half its size.

Its green body was covered with branches and twigs that seemed to have grown out of its skin somehow. It had long, slim arms ending in strong-looking hands with long, bony fingers. Its legs, folded underneath it, looked powerful, as if it was capable of leaping great distances. Amidst the branches covering it was a large head—impossibly large for the size of its body—with almost no neck, a wide mouth, and huge, bulging eyes set atop an emotionless face. Draped around its thick, meaty neck was a necklace of intricately carved wooden beads and a single teardrop-shaped blue stone that gleamed opalescent in the firelight. It was a mighty pearl taken from one of the mollusks that lived in the river ways. The smaller creature had a similar necklace, although the pearl was half the size, with a pinkish hue.

Beyond them both lay the bodies of the two dead rhakha, and a chunk of meat had been cut from the body of the smaller one. The meat over the fire had come from there. He focused again on the two creatures who squatted across the fire from him. They looked like the goddess Amarassa had crossed men with frogs, or perhaps toads. Neither Ty's father nor anyone in his village had ever even hinted that such creatures existed.

The large creature held Ty's spear, the butt of the weapon in the ground, and it seemed to be leaning against it lightly. Ty's dagger lay on the ground beside it. As it met Ty's gaze with those large eyes, its head cocked to the side.

"*Do you feel my words?*" ShakTi asked.

"I do," Ty replied. "But how? I hear nothing but the forest."

"*The voice of the X'in'Kutal has not been heard since before the Sundering. Our thoughts are our words.*"

The statement made little sense. Ty guessed the X'in'Kutal were the creatures that seemed to be all around him, but he had no idea what the Sundering was, nor why their voices couldn't or wouldn't be heard. He sat up slowly, not wanting to appear threatening. He winced in pain and realized a rhakha spine was stuck through his thigh. A green paste had been wadded up around the spine where it pierced his flesh, and it seemed to be keeping his blood from flowing out.

ShakTi stiffened as the great lids of its bulging eyes narrowed to mere slits. There was a shifting in the trees above, and Ty heard the creaking of bows being pulled taut.

"I have no intention of hurting you," Ty said, holding up his hands. "Not that I could if I wanted to. I'm not even sure I can get up off the ground right now."

"Yes, the beast you killed nearly took your life in exchange. We have stopped the bleeding...for now." ShakTi seemed to relax somewhat. It raised a hand, and the bows above creaked again as the strain on them was released. *"Know this: I will question you, and we will sense any deceit. A single lie and your life will be forfeit. Do you understand?"*

Ty swallowed hard. He had no intention of lying to them. His people didn't do that. However, if they misunderstood him, or if he tried to dance around the truth like he had with his father, they might just fill him with arrows and be done with it.

"What brought you to the X'in'Kutal?" ShakTi asked.

"If I understand what you mean, nothing brought me to you and your people," Ty replied, letting out a weak breath. He was going to be as careful as he could with his answers. "At least, not directly. I didn't know the...X'in'Kutal...even existed until I opened my eyes a few moments ago. I came to the Nil'Saur forest to slay a rhakha."

"The beast." ShakTi settled back slightly on his haunches. *"You came to take one of the great hunters of the forest."*

Ty nodded. "I came to take the smaller one for my Tokonn—the rite of passage that ushers me into adulthood among my people. I didn't expect to encounter two of them, and certainly not an adult."

"We have a similar custom." ShakTi reached up and scratched beneath his wide chin. *"It is called the VaSukai."*

"End this," KroSoon said from somewhere above. Ty was getting a sense of how their thoughts—their *words*, as ShakTi had put it— worked. He could feel the animosity and fear above him, not as any sort of sense he possessed, but as the recipient of their thoughts and feelings. He'd never felt anything like it. *"Not only is the human a trespasser, it is a thief,"* KroSoon added.

ShakTi, the creature holding Ty's spear, looked sharply up at a pair of eyes in the tree above.

"It is, at worst, an ignorant hunter, and while that may require we end its life, there is still the Debt." Ty still didn't hear the words, but he understood ShakTi was frustrated by the other's impatience. It returned its gaze to him. *"You say you didn't expect to find an adult."*

"Yes," Ty replied. "I only wanted one of the younger ones. They're dangerous enough, and only a fool would hunt an adult rhakha alone."

"You're not wrong. Are you saying you're a fool?"

"I wasn't hunting the adult. I followed the smaller one here and hoped to slay it with the spear you hold."

ShakTi glanced at the spear in its hand and then returned its gaze to Ty, blinking its eyes slowly. It seemed as if it were pondering Ty's words carefully.

"And yet, you did what you did. We saw…from above. You risked your life to take the adult." Again, ShakTi tilted its head to the side. *"I find myself asking why."*

"I had no choice," Ty replied. He was confused, though. They'd been watching…?

"No choice?" ShakTi asked. *"You could have left ChulaKai's grove—"* it motioned toward the smaller creature beside it, *"—and run far from here to hunt a smaller rhakha elsewhere.*

"Honestly, I was about to," Ty said a bit sheepishly, "but when I saw the rhakha tearing out chairs and a blanket, I knew it was after something other than an animal. My people don't let others perish when danger threatens them. We help."

"But you don't know the X'in'Kutal."

"It doesn't matter," Ty replied simply. "At least not to the Sakari. I don't need to know a person or a people to feel obligated to help."

"That has not been our experience with humans." There was an edge in ShakTi's words. *"There are those who even hunt us."*

"I'm sorry," Ty said, meaning it. "I don't know what humans you've encountered, but I doubt it was a member of the Sakari. We'd never hunt intelligent beings for sport, and we're not at war. What's more, we consider the Nil'Saur forest to be forbidden, so my people generally don't come here. At least, I know of none who have."

"And yet you are here."

Ty felt a pang of guilt and embarrassment flow through him. When it came right down to it, he'd disobeyed his father, and done so knowingly. That was bad enough, but he'd found a race of beings that might very well kill and eat him. He was beginning to understand much better why the Nil'Saur was forbidden.

"True," Ty finally admitted, "but for my Tokonn, I wanted to do something none other had. A rhakha would have been a mighty achievement, and I was willing to take my father's beating if I succeeded, or die out here if I failed."

"Why?"

Ty's eyes widened. He hadn't been expecting such a question, and as he thought about it, he wasn't sure he knew. Heartbeats passed as he considered it. "I suppose because I believed I could...because I've always tried to do better than those before me...not to beat their achievements, but achieve for myself. It's just the way I've always been." He shrugged. It was as good a reason as he was likely to come up with, and having answered, he realized he knew a little bit more about himself than he had a moment before.

"You said the Nil'Saur was forbidden. Have you also always broken your own laws?"

Ty stiffened. "I've never broken the laws of the Sakari," he replied defensively, "nor those laid down by our goddess Amarassa. It's not against our laws to come here, only something to be avoided because of the danger. It's a thing fathers use to scare their children with."

ShakTi looked up to the trees again.

"It has courage, and it deliberately intervened on behalf of ChulaKai, even though it knew nothing of our people. Do any sense deceit in its words?"

For long moments, there was no reply.

Finally, KroSoon's words drifted down, *"The Law is the law. It hunted in our lands and would have taken—"*

"Did you sense deceit?" ShakTi asked sternly.

Several heartbeats slipped past.

"No," KroSoon finally replied.

"Then we have an honorable act of courage that saved a member of the tribe, creating a Debt. The Law is clear. It's earned its life, if it agrees to take the Vow."

"What vow?" Ty asked, suddenly concerned they might ask him to do something bad. "I wouldn't break any of my own laws, but I'll otherwise make any vow you require of me. I truly wish you and your people no harm, and I'd be happy to leave this place, if that's your wish."

"I believe you, but there's more to it than just the Vow. It's our custom that you keep what you kill, but payment must be made to the tribe first…for the right to hunt in our territory."

"What sort of payment?" Ty asked. "Except for a canoe, you've seen all I possess…at least out here."

Is that how you intend to take your kill with you? ShakTi asked. *A rhakha is a large beast, indeed.*

"As I said, I'd only planned to kill a small rhakha. I would have taken the head of the smaller one as proof of my Tokonn and most of the meat for my family. I must admit, however, that I wouldn't have been able to take it all. Some would have been left for the forest to reclaim. My people don't believe in wasting a kill, if we can help it." An idea popped into Ty's head. "If you like, you're welcome to take the meat as payment."

ShakTi cocked its head to the side again.

"*I think you misunderstand me. The large rhakha killed the smaller one, making that its kill. You killed the larger one, making both yours to do with as you please.*"

Ty's eyes went wide. He'd fully expected that the larger one would go to the X'in'Kutal.

"ShakTi, as payment, I would gladly give you all the meat. All I really require is the smaller rhakha head. I came to complete my Tokonn, and I've done that. It matters little which head I bring back, and to be honest, I don't believe I could get the larger one into my canoe."

ShakTi looked up to the trees. There was a long silence, although Ty felt a strange sensation, as if words...or thoughts...were being exchanged by the X'in'Kutal without him knowing what they were saying.

"*The X'in'Kutal accept payment in the form of the large rhakha. It is more than enough to grant your passage into and out of our lands. You may do with the smaller one as you see fit. That leaves only the Vow.*"

"What is it?"

"Using our majea, we shall bind your thoughts as you speak the Vow. You must swear to never speak of the X'in'Kutal for so long as you live, and never reveal to any outsider what you have seen here, or even that we exist. Once bound, breaking this Vow will result in your death. Will you agree?"

"Of course," Ty said without hesitation. "If there are humans who hunt you, then the best way to protect yourselves is to remain hidden."

ShakTi's head tilted to the side again, and it peered at Ty for a long time. *"You surprise me. You have wisdom beyond your years."*

Ty blushed and gave ShakTi a slight smile. "I like to think my parents raised me well, and the teachings of Amarassa are clear on such matters," he replied. He was humbled by the strange creature's words, but he also felt a well of pride. He suddenly wished he'd be able to tell his father of this day, but he understood the need.

"Indeed," ShakTi said. *"May I have the honor of your name?"*

"I'm Ty Kotha, born of my father Sarat and my mother Keeley. They would be honored to hear your words."

"Well, then, Ty Kotha," ShakTi said, stepping closer, *"are you ready to take the Vow?"*

"I am," Ty said. A sudden pang of worry hit him. "Will what you're about to do hurt?"

ShakTi held out his hand, his palm only inches from Ty's forehead.

"Not even if you break the Vow." It placed its hand on Ty's head and closed its large eyes. Ty felt a strange sensation, a warmth and tingle that seemed to flow from ShakTi's hand through his head, and down across his neck and shoulders. It wasn't uncomfortable, let alone painful. For a flicker of a moment, he felt ShakTi's thoughts. He saw a flash of images—the forest, the rhakhas, ChulaKai—and then he

felt the thoughts of others. He couldn't count them, but he felt that they were the others in the trees above. All of them had joined their thoughts with ShakTi. "*Now, speak the Vow,*" ShakTi said.

Ty drew in a slow breath, trying to remember what ShakTi had said. "I swear to never speak of the X'in'Kutal for so long as I live. I will never reveal to any outsider what I have seen here, or even that you and your people exist. Once bound, I know that breaking this Vow will result in my death. I swear it on my life, my family, and upon Amarassa, from which all things flow."

A sharp tingle coursed through Ty's body. He felt no different, but he knew deep down that if he broke the Vow, he would, indeed, die.

ShakTi pulled his hand away and stepped back, the pendant around his neck gleaming. "*It is done.*"

"ShakTi," Ty said, "I was wondering about something."

"*What is that?*"

"You said before that you were watching me, which meant you were watching the rhakha tear into that den to get at ChulaKai. Is there a reason you didn't try to kill it yourselves?"

"*A fair question. There are two reasons, actually.*" ShakTi glanced at the smaller creature beside him. "*Our dens are deep, and it was unlikely even the adult rhakha could reach her. There's always a risk, but she needed to feel the fear. She disobeyed me this morning and went gathering berries when she shouldn't have. That created this lesson for her. Fear is the best teacher of all, after pain.*"

"That's true enough," Ty conceded. "What's the other?"

ShakTi's thoughts took on an almost sad feeling. "*Our arrows cannot pierce the armor of large rhakha. We must, therefore, hide from them. When I saw your weapon pierce the adult so readily, I must admit, I was envious. Such a weapon would be of great benefit to our people, but we lack both the metal and the skill."* ShakTi held out Ty's spear. *"You have taken the Vow, and I believe it is now time to return this to you. I will be able to heal your leg, as well, so that you may return to your canoe and home once again."*

Ty smiled. "Would you consider a trade?" Ty asked. "My spear for that necklace of yours?"

ShakTi's head tilted to the side. *"What would you do with such a thing?"*

Ty let out a long breath. "Because of the Vow, I will only have my memories of this day. I can never tell anyone about it, other than that I slew a rhakha, and I must bury the head once my Tokonn is accepted by the council. The necklace would be a keepsake for me, something to mark this day. I would simply tell my people I encountered traders during my Tokonn." Another idea popped into his head. "Although, now that I say it, do your people make such necklaces regularly?"

"We do," ShakTi replied. *"They are trinkets to us only, but the mollusks of the rivers often have these stones inside."*

"Then, would you consider making more of them and trading them for arrowheads made of the same metal the spear is made of? I could come back from time to time and exchange the arrowheads for the necklaces. Your people might be safer if they could kill rhakha."

ShakTi looked up to the trees. *"What say you all? You have felt the mind of this one and know his heart. His offer would make the X'in'Kutal stronger. Is there a dissent?"*

Ty expected the thoughts of KroSoon to slam down from above, but there was only silence and the chirping of insects in the forest.

"It is agreed, then," ShakTi said. He lifted the necklace over his broad head and held it out. Ty took it and was astonished at how

intricate the carving was. The patterns and shapes in the wood held the smallest details, and the pearlescent gem gleamed in the firelight. ShakTi hefted the hunting spear, tested its weight, and then handed it to ChulaKai.

"You should find that the metal doesn't rust, either," Ty said. "It'll take me a while to get more ore, but now that I know what's required, I'll be able to make such things whenever I want. How can I find you once I have the arrowheads?"

"*Return to this place and light a fire. Within a day, one of us will see it and come to you.*"

"I will," Ty said. "It may be several months, but I'll return, alone, with the arrowheads."

"*Then let us feast,*" ShakTi said. "*There's plenty of rhakha to eat, and we must still heal that leg of yours.*"

"How will you do that?"

"*It's not unlike what we did when you took the Vow, only we'll affect your body, not your mind.*"

"Then let's eat," Ty said. "I'm starving."

* * *

Ty stood next to his father as they watched the village elders disappearing down the path away from his home. There'd been raised eyebrows when they first saw what he'd slain for his Tokonn, and a few of them glanced at Ty's father with eyes that insisted on the beating all Sakari received if they entered the Nil'Saur. When the last of the elders was out of sight, Ty's father placed a firm hand on his shoulder and stared into Ty's eyes.

"Are you prepared for your punishment?" he asked.

"I am, Father."

"Hands on the shed," his father said firmly.

Ty nodded and walked over to the shed where their forge, anvil, and other tools were stored. He placed his hands high on the wall, leaning forward slightly. His father grabbed the thick switch leaning against the shed. It had been years since his father had needed to punish him, but he was happy to take it. He'd completed his Tokonn, and nothing could ever take that away.

Ty glanced over his shoulder and spotted his mother looking out the window, a worried look upon her face. He gave her a smile and a simple nod to say that it was alright.

"This gives me no pleasure," his father said gently, "and I want you to know that I'm proud of you for how you completed your rite. Your courage and skill have surpassed my greatest hopes."

"Thank you, Father," Ty replied. "It was your teaching and the lessons of Amarassa that made it possible." Ty thought back to his experiences with the X'in'Kutal, and a smile crossed his lips. Everything about those events would stay with him for the rest of his life, and he looked forward to seeing them again.

"Ready yourself," his father said, raising the switch high over his head.

Ty closed his eyes and waited. Heartbeats passed. What was his father waiting for?

Moments later, he felt the switch laid gently across his shoulders, and then it was gone. He heard the switch leaned against the shed, followed by his father's footsteps moving away. Confusion filled him. He turned his head around, keeping his hands against the shed, and saw his father standing over the canoe where the adolescent rhakha head sat in front of large slabs of its flesh wrapped in hide.

He met his father's gaze, and there was no anger there.

"Help me unload this so your mother can work with the food you've brought home for us," his father said, a strange look upon his face. "There's much here to be roasted, smoked, and turned into jerky. We must also bury the head so none know of your victory."

"Father?" Ty asked, turning around.

His father stared at him for several heartbeats as a slim smile slowly spread across his face.

"How could I beat you for completing the Tokonn in exactly the same way I did? You're not the first, son."

Ty gave his father a surprised smile. He'd never imagined his father had been willing to endure punishment by braving the Nil'Saur. His father had always been stoic and practical. In that moment, Ty understood his father better—at least a little. He walked over. Together, they lifted the rhakha meat, each large chunk wrapped in a wide swath of scaly rhakha hide, out of the canoe and carried it into the house. It didn't take long, and when they were done, they both stood over the canoe. His father reached down and grabbed a folded-up piece of hide. As he did, ShakTi's necklace fell out and dropped to the ground.

Ty's eyes went wide as his father turned surprised eyes toward his son. His father picked up the necklace and handed it to him.

"Follow me," his father said, a curious smile upon his face. He turned and headed into the house, Ty following close behind. They moved through the house and into his parents' bedroom. There was a large bed against one wall, a tall cabinet for clothes to the side, and a low table opposite the bed where a wide mirror sat. At the foot of the bed was a large wooden chest Ty knew held his father's most prized possessions. He'd been taught to never go into it, and in his whole life, he never had.

His father opened the chest and rummaged around. He pulled out a suit of hard leather armor, dyed black, with a strange yellow crest embossed on the chest piece, and laid it on the bed. Ty didn't recognize the crest and wondered where the armor had come from. His father then pulled out a longsword and matching dagger, and set them beside the armor. Finally, he pulled out a piece of heavy cloth and carefully unfolded it. Ty gasped when he saw what was contained within.

His father held out a long necklace of intricately carved wooden beads with a shimmering, pearlescent yellow pendant at the bottom. It had obviously been crafted by the X'in'Kutal, but the patterns were somewhat different from the one Ty held.

"Vows can never be broken," his father said.

* * * * *

Quincy J. Allen Biography

Quincy J. Allen is a national bestselling, cross-genre author with a growing list of novels and short story publications to his credit. His novel works include steampunk fantasy, military science fiction, military fantasy, and a post-apocalyptic media tie-in, all of which have been received to critical acclaim. Going in several directions at once, he is actively engaged in new novels in five different universes, including two of his own. He is one of five Founders of the *Eldros Legacy* and hopes to devote a good portion of each writing year to that property. Working from his home in Charlotte, North Carolina, he continues striving to create great new fiction for his growing list of fans.

You can find him at QuincyAllen.com or follow his exploits on Facebook at both facebook.com/Quincy.Allen.Author and facebook.com/QJABooks.

* * * * *

Trust Not the Trickster
by Jamie Ibson

An Eldros Legacy Story

The sun had blessedly set, taking with it the scorching rays that sent lesser creatures scrambling for their burrows and dens.

Truth be told, Ka'Deryn had sought refuge himself. It was a hot one today. He'd slung his hammock under the generous limbs of his favorite river birch along the gentle banks of the Ramar River and dozed off. The shaman woke as the sun set, and he gave thanks to Kari'Maro for the bounty of fresh-caught spiny catfish he pulled from his net. With the deft expertise of long practice, he cleaned them quickly, sliced them into cubes, and dashed them with a pinch of Ka'Roklin's homemade finspice. The fragrant white meat skewers went over an open flame, and Ka'Deryn moistened his throat with a swig of mead from his skin.

He moved upwind so dinner wouldn't affect his senses as it sizzled, and he tasted the breeze. It seemed Kari'Maro favored him—it was a good night to hunt.

The Doompelt Walkers tended to be most active in the cooler evenings and the early morning, and Ka'Deryn was no exception. If he was going to reach the snares he'd set by full dark, there was no time for dawdling. He chomped down on one of his skewers and drew it out between his canines. He stripped the tender, flaky meat free, chewed twice, and swallowed it back with the last of his mead. He descended the banks of the river, filled his skin with the cool water, and whispered a quiet urging to purify the drink. Again, he gave thanks.

The hammock and skins went into his pack, and he took a quick dip in the river. He had a long lope ahead of him, and the waters would help keep him cool in the evening heat. Once out, he shook himself and stripped the other half of the meat off the skewers for his coconspirator, Koreus. The lazy bum still snored beneath the tree, and probably would for a while yet.

Ka'Deryn cinched the straps of his pack, put the sun at his left flank, and set out at a brisk, loping pace. An hour later, his endurance began to flag. He cast his senses about and detected an invasive patch of jiandimar weed a quarter-mile distant.

Two days earlier, he'd have cursed the weed. They were noxious, unwelcome invaders from beyond the mountains to the southeast. Not unlike the humans of Pelinon in that regard. When the weeds put down roots, they claimed the territory for all time and resented any pushback by the native flora.

Ka'Deryn veered toward the weeds. It was still early in the season; their burnished bronze flowers had only just started to bloom and hadn't yet become the white fluffs carried by the wind, bypassing grassland grazers, wherever they could catch a ride. In that sense, they too were like the humans.

There. The stalks' root went deep and had leeched the soil of its nutrients such that the grasses wouldn't grow in a patch now a dozen paces across. He'd put a stop to that. The shaman cut his pace short and walked into the circle of jiandimar blossoms, breathing deep, but not hard. It helped him calm the beating of his heart and draw upon the gifts Kari'Maro had given him.

But only for a moment.

He shut his eyes, splayed his fingers, and *felt* for each of the noxious, all-consuming floral stalks. As he'd suspected, they were all linked together deep beneath the soil from a single taproot. Just ripping the heads off the stalks would do no good. Not even ripping it out by the root would do—the roots went two or three feet down before they produced mature flowers.

The shaman began at the outside of the ring, found the *Ka* that went down beneath the soil, and snuffed it out. He circled, cutting each of the roots off from the bulb, and soaked in that energy, reinvigorating himself a little each time. When the largest of the jiandimar stalks was all that remained beneath his feet, he traced it down to the root, and from the root to the bulb. He reached into the bulb itself and closed his spiritual fist around it, crushing it entirely. The life energy flowed back, and Ka'Deryn's fur *sang* as though electrified by another midnight thunderstorm.

The weed blackened immediately and fell to ash as though scorched. Ka'Deryn was shaman, curator, gardener, and warden all in one. It was a rare thing for him to harness Kari'Maro's gifts for outright destruction, but jiandimar weeds had their place—on the far side of the mountain—and the grasses would reclaim this spot, eventually. That he was now energized as though he'd slept the whole night through was a convenient side effect, nothing more.

Ka'Deryn redoubled his pace. The golden hues of the sun setting far beyond Kari'Ghos Bay had faded through reds, purples, and now the deep indigo of night was truly upon him. He navigated as much by memory as by feel. His feet remembered each hillock, each crest as he strode up the rolling hills and down again. At last, the foreign lights of the human forts twinkled on the horizon like distant fireflies.

The human fortresses perched above the valley floor like a hawk might survey a field from atop an oak. The fortresses themselves were predatory edifices carved into the very faces of the rock. They, and their seven brothers and sisters all along the eastern mountains, all too frequently promised violence, war, and death. The Doompelt Walkers patrolled these lands and held the humans in check, just as Ka'Deryn stamped out any weed blight that might have caught a ride across the mountains with a supply train.

The Walkers' shaman gauged the bearing to the mountain keeps, veered right, and found the footpath the invaders had used each of the last three nights. It paralleled the riverbank and emerged from the tall grasses by the shallow ford that crossed the river onto the Pelinese side. Forty paces more, and he found the first snare, still tightened into a little wire knot, just as he'd left it that morning.

Good. The humans haven't returned in my absence. He suspected as much. The humans thought the shadows of the night hid them from his senses, wholly ignorant of just how well Ka'Deryn's eyes pierced that veil. The second snare reflected the faintest hint of starlight, and so did the third. The fourth…all were as he'd set them.

Ka'Deryn retreated behind a thatch wall of scythegrass and hid his passage, so no bent stalks or crumpled leaves betrayed him. He reclined, closed his eyes, and let his ears take over. Gnats buzzed, and his ear flicked, but there was nothing to be done about the tiny bugs. A savvy tracker might notice them, but if the string of snares was any indication, these humans were anything but savvy.

Half the night passed, and the moon was high overhead when the snap of a branch betrayed the humans. Ka'Deryn's lips curled back in a toothy smile, but he didn't rise. Not yet. The rhythmic crunch of their hobnailed boots allowed him to track their approach as clearly as if he'd been a night-sighted owl overhead. They paused.

"Aww, by the Giants, Kreese, I told ye! I told ye, didn't I? There's sommat out here, and it's found the snares. See?"

"Shut your gob, Grieg, I can't see nothin' in this dark, and you didn't want no torch, did ye? Blind as a bat, I am. Whatcha mean something found the snares?"

"Jus' what I said. The snare's been pulled tight, but nuffin's in-nit." A pause, with more crunching. "And so's this one! We should go. If it's one of those blasted Kari'Ma warriors, we'll be in so much trouble."

"What, you're more afraid of one of those mangy coyotes than Captain Hibersen?"

"Of course! You mean you're not? Hibersen might throw us in the stocks, or give us a whipping, but the Kari'Ma will *eat us alive.*"

Ka'Deryn nearly stood up. What had those fools in the fortresses been teaching the Pelinese about the Soo Kari'Ma? One didn't *eat* a human, or a Kapros, or even an Elwhari, no matter how much the latter looked like an overlarge plains grouse. It simply wasn't *done.*

No matter. Words are just words, whether spoken by the wisest shaman or the most ignorant pup. They'll learn soon enough.

"The third snare's just like the first two, Kreese. I'm telling you! We need to go, and we need to go now!"

Ka'Deryn willed them to continue on just a little bit further. Just a little more along the path. Don't let these fool poachers have a sudden attack of intelligence...

Snap!

"Somefin's got me!" the voice belonging to Grieg cried. "It's got me leg! Help me, damn you!"

"Awright, awright, keep yer knickers on. Lemme see," Kreese said.

Ka'Deryn flowed to his feet, threaded his way through the grass, and was upon them. He channeled a touch of Kari'Maro's gift, just enough to give his eyes a hint of glow. Kreese had his back to Ka'Deryn, with his head down, trying to work the snare loose.

The shaman cleared his throat. Grieg screamed. Kreese cursed, fell over on top of his co-conspirator, and the Kari'Ma loosed a feral howl that would carry for miles. When the shrill cry's echoes had faded, Ka'Deryn took a deep breath and wrinkled his nose. He'd even prepared a speech, but the air carried a new, acrid odor. He laughed and took another sniff—yep. There were *two* distinct odors coming from the men.

"Really? You *peed* yourselves? In unison?" The humans' eyes bulged, and the whites shone in the darkness like a full moon over a still pond. He laughed even harder.

Kreese collected his wits like a sheepdog collected sheep—that is to say, slowly, with much noise, and very little accomplished.

"Please…don't eat us."

"*Eat* you? What kind of a savage do you take me for?" Both wore blank looks of terror on their too-flat faces. Apparently, the Pelinese didn't speak Kari'Marese nearly as well as Ka'Deryn spoke Pelinese, so he switched tongues and tried again. "Barracks-tales to the contrary, the Soo Kari'Ma do not *eat* the sentient races." Grieg let out a deeply held sigh of relief, and Ka'Deryn leaned in close to grab the human by the beard. "But in the case of *poachers*, we have been known to make exceptions."

The shaman held Grieg's eyes for a moment, then barked in his face. "Tell me of this Captain Hibersen, Grieg? How is he likely to react to the news that two of his troops have caused an incident with the Soo Kari'Ma?"

"If you harm us, he's not likely to take it well at all," Grieg said. He mustered what little dignity and courage he had left. "Let us go, and you'll never see us again."

"Brave words from one whose guilt stains his trousers. No, I will not just let you go. You have trespassed each of these last three nights, treading on land that isn't yours to tread, setting snares for game that isn't yours to catch. I think we Soo Kari'Ma are better stewards of these lands than you could ever be, and I'll not have you steal what you could have traded for instead. I'll see you returned to that cave you call a home and have a word with your captain. Do you believe me when I say I could catch either of you in the dark should you run off?"

"Y-yes," Grieg stammered. Kreese nodded dumbly.

"Good. Know this: if one of you runs, you kill the other. The first one I catch, I will open your throat and let your lifeblood water the scythegrass. Then I will kill the runner and dump your corpse at the foot of the SunJim portcullis. A terrible way to suicide, don't you agree? Yes? Good."

Ka'Deryn found the long iron spike he'd set into the soil as the anchor for his snare and heaved it loose. He pulled Grieg to his feet, wrapped the length of wire around his waist once, and handed the human the spike. "Don't go swinging that around too hard, else you cut yourself in half."

Grieg whimpered. "You can't cut me loose?"

Ka'Deryn shook his head. "Do I look like I carry cutters for wire like that on me? Don't be daft. Your Captain Hibersen can decide when—*if*—to cut you loose. Now, let's revisit the only good idea you had all night, and return to the fortress."

* * *

A quarter mile from the footpath that led up the hills to the twin fortresses of Strakha SunJim and Strakha SunJo, Ka'Deryn called them to a halt.

"Why are we stopping?" Kreese whined. "It's just a little farther."

"Would you believe me if I said I just wanted you to walk most of the way back before I slaughtered you and left your corpses for your captain to find in the morning?" The looks of terror on the men's faces told Ka'Deryn all he needed to know. "You would? Good. I won't, but it's good to keep you on your toes. Now, no human-business, I'm lighting a torch so your guards don't fill us full of quarrels when we march up to the fortress gates in the middle of the night."

Ka'Deryn produced a cloth-wrapped bundle from his pack, and from the bundle he withdrew a cattail. They grew along the banks of the many creeks, streams, and rivers that flowed out of the mountains, and he quietly thanked Kari'Maro for her wisdom in planting such a useful reed in such abundance. He drew upon a sliver of her firetail hawk aspect, compressed it into a tiny spark, and lit the top of the oblong reed. It sputtered and smoked for a moment, then caught. Ka'Deryn breathed on it, feeding the flame life-wind until it blazed merrily. The shaman pulled up his hood, held the torch aloft, and gestured for his prisoners to continue.

A few minutes on, one of the soldiers atop the barbican hailed them. "Hold there, stranger! Strakha SunJim is closed for the night!" Ka'Deryn's heart sank. The guard wasn't human, but one of the Kapron, the wooly, horned mountain folk, and they held grudges for generations. The deep purple of the soldier's fur had blended to look like shadows, but now that he'd stepped into the light, Ka'Deryn wondered if perhaps he'd made a mistake.

It mattered not. In for a nek, in for sepik, as the Pelinese would say. Ka'Deryn threw his cloak's hood back to reveal his face in the torchlight. He knew what the guards would see, and he'd make no secret of it. The Soo Kari'Ma bore passing resemblance to some of the dogs the Pelinese kept. Not the baying, floppy-eared scent-hounds they used to find foxes and muskrats, though. The Kari'Ma were more akin to the lean, knife-eared coyotes that ranged the grasslands in packs.

His pointed ears stood proud atop his skull, and his muzzle didn't yet bear the grey fringe of an elder. His symbol of office gleamed in the cattail torchlight—a leather-wrapped bronze torc around his neck, with feathers and freshwater pearls hanging from it in strings. Unlike the torc's bright colors, his cloak, tunic, and tabard were a mottled blend of tans and browns, made darker by his brief dip in the river.

"I am Ka'Deryn Ko'Ryna Kallatock of the Doompelt Walker Clan. The Doompelt Walker Clan is duty bound to patrol the grasslands that border the Demon Spine Mountains and dissuade trespassers of both sides. Thus have my ancestors straddled the divide between Pelinon and Soo Kari'Ma since the last peace. Thus do I. These men are guilty of trespass. They set snares in my territory to poach and have given me the name of Captain Hibersen as their commander. Bring the commander out so that he may take custody of my prisoners."

"Bring him out?" the Kapros scoffed. "Bring him out? Who are you, cur, to make demands of the captain? Why should we not stitch your hide to the earth where you stand?"

"Does the colonel of the garrison not believe in honor anymore?" Ka'Deryn retorted. "I have kept the peace, and I have met my obligations under the treaty. How think you the rest of the garrison would treat you and yours, knowing Grieg and Kreese here died for no good cause? Or do you honestly believe you could kill me, a bearer of the torc, before I could finish these two off?"

Ka'Deryn yanked on the snare wire, eliciting a yelp from Grieg. He stepped behind Grieg, using the poacher's body as a shield, and let the moonlight fill his eyes again. When they glowed more brightly than his cattail torch, he threw his head back and filled his lungs. He howled, and with Kari'Maro's aid, it chorused as though he'd brought an entire war party with him. The volume ensured he'd wake every sleeping resident of the fortress, and perhaps those in SunJo, as well. As his howl echoed and faded across the valley, Ka'Deryn gazed at the fort and waited.

A tense minute passed, with neither side making a move. Troops rushed onto the elevated platform from both ends. By the cacophony, Ka'Deryn judged no one senior had yet taken command, so he ducked low behind his prisoner and made no other move. Then a baritone-voiced human strode onto the parapet, a gambeson and chain shirt over his nightclothes. "Is that your Captain Hibersen?" Ka'Deryn whispered in Grieg's ear.

"It is," he replied fearfully.

"Good. You may yet live out this night." Ka'Deryn raised his voice. "Captain Hibersen? I have something that belongs to you, but I would beg you to replace your Kapros guard with one who is rather less trigger happy first!"

"What do you want, dog?" Hibersen replied.

"To turn over prisoners without suffering a murder! Your Kapros thug threatened to, and I quote, 'stitch my hide to the earth where I stand,' when I approached unhidden to return your people unharmed! Rather awkward way to converse, wouldn't you say?"

The captain issued a few low orders, and the sheep-headed warrior left the barbican. Crossbows lowered, and Ka'Deryn reintroduced himself and his prisoners.

"And you wish to release them to us?" Hibersen asked.

Ka'Deryn bowed low. "I do."

When the shaman straightened up, Hibersen had already turned on his heel and was marching away. The portcullis ratcheted up, clank by steady clank, to the tune of the guardsmen's curses from above as they struggled with the winch. The captain emerged in his incongruous chain shirt and nightclothes. He clomped out in unfastened hobnail boots like those the prisoners wore, and Ka'Deryn struggled to keep a straight face. Two more soldiers who were rather more appropriately dressed flanked the captain. If he recalled his lessons properly, the younger one wore a lieutenant's stripe on his pauldron, and the older had the chevrons of an experienced sergeant.

He waited for the men to come to him. "Not that it's any of my business, Captain, but I must say I am concerned for your men's well-being. Guardsmen slipping away for a quick bit of foreign theft in the dead of night. Sheep-shagging arbalesters threatening your neighbor when he's come to return the aforementioned fools, *un-*

harmed, and you might have moon fever sweeping your camp, sir. It seems anyone still awake after dark transforms into an idiot."

Hibersen grimaced. "What's this about theft? They've stolen nothing."

"Not for lack of trying, Captain. Mister Kreese, what *exactly* were you in the process of doing when Mister Grieg found himself caught in the wire trap currently wrapped around his leg?"

Kreese shifted uncomfortably. "We was, uh, we was checking some game snares we'd set, Cap'n. The first three'd been tripped with nothing caught."

Hibersen cocked an eyebrow but said nothing. Ka'Deryn crossed his arms. "What was your catch last night, Mister Grieg?"

"Nuffin'," he said, and kicked at the dirt like a sullen child. "Ten snares, all ten were tripped, nuffin' innem."

"You had *ten* snares set, they were all tripped, and you went back again? Into enem—ahem. Into foreign territory?" Hibersen corrected himself. "Lieutenant Lindemann, arrest these men for Absence without Leave."

"Sir," the younger officer barked. He and the sergeant stepped forward, brandishing manacles.

Ka'Deryn caught a hint of something on the breeze and looked away south. "Do you hear that?" he asked. The humans frowned quizzically and shook their heads. The wind-mother carried a warning, a rhythmic thumping that could only be the beat of heavy wings as they swept the air. Though the humans had been facing the direction of the attack, the Kari'Ma was the only one who'd heard them, and he dove aside.

A massive shadow swept through, just barely over his head, and sent the humans sprawling like reeds in a spring flood. Taloned hands raked the dirt and carved deep furrows in the soil. Ka'Deryn regained his feet just in time to catch a glimpse of the winged beast as it swooped upward and crested the battlements to perch on the tower. Its body was long, lean, and leonine, with powerful shoulder muscles supporting wings each as broad as any four Kari'Ma were tall. Aside from the mane and tail tip, which were a deep muddy brown, the beast's fur rippled tawny in the fortress's lanterns. It wore a canine face, and when it roared, long white fangs caught the torchlight.

"Canisphinx!" Ka'Deryn shouted and hauled Hibersen to his feet. "Do you have a ballista? Anything that can hurt that thing?"

As if in answer, the troops above the portcullis raised their crossbows, but the jackal-headed beast leapt clear of the battlements, and quarrels snapped through the air where it had just been.

"No, nothing larger than a heavy arbalest," Hibersen said. It swooped low, and Ka'Deryn briefly lost sight of it. Then the winged beast cleared the wall again, rolled to avoid another volley of crossbow bolts, and beat the air to regain altitude. It climbed higher and higher, until it reached a clifftop outcropping above the fort. Ka'Deryn shook his head sadly.

"I think you've got a problem, then. It's nesting."

"It's *what?*" Grieg whimpered from behind them.

"How much do you know about canisphinxes? Or sphinxes in general?"

"Not much," Hibersen admitted. "Generally, they attack us, we pincushion it to bring it down, and apply fire. Or that's what we did in Strakha Romish."

"Those would have been saurosphinxes, then? The ones that are scaled, like lizards?"

Hibersen nodded.

"Different creatures altogether, then. The saurosphinx lives in the lowlands and suns itself on the rocks. Did you lose many men to them?"

"No, never."

"Curious, then. When roused, a saurosphinx would normally ambush at sunset, pierce a being with its talons, carry them aloft, and drop them from a great height before devouring the remains. You said it would attack you?"

Hibersen nodded. "Aye. Well, they would circle the fortress all afternoon. Then when one descended within bolt range, we'd pepper it, bring it down, and dispatch it before it could harm anyone."

"Meaning it didn't actually attack you at all." Ka'Deryn's tone turned acidic. "Meaning it had adopted your fortress as its territory, and it was scanning its territory, *your* territory, for threats before retreating home for the night. And you killed it because you didn't understand it. You ignorant fool." The shaman shook his head sadly. "Seems the moon fever's catching. Such a waste."

Hibersen rounded on the Kari'Ma shaman, indignant. "How dare you, sir! How dare you! I'll have you know I run a well-disciplined, well-trained barracks, and they brook no threat from anyone or anything. Why, four times that season, we repelled raids by the Bhirtas'Vuoda!"

"Well-disciplined, Captain?" Ka'Deryn crossed his arms and cast his gaze pointedly at Grieg and Kreese. "Perhaps my understanding of the word in your tongue is incomplete. Normally, I wouldn't describe truant guardsmen poaching and trespassing in foreign territory *well-disciplined*. What would you say if I told you that had you allowed your saurosphinx to remain your fort's self-appointed guardian, your water goblin problem would have been taken care of long before your men risked their hides in battle?"

"Don't be ridiculous," Hibersen spat. "They're enormous, scaly, fork-tongued *monsters.*"

"Says the man who slew a proud beast who'd offered no offense, issued no provocation. I see how it is, Captain; you are a warrior and understand the natural order of things about as well as you understand Kari'Maro's blessings. Your blade lets you stick your nose where it has no business, and your arbalests merely give you greater range to do so."

"Your point?"

"Allow me to give you this one warning, then, and I will depart. That canisphinx is more cunning than you give it credit for. It has adopted that peak as its home. It knows you turn out your livestock into the river valley below in the mornings. It is a simple creature, with simple needs. A goat or a sheep every so often will sate it, and it will leave you in peace. At the same time, it will defend this valley with its life, warding you against the river-going water goblins, predators, and worse. Its ears are keener, its sense of smell sharper, and it can spot a still hare in the grasslands from hundreds of feet in the air. Your troops will not be able to sneak up on it. If you are determined to make an enemy of it, you are a fool. You see, unlike the saurosphinx, these jackal-headed beasts remain packmates with their siblings for life. If you harm this one, you'd best keep your guards under shelter at night, lest they be plucked from the walls and dashed on the rocks."

Ka'Deryn turned on his heel and strode away from the human trio. He summoned Kari'Maro's blessing to harden his skin to the density of riverstone as proof against the *twang-hiss* he expected to come at every step. He'd pushed the captain hard, harder than he'd intended, but the senseless murder of the saurosphinxes had set his fangs on edge. *Humans.* So like the jiandimar weed, invading lands where they had no place, and choking out the life that naturally dwelled there.

To his surprise, the humans fired no bolt, and he departed unharmed. The darkness drew a cloak around him, and he passed the point where he'd lit his cattail torch before he looked back.

Then he *changed.*

The journey of following in Kari'Maro's footsteps had many milestones along it. For those blessed enough to sense her presence and hear her voice, with enough knowledge, skill, and practice, they eventually unlocked the secrets of living—for a few hours at least—as all Kari'Maro's children did: wild and free.

The shaman leapt into the air and didn't come down. In an instant, his body shrank into itself, his furs and skins became feathers, his bones realigned, and he caught the evening breeze on feathered wings. He flapped a few times, then Kari'Maro's breath was with him, and he glided silently back to the fortress.

From this vantage, he had a much better view of the fort. The humans who'd built the place must have had an *ido'maro* among their ranks to make such precise carvings out of the cliffside. The walls were sheer and free of toolmarks. They hadn't piled up masoned bricks; they'd physically reshaped the stone on a massive scale. Ka'Deryn had never crossed the eastern mountain range, but he'd scouted the entire downslope edge by wing, and knew all the paths. He'd even heard there were great stone paths threading their way through *all* of Pelinon that had been created in the same fashion.

An unfortunate waste.

The view confirmed what Ka'Deryn had suspected—the humans had few livestock in the first place, and there was precious little land for them to graze on. Most of their fort had been carved from the guts of the rock; the only structures outside in the yard were a small pen for their livestock and a stable for horses. He spied a window on the highest tower with torchlight spilling out and swooped low to perch on a banner pole just outside. Inside, Captain Hibersen was dressing down the idiot poachers.

"…and what's worse, *you went back*! Bad enough that you violated the border treaty, but after your snares were tripped, you kept going back? What animals do you know that are clever enough to trip *thirty* snares without getting caught?"

"I tried to say, Cap'n—" Grieg said, but he physically recoiled as Hibersen crossed the chamber to bellow in the man's face.

"*I don't care what you tried to say, Guardsman! You two clodnoggins very nearly dragged us into a skirmish we cannot afford to fight!*"

"Yes, sir." That was Kreese.

"I've half a mind to set you two to post atop the portcullis permanently. Or maybe guarding the sheep when we turn them out."

"Yes, sir," Grieg replied.

Captain Hibersen paced back and forth. Then he stopped and came right to the window where Ka'Deryn, as an owl, perched. "Could he be telling the truth?"

"Who?" the owl replied, and he flapped away. Ka'Deryn circled the tower and landed on another banner pole on the far side of the room. This time, he hopped as far out on the pole as he could so the lantern light from inside the room spilled past him and kept him in shadow.

"...exactly have a lot of livestock to spare. Even one a week would leave us starving by summer eve."

Come on, you fools. Speak up!

"Sir?"

"What is it, Guardsman?" That was Kreese again.

"The coyote shaman...he said something about not letting us steal what we coulda traded for. What if the fort traded with him? Or his people? What if we traded...some kind of bauble, something shiny but of little value, and we bought livestock from them?"

"I'm not thrilled with having that...beast perch over our heads like that, Guardsman. No, I think I'll have our Kapros striders mount an expedition up the mountainside tomorrow and see if they can drive it off. I'm not convinced we wouldn't be able to sneak up on it."

The shaman had heard enough and took to his wings again. The 'expedition' was doomed to fail, but it would be hilarious to watch them try.

That was enough for the night. The knucklebones were cast, and the humans had no idea they were loaded. He had other stops to make, and many miles to travel before the sun rose.

* * *

The worst part of having to wait on the mountaintop for the Kapros patrol was there were no trees to sling his hammock. Instead, he lay his pack down in a hollow beside the goat path the Kapron would take to the crest and summoned some of Kari'Maro's *Ka* to thicken the grasses that grew at this altitude.

The grasses gave him some privacy, and his pack granted him enough cushion he could sit comfortably on the rock for some time.

He relaxed into a meditative trance until the *clip-clop* of the Kapron's hooves stirred him.

He let them pass, then rose from his hide and followed. The path was narrow. Only one of the horned sheep-men could follow it at a time, with sheer cliff rising on their left, and sharp granite projecting up on their right, before dropping away to the valley floor.

Ka'Deryn pitied the Kapron, in a sense. They hadn't been blessed with Kari'Maro's spirit and had to patrol this route regularly—the hard way. If they'd had a skilled Ka'maro like him, their shaman could have patrolled this entire peak in an hour, and more besides.

But then again, if they'd had a Ka'maro, they wouldn't be in this situation, so the joke was on them.

The path bent away to the left to follow a wide curving 'C' in the mountainside that would take the Kapron directly over the ledge where the canisphinx had staked its claim. It was there now, in fact; he could see it from this bend in the path.

This will do. He set his pack down again and waited for the inevitable, as the Kapron dutifully followed the path to the precipice.

They actually made it further than he'd expected. Sure enough, as they passed the mid-point of the C, one of the Kapros dislodged some stones, which drew the sphinx's attention. It got to its feet, leaned around the corner of the ledge, and leapt off. It flapped three times, buzzed the patrol, and passed them before they could even string their bows. It followed the arc of the C, flapping all the way, and Ka'Deryn was buffeted by the powerful wings for the second time in a day.

The patrol, meanwhile, dissolved into anger and pointed fingers at the Kapros who'd dislodged the stones.

The Kari'Ma shaman snacked on smoked boar jerky and enjoyed the show until the sphinx lit on a ledge above the patrol and began knocking small rocks and stones down at them. They barely noticed at first, until one of the ones doing the finger-pointing took a good-sized rock on his pauldron. That caught his attention, he looked up, and shied away from the stone that bounced off one of his horns. With that, the patrol turned and fled back the way they'd come.

The first in line pulled up short when the mottled grey, tan, and brown formation at the corner wasn't a strange pile of stones, and Ka'Deryn got to his feet. "I did try to warn you," he said. "A sphinx is a cunning creature, and it chose that roost for a reason."

"Blasted coyote! It could have killed us!" the lead strider shouted.

"It could have, true, but it didn't. I don't imagine there was a shortage of rocks up on that ledge, so why do you suppose that is?"

The Kapros had no answer to that, so Ka'Deryn bowed low. "I will let you ponder life's mysteries on your walk down, strider. Don't let me block the way."

Ka'Deryn pressed his back to the cliff face, and the patrol passed by warily. He watched them all the way down to the next bend, and then the switchback below that. Each time they'd scanned his little bend in the path, and each time he'd been there. The ascent had taken hours, and the Kapron would only return to the fortress in time for dinner. The shaman had plenty of time, so he assumed the raven's mantle and rode the thermals. With enough altitude, he got a good look at the sphinx's new home, the trails that led to it, and then drifted lazily back down to the valley floor.

The stone path reached the valley floor inside the fortress walls, and was clearly marked with a wooden signpost, just past the stable. The signpost denoted an estimate of the marching distance to the pass and the total distance to make the hike to Strakha SunJo on the far side. Few ever made the trip, but it would be a useful trail if, say, the fortress was ever besieged, as an escape for those inside, or a means to smuggle food and supplies inside.

* * *

The sun had begun its final descent when the patrol followed the final bend down from the pass. Ka'Deryn perched on one of the stable's stalls and counted heads as the defeated patrol returned. He hopped free of the wall and returned to his natural form. He emerged from behind the stable just after the last of the striders passed and fell in with them as they marched across the fortress courtyard. One of the fort's several lieutenants, a Kapros like the patrol, called them in, and they gathered around the officer. He spoke to the patrol in their stuttering language, one Ka'Deryn had never learned, and they departed.

As they broke off, though, the lieutenant spied the shaman and brayed an alarm. Ka'Deryn held his hands low and to his sides, clearly unarmed, and made no threatening gestures. He didn't understand the orders shouted at him, but the body language was clear. A Kapros joined the lieutenant and leveled a crossbow at him. They all looked the same to the shaman, but he could have sworn it was the same one who'd challenged him the night before.

Captain Hibersen came running at the alarm, this time properly dressed and armored. When he caught sight of the shaman, *inside* the walls this time, he drew his blade. "Now who trespasses, dog?"

"I have taken nothing but breaths, and left nothing but footprints," Ka'Deryn replied. "And as you can see, I am unarmed. Your patrol failed, Captain. They didn't get within a hundred paces of the sphinx's lair before it took wing."

"And you snuck down here behind them?" the captain replied.

"Hardly. I've been here for hours, waiting for your patrol to return, to make you an offer."

Hibersen gestured to the arbalester to lower his weapon, and he sheathed his sword. "What kind of offer?"

"Perhaps we could continue this discussion in your office?" Ka'Deryn replied. "The one on the fourth floor of the tower, with the oil painting of Corsia on the wall?"

"You're too clever for your own good, shaman. But yes, I'll hear this offer."

Hibersen led Ka'Deryn into the face of the fortress, down a hall, and up some stairs. As the shaman suspected, much of the interior had been shaped with *ido* magic, not quarried and worked with chisel and hammer. He followed the human up the stairs, and on the second level, Hibersen called for the sergeant who'd arrested the poachers the night before. He came running.

"Join us," the captain ordered, and they continued their ascent. Once inside, Hibersen seated himself at his desk, pointedly not offering the shaman a chair. "Make your offer, then."

"It occurred to me, after our discussion last night, that you are a long way from home, and supplies of fresh meat must come from the pen inside your walls, not carted here by oxen." Ka'Deryn had, in fact, come to this conclusion weeks ago, but they did not call the coyote people 'tricksters' for no reason. "Thus, your concerns that the canisphinx will prey on your flock. I, of course, understand that an army fights on its stomach, and without fresh meat and vegetables, your position here would quickly become untenable."

"Would that the decision-makers in Pelinon had your foresight," Hibersen replied. "Do I detect a hint of a trade offer in the making?"

"You do," Ka'Deryn replied. "My people are of the plains. We have little metal, but we have ample pens of sheep and goats, and our plains stalkers bring down broadhorns without too much difficulty. Part of my role, as warden, is to ensure the herds remain well-fed and healthy. Thus, my interest in the canisphinx. They are not cruel or mercurial, and can be of great utility to the region. It will protect its lands, and hunt anything vaguely dangerous, for some distance around. It would not be unwelcome if you would trade, say, tool steel in exchange for livestock, on a semi-regular basis, in the interests of keeping the canisphinx here, and sated. Perhaps one hundredth-weight of steel per weight of livestock?"

"I'm not comfortable making that trade," Hibersen said. "Present company excepted, your people and mine have a lengthy history of conflict. Equipping you with steel that can be forged into weapons and armor could prove disastrous, should hotter heads spark off a confrontation."

"Fair," Ka'Deryn said. "Unfortunate, but fair. Do your people still use bronze?" He tapped the torc around his neck. "It need not be steel, or even iron."

"That may be more likely," Hibersen said. "Bronze weapons or armor would have little utility against proper water steel. I'll have to convince the colonel of the value, and he's currently across the valley in Strakha SunJo, but I believe it's doable."

"Very good! In the short term, I will speak to my people about bringing a few goats down as a sign of good will. Whether you milk them, slaughter them, or stake them out for my winged friend up there is up to you."

"That's very generous of you," Hibersen said, "and I cannot help but wonder what, exactly, are *you* getting out of the deal?"

"I have told you. I am a steward to all Kari'Maro's creatures. The canisphinx is particularly holy to my people, given the resemblance between them and us. So, I consider it a duty from Kari'Maro herself to see that they are not misunderstood and hunted or slaughtered when they pose no threat."

He stood. "I apologize for intruding earlier; that was rude. I'll ensure I use the front gate from now on. I'll return tomorrow evening with the goats and hear your colonel's decision then."

Hibersen stood. "Before you go, a question. You claim you met the patrol up on the path above the beast's lair, yet you claim you were here for 'hours' before they returned. You appear to have lied your way into a corner, shaman."

Ka'Deryn bared his fangs in a smile. "I haven't heard a question yet."

"Just this—how can both be true?"

Ka'Deryn barked in laughter. "This fortress is living proof that incredible things are possible for one who is blessed with *maro*. I will see you tomorrow evening, as the sun sets." He moved to the window where he'd perched as an owl the night before and leapt. Hibersen raced to the window after him, but there was no broken body on the stone below them...just a raven gliding away, its black feathers gleaming in the sunset's orange light.

* * *

Ka'Deryn, as a raven, flew west into the sinking sun until he reached the Doompelt Walkers' encampment. He circled, descended, and returned to his canine form just before touching down on the edge of the communal fire at the center of the camp.

"Gentle skies, Ka'Deryn," Ka'Roklin said without looking up. "A little birdie tells me your maneuvers at the twin forts goes well?"

"It does," Ka'Deryn said. "The captain's ignorance astounds me, and I thank Kari'Maro he has the cunning the Goddess gave a baby goose. If he'd known the canisphinx are *not* the dumb animals they presume, the entire scheme would have collapsed from the beginning. Or if they had ballistae. I had not seen any before when I scouted the fort last, but he readily admitted they did not in the heat of the moment. No, so long as they are surrounded by stone, they are content to assume any creature on four legs is as dumb as the rabbit I smell roasting on the fire."

"What's the next step in your scheme?"

"Please, Ka'Roklin, allow this humble druid *some* secrets."

A moment passed as they chewed in silence and let conversations between other Kari'Ma fill the silence. "The *ru'maro* on the coast sent this ahead to you."

The senior druid passed his protégé a leather-wrapped bundle, and Ka'Deryn grinned ferally in the campfire light. He undid the leather thongs that tied it at top, center, and bottom and unrolled the protective skins reverently.

"Gorgeous," he breathed. The skins protected a burnished, polished walking staff of fireoak with a gnarled knot at the top as a grip, and the base flared out in a V at the bottom. Runes and sigils had been etched into it, and a braided leather wrap with a broad loop hung from the shaft just below the cap. He slipped his wrist through the loop, doubled it again, and stood to test the staff's length. It came to just above his waist—perfect.

"Nice stick," Ka'Roklin said. "You couldn't find a length of deadfall on the riverbank?"

"This comes from Ru'Jimothy's workshop, old dog. I traded him a hand of potions and healed that old hound he loves so much—it had fluid in its abdomen and couldn't breathe. Observe."

Ka'Deryn got to his feet and collected a log round from the firewood wagon. It was thicker than his thigh and a pace long. He set up two other half-cut logs as a base and laid his object lesson on top of it. Then he took up his staff and swung it in an arc over his head. Centrifugal force slid the braided leather wrap all the way down the polished shaft to the flared base before he'd drawn half an arc in the air, and he brought the staff's heavy burl down on the log. The impact cracked the log and bent it nearly in half.

"These sigils aren't just for show, but this one here—" he tapped, "—means the *maro* will only cooperate for me. Given our dearth of metal weapons, this ought to be the next closest thing to one of the heavy maces the Pelinese knights sometimes carry."

"I take it back," Ka'Roklin said, "it's a beauty. I've got one of De'Petrine's stone daggers, but a warclub that strong could tilt the balance. Is that your plan if the deal tomorrow fails with Strakha SunJim? Are you going to brain each of them and start the war single-handedly?"

"Of course not." The junior shaman snorted. "If things go horribly wrong, that's what Koreus is for."

* * *

The next afternoon, Ka'Deryn strode purposefully across the grasslands, with half a dozen younger pups shepherding their 'gift.' Four rams, three ewes—one heavy with kids—and two fat lambs nearly full-grown. The winged silhouette of the canisphinx soared lazily on the breeze far overhead, cruising the river valley for dinner. The ram bleated, frightened, and Ka'Deryn quieted it with a touch of Kari'Maro's whispers to calm it. At the river's edge, he scooped up two of the animals and waded across at the shallow point. The pups did likewise, and then they were on the path up to the fort's gate.

"Halt there, Druid!" a guard shouted, and the Kari'Ma delegation halted in place.

"What now, Deryn?" young Kali asked nervously.

"Patience, pup," he replied. "Kari'Maro watches over us. If the humans do something *incredibly* foolish, like open fire with those arbalests, you six run home as fast as the winds can carry you. I will be fine."

Captain Hibersen, the sergeant from the meeting the previous night, and an older greybeard who could only be the colonel of the camp marched out with a squad of armsmen on each flank. The shaman's keen eyes picked out the same angry Kapros lieutenant on the walls again.

"Good evening, Captain, Sergeant. Do I have the pleasure of meeting Colonel…?"

"Baron Lindsay Jiandichor, yes," the older man rumbled. He had a voice like an avalanche. "I command Strakha SunJim. I don't believe you made yourself known to my soldiers here, though."

The shaman smiled and bowed low. "On the contrary, Lord, I did, but the Kapros I introduced myself to seemed more interested in filling me with crossbow bolts than noting my name. Ka'Deryn Ko'Ryna Kallatock, of the Doompelt Walker Clan."

"Do I understand correctly that your name's prefix, Ka, denotes one who is gifted with the Life Magic?"

The shaman bowed again. "You do, Lord. Your understanding of my people's naming conventions does you credit."

"That does explain the means by which you departed yestereve," the baron said. "Captain Hibersen and I have consulted for some time on the nature of your trade deal." He made a moue of distaste, as though the very thought of trading with the Kari'Ma was somehow offensive. "And my answer is no. I won't trade with your people, shaman, and provide you with resources you could turn against us. We'll do our level best to drive the canisphinx off. Let it find some other craggy peak to make its home. If the beast attacks, we'll defend ourselves. If it seizes our livestock, we risk starvation—and we'll defend ourselves."

Ka'Deryn bowed. "Although your decision merely reinforces the Kari'Ma's perception that humans are short-sighted, unreasonable, parasitic, and foolish, I will respect it." He looked past the baron to Hibersen. "Good day, Captain. Give my regards to your poachers. I'm rather regretting now that I brought them in unharmed." He cast his eyes up toward the circling canisphinx. "Perhaps shattered limbs and broken bodies will be rather more compelling."

Jiandichor's face reddened, and he blustered something about respecting one's betters, but Ka'Deryn ignored it. He strode away without another word.

* * *

"Kali, take everyone home. I have other mischief to attend to."

The eldest of the pups nodded so seriously, Ka'Deryn had to stifle a laugh. "I will, Deryn. What should I tell Ka'Roklin?"

"Tell him the overstuffed Pelinese is almost as bull-headed as I am. He'll understand."

After the younger Kari'Ma had turned tail, Ka'Deryn loped away south. He followed the Ramar's banks for an hour, then tucked into a light bite of trout, before carrying on. A little further, a babbling creek flowed out of a narrow valley in the mountains, crashed over a series of short waterfalls, and joined the Ramar. As the sun set behind him, he followed the creek up into the valley.

The scent of steamed fiddleheads spiced with fennel reached his nostrils, and Ka'Deryn followed it to the goblin camp. He crept closer, staying in the long shadows, until he could discern the crackling of the fire. He'd studied these Bhirtas'Vuoda before, but they'd never been so foolish as to trespass on the Kari'Ma side. The humans, lacking any sense of ambition or duty, had allowed this tribe of water goblins to fester like an untreated boil.

The long shadows at his back made sneaking nearer impossible. He'd be silhouetted and noticed immediately, so he threw caution to the wind, and strode forth, summoning Kari'Maro's avatar as Goddess of the Hunt. He grew in size, nearly half again his normal height, and willed broad, palmate antlers to sprout from his forehead. His claws lengthened into vicious parodies of their former length, as did his canines.

At the edge of the clearing, the shaman halted. "Where is the one called Chieftain?" he called. His Vuodanese was badly accented, but passable. "I, Dubok, Chosen of Urag summon you! Come forth!"

A score of heads swiveled his way at once. These goblins had blue-green scales, and whiskers like catfish. Their pointed ears were webbed like fins, as were their fingers. They wore a motley collection of rags and hides, and most of them had short spears within arm's reach.

Two of them, their nerve broke at once. They dropped their wooden bowls of stew and fled into the trees. A half-dozen fell to their knees and prostrated themselves before the mighty being. Three looked directly to their chieftain; the rest were too stunned to even do that.

Water goblin chieftains rose to their position through cunning and political acumen, though what passed for politics among the Bhirtas'Vuoda generally involved wars to the knife, and knives in the guts. This chieftain had demonstrated himself to be cleverer than others; he at least knew to stay out of Kari'Ma territory, and not to pick fights with the humans, either.

That was about to change.

"This one is Xago," the chieftain declared. To his credit, his voice didn't betray a hint of fear. "This one leads the Bhirtas'Vuoda Garakh now, for six summers and six winters. This one slew the Kugu Drake and killed seven humans in fierce battle."

More likely murdered a family of farmers in the dark of night, but no matter.

"It is the gods' will that Xago will slay more," Ka'Deryn replied. "A sphinx has laired in the cliffs above Strakha SunJim. Some time in the next many days, the humans and their Kapron lackeys will sally forth, up long, arduous mountain paths to kill it. They will leave only a token guard behind. It is the gods' will that the one who leads Garakh shall be ready when the opportunity presents. The fort has weapons, armor…" Ka'Deryn cast a derisive glare at the soup pot over the fire. "…food, livestock, and more. Should one of the waters be prepared, one could reap a glorious harvest."

"This one will be prepared, Chosen of Urag," the chieftain replied eagerly. "Glory awaits! This one will dispatch scouts and runners tonight, and be ready tomorrow!"

"It is well, Chieftain. Urag watches over you."

Ka'Deryn turned and strode back into the forest. As the last rays of sun were disappearing beyond the horizon, he shifted from his avatar guise to owl and took wing. He returned to one of his riverbank camp sites, ravenous from channeling as much *Ka* as he had been. The forest avatar was unnatural and sapped his reserves more deeply than any natural creature would, but nothing less would have convinced the goblins to take such bold action. Ka'Deryn tore into some salted mutton he'd cached at the camp; he'd need plenty of food and rest for the coming days.

It was only as he got his fire started that he wondered what Xago would need "runners" for?

* * *

Three days later, in the quiet stillness of a crisp morning, the baron sent his men up the mountain path. Well before the sun had crested the peaks and cast its gleaming yellow beams upon the Ramar, they stole up the path like thieves in the night. From his perch above the fort, Ka'Deryn snorted in amusement.

"What?" rumbled Koreus, the canisphinx.

"Here they come." Ka'Deryn twitched an ear and bared his teeth. "Took him longer than I thought it would."

"It astounds me how ignorant this noble and his men are," the canisphinx replied. "Do they honestly believe I'm but a dumb animal?"

"They do," the shaman replied. "They spend all those hours waving around those pieces of steel and loosing bolts at bales of straw, and not one moment studying the world around them. I'd be surprised if half of them even know their letters."

Koreus yawned and rolled over, with his back to the precipice. "Wake me if breakfast arrives."

Dawn arrived first, and the sun's rays shone bright on the grasslands Ka'Deryn called home. The shadows grew shorter as the sun rose higher, and Ka'Deryn maintained his vigil. Around midday, when the shadows no longer concealed the human troops as they climbed the switchbacks, Ka'Deryn caught the first hints of movement on the riverbank.

The water goblins flowed forth, their skins slippery and wet from hiding in the waters, reflecting the sun's rays like the tide as it rises. Ka'Deryn poked Koreus with the knobby end of his walking stick. "Chieftain Xago is a cunning one. He waited until the humans were most of the way to the top before leading the charge. Hmm…"

"What now, Shaman?" Koreus rolled onto his paws and glanced out at the approaching host. "I thought you said Xago had twenty or thirty in his clan?"

"He did. Does."

"That is rather more than thirty," Koreus observed dryly. "I count twenty hands, maybe more."

"Indeed. He must have summoned clans from up and down the river."

Near the front, he spied Xago's blue-green, whiskered goblins. To their left flank was a slightly smaller mob, whose scales were a ruddy brown. On their right, a larger one, whose navy skin and white underbellies looked more akin to a shark's than a fish's. Those were slightly larger, and instead of webbed hands and arms, they had tentacles gripping tridents and nets.

"The river?" Koreus chuckled. "He brought in their seaside brethren, too. Ambitious. He got one little visit from an avatar of the wilds, and it went straight to his head. I'm puzzled how they plan to breach the walls, though. I don't see a ladder among them."

Below them, the half dozen guards atop the battlements who hadn't gone up the mountainside blared a war horn. The low, fat tone reverberated throughout the valley—and was abruptly cut off. The tentacled goblins had used their suckers to scale the sheer walls without the need for siege equipment, or even ladders. The soldiers quickly found themselves surrounded and formed a hard knot of armor, pressed from all sides by the squat Bhirtas'Vuoda.

"I may have erred," Ka'Deryn announced.

"You *may* have?" Koreus echoed. "Those guards are about to be overwhelmed. If I'm to 'save' them, I'd best get going. And you'd best help."

"One moment," Ka'Deryn cautioned him and lay prone to peek over the edge. He brayed a laugh and pulled his head back. "They just threw that Kapros who threatened me over the edge! Now we can go."

Koreus jumped clear of his lair, let the wind fill his wings, cut right, banked left, and barreled into the tentacled goblins, sending them flying like reeds in a storm. He emerged from the scrum with bodies clutched in each of his four talons, and released them on a ballistic arc that turned them into deadly projectiles to plow into the goblins still outside the walls. He circled and returned for another pass.

Ka'Deryn shifted to his preferred raven form and soared down as well. He lacked any kind of offensive capability, but he spied Xago at the center of his tribe, shouting encouragement at more of the tentacled goblins who were squelching their way up the keep's walls. Ka'Deryn swooped low and shifted back into his natural form just a few feet above the goblins' heads. He landed just behind Xago, raised the war staff, and brought it down on the knobby back of the chieftain's neck with all his might. He felt the *crack* as bones broke under the impact, Xago collapsed, and the battle was joined.

Ka'Deryn hated this part. He rarely engaged in brute hand-to-hand combat, much preferring to manipulate others from a distance, or at the very least, brawl as one of Kari'Maro's chosen predators. But given how much he'd been shifting over the last many days, he was near his limit. He jabbed forward with the knobby end of his staff as though thrusting a spear, and a goblin fell, its rib cage staved in. Ka'Deryn reversed his grip and thrust backwards, then took the staff in two hands and shoved against the mob to clear some space. He whipped the club back and forth, forehand and backhand, battering goblins with every swing.

He was taller than they were, and hammered his way through the mob, headed for the ruddy brown tribe, searching for their chieftain or war priest. He stayed on the move, deflecting thrusts from spears and tridents as he went. He moved too slow, and a slate-tipped axe cut him deeply across the thigh. He howled in pain and killed his attacker with an overhand smash. A spear tip skated across the surface of his leathers, but the stone tip failed to penetrate. He trapped the spear under one arm and smashed his forearm across the weapon to shatter it. He reversed the damaged half and drove it into the offending goblin's chest. He was heartened to see Koreus was down off the wall and among the remnants of Xago's tribe. Goblin morale had been shattered along with Xago's neck, and most were fleeing back to the safety of the river.

The ones to Ka'Deryn's front, however, hadn't gotten the message yet.

He smashed, shoved, and battered his way through the goblin lines, but the wound to his leg troubled him. The brown goblins had much longer arms than Xago's tribe, and he found he'd misjudged their reach as he went. It also meant their stone hammers and slate axes had more strength behind them when they swung. He gasped in pain as a hammer struck him in the chest, knocking the breath from his lungs. He stepped back, and a shadow fell across him as Koreus leaped over him to pin the attacker to the dirt with his claws. That gave Ka'Deryn the respite he needed.

"You *may* have erred?" the beast roared. A goblin tackled Koreus' leg, and Ka'Deryn did likewise. He snatched the goblin by the ankle, tossed it bodily into the air, and brought his staff across in a two-handed blow that broke bones and sent it flying.

"I suppose I deserved that!" Ka'Deryn shouted back. "Do you see the chieftain?"

"I do!"

"Kill him, and they break!"

Koreus jumped free of the mob he was savaging, caught the wind, and scooped up a goblin wearing a ragged set of armor made of lacquered linen. If Ka'Deryn understood the dialect, the chief had been shouting orders at his "cowardly" warriors to quit running. Koreus carried him high into the air and dropped from a height inside the keep. A gift, Ka'Deryn supposed, for the humans to find when they returned from their failed hunt.

The last of the goblins' morale collapsed, and they ran. Ka'Deryn let them go and retreated until the fort wall covered his back to be sure none of the conniving little things stabbed him on their way by. The sphinx touched down next to him.

"You're bleeding," Ka'Deryn observed.

"So are you," Koreus replied. Their chests heaved as they panted. Sweat steamed off the canisphinx's flanks, and the heat behind Ka'Deryn's eyes told him he ought to cool himself in the river, and soon. Soo Kari'Ma didn't sweat like the humans did, and panting could only accomplish so much; overheating in combat was a very real danger, and Ka'Deryn had come to this fight ill-prepared.

Ka'Deryn channeled more of Kari'Maro's energy into sealing Koreus' wound and bound up his own leg with a leather tie from a pouch. "I'm not sure Kari'Maro would approve of this particular mess," he said. "I won't ask for her help with it this time. I underestimated Xago's cunning, and this is the penance. A lesson to be learned."

"That was nearly a disaster."

"Yes."

Koreus took hold of a goblin body in one claw, and the dead Kapros guard whose body lay in the dirt nearby. "I'd best be gone before the Pelinese return if I'm to enjoy the fruits of my labor. And you'd best not underestimate them again in the future. Or the humans. If you *err* again, you may get that disaster after all."

* * *

"Misters Kreese and Grieg, as I live and breathe. What have I told you about trespassing on this side of the river?" Ka'Deryn favored his wounded leg and leaned heavily on his walking staff.

"Beg pardon, Shaman Kallatock…" Kreese began.

"…of the Doompelt Walkers?" Grieg continued, formally.

"Baron Jiandichor sent us," Kreese cut in again. "We're the only two who've been on this side of the river, and he tasked us to find you."

"Follow me," Ka'Deryn said. He limped down a short path through the scythegrass until they reached his camp, where lunch was roasting. He lowered himself slowly onto his log and let out a hiss of pain as his wounded leg protested. "Tell me more, young soldiers. What does the baron have to say now?"

"We were on the wall when the Bhirtas'Vuoda attacked," Kreese blurted. "The beast saved our lives."

"Without its help, the goblins could have raised the portcullis, and the rest would have stormed the bastion," Grieg interrupted, and Ka'Deryn wondered if they shared just one brain between them. "When the sphinx was through with them, we could see you, alone, fighting the goblins as though you had a whole army at your back."

"I have Kari'Maro at my back," Ka'Deryn replied, "and that is enough."

"But, why?" Kreese asked. "Please don't think we're not grateful, but…"

"…but the baron was a bit of an ass. You might have even thought it well-deserved if they'd sacked the fort."

"He was," Ka'Deryn allowed. "I believe I've been clear that I value the sphinx's life well, and all the natural beasts of the mountains and the grasslands. It was entirely possible the sphinx would have been overwhelmed as it fought to defend its territory. I helped."

That seemed to satisfy the two of them, and Kreese forged on. "Yes, sir, and you have our personal thanks as well." He cleared his throat. "Baron Jiandichor has come to the conclusion that the water goblins are a more serious threat than he initially estimated, and…"

"…and he's wondering if the offer to trade bronze for livestock is still on the table?"

"It might be…" Ka'Deryn replied. He gestured for the humans to pass him the haunch of lamb from the campfire, and Grieg obliged him. Ka'Deryn took a bite and chewed for a moment. "…but I believe the cost of mutton has gone up since we last met."

* * * * *

Jamie Ibson Biography

Jamie Ibson is from the frozen wastelands of Canuckistan, where moose, bears, and geese battle for domination among the hockey rinks, igloos, and Tim Hortons. After joining the Canadian Army Reserves in high school, he spent half of 2001 in Bosnia as a peacekeeper and came home shortly after 9/11 with a deep sense of foreboding. After graduating college, he landed a job in law enforcement and was posted to the left coast from 2007 to 2021. He retired from law enforcement in early 2021 and moved clear across the country to write full time in the Maritimes.

He's pretty much been making it up as he goes along, although he has numerous writer friends who serve as excellent role-models, mentors, and occasionally, cautionary tales.

Jamie's website can be found at https://ibsonwrites.ca, where he has free short stories available for download.

He is married to the lovely Michelle, and they have cats.

* * * * *

The Truly Monstrous
by Rob Howell

An Eldros Legacy Story

"I've never seen a valley stare back at me," Jaime Muniotz said.

Rabah, Jaime's older brother, nodded without taking his eyes off the glorious vista in front of him. Many a poet had described the beauty of the Transtochalian Mountains, but Rabah knew they'd never seen *this* valley.

He fought to keep his focus on the area around the deep blue tarn at the bottom. After a long moment, he lost the battle of wills. He turned to his brother. "Something's down there."

"That's where a monster keeps its lair," Jaime agreed.

Falcons had soared overhead throughout their trek, which had always seemed promising to the two. Rabah searched above, hoping for their taloned blessing. He saw no birds at all.

He gestured at the empty sky. "May Wyrd and Ekhi of the Endless Light stay with us, unlike our escort."

"The birds of prey feel the evil of this place, too." Jaime snorted. "The Reader in Amaranth will be pleased we're heading into peril."

Rabah laughed, and for a moment, the power of the valley lessened. "He didn't hide his feelings, did he?"

"Good thing the precept had personally instructed him to help us."

"Almost as if her magic said we'd need it," Rabah mused.

"It surely did."

The brothers sobered, and the valley reclaimed its power. It wasn't just the valley, though. They'd been Readers until they'd broken their oaths to save the villagers they'd grown up with. A Reader who broke his oath played false not just with the order, but also with Wyrd, the personification of Fate. Who wanted to be on Fate's bad side, other than two brothers with more honor than sense?

The precept had pronounced Wyrd's Doom upon them when she'd cast them out of the order. Why she'd used her magic to proclaim that doom, they still didn't understand, nor did they understand why she'd insisted the order continue to help them despite their oathbreaking.

That was theirs to discover, she'd said. Then she'd made them swear a new oath. It had seemed easy to promise at the time: "Find the oath that lets you defend the innocent and keeps you faithful to Wyrd."

But how does one find something like an oath? Their homeland of Euskalerria held no answers, so they'd made their way to Amaranth, the great trade city in the heart of Shijuren, as the precept's magic had apparently anticipated. There, a Reader had informed them, "A great monster or some such is troubling certain mountain folk," in a tone that suggested he didn't really believe the tales. It was simply a quest that might get these brothers out of his hair.

They'd known the Reader wasn't telling the whole truth. Readers usually didn't tell people outside the order everything, even if they didn't despise the people asking the questions, but if the rumors were true, the victims were innocents the brothers had sworn to protect.

When they'd gotten to the border of the Empire of Makhaira, however, Imperial legionnaires had corroborated the villagers' reports. Two merchants said *something* had raided their caravans, taking both horses and men. A number of trappers and woodcutters from this part of the mountains grew quiet when told about this valley, all stating they'd never come to it.

So here the brothers stood, staring down at a valley that somehow hated them. They shifted their shields slightly, placing them where they could bring them into position quicker. They made sure their swords would come out of their sheaths smoothly. Checked all the straps on their armor.

"Are you ready, brother?" Rabah forced his eyes downward, battling the valley once more. He snarled, "Ready for whatever *that* is?"

Jaime searched for a way downward, finding only rough paths made by goats, deer, and other wildlife. However, they didn't look well-worn. "These paths haven't been used in a while, brother."

Rabah studied them. "You're right. There are no prints. No scuffs. Just patterns of wind and rain."

As if to emphasize the point, their pack mule stopped, totally refusing to go further into the valley. With wide eyes staring anywhere but down, it dug its hooves in and twisted away, no matter that it had been quiet and amenable on the trip so far.

"Do we need it?" Jaime asked.

"Not until we're done. We'll take what we need and leave it here."

The younger brother tied the mule to a tree up the slope a bit, near a trickling bit of mountain runoff. The brothers took food, water, and whatever seemed useful.

"Take all our lightstones," Jaime said.

"All of them? That's a full, heavy pouch for each of us. Might get in the way."

"I know." Jaime waved at the bottom. "There's a darkness down there."

"They're just lightstones. It isn't that kind of darkness."

"They were blessed by those beloved of Ekhi. I think I want all of the Sun Mother I can have with me."

Rabah shrugged, and they added the bulky pouches to their belt. "Anything else?"

Jaime considered. "No. If this isn't enough, we'll see Ekhi's light sooner than we want."

"Wyrd will have her way," said Rabah.

They headed down.

The mule's plaintive braying didn't echo; the valley's wrongness seemed to swallow all noise. With every step downward, the silence grew.

"You don't really notice the sounds of animals, do you?" Jaime mused.

"Not until those sounds aren't there," Rabah agreed.

"What could live here without animals to hunt?"

"That's a good question." Rabah peered around. Nothing moved, not even the grass. "I suppose a beast could range outside the valley for food."

"Every day? Wouldn't it then migrate to where food is more plentiful?"

"And yet those we talked to in the last village can't remember a time when *this* valley wasn't haunted."

The pair proceeded down to the tarn at the bottom of the valley. Its water carried the crystalline clearness of something rarely disturbed.

"Perhaps it eats fish," Jaime said after a moment.

"Perhaps." Rabah's tone clearly indicated he doubted the possibility.

The two brothers searched the tarn for any hint of trout jumping, or ripples where fish came to the surface, but the surface looked as smooth as glass. The reflection off the water tore at their eyes.

Rabah muttered, "If it eats fish, it can't eat that much."

"I don't like what that means," Jaime said. "Magic."

"Just what that Reader in Amaranth didn't want to tell us. You were right about the lightstones."

"Perhaps."

They walked around the lakeside, searching the mountainsides rising from the valley floor.

"Do you see any caves?" Rabah asked. "Any good places for a lair?"

Jaime pointed. "Maybe over there. It looks like there's a bit of a bend around the mountain."

"Have you seen any tracks yet? Of anything?"

"No, and I've been looking."

"Me too," Rabah said.

They continued following the lake's edge. Even here, where midges and dragonflies should have flitted about in great clouds, no animals stirred.

The sun, now almost at its peak, hammered down on them. Sweat trickled down their backs, and the black tunics they wore grew hot and itchy.

"I'd like maybe a little less of Ekhi's gift right now," said Rabah.

"There's something about this place that turns all that is good to evil," Jaime said. "Ekhi's light burns. The tarn's deep blue promises something awful. Animals should fill this valley, yet none feed here. The gods who once blessed this place have been defeated."

He continued forward, Rabah in his wake. With each step, the valley seemed to fight them. The something Jaime had described forced their gaze to move constantly, preventing detailed examination. The grass of the meadow pulled at their boots. Rocks shifting underfoot unexpectedly, combined with the angle of the hill, made their calves and ankles ache. Neither could stay in fighting balance, though with each step they felt the need.

Around the bend, a chunk of the mountain had slipped down to create a pile of rock and expose many layers of stone. Some of the rubble gleamed red in the sunlight, brighter than any other sandstone they could recall.

They saw no obvious item of interest, but again, they had to force their eyes to look closely.

"We continue," Rabah growled.

"As you say, brother."

When they reached the southern side of the tarn, the grass seemed higher and tougher. Not only did the blades try to grab them with every step, as before, they also stabbed through their pants into their calves above their boots, causing them to curse in pain from time to time.

Rabah fell to his knees after one particular curse, but Jaime could see he'd done so purposefully. The younger brother went to his knees at his side.

The ground and grass took the opportunity to make them hurt, but the two brothers began reciting an old prayer. Simple words beseeching Ekhi, the Mother Sun, to aid and strengthen them.

It wasn't a battle prayer. Rather, it was the first prayer nearly all in Euskalerria learned. A bedtime prayer, usually, requesting that the sun bless them the following morning.

A prayer of children.

But here, in this cruel valley, two warriors, as if still children, asked for Ekhi's love and light.

By the time they finished, the pain caused by the ground and grass made them struggle to stand up, but once the brothers had managed to rise, a wisp of a cloud slid over the sun. It didn't block its glory, but cooled its power enough that it caressed instead of attacked.

The valley didn't relinquish its hate, of course, but it no longer had its ally in wrath.

The brothers forced themselves through the grass. When they reached the rockfall, Jaime saw a sharp angle. "That's been shaped."

Rabah ran his hand over the stone. "Yes. By a skilled mason."

"This one, too," Jaime said. He lifted the stone, then staggered back, dropping it and falling to his knees.

"What?" Rabah rushed to Jaime's side.

"There. Underneath it." Jaime caught his breath and stood up. "I'm fine now. It was just the surprise of seeing that block."

The two looked at what lifting the stone had revealed. There was another stone, this one carved into an intricate, swirling pattern with a face in the middle. An alien face, but one that clearly despised those who gazed upon it.

Rabah leaned in. The effort was palpable, but he stared into the face for a long while.

"Good thing we're zalduns of Euskalerria," Jaime muttered.

"Yes. No zaldun is ever fearful," Rabah replied in a clipped tone. "Whoever made *that* deserves to taste our steel." He leaned up and gestured at the rock pile. "A nuraghi."

Jaime nodded. "Has to be. It's the only type of place where I've seen anything like this."

"That explains why this valley seems odd. The evil of the Giants remains powerful here."

The younger brother looked around, twisting his lips in thought. "Not entirely," he mused after a moment. "Oh, it's surely the cause of the strangeness of this valley *now*, but that hasn't always been the case."

"What makes you say that?"

Jaime pointed up at the mule and the paths they'd used to come down to this point. "Animals made those paths over hundreds of years, and then stopped. Stopped not too long ago, or the paths would have become completely overgrown. What made animals stop coming here? Every other nuraghi I know of has been around since the time of the Giants a thousand years ago. And this doesn't look any newer than other nuraghi we've seen. So what happened recently?"

"Maybe this rockfall changed something. Blocked a cave, perhaps, of a warden who can no longer fight off the curse here?"

"No way to tell, so let's go to that overhang down that way." He pointed southward, where the mountain's base lay hidden in shadow.

"I don't see anything better," Rabah answered.

At the overhang, the *something* of this valley pushed back hard. Rabah took a step back, but with a snarl, he slashed through the empty darkness with his sword.

As if it were a physical cloak defeated by the sharp steel, the something receded, and Rabah jumped forward into the shadows. Jaime followed at his heels.

Suddenly, rage filled both of them, and they charged forward toward the deepest part of the darkness. Fortunately, both managed to gain some control of the rage before running into a wall or striking at each other.

With deep breaths, both brothers pulled out lightstones. Once activated, the stones illuminated the cave they'd entered.

The opening looked natural, formed of sharp granite strata, and curved only a few paces inward.

However, immediately beyond the curve, the granite smoothed into a tall, man-made passage. Whoever had created the passage hadn't formed it out of blocks, but simply cut straight through the stone and polished it. The layers of the mountain, thus exposed, would have been beautiful, gloriously beautiful, had not the rage bestowed on the brothers by that something forced them to keep tight control of their emotions.

They moved forward to a larger opening. A room, in fact. It seemed to be a precise cube cut out of the stone, each side about ten paces long.

The room held nothing they could see. In fact, it didn't even hold the layer of dust or dirt one would expect. All it had were passages going out the other three walls. They, like the one they'd used to enter, lay exactly in the center of the walls.

Rabah looked at Jaime.

Jaime pointed at the right passage.

"Why?" Rabah asked.

"Don't know that I really have a reason, to be honest, but yes, I think we should go that way first."

Rabah considered, then shrugged. "I can't see why not."

When they reached the doorway, they saw a series of runes etched into the stone.

"I don't recognize these," Jaime muttered.

"Me neither." Rabah snorted. "With all those different scripts the Readers pounded into our heads, you'd think we'd at least see something familiar."

"Maybe this one?" Jaime traced a rune. "Old Akkermanian?"

Rabah snorted again. "You paid attention to that tutor, not I. What rune do you think it is?"

"If I had to guess, I'd say 'servant' or something like that. I think 'Lehpoy' was the actual Old Akkermanian word."

"The servant's quarters?"

"Only one way to find out." Jaime stepped forward.

Or rather, he tried to step forward. The something that had bothered them surged as if tied to the runes. It held him in place. Then he heard words echo into his mind.

"*Enter not. Leave, as thou desireth life.*"

The look in Rabah's eyes told Jaime his brother had heard the same words.

"*This is no place for thee,*" continued the voice.

For a moment, the brothers began to follow the voice's instruction.

Then Rabah growled, "By Ekhi of the Endless Light, I will *not* flee." He pushed forward into the passage, with Jaime at his heels.

"*So be it*," echoed in their minds.

The passage only ran about five paces before opening onto another room.

The brothers had been warriors most of their lives. Enemies had fallen to their steel, and both had held kin and comrades as their intestines fell to the ground like so many worms. They'd seen blood by the gallon, along with limbs strewn about like a child's playthings on the battlefield.

Those things no longer bothered them, not after the choices they'd made. This was their life, and they accepted them as part of the price.

But the sheer butchery in this room stopped them cold. They felt their gorge rise, and Jaime put a hand on the wall to steady himself.

In the center of the room was a blood-soaked wooden table. The floor around it, not surprisingly, showed similar crimson stains.

That wasn't the real horror, though. Racks of knives, pliers, and other tools beyond description occupied one wall. In one corner, limbs had been stacked neatly. They came from bears, tigers, deer, and a myriad of other beasts. Human limbs, too. Tall shelves held various organs in jars, suspended in some greenish liquid. Heads of various creatures were arrayed neatly on another set of shelves. A third set held unidentifiable chunks of bodies. Sheets of skin, not tanned or prepared for use by a leather-worker, hung on racks like rugs.

Each item had a tag.

There was no beast here, but clearly it was a home for beasts.

"I've seen all I need to," Rabah said.

"I as well." Jaime stepped into the passage.

A creature flew at him out of the darkness. Its talons raked at his head as it slashed by.

Jaime crouched and threw up his shield just in time.

It dove at Rabah, but he was ready, and his sword flicked out to slash through a wing.

Another creature flew at Jaime. In the hallway, he couldn't swing his sword, so he pushed up with his shield again. It slid past the steel-edged linden wood, and a face on a sinuous neck struck at him. Fortunately, by avoiding the shield, its fangs couldn't quite reach Jaime as it swept past. With a screech, it circled back.

This time, Jaime was ready. He released the shield's handle and swung it by the edge at the creature. It bounced off the shield, then slammed into the wall. It fell to the ground, moving, but clearly stunned.

Jaime picked up the creature, and again, he nearly retched. It looked as if a bat had grown an eagle's talons and added an asp's head.

Venom dripped down the asp's fangs as it tried to bite him.

However, it hadn't yet completely recovered, and Jaime simply slammed it into the wall again. Then again. He dropped it, put his foot on the body, and chopped through the neck.

The pieces took far too long to stop moving.

Rabah checked the one he'd winged. It was still alive and crawling for him. He sliced its head off, too.

"What are they?" Jaime asked.

"I don't know."

"Good thing we're courageous zalduns of Euskalerria," he repeated, almost as if it was a mantra.

"Yes."

They returned to the main room and stepped over to the left door. It, too, held runes around the opening, and they tried to recognize anything as they approached.

Before they could, another beast exploded out at them.

The creature that drove them back to the center of the room was nothing they'd seen before but, oddly, seemed somehow entirely familiar. Its arms and chest were those of a bear. Its body had scales, almost as if a snake had been attached to the bear. From that body came the four legs of a tiger, with stripes growing down from the scales, and sharp, wicked claws on each paw.

It was, however, the head and face that made the creature truly monstrous. It was a man's face, with a wild, stick-filled beard and clear, blue eyes that would have perhaps seemed intelligent if rage hadn't clouded them.

Its rush surprised them, sent them spinning out of the way, and caused them to drop their lightstones. Fortunately, the stones still provided enough light for them to see the monster's lightning-quick slashes with its bear-like foreclaws.

Rabah managed to bring his shield around quickly enough to block the blow, but the sheer power sent him staggering against the far wall.

Jaime jumped in to slash at one of the striped legs. Somehow the creature avoided the blow, twisting on its side and raking its hind claws along Jaime's shield and thigh. Jaime's attack had cost the creature its full reach and power, making the gashes on his thigh shallow, though still painful.

The creature whipped back to its feet before either Jaime or Rabah could do anything, and it squeezed through the passageway heading outside.

Jaime started to chase, but Rabah said, "Wait."

He quickly wrapped a bandage around Jaime's leg. "You're going to need to be able to move fast with that thing in open space."

"True. Besides, if it's fleeing its lair, we couldn't keep up. I bet even if we were on horses, it would outdistance us."

"Yes. It's truly monstrous." Rabah finished the bandage. "But I don't think it fled."

"Me, neither. It's out there waiting for us to stick our heads out."

"Ready to pounce, where it has all the advantages, instead of in here where it can't use its swiftness and reach."

Jaime nodded, considering their options. "Even though we didn't follow immediately, I bet it's expecting us to charge out as fast as we can."

"Speed is not the answer." Rabah paused, then continued, "However, if one of us charges, expecting to be pounced on, the other can follow up. Maybe we can trap it between us. I'll make the charge since I'm not wounded."

"I can't think of a better idea." Jaime grimaced. "Not that it's a *good* one."

"How many *good* ideas have we had since that day at the Library?"

"Wyrd watches us, no doubt. She doesn't like to give us good options."

"No," Rabah agreed. "At least we can take some comfort that she still wants something from us."

"If only we knew what it was."

"Not going to find out in this lair. We've dawdled enough."

Jaime didn't answer, but waved Rabah forward.

The older brother brought his shield around, and they crept through the passage leading outside. He peered around the curve just before the entrance.

"I don't see anything," he said.

"Waiting to pounce, as we thought." Jaime took a breath. "I'm ready."

Rabah charged out, twisting as he did to bring his shield around, ready for the monster's attack.

He wasn't disappointed. The monster landed on him, sending him sprawling. However, the shield took the brunt of the blow, and the creature's claws and teeth didn't claim any of his blood.

Jaime jumped forward, aiming at one of the creature's legs.

The creature twisted as if it had anticipated Jaime's attack. Jaime's blade struck the creature, but in the flank. The creature's scales blunted his strike. His blade sent a small spray of crimson into the sunlight, but did little more than scratch the beast.

The creature swiped at Jaime, claws rending.

Jaime rolled out of the way, coming up next to his brother, who'd also regained his feet.

Together, they advanced grimly, step by step, shields locked together.

The beast considered for a moment, tail lashing. It clearly possessed more than simple animal cunning, and it prowled to the side, forcing the brothers to work to stay in formation.

Then it jumped, paws spread wide as if it wanted to catch both of the brothers under its bulk.

The brothers separated swiftly, allowing the beast to land between them. Their swords glittered in the sun and bit into the beast's sides. Still, the heavy scales resisted their blows.

The creature chomped at Rabah.

He punched out with his shield, but again, the power of the creature sent him sprawling.

It spun to pounce on him, but Jaime thrust the point of his blade deep into its rear haunch.

The creature yelped and bounded again to get out of the middle. Its leap spun Jaime around, nearly yanking the sword out of his hand.

It jumped back in, and with a swipe, it sent Jaime sprawling. It slammed a paw down, barely missing Jaime's face. The paw rose for a second strike, spraying him with dirt, gravel, and grass.

Jaime desperately rolled away.

Then Rabah struck at its flank, pounding the beast twice in the scales with his blade. The steel, again, did little, but it did make the beast turn beast away from Jaime.

With claws extended, it swiped across Rabah's shield, catching the edge in a screech of torn metal. It ripped the shield out of the zaldun's hands, sending it spinning across the meadow.

Rabah fell to his knees, barely raising his sword in time to deflect the following strike.

The beast bounded away before either Jaime or Rabah could attack again. It turned with a swishing tail and prowled back into the fight as the brothers caught their breath and prepared for the next round.

"Go left, brother," Rabah snarled.

"What are you going to do?"

"Just do it—now!"

Jaime charged left, shield held high, aiming at the right shoulder of the beast.

Rabah faked like he was going to follow, and when the beast committed to Jaime, he ran back and retrieved his shield. The pain in his left arm meant he could no longer hold it as steady as he wished. However, it could, and did, serve in another way.

He spun it with everything he had at the beast's head, like a large discus of sorts.

The beast, of course, saw it flying and batted it out of the air easily.

However, in so doing, it left an opening. Jaime saw it and struck. His blade ripped through the fur of a bear-like arm.

The arm was simply too massive for Jaime to cut completely through, no matter how strong and well-trained he was after a lifetime of sword drills.

Still, his blade bit deeply, and the beast howled in pain.

With its other paw, it struck back.

Twisting to a knee, Jaime managed to get his shield up to block the blow.

The beast performed a strange, graceful twirl, putting his hindquarters toward Jaime. Then it kicked like a mule, its tiger legs slamming into Jaime's shield and sending the warrior flying.

Jaime landed in a patch of grass, wind knocked out of him.

Rabah charged to get the beast's attention, blade fending off the claws of the monster's unwounded arm and its tigerish forelegs. He slashed twice, then jumped out of the way as the beast's teeth chomped right where he'd been.

He tried to jump back and slash at the creature's outstretched neck, but he could only reach the all-too-human cheek of the beast, and his blade merely scratched it.

However, that earned him a roar and a back-handed swipe of the good paw.

Rabah ducked under the swipe and charged in to strike at the tiger-like forelegs. He sliced into one, but didn't stay to determine how deeply, fleeing in the direction of his charge.

He almost made it, but the maddened beast slashed across his back, ripping rents in his hauberk and sending a spray of blood and chain links to glitter in the sunlight.

Rabah stumbled and fell.

The beast pounced, but the fresh wound must have affected its balance slightly, as it landed just to Rabah's left instead of on top of the warrior.

He saw an almost human expression of frustration pass across the beast's face. Nevertheless, the beast recovered to claw along Rabah's left arm as the warrior frantically tried to get out of the way.

Jaime had finally caught his breath and charged in to help. He struck at the seam where the scales turned into tiger stripes on the beast's left haunch.

The beast's hide in the section was far tougher than it should have been, more than any natural beast's was, but Jaime's desperation drove his blade deep.

With a howl echoing off the hills, the beast rose and twisted. It landed on Jaime's shield, sending the warrior stumbling back toward the mountainside.

It tried to pounce, but stumbled as it pushed off the hind leg on the wounded quarter. It landed next to Jaime, face-to-face with the warrior.

The face held such a normal expression of exasperation that Jaime hesitated. But the exasperation turned into rage just as quickly as it appeared, and Jaime frantically brought his shield up. It warded off the beast's rending teeth, but did little against its hot, fetid breath. He jabbed with his sword, striking something, but with little strength and power.

Then the beast turned, anticipating Rabah's attempt to save his brother. With a swipe, it sent Rabah's sword flying. Then with a scream, it bounded out from between them to circle around again.

This time, as it prowled, it limped, clearly suffering from the brothers' steel. However, it paid even the worst of its wounds little attention. Its eyes, far too cunning for their comfort, considered the brothers.

With Jaime shielding both, they backed up to where Rabah could retrieve his sword.

The moment Rabah's hand touched the hilt, the beast charged. With its wounds, it was less a graceful pounce, and more a ponderous, bounding rumble.

Nevertheless, there was no way Jaime could stand up to it, so the brothers split again.

The creature seemed to have anticipated this, and it jumped on Rabah before he could fully regain his balance and position. It stood over the warrior, hot spittle drooling on his face. Its eyes, intent, hard, full of hate...and something else, stared at Rabah. It slowly opened its mouth to rip chunks out of the zaldun's body.

But before it bit down, it turned to swipe at Jaime, clearly knowing when the brother would be in reach.

The speed of the attack almost overwhelmed Jaime, but he'd expected something, given the way the beast had tried to bait him earlier. He dodged—mostly—out of the strike, sending his steel back in return.

The blade slid along the healthy bear-arm, but did little more than ruffle the beast's fur.

Still, the beast bounded out to circle once more.

"That was close," Jaime said, trying to catch his breath. "Thank Wyrd it was merely aiming to trap me. But I wonder—"

Before he could continue the thought, the beast came back in for another pass. This time, the beast lumbered past and swiped, not allowing the brothers a chance to strike.

It circled back around to repeat the process.

Even wounded, the beast's charges came in with such speed and power, the brothers could do little but fend them off.

Gradually, the beast pressed them farther and farther away from the mountainside into the center of the meadow.

"It's trying to get us where we'll get too separated," Jaime gasped.

"You may be right," Rabah said, pain filling his voice.

"You have something else in mind?"

Rabah had no time to answer as the beast swirled in, again swiping and getting out of range before the brothers could reply with steel.

He opened his mouth. "I—"

But the beast didn't slow this time. Instead, it came in again…and again. Four times in a row in all, never pausing.

Then it stopped with a broad, eerie grin on its face. It made a strange huff-huff sound.

This, even more than the beast's visage, chilled the brothers, because it was obviously a laugh, the kind of laugh a gruff man might make.

The brothers took a moment to glance at each other in horror before snapping back to defend against the next swirling charge.

And the next.

The beast's wounds didn't seem to affect it, while both Jaime and Rabah could feel fatigue slowing their reactions and making their swords heavy, so heavy.

"We have to do something," Jaime said.

"It's leading us away from the wall," Rabah replied after the next swirl.

"So we go back."

"Yes. You head that way. I'll give you the chance."

After the next swirl, Rabah charged obliquely to interpose himself in the path of the beast as it circled around.

Jaime turned and ran straight toward the mountain wall. When he got there, he brought up his shield to deflect an attack, assuming the beast would get past Rabah quickly enough to pounce at him.

He was right in his assumption. His shield stopped the blow with a *crack* that echoed off the wall as the laminated linden boards in the center of the shield gave way.

The edge of his shield now curved back in on itself, that section of the wood held in place only by the steel rim on the shield's edge.

Still, it had served its purpose, and Jaime held his ground.

Rabah had reversed his charge the moment the beast went around him to attack Jaime. He made it to his brother's side just as the beast came around for another pass.

"What's it thinking?" Jaime gasped.

"I don't know, but there's something it knows that we don't."

"Yes, I think—"

Again, before Jaime could complete his thought, the creature jumped at them. With flashing steel, the brothers fended off the beast's claws.

This time, to their great relief, the beast took a few moments to prowl back and forth to determine its best strategy. Blood covered its back haunch, scales flapped where the brothers' swords had ripped them away, and its wounded arm hung limply.

Yet the beast seemed undeterred, and it stalked around them, moving to the side of the mountain to their south.

"It's coming again," Rabah snapped.

Rabah's prediction came true with a sudden rush. This time, though, the beast didn't curve to swirl around, but instead charged straight through.

The brothers tried to slash at its flanks, but the beast forced them away from the mountainside. The beast turned around with a roar and charged in again, this time stopping between the brothers and the mountain.

"What's *in* there?" Rabah asked, leaning on his sword as he watched the beast rake the ground with its forepaws.

It pounced at them with bear claw, tiger claws, and human-like teeth flashing at the brothers.

Swords slashed in reply.

Fatigue had claimed some of each combatant's defensive skill, so blade, claw, and tooth struck their foe.

The beast's teeth tore into Jaime's shoulder, ripping away mail, and crunching into his bones. Fortunately it was Jaime's left shoulder, and the exchange had ruined his shield beyond use, anyway.

Even better, Rabah had ducked under the rearing forepaws to thrust deeply into the beast's belly. The beast roared and twisted quickly, but he yanked his sword back fast enough to keep a hold of the blade.

"That one hurt it," he growled as it staggered off to prepare another assault.

"Yes," Jaime agreed. He let his shield fall to the ground.

"Can you still wield your sword?" Rabah asked as he grabbed Jaime's shield.

"Yes, but my left side feels wrong."

"Poison?"

"Maybe. No way to tell yet. More interested in why it's doing what it's doing."

"Me, too."

The beast cut off their discussion with another charge.

Jaime slashed at it, but missed, flat out missed, as his body seemed to respond slowly, and he felt off balance.

Then the beast turned and knocked him down.

He lay at its mercy and stared up at it.

The beast stared back, but for no clear reason, it turned to Rabah rather than finishing him off.

Rabah thrust his sword again, but a tiger claw brushed the blow away. He tried again, but the beast backed off and prowled around them.

"It's playing with us now," Rabah said, helping Jaime to its feet.

"Is it?" Jaime's words came out in a cough. He caught his breath, though, and straightened. He moved his sword around in a few passes, getting a feel for his balance again. "Let it," he said with a determined snarl. "It's given us time. I'm ready for it now, and I know it's still got something human in it."

"Yes. Something human. That means we can kill it," Rabah's tone was soft, musing.

"And maybe something more," Jaime continued as he peered around the meadow, considering.

"Daydream not, brother; here it comes again," Rabah growled.

"Not daydreaming. Follow me." Then he turned and ran toward the cave opening.

Rabah was startled, but he followed at Jaime's heels without hesitation.

The beast chased and swiped at them in a running battle. Claws glanced off blades. Blades swirled to find an opening.

The beast was faster than the brothers, but at one point Rabah rolled *under* the beast, dodging the tiger claws as they stamped at him.

Then Jaime was there, slashing at hamstrings and foreclaws.

The beast, focused on Rabah, didn't dodge Jaime's blade quickly enough, and Jaime managed several solid strikes on the beast's legs.

As he struck, Rabah tried what Jaime had done and ran toward the cave himself.

Instead of swiping at Jaime, the beast chased after Rabah.

Jaime got one chance to chop into the same rear quarter that had been wounded before, sending a spray of blood flying.

The beast didn't seem to notice. Still, it clearly couldn't run as fast as before, and Rabah had almost reached the cave before it could catch him.

The beast swiped at his legs with his remaining bear arm, apparently hoping to trip the warrior. The beast's wounds made the swipe awkward and off-balance, though, and Rabah managed to avoid it.

He stumbled toward the opening.

Jaime caught up and slashed into the beast's other hind leg. Again, blood flowed, but the beast merely snarled at him and turned back to Rabah.

Rabah fended off another attack made awkward by the various wounds. Its focus on the older brother gave Jaime yet another opening.

However, Jaime's fatigue and the valley's footing threw him off balance, as well, so his strike landed with full force, but with the flat of the blade.

The beast didn't even acknowledge the blow, striking at Rabah.

This time the blow came in too fast for Rabah to parry with his blade, so he repeated the earlier trick he'd used. He scrambled under the beast, hoping its wounds would prevent the beast from rending him to pieces.

The beast realized it couldn't move as nimbly as it normally would and tried the simple maneuver of plopping down on the zaldun.

It landed a full forepaw on Rabah, but he slashed down on it, severing something inside the tigerish limb.

At the same time, Jaime stabbed once, twice, and a third time into the right rear hindleg.

This earned a cry of agony from the beast and a terrific kick with the other hindleg. The tiger claws hammered into Jaime's hauberk, slicing through its steel, his padded gambeson, and rasping along his ribcage.

"Take its legs," Jaime said with a cough.

Rabah shifted his aim. He stepped to the right and slashed at a foreleg. The beast batted his blow to the side and attacked with its bear claw.

He ducked, and the claw whistled over his head.

Jaime stepped left and feinted at the foreleg. The beast swiped to block the blow, but the warrior was already moving to hammer the paw of a rear leg.

His blade chopped through the tiger-like ankle, and the beast nearly collapsed on top of him.

He skittered back while Rabah raised his blade to strike at the beast's suddenly exposed neck.

"No!" Jaime commanded.

Rabah faltered, clearly astonished. He backed off before the beast could rend him. "Brother, I had him!"

"I know."

They watched as the beast tried to stand on three paws, eyes having lost none of their hate.

"Don't kill him," Jaime added.

"Him?"

"Yes, him. Trust me, brother. He's not a threat, at least not at the moment, and he did the same for us." Jaime pointed at the cave. "Our foe is in there."

Rabah rested on his sword as he considered, looking deep into the beast's eyes.

Its eyes held hate and....

"It almost looks like it's pleading with us," Rabah said. "Wants us to kill it?"

"Maybe," Jaime said. "Maybe not."

Rabah considered again. "I'll lead, but you clearly have an idea."

"We'll see if I'm right.

Rabah stepped into the cave, sword and shield held at the ready.

The strange, uncomfortable something that had hammered at them the first time they'd entered the cave attacked again, but they'd been expecting it, and they pushed into that evil. They'd also expected the surge of rage. This time they used the rage to help fend off the something.

They reached the cubical room where the beast had attacked them. Again, the doorways faced them.

Jaime picked up the lightstones they'd dropped earlier. "I can't hold a shield, but I can hold these."

"Good." Rabah took a deep breath. "Now which door?"

"I'd guess the left is the beast's lair, so I think Wyrd wants us to go straight."

Rabah said nothing, but went as directed. This door, like the others, bore many runes. He ignored them and tried to step through.

Only to find these runes held more power, or else the battle had taken away too much of their strength.

Both brothers turned away, left the room, and had almost reached the cave entrance before they realized what they were doing.

Without a word, they turned around and retraced their steps to stand in front of the door.

"The door will try to drive us away," Rabah said. "Pay attention for the moment it starts to work. Maybe we can realize what it's doing and counter it."

"Agreed."

Rabah stepped forward.

The moment the magic forced them to turn, they focused their will. Still, both took several steps toward to the entrance.

Jaime raised the lightstones and snarled, "I will not flee."

The light seemed to hold back the *something*, and they stood there for a long moment, muscles trying to turn, courage trying to keep them as they were, light straining against the darkness.

Rabah stared up at the stones, then growled, "Ekhi, may your light fill me against this evil. May I die in a manner pleasing to you. Help me be worthy of all my oaths, even those I've foresworn."

"This I ask as well, Lady of the Eternal Light," Jaime responded.

The brothers found they could turn around.

They stepped toward the door.

"Let me," Jaime said. He pushed the lightstones forward into the opening. It was like pushing into a brick wall, and the pressure on his hands almost made him drop the stones. His blood dripped on the floor.

Then Rabah said something. The warding magic prevented Jaime from understanding the words, but he could hear the voice. The voice he'd known his whole life.

He pushed again, thinking of Ekhi's light and a brother's love.

Then he was past the barrier, falling to his knees at the effort.

Two snake-bats flew at him, but before they could reach him, Rabah was there, shield held high and sword slashing. Wyrd, or Ekhi, blessed him and he sliced through a wing. The snake-bat fluttered into the wall and landed on the ground with a thud.

The other twisted past his shield, and venomous fangs raked across his chest. Fortunately, they didn't penetrate through the links of his hauberk.

Jaime, on his knees, slammed the beast with his blade. It bounced off the wall, and the moment it landed, Jaime's steel sparked off the stone floor after chopping through its neck.

Rabah finished off the other.

"I'm going to need time with a whetstone," Jaime said ruefully. He pushed to his feet.

"Our father would have words to say for the way you treated that sword. And more than words."

Jaime chuckled. "I don't think you need to tell him when we see him next."

Rabah snorted. "Ready?"

"Yes."

They stepped forward. Ahead, they could see that the passage opened into another room. When they reached the opening, however, the light from the stones seemed to fight against the room's darkness, spreading only a few feet around them.

The something was back. Their first step into the room felt like they waded in the heavy surf of the Piperimar Ocean.

"Follow the wall," said Rabah, who started edging to the right. "You watch that way, I'll watch for more of those flying creatures."

They crept around the outside of the room. Runes covered the walls, and Jaime thought he might recognize one here or there, again from the Old Akkermanian alphabet the Readers had pounded into them.

Occasionally, they passed geometric designs that surrounded images. The images held prosaic scenes of people at dinner tables waited on by their children, or artisans at work assisted by what looked to be their young.

The first corner was some ten paces from the door. Around the corner was a tapestry holding a picture much like those inscribed on the wall. The sheer normalcy of the images bothered Jaime.

Rabah stopped.

"What?" Jaime whispered.

"I don't know." He shrugged. "I thought I heard something. In any case, the answer you seek isn't along the wall."

"I think you're right. Let's return to the door and go straight across."

Rabah nodded, and they retraced their steps. Then he stepped forward.

Five paces in, they could see only the shaped stone floor. No door. No nothing. Just darkness and floor.

The darkness pressed in on them, reminding them of their loneliness, their oathbreaking, their failures.

Ten paces, and still they saw nothing. Their guilt, both from the oathbreaking and all the other shame they carried, caused them to weep, yet they pressed on.

Fifteen paces and exhaustion, combined with their guilt, made them stagger.

But they helped each other stand firm, and with Ekhi's name on their lips, they made five more paces to find the back wall. The wall held a long, low altar with a metal statuette.

The statuette was of intertwining metal bars. The bars twined in a pattern much like the chunk of sandstone that had so repulsed them in the valley. It held all that is wrong: rage, sickness, hunger, death.

"Few are those of your kind who have beheld this," came a voice out of the darkness. A figure, hidden in shadow, stood at the edge of the light. All they could see was that it was tall and slim.

They turned, and Jaime lifted the stones and said, "Ekhi, I beseech thee that we might see that which is hidden."

The stones quivered in his hand, and the light extended far enough they could see the figure's angular face.

Its black eyes narrowed. "So. You are of that line. Another mistake by my northern cousins. It is of no matter. Do you think to challenge me in my home?"

"We are tasked by Wyrd to face all that strikes at the innocent."

"The innocent? Then you should welcome finding me. None of your kind is innocent, of course. It is your treachery that has brought me to this place." It shrugged. "Not that you have any true understanding of such things."

"We understand that you butcher things to create abominations," Jaime said.

"Abominations? I think not. It is true my magic has shaped and joined that which nature has not, as yet, seen fit to combine. However, are they not beautiful in their own right?" It stepped forward and smiled. "And are they not *innocent?* You came into their home and attacked them."

"The beast outside has attacked many around here. Many who have done nothing to it or you."

"And yet, I say again, are any of your kind innocent?" It peered closely at them. "I see Lore Magic around both of you. Is that what drives you here?" It paused. "I see that it is. Fascinating, and far more subtle than I would have expected. I will enjoy studying you."

"We left the Readers for a reason," Rabah snarled. He whipped his sword out in a lightning-swift rising snap.

The figure merely lifted his arm and blocked. The blade clanged off its arm as if it had struck the strongest steel.

It said nothing, but a tentacle came out from under its robe and wrapped around Rabah's wrist.

Jaime chopped down with his blade, and it rebounded as well, but the power of his strike forced the tentacle to loosen, and Rabah spun away.

Then Jaime had a tentacle of his own to deal with. And another. And a fourth!

A pair of tentacles now faced each brother like two swordsmen with twin blades. They whipped in intricate patterns at the brothers.

They parried the tentacle tips, which rang like steel, searching for an opportunity to counter. However, each apparent opening turned out to provide the figure with an opening of its own.

Small touches from the sharp edges of the tentacles nicked the brothers' arms, shoulders, and whatever else the slashing limbs could reach. None of them were deep cuts, but they were painful, and the figure smiled each time one of the brothers cursed in pain.

Rabah jumped back to get out of a series that had completely eluded all his blocks, and the tentacles originally aimed at him slashed quickly at Jaime.

The unexpected attacks landed, ripping through Jaime's already damaged hauberk to bite into his ribs.

Then Rabah was back in the fray, and his blade slid along the creature's leg.

Again, his blow rebounded as if it had hit steel.

The figure's tentacles riposted, tearing at Rabah's hauberk this time, sending him spinning away to his knees.

Jaime stepped over to shield him, earning three more nicks.

Rabah returned to his feet, this time with a more calculating eye. He parried without seeking opportunities to strike, just judging the foe in front of him.

"We have our strength and the light of Ekhi," he declared after a moment. "You cannot defeat us, though you take all our flesh."

The figure laughed. "Then take all your flesh I shall." It sent its four tentacles at them in a flurry so quick and complicated that each tip scored at least once on the brothers.

"To me, brother," Rabah said.

Jaime slipped out of the next attack and followed as Rabah circled.

"Now!"

Jaime didn't know precisely what Rabah intended, but understood he needed to engage closely once more.

While Jaime covered his brother's back, Rabah ran toward the altar, frantically scrabbling in the pouch of lightstones. One fell to the floor in his haste, darkness swallowing its power before Rabah could activate it.

He reached the altar, saying the activation words for each in his hand in a sequence.

The *thing* on the altar pushed him back two steps.

Meanwhile, the figure's tentacles had penetrated Jaime's defenses three times. The strikes came in with more purpose as the figure tried to bash the brother out of the way to get to Rabah.

But Jaime's sword flickered, defending him, as he danced through the web of razor-tipped horror.

"Move, little one!" the figure snarled.

"I'll move as Wyrd wills it," Jaime snarled back.

Rabah lifted an activated lightstone in each hand and *leaned* into the power of the altar. He took a step. Another. Within a pace. Almost within reach of his arms.

A tentacle struck Jaime and sent him sliding away.

Rabah half-turned, and it was enough to allow the altar to push him back.

He threw a lightstone at the figure.

His throw connected, earning him the first bark of pain they'd heard from the being.

Rabah dug for another stone and turned back to the altar.

The figure stepped forward, sending his tentacles at the older brother.

Then the younger brother slashed at a tentacle from behind, where it lifted the base of the robe, instead of the razor-tipped forward portions. These held less armor, and his blade chopped into this portion of the tentacle. He didn't—quite—slice the tentacle completely off, but the result might have been even better than if he had.

The figure whirled about to slash him down with the other three tentacles, but the still-attached fourth threw it off balance.

Jaime deflected the blows easily this time.

Rabah pressed toward the altar again. He got within arm's reach and pushed a stone forward. Eyes intent, teeth bared, he leaned into the shadow.

Then he reached it. He dropped the stone next to the strange statuette, and its light almost disappeared in the shadow of the thing.

But only almost.

He pushed forward a second stone. This time, the first stone's light helped, and he managed it with an explosive breath.

The effort wearied him, but he stood forth with a third stone.

And suddenly the sinuous, twisting, horrific statuette stood in bright light. It wasn't something that should have ever been seen in bright light, but it would have been worse had it remained in the darkness.

"Ekhi hold you!" Rabah shouted at the statuette.

A cry behind Rabah told him the being had wounded Jaime again. He twisted around to face the figure, who charged toward the altar.

Rabah stepped forward to meet it with his sword and shield. "Go, brother! Go, get the one who will finish this."

Jaime hesitated, then laughed. "Right you are, brother." He ran out of the chamber, through the central room, and outside to face the wounded creature.

The rage and hurt in the creature's eyes almost pushed him away, but he ignored it. He glanced up at the sun, measuring its direction. He pulled out a new lightstone, activated it, and put it as close as he could to due west of the creature.

He then ran south to place another on that cardinal direction, then to the east, and finally to the north.

Then he stepped into the circle, sword raised high.

Point down, hands on the blade.

He approached the creature. "Ekhi, I see your light to the east, where it gifts us every morning. I see your light to the north and south, where it holds away shadows. I see your light to the west, where you leave us to learn from your absence."

With each phrase, he stepped closer to the creature. He was now within reach of its tigerish forepaws.

Yet the creature didn't strike, seeming mesmerized by Jaime's words and actions.

Jaime laid the hilt of his sword across the creature's face. "Ekhi, here within your light, I ask that you aid the innocent. That you give them the life and health they have never had."

Nothing happened.

At least, nothing happened to *Jaime*.

But the wounds on the creature stopped flowing blood. Muscles knit, and sinews returned. The creature staggered to its feet.

It loomed over Jaime, claws outstretched.

"You've had the chance to slay me," Jaime said. "You chose not to then, and you won't now."

The creature leaned its head back and howled. Then it bowed it head and lowered its claws.

"You are truly innocent," Jaime said, "but the innocent aren't prevented from striking back at those who've harmed them. I know what you are, and what you have been. And so do you."

The intelligence that had peeked through from time to time flooded the creature's eyes.

With amazing speed, it bounded toward the cave.

Jaime raced to catch up. When he reached the large room, he saw the creature rolling on the floor, entwined with the figure. Its claws, both bear and tiger, raked the figure. The figure's razor tentacles ripped through the snake-like scales.

Rabah was on the ground, trying, and failing, to push himself to his feet to rejoin the fight.

Jaime ran over to help him up.

Rabah lifted his sword wearily. "Let's finish this."

Together, the brothers advanced into the fray yet again. They circled toward the heads of the two writhing, bleeding beings.

Jaime saw a chance to slash at a tentacle near the figure's body, where it had been all but unarmored before. He slashed through the tentacle completely, and it flopped away.

Rabah stabbed toward the being's face. He missed, but its flinch gave the creature a chance to scrape down the being's face with a bear claw.

Then the creature leaned back and ripped into the figure's throat with its human-like teeth.

The figure yelled and slowed as its lifeblood spilled in front of its altar. The pool of blood gleamed in the light from the stones, shimmering as if a living creature all its own.

Jaime and Rabah struck at the same time. Rabah stabbed straight through the figure's left eye. Jaime, his blade already notched, chopped through its neck, and the head spun away. It came to rest vertically, as if the ground itself were the figure's shoulders.

The being's mouth moved like it wanted to say something for a moment, then stilled.

The creature howled, a deafening sound in the enclosed space.

Jaime and Rabah leaned on their swords, trying to catch their breath.

Then the beast stopped, and the echoes faded away.

The brothers stepped toward the beast.

"Come, brother of ours," Rabah said. "We must leave."

The beast growled and crawled toward the figure's body.

"This is no place for you," Jaime said.

The beast growled again. With a pained grunt, it flopped on the figure's body, embedding its claws in its creator and torturer.

"We must close this place. We would not leave you to rest here. You deserve better."

The creature stared at them with knowing eyes, then settled on top of the figure's body.

Rabah placed a hand on the creature's shoulder. Jaime matched the gesture.

The great beast—teeth bloody, wounds across its monstrous form—whickered, then laid its head on the truly monstrous.

* * * * *

Rob Howell Biography

Rob Howell is the publisher of New Mythology Press (https://chriskennedypublishing.com/new-mythology-press/), including his work as editor of the *Libri Valoris* anthologies of heroic fantasy. He's one of the founders of the *Eldros Legacy* (www.eldroslegacy.org) and an author in the *Four Horsemen Universe* (www.mercenaryguild.org). He writes primarily epic fantasy, space opera, military science fiction, and alternate history.

He is a reformed medieval academic, a former IT professional, and a retired soda jerk.

His parents discovered quickly that books were the only way to keep Rob quiet. He latched onto the *Hardy Boys* series first, and then anything he could reach. Without books, it's unlikely all three would have survived.

You can find him online at: www.robhowell.org, on Amazon at https://www.amazon.com/-/e/B00X95LBB0, and his blog at www.robhowell.org/blog.

* * * * *

Engraver of Bones
by Elowyn Fahnestock

An Eldros Legacy Story

O NOT ENTER. DO NOT DIE.

Orin read the words one more time before stepping inside the Gilded Door of the nuraghi. She inhaled the scent of forgotten earth and withered paper. Heroes came here to fail, and the dusty display items gleamed in the weak torchlight to remind everyone: the Sleeth Slayer's broadsword, Dorian Evermarch's famous cape, and so many other tributes to the people who'd died within these walls.

Orin had never paid much attention to the rumors, to the missing people and the deaths, not until the most recent failed hero had been Mother.

The buried nuraghi had been discovered by Mother decades ago, a Giant's home forgotten by the ages. As the village council gathered groups to venture in, they slowly unearthed, explored, and documented the nuraghi. The process had gone smoothly, one remarkable discovery after another, until Mother and her team had found the Gilded Door. Ignoring the warning carved above the door, the town put together a team to venture inside without Mother at the start of summer. They said they'd only be gone a day.

They never returned.

Instead, three days later, bones were found under the Gilded Door—and not just any bones, but human ones, piled with the personal items the excavation group had carried with them: the team leader's notes, the cartographer's maps, and the soldier's wedding ring.

The bones had been picked clean, stripped of flesh, and polished to a careful gleam, each one carved with a neat patchwork of words. 'No more,' or 'Killed,' or some other vague description of death. Each person's remains were marked differently, but every skull had 'ended by the very walls' engraved front and center.

Thus, the nightmare had begun. A threat for some, but strangely a challenge for others. Every dragon slayer and hometown hero marched into the Gilded Door, and only engraved bones and personal knick-knacks returned, as though the beast inside wanted to boast about all who perished in his lair. The locals took to calling the monster the Engraver.

Mother had tried to stop the parade of doomed adventurers. "Idiots. Not one of them learns," she'd said. "If there's a place none can survive, we stay out of it until we know why." But no one listened.

That's why it didn't make any sense that she'd gone through the Gilded Door herself.

In the last week before her death, Orin had heard Mother raving about some map, but she'd never thought she'd walk through the door! Orin hadn't believed she'd leave behind her family.

Yet that morning, Orin's sister Rory had come rushing into the house, babbling about Mother. Between panicked breaths she broke the news: a fresh pair of bones had been placed under the Gilded Door. Among them were Mother's rings, scraps of her favorite bag, and a journal—her complete notes on the nuraghi and all that was inside it.

As Orin, Rory, and their brother Finnick retrieved the bones, the siblings bickered. Mother's locket was missing from the items.

"It's unfortunate, but there's nothing we can do about it," Orin's brother Finnick, said. "None of us are going in there to fight the Engraver."

"She won't be put to rest without her locket," Orin protested.

Their mother had loved that locket more than anything else, and everyone knew souls needed their favorite item to be preserved, encased in clay, in order for them to move on and for the living to remember them.

Rory took Orin's hand.

"She'll fade! She'll be forgotten," Orin continued. "Is that what you want? We could get the locket back. I'm small; I could be quick. In and out. I can get it for us."

"Don't be *stupid*," Finnick sneered. "You can't even *hold* a sword, let alone fight! You think a tiny thirteen-year-old is going toe to toe with something that took out the Sleeth Slayer? It's not worth it."

"But—"

"Orin!" Finnick snapped. "Let it go."

Rory clung to Orin's arm, but Orin shook her off. "I'm not going to just let Mother be forgotten because you're too much of a coward to do anything about it!"

"You're so dense!" Finnick threw his hands up. "You always do this, run headlong into danger because you can't get a hold of yourself. I'm not always going to be here to save you!"

"I don't need you to save me!" Orin shouted.

"You're not going." Finnick moved across the room as if it was decided.

"You're not Mother, and just because she's dead, it doesn't mean you can pretend you are!" Orin spat.

Rory smacked Orin on the arm.

Finnick looked up, face darkening. "If you go into the Gilded Door, you get what you deserve. I won't go crawling in there to drag your bones out." He left without another word.

Rory took Orin by the shoulders. "Listen to him. He's right. There's nothing we can do." With an apologetic pat on Orin's cheek, Rory left, and that was the end of it.

Orin came out of her reverie and looked at the room of fallen heroes. It was too late now. Orin had crossed the first threshold, and she wasn't going back. She clutched Mother's journal to her chest. Mother had been a brilliant woman. She'd been sharp, efficient, and every bit the mind people thought her to be. Orin couldn't bear the idea of her fading away.

She pulled the map out of Mother's journal and spread it across the dusty floor. Neatly inked lines detailed what Orin would find just a few feet past the room with the warning, which the map had labeled 'the trophy room,' and what they would find in the noktum.

The noktum was a swath of complete darkness that bisected the mostly-buried manor—even underground—cutting the trophy room in two with a solid black wall.

Noktums were full of monsters, all different in make, and every single one hungered for human flesh. But if mother's map was accurate—and Orin was sure it was—she'd only have to walk through ten feet of a noktum covered cavern to reach the other side.

Easy. Quick. In and out, she thought.

Orin measured the distance between the Gilded Door and the start of the noktum to confirm Mother's maps before reaching behind herself for the pole and twine she'd brought with her. The pole was exactly eleven feet long, and Orin intended it to serve as a guide through the darkness, tying herself to it with a bit of twine to make sure she moved forward in a straight line.

She stuck the pole into the noktum, and it pushed in with no resistance for about ten feet. *That ought to be enough to cross through this branch of the noktum to another doorway on the other side.*

The torch flickered as Orin set it down. She didn't dare take it with her. Everyone knew a torch in the noktum was a beacon for hungry monsters. It was like ringing a dinner bell.

Orin turned to the monument of fallen heroes. She pulled the newest looking broadsword—still nicked in half a dozen places and pitted with rust—off its display. The tip instantly slammed into the ground as Orin struggled to hold it upright. She huffed angrily as she marched back to the twine, trailed by the dry scrape of metal on stone.

She took a shaky breath, then a flying leap forward. The darkness swallowed her, paired with a sudden harsh cold.

She'd been in the dark before. She'd spent nights in quiet whispers at the edge of the woods with her siblings. The night was thrilling, offering the allure of the unknown. The noktum wasn't that kind of dark. Orin couldn't see any indication of the wall or her own arms. She wrapped her fingers tighter around the twine to reassure herself, shivering at the temporary loss of vision.

The string tugged along the pole in a slow and jerky fashion, yanking her backward, and making the sword hit the stone. Each small noise made Orin's breath hitch.

The ground sloped downward. Orin leaned heavily on her back foot to keep from falling forward.

She had no wall to lean on, no way to see—let alone avoid—any dangers in front of her; she just had to trust the twine.

A sharp, loud yip cut through the silence, startling Orin off balance. Her foot hit a jagged outcropping and, sword splayed to the side, she fell.

Her fall yanked the pole off course, and Orin dropped the string. The pole rolled away with a few soft thuds. Orin tucked her knees to her chest, trying to turn the fall into a roll, and twisted to avoid landing on her own sword. The tip of it slammed into a wall with a *clang*.

She swore under her breath and pressed a hand against the wall, drawing back in surprise as she felt something soft and fibrous. A rope of some kind? Orin hauled herself up, trying to steady her legs. Her heart beat so hard it threatened to break out of her chest, and every draft of air felt like some nefarious creature was breathing down her neck.

Orin groped at the strange rope, following it until her hand closed around something round and bulbous. She recoiled at the rough, jagged texture.

The bulbous thing, whatever it was, burst open with the sound of cracking leather. A glob of bright golden light shot up from the bulb and stuck to the ceiling, suddenly illuminating the wide hall Orin was traversing. She stood in front of a wall covered with large slashes, pockmark holes…and creeping purple vines. The vines ended in puckered bulbs, and apparently the one Orin had touched had split open. The bright bubble of golden light pulsed twice above her, and then winked out, leaving her in pitch blackness once more.

Orin flinched at another high-pitched yip in the distance. Both hands went to her blade.

She bolted, hopping over rocks and ducking under vines, sprinting with all her might toward the supposed exit of the noktum. She was supposed to stay in a straight line for ten feet, then find the door out, but the fall had left her directionless.

Every step was uneven, every stone jagged, as if the very ground fought against her. She stumbled, staggered, and the remaining five feet felt like miles.

More yips sounded in the dark, closer this time. Off to her right, a second round of short yips began, responding to the first.

Orin reached where the map had indicated the exit, but her hand hit stone. A dead end. Her heart dropped into her stomach.

"Oh no, no no no." She stepped sideways along the wall, searching for the promised doorway. Had she missed it? Had she gotten turned around somehow? Had she read Mother's map incorrectly?

The next bark sounded like it was right behind Orin, and she winced. Whatever the things were, they weren't far off.

"Come on," Orin whispered, pounding against the stone of the wall. "Where is the door?" Her hand collided with wood.

Frantically, Orin felt about, seeking the doorknob, then gave up and threw her full weight against it. The door swung open, and she dove out of the noktum.

Orin, her clunky sword, and Mother's book tumbled to a stop in an unremarkable heap. She scrambled backward out of reach of whatever was in the noktum, then put her head between her knees until she could no longer hear the roar of her own heartbeat.

A few moments later, she'd calmed herself enough to raise her head. The door she'd exited loomed behind her like a threat, old, rotting oak opening to a solid wall of black.

To Orin's left was a small, crudely carved tunnel rimmed in bright green grass. A pleasant draft came through it, brushing across Orin's ankles.

To Orin's right was a long wood-paneled hallway, lacking the rot and overgrowth inside the noktum. Several sconces with torches lined the walls. The dim light had never looked so welcoming, but Orin could only worry about what had lit them.

Further down the wooden hallway, another door of old oak lay open. A piercing metallic sound echoed from inside.

Orin snuck forward, curled one hand around the door's edge, and peered in. A horrible monster filled the space, his long body bent at odd angles to fit inside the room. Spindly arms led to two large, clawed hands, which were busy fiddling with a metal contraption. Hundreds of keys lay out in front of him, all with needle sharp spindles pointed toward the ground. The monster carefully pressed a few down.

The creature's back sported pale, twisted scars, each different in make and age, as though to show that the dead heroes hadn't gone without a fight. The freshest encircled his thin wrists, a pair of dark rope burns.

The keys on the contraption moved up and down, forcing large spindles onto…what? A white cloth? Orin craned her neck forward to get a better view and stifled a scream. It wasn't cloth; the spindles descended onto *bone*.

This was the Engraver! He *was* real, he was enormous, and Orin was just a stone's throw away. She gulped.

The skull the Engraver worked upon belonged to something that wasn't human—it had an elongated snout, and what looked like small tusks at the tips—but Orin couldn't help but think of Mother under the same machine.

Orin pushed herself back and against the door. The broadsword's worn leather hilt pressed into her clenched fists. Arms and shoulders taut, Orin tried to focus on what was in front of her, not the deafening roar in her ears.

You think a thirteen-year-old is going toe to toe with something that took out the Sleeth Slayer?

Orin peered back around the door.

The Engraver's face was nothing but a circular pit with rows upon rows of teeth, and the creature held one of the thick, purple vines with the glow bulb above that jagged mouth. The Engraver lowered it, and Orin watched as the razor jaws shredded the thick plant. Orin's heart pounded in her ears.

Despite the horror in front of her, Orin's eyes searched desperately for the object of her quest...

And found it! On the wall just above the Engraver's machine, Mother's locket gleamed, hanging from a hook.

Orin clenched her teeth, hefted the sword overhead, and charged into the room—

—but her arms weren't strong enough. Her muscles gave out, and the sword slammed back down into the wood, splintering the edge of a plank.

The Engraver's head whipped around, baring that cavern of teeth in a horrible hiss. His enormous clawed hand reached for Orin's head. She dove sideways, ducking under the beast's elbow, and jumping high to reach for the locket. Orin's hands closed on the cold metal. Victory swelled in her chest as it lifted free of the hook.

The Engraver's claws buried in the wall where Mother's locket had hung, just missing Orin's retreating hand. Even with no eyes, the Engraver seemed fully aware of Orin's presence. The creature turned and faced her.

"What do we have here?" the Engraver asked. He sounded like frozen wind in a canyon, like a cold marble statue that had grown a voice.

Orin ran, tripping over herself to get away from this nightmare. She had Mother's locket—she'd done it! All she had to do was get back out. There was just a few dozen feet of hall and noktum before she'd be safely out of the nuraghi and gone from this place forever.

Cracking joints behind Orin told her the Engraver was following. Clutching the locket, she dragged the sword—bumping and bouncing across the planks—behind her.

Orin was only a few feet away from the rotting door to the noktum when the long arms of the Engraver stretched out above her. The creature threw himself in front of the door, spread his arms, and hissed from the pit of razors that was his mouth.

Orin stuffed the locket into her pocket and shakily hefted her broadsword. It dipped up and down as she attempted to point it threateningly at the Engraver.

"Oh, please." The creature's giant round mouth twitched. "Put that down. You'll hurt yourself."

Orin charged, but the waving sword pulled her off balance. The Engraver lifted his giant claw and knocked the sword away. It clattered to the ground.

Orin curled into a ball as she fell and rolled underneath the Engraver's outstretched arms, through the doorway...

Back into the blackness of the noktum.

The darkness rushed in about Orin, and so did the sharp sound of the yipping creatures she'd fled earlier.

Snapping teeth sounded right in front of Orin. Warm breath wafted across her cheek, and she skidded to a halt. Tentatively, Orin reached out, and her hand closed around a leathery bulb. It cracked open, and a globe of golden light shot upward, stuck to the ceiling, and illuminated the room.

Orin stood inches away from what looked like a solid wall of teeth. The pointy-faced, slathering thing clung to the wall and snapped *four sets* of jaws together, each stacked on top of another, from its long chin all the way up to the tip of its snout. The jaws came down in a chorus: *snap-snap-snap-snap!* Its jagged teeth fit together unevenly, creating a horrible jigsaw of serrated spikes with the blood of last night's dinner still smeared across them.

Orin took a shaky step back, drawing a thin, terrified breath, and the creature pursued, thick black paw clenching the stone of the wall. Its wolf-like ears twitched erratically. Orin looked to her left to find another wolf-creature, and another, and another. All of them hunched together, using claws and the sharp points of their tails to cling to the walls. Orin looked up, her wide, trembling eyes meeting the dead gray eyes of the beast in front of her.

The glowing globe pulsed once, and then went out.

Orin stumbled backward toward the doorway, stuck between the Engraver and a pack of new nightmares. Orin didn't know which way to run—

The wolf-creatures barked a threat in the blackness. Then three more bulbs opened with dry cracks, shooting lights into the sky and revealing the monstrous form of the Engraver with his claw splayed across the vines.

The Engraver roared at the wolf-jawed creatures, and then he charged.

One of the wolf-creatures dove for Orin, only to be met by the Engraver's vicious claw. Blood sprayed across Orin's face. She gagged, trying to wipe away the warm liquid.

Another creature charged for Orin's arm, but she drove low and met the charge, slamming into the surprised wolf-creature's legs. The thing cried out as they both tumbled to the ground. With its jaws just missing Orin, she rolled off of it.

The next several instants passed in flashes. More globes of light blossomed, shot to the ceiling, stuck, then went out.

In that flashing light, the Engraver's hands slammed down again and again, smacking away the wolf-creatures. Blood and fur flew. The Engraver's claws tore through one creature's throat as his horrible mouth dipped low and ripped open the stomach of a second. Both howled and died. Then the Engraver roared as one of the wolf-creatures slipped past his guard and sank four layers of teeth into his back.

Too fast for Orin to react, the Engraver spun, wrapped its huge claw around Orin's waist, lifted her from the ground, and charged toward the doorway. A wolf-creature lunged and bit into Orin's boot, teeth sinking into her foot, but the Engraver twisted, lashed out at the wolf-creature, and Orin heard a neck crack. The wolf-creature fell away, taking Orin's boot with it.

With Orin in hand, the Engraver stepped out of the noktum and back into the light of the wood hallway they'd just left.

Orin clawed at the Engraver's hand, and the monster dropped her unceremoniously onto the floor. It turned back to the noktum, spread his claws, and roared so loud, it rattled the door. The sound of panicked yips behind the dark wall of the noktum faded until they were gone.

The Engraver rounded on Orin, seeming to fill the entire hallway.

"What kind of idiot runs headfirst into a Quadjaw nest?" the Engraver bellowed.

Orin's eyes darted frantically from the blood on the monster's teeth to the open wound on his back. Orin pushed herself away from him, looking for some kind of escape.

"There was a perfectly good tunnel right there." He inclined his head to the left and paused, as he and Orin both realized the crudely-carved, grass-lined tunnel was no longer there.

The Engraver sighed. "Or rather…there was." He hissed, then, seemingly more to himself than to Orin, he said, "Of course."

As she watched, the wooden hallway to their right shifted, planks creaking like it was laughing. The hallway was *moving*. Orin turned in horror to the Engraver, but the big monster was focused on gently assessing his new wound. The wolf-creature's bite had made a deep gash that dripped blood onto the ground. Orin's own foot throbbed in pain, red seeping through her torn sock.

The Engraver picked up a white cloth from under the machine and shredded it, wrapped his own wound, and passed a strip to Orin. "For your foot."

Orin scrambled away from the Engraver's outstretched claw. "Don't—don't come any closer!"

The Engraver cocked his head like he was seeing Orin for the first time. "You're a *child*, aren't you?" The surprise in the monster's cold marble voice sounded very out of place. "What are you doing here? Don't people tell their newlings the noktum is dangerous? Surely they *must* tell you it's dangerous."

What kind of game is the beast playing? Orin wondered. *It protected me from the wolf-creatures like a lion protects its kill from mongrel dogs. Is this pretend kindness some kind of belated lure? How long will the beast keep this up? Did Mother die this way?*

Orin pushed herself further away from the monster, wincing every time her wounded foot touched the floor. The Engraver silently pushed the cloth closer to her.

She hesitantly leaned forward and snatched it, keeping one eye on the Engraver's horrible circles of teeth. "The noktum is dangerous because of *you*."

"Because of *me*," the Engraver echoed. "I see. Why are you here, little newling?"

Orin looked up at the monster accusingly. "You killed my mother."

"Oh." The Engraver's voice softened.

"You killed my mother!" Orin repeated, stepping forward. She cried out and fell back down, clutching her foot. "And then you took her locket so we couldn't put her to rest."

The Engraver slumped into a sitting position, purposely putting distance between the two of them. "Oh, little newling." He sighed. "I didn't. Not her. I didn't want *any* of them to die."

"Liar!"

"I never laid a hand on those foolish humans. Not a single one." The sound of heartache was clear in his voice, even twisting out of a monster's mouth.

Is this another ruse? To what end? What is this creature?

Orin stopped crying. "But the bones. You were carving on bones!"

The Engraver shook his big, scary head as though he hadn't even heard Orin's accusation. "I just don't understand what else I have to do to stop you people from coming down here. No one has ever emerged from the nuraghi alive. I even put a warning up. Are humans just incapable of learning?"

"*You* put up the sign?" Orin asked, stupefied. "But…if you didn't kill them, what did?"

"There are things in this place far more dangerous than me." The Engraver sighed, his frightening face still managing to convey pity. "I'm sorry, little newling. It's been a long day for you, hasn't it?" He glanced around the hall. "Perhaps we should focus more on getting you home, and less on the things that haunt these halls."

"Wait—"

"Would you let me carry you? That foot's no good. It'll need human medicine."

"No!" Orin pushed herself up, leaning on the wall. "Carry me? No!"

The Engraver nodded, fumbling around in the machine room and retrieving a short stick. "Very well. Lean on this. It's not too far, assuming the nuraghi is kind. Stay close to me." The Engraver looked at Orin directly for the first time since he'd rescued her. "Do you understand? Don't wander. There are worse things in this nuraghi than Quadjaws, even."

Whatever the Engraver was, whatever he wanted, Orin didn't know. Not anymore. She spotted her broadsword discarded on the ground, and using the stick, she limped over to get it. She struggled to keep her balance, tried to pick up the broadsword, then finally abandoned it in favor of not falling over.

"You're not going to be able to carry that," the Engraver said. "Here." In the time it had taken Orin to hobble over, the Engraver had retrieved a large knapsack with one of his impossibly long arms. He scooped up the sword and placed it inside.

"Follow me." The Engraver started down the new hallway, hunching on all fours.

Orin glanced back to the large door and the wall of the noktum beyond it; she could still hear the snuffling of wolf-creatures. Orin's foot throbbed, and her shoulders ached. Dirt and tears stained her cheeks, but she still had the locket—

The locket! Orin frantically checked her pockets for the locket. It was still there! She pulled it out and pressed a relieved kiss into the center of it. With renewed courage, she set off after the Engraver.

The two continued their walk in silence, and every now and then, the Engraver would check to make sure she was following. The hallway eventually ended in a large, stately arch, opening up into a massive room. Orin glanced up at the wooden rafters, trying to find an exposed window, but all of them were still blacked out with dirt, and only the torch in the Engraver's hand cast a warm glow on the walls. An old ladder leaned up against the far wall, stretching down toward a small pit. Stained glass statues danced in a circle in the middle of the room, a trio of smiling women.

Orin stared at the glass folds and faces. "These are beautiful."

The Engraver turned in their direction, poking one of the statues disdainfully. "Don't wander. And don't get distracted. Remember, you haven't seen the worst this place has to offer. We're headed this way."

One corner of the room had caved in, and a small crevice snaked across the floor. A corner of the noktum seeped out from below, filling a part of the crevice.

"Hold on." The Engraver paused on the edge, and there was a new lilt to his voice that Orin couldn't place. It was...disarming. "You'll like this." He pulled a few of the strange bulbs out of one of his bags, cracking one open and pushing the light toward the noktum.

The wall lit up, covered in thousands of small, shiny forms. The Engraver reached down and plucked one off the wall before the light winked out again. It uncurled in his massive palm, revealing a rounded nose and two broad, armored wings. The thing yawned, with small fangs and a smaller squeak.

Orin gasped with delight before trying to pull her face back into a scowl as the eyeless Engraver seemed to look at her. The small creature shook water from its wings and chirped again. Orin's face twitched as she struggled to maintain the façade.

The beetle-like thing meandered around the Engraver's hand, sniffing his long nails curiously. The monster regarded it with a strange reverence.

"Would you like to hold it?" He extended his claw to Orin, and the small creature looked up expectantly, moving two fuzzy antennae back and forth.

Orin kept one eye on the Engraver's claws and reached gingerly for the creature. It perked up and flew onto Orin's hand, squeaking at the much smaller seat. Its smooth skin felt nothing like Orin had expected. The creature was slick and soft, like velvet. One of the antennae brushed Orin's wrist, and she giggled. The Engraver laughed, too, and the rattling sound seemed so unnervingly human.

"What's it called?" Orin held the small creature up to her eyes, examining its broad wings.

"I've always called them gembugs."

"Wow." Orin leaned over the lip, staring at the sleeping gembugs. "I didn't know the noktum had things like that."

"The bigger, scarier monsters need things to eat when dumb human children aren't wandering about."

Orin laughed, and her mirth pushed against the knot in her chest, the heaviness of how lonely the past day had been. The gembug butted its head against her hand.

The Engraver reached across the crevice. "You two keep each other company. I'm going to check ahead." His voice darkened. "Stay. Put." The monster vaulted across the crevice and into the shadows.

Orin glanced at the Engraver's retreating form, and she slowly crept back to the stained glass statues. The three women seemed to smile welcomingly as Orin limped toward them.

The small gembug chirped and flew onto Orin's shoulder, then flew urgently around her head twice. Orin waved it away, focused on the statues. The gembug took off, flying in the same direction as the Engraver.

Orin drew nearer the stained glass statues. Each had such a defined look, delicate panels of colored glass coming together to form faces as complex as an actual human. Orin paused before the third statue, staring at the round black glass eyes lined with pewter wrinkles. The expression she wore created a spreading warmth in Orin's chest.

Orin's eyes fell on the glass necklace she wore. It was identical to the locket in her pocket. "Mother?" Orin barely realized the word had left her mouth, and it echoed down the chamber.

The glass statue smiled, rainbow panes folding in on each other as she came to life and stepped away from the others. The glass imitation of Mother's face moved to form words, but no sound came out.

"I don't understand." Orin's voice cracked. There was a painful tugging in her chest.

Cool glass hands tucked Orin's long hair behind her ear. The statue's—Mother's—hand closed around Orin's wrist. She gently tugged her across the room, away from the crevice and toward the old ladder.

"Is there something over there?" Hope bloomed in Orin's chest, intoxicating after the past few hours. She led her, and they walked faster.

Stained-glass Mother held a finger to her lips, and this time Orin could see what she was mouthing: *Quiet.*

She tugged again on her arms with such a surprising force, Orin stumbled, but as she looked back up at her, she couldn't bring herself to care. The wrinkles under her eyes, the gentle curve of her smile. It looked so much like her. And if Mother urgently wanted to show Orin something, she wanted to see it.

"I'm sorry Rory and Finnick wouldn't listen to me," Orin whispered, clinging to the warmth in her chest. She drew closer to the ladder. "But   I   knew   I   could   do   it."

Stained-glass Mother smiled widely, like she'd never had a doubt, like she'd always believed in Orin—

Two large claws wrenched Orin away from Mother.

Orin hollered in anguish. She pushed against the massive claws. "Let me go!"

The Engraver moved quickly, the gembug chirping like an alarm behind him. Orin leaned over the Engraver's claws, craning her neck, straining to see Mother—

But when she looked back, none of the statues had moved at all. The third one—Mother—was still frozen in the same dance. Only her laughing eyes seemed to follow Orin...and she did *not* look like Mother anymore.

The Engraver leapt across the crevice, carrying Orin with him this time. The warmth of seeing Mother vanished, leaving Orin shaking.

"Wait!" Orin cried.

"I think not." The Engraver panted, chest heaving, long fingers trembling. He sounded panicked.

The room across the crevice stretched out around them, and darkened windows made from the same stained glass seemed to chase them.

The Engraver clutched Orin closer as a resounding *creak* echoed through the room. Orin turned back to see a flurry of gembugs erupt from the crevice, swarming together in a frantic escape from the crevice. Orin's ears filled with the cacophonous sounds of hundreds of frenzied chirps.

The Engraver dared a glance backward, and with a sharp gasp, he ran faster. "Keep your head down!"

Orin went silent and let the Engraver carry her away from the statues, away from the crevice. Twisting her arms into her pockets, Orin pressed the locket into her palm. The delightful warmth in her chest faded as the gembugs chirped and the room creaked.

The Engraver aimed for a broken window at the end of the room, a cracked sill leading to what looked to be a natural cave. His claws tightened around Orin as the first window shattered.

One by one, the windows behind them burst, sending sharp sprays across the room. Orin covered her face as glass blasted across her and the Engraver. Shining flecks of glass cut into her skin. Orin winced. The Engraver twisted his massive frame and leapt through the window, leaving the sound of cascading glass behind them.

The warmth dried up completely as Orin stared wide-eyed at the new crisscrossing of cuts across her and the Engraver. In its absence, Orin suddenly realized the stained-glass statues must have cast an enchantment on her!

"You can put me down now," Orin said, dejected. Even though she now knew the statue hadn't been Mother, she still longed for it to be true. To have seen Mother again, to have felt her warm hands on her arms. For her to be proud she'd found her locket. Instead, she'd just been put through another deadly chase.

The Engraver slowed, then cautiously put Orin on the ground as though he expected her to bolt. "Just stay focused. We've run out of time. We have to keep moving."

Orin took a few shaky steps forward, leaning on her stick as pain fired through her injured foot. "I'm sorry." Her breath was ragged. The gembug butted into Orin's shoulder comfortingly.

"Not your fault," the Engraver said. "I shouldn't have left you alone." The Engraver considered her. He twisted uncomfortably, blood seeping through the bandage on his back. "I try to give back items of importance, whatever this place doesn't claim first, but…I confess, I liked the locket. I'd hoped no one would miss it. If I'd known it was so important, I wouldn't have kept it."

Orin didn't know what to say. She blinked, stunned. The Engraver—the supposed scourge of their village—had just apologized to her.

He ducked his massive head. "I actually quite liked your mother. She was smart," the Engraver continued, starting down the cave as he talked, keeping a massive claw behind Orin's back to shepherd her along. "She knew what she was after when she came down here; one has to admire her ability to plan ahead. She wanted to know what made this part of the nuraghi different, and she wouldn't accept me as an answer. She was polite, though; she didn't hurt me as bad as the others." He gestured to his many scars. "I almost got her to listen to me. Almost." A single large finger twisted around the rope burns on his wrist. "I didn't know she had a family."

Orin sniffled. "No. She wouldn't have mentioned us."

"Us?"

Orin worked the locket chain between her two fingers, remembering the bitterness between her siblings that morning. "I've got a sister and a brother."

The Engraver pressed on Orin's shoulder, glancing behind them. The place after the crevice was a wide, flat stretch of cave, all roots and stalagmites. "Would you like to tell me about them?" He offered the question as though it would provide some form of protection.

She glanced up at the Engraver. "They didn't want me to come down here. None of them cared that Mother's soul would be torn apart without the locket," Orin said sourly. "Finnick wanted to stop me from coming, and Rory wouldn't say a thing against him. We argued. I left."

"Smart siblings. You should never have come here."

"You shouldn't have taken what wasn't yours!" Orin snapped.

"Perhaps that's true."

"It doesn't matter. I did it, and I'm glad. I have the locket. I—I don't care about anything else," Orin said, though that wasn't true.

"And yet you're not happy," the Engraver noted.

Orin raised her head, surprised that the Engraver had noticed. The thing had no eyes; how could it know? "Finnick told me if I came down here, I shouldn't bother coming back."

"Finnick is your brother."

"Yes." Orin watched the gembug settle into her shoulder.

"Ah. Then I doubt he meant it."

"He meant it."

"As you say," the Engraver said, though his voice clearly indicated he didn't think so. "Is Finnick usually the one in charge?" the Engraver filled the silence once more.

Orin gave a small smile, and her heart ached, thinking about Finnick and Rory. "Well, sort of," Orin said fondly. "He's the eldest, though only a few months older than me and Rory. Well, maybe not even that, really. None of us know exactly how old we are, but we think of him as older. Since Mother adopted Finnick first, Rory and I agreed to let him be in charge. He's good at it, too. Mother worked a lot of the time, so Finnick kept track of us."

The Engraver hung on her every word, gently pushing her forward. "You and Rory are the troublemakers, then?" He held a curtain of roots aside for Orin to duck under.

"You have no idea!" Orin giggled at a memory, exciting the gembug on her shoulder. It chirped and wiggled about. "One time we stole all seven of Sir Lebrag's frivolous bonnets and hung them in the town square." The story rushed out of Orin in a blur. "Rory was so smart in planning it—she's much smarter than me—but we got caught anyway. I had to keep her calm when Finnick found out, but he's never as angry as he likes to pretend." Orin's face wilted. "I wonder if they're thinking about me right now."

"I'll get you home safely," the Engraver reassured her, though the end of the sentence trembled.

Orin looked up, past the Engraver's twisted limbs and clawed hands, past the circular forest of teeth and the blank, eyeless face. "Do you have a name?"

"I'm sorry?"

"A name. People in the town call you the Engraver. That doesn't fit anymore, so what's your name?"

The Engraver sighed. "Best for you not to know it."

Orin opened her mouth to protest, but the words dried up as a loud cracking noise came from behind them. The Engraver whipped around, pushing Orin behind him. The gembug flew back with them, making a weak chirping noise that was much closer to a whimper. Peeking out from under the Engraver's arm, Orin watched with horror as the cave walls began to change.

Bright wooden planks unfolded themselves across the stone, each one burrowing into the ground with a harsh *crack* until it looked like the area had been wood all along.

"What-what is going on?" Orin could feel the Engraver shaking in front of her; he seemed transfixed by something in the distance.

Step by step it emerged, tall and angular, with limbs too long for its body, and arms ending in massive claws. It could've been the Engraver's twin, if not for the way it moved down the hall. Each step was jerky, moving without any real consideration as to *how*. It yanked itself forward by the chest, like a clumsily controlled puppet. Its skin seemed to ripple, sliding across it as if what was underneath wasn't solid enough to hold it down.

The Engraver made a strangled noise in the back of his throat and turned them both around to run. They only made it a few feet before Orin heard the sound of wood beneath the Engraver's feet.

"Duck!" the Engraver cried. Orin flattened herself to the ground as a claw sailed above her head. The Engraver tackled the monster away from her. The two rolled away, clawing at each other.

The Engraver leapt back up, shoving the imposter aside. The creature didn't even stumble, just bent backward for a moment before lunging forward. Moving too fast for either of them to react, the imposter reached out and grabbed Orin. The gembug shot forward, flying around the imposter's face. It raised one hand and flicked it across the room, and the gembug slammed into the wall with a chirp.

Orin swung her walking stick at the imposter's head. The tip slammed solidly into its cheek, and while its head snapped back, the creature didn't seem hurt.

The Engraver snarled, shredding the weird loose skin on its hands in an attempt to loosen its grip. With a horrible *crack*, the Engraver pulled one of its fingers backward, allowing Orin to pull herself free.

The Engraver slashed across the imposter's face, trying to grab its attention. "Run! Get off the wood!"

Orin looked up to where the wood floorboards ended, just a few feet away from them. She scooped up the injured gembug and limped forward as fast as she could. She glanced back to see the Engraver fighting to keep a hold of the imposter.

The floorboards seemed to buck as she stepped forward, pitching her backward. With the added balance of her walking stick, Orin managed to stumble her way back onto stone just as the Engraver lost. The imposter twisted its neck sideways and bit the Engraver's arm. He roared, and his grip loosened just enough for the Imposter to turn and grab him by the throat. The Imposter slammed him twice into the wall before dropping him in a breathless heap.

Orin backed away from the wooden panels, scanning the area for another weapon. The Imposter stalked up to the edge of the floorboards and...stopped. It stood completely still, toes just resting on the edge of the wood.

Orin steadied her breathing. The creature wasn't able to step off the wood. With one hand she set the gembug down. It let out a weak chirp.

The Imposter, seeming to realize Orin was out of reach, turned back to the injured Engraver. Baring its teeth, the Imposter yanked the Engraver to his feet again. Orin was sure she was about to watch him get torn apart.

She wasn't going to let that happen.

With its attention now fully on the Engraver, Orin moved silently back toward the wood. Wincing as her foot hit the floorboards again, Orin crept toward the monsters, walking stick held out in front of her horizontally.

It was just a hunch, but if the Imposter wasn't able to step off the wood, it probably wouldn't like being thrown off of it.

The Imposter's claws were carving slow and painful paths across the Engraver's chest. On Orin's ninth step, the Imposter turned his head slightly. Orin froze, and just as she thought she was about to be caught, the Engraver grabbed the Imposter's face and spun it back toward him. Sensing her opening, Orin ran the last few steps, nearly blacking out from the pain in her foot. Throwing her full weight forward, Orin slammed the walking stick into the back of the Imposter's knees. The two tumbled off the wood and onto the stone cave floor. The Imposter let out a cry and burst apart, the rest of the wood disappearing with it.

In a moment, it looked like nothing strange had happened at all.

The gembug flew up, looking somewhat recovered, and hovered over the Engraver worriedly.

"Are you all right?" Orin asked.

The Engraver stood, wincing. "I will be. But more importantly, we're here." He slammed one of his claws against the stone ceiling, and a chunk of it fell away, revealing a small hole that let in just a bit of moonlight. He opened his palm, and Orin stepped onto it, bracing herself against one of the claws. Slowly and carefully, the Engraver lifted Orin and the gembug up to the hole.

Fresh air brushed Orin's hair and clothes, and she scrambled onto the grassy ground of the normal world. The moon winked welcomingly down at them. Orin pulled herself onto the grass and inhaled the sweet smell of dirt and summer wind. The gembug hopped off her shoulder and rolled around, stumpy feet wiggling in the air as though it had never felt grass before.

The Engraver's voice drifted up past them. "I think.the gembug wants to go with you."

Orin looked over at the small creature. "You think?" She reached out tentatively toward it, running a finger along its nose. The gembug chirped happily, rolling over to let Orin stroke its wings. She giggled. "All right, buddy, do you want to come home with me?" She picked up the gembug and held it close to her chest. Turning back to the Engraver, she said, "I'll take good care of it."

Letting the gembug go and rolling onto her belly, Orin looked back down through the hole in the side of the hill. From this angle, the Engraver looked smaller, alone, and forlorn. He pulled Orin's broadsword out of his bag and pushed it up to her.

"I think you could be good with that someday." The Engraver lowered his hand. "You have the determination, and plenty of courage. The arm strength will come."

"Thank you." Orin's voice came out choked and raw. She lifted a hand and waved, the gembug moving along with it. The Engraver waved back and stepped out of sight.

Orin crawled as far away from the hole as she could before the pain overtook her, and she slumped to rest. Maybe she'd spend the night here, try to make her way back to the village in the morning—

Orin saw bobbing yellow light over the next knoll. Those were people. They were looking for her!

"Over here!" Orin yelled. "I'm over here!"

Rory's ebony curls and dark eyes bobbed over the nearest hill. "Orin!" She ran to Orin, dropping the lantern and pressing a kiss to her temple. The gembug chirped, excited by new people. It flicked into the air and circled the pair.

Finnick followed quickly after and skidded to a stop right behind Rory, fists clenched and face flushed from crying. "I can't believe you did this, you idiot! What did you possibly think—"

"I got it." Orin held the locket up triumphantly, the chain tangled in her shaking fingers.

Rory gasped.

"I got it," Orin repeated, then buried her face in Rory's shoulder. "Mother can rest now. She's going to be all right now."

* * * * *

Elowyn Fahnestock Biography

Elowyn Fahnestock is a writer of fantasy, a massive nerd, and has a small collection of ornate daggers. Her passions are Dungeons & Dragons, fantasy stories, and spending time with her close-knit group of friends. When she's not writing, she attends Englewood High School as a senior, cuddles with cats, and dodges Galahad the Weimaraner (who tries to jump on her far too much). Engraver of Bones is Elowyn's first published short story.

* * * * *

The Darkest Door
by Todd Fahnestock

An Eldros Legacy Story

"This is it." Rhenn held up the huge silver key to Lorelle in the yellow light of the lantern, turning it so it was sure to glimmer, like it was magic.

Rhenn had brought Lorelle here, to her father's study, because it stood at the end of the hall—the furthest room from the bedrooms of the royal wing. In the study, it was less likely their parents would wake at their whispered voices. Rhenn loved Father's study; it smelled of oiled wood, leather, and old paper. It smelled like secrets, and a future queen should know secrets. She should know more of them than anyone else.

Books lined the walls, rising to the ceiling, and a thick wooden desk stood at the back of the room with Father's cushioned leather chair behind it. Of course, Father had told Rhenn a hundred times that his study was not a place to play, but a warning like that was just another way adults hid secrets from children.

Lorelle, Rhenn's best friend, looked wonderingly at the key. The beautiful Luminent already stood taller than Rhenn by half a foot—a fact that annoyed Rhenn. Princesses really ought to be taller than those who weren't.

Of course, Luminents were taller than humans. That's just the way it was. Luminents were also lighter and more graceful. They could tiptoe along the edge of a rooftop and never fall. And even if they did fall, it wouldn't hurt them like it would hurt Rhenn. They also had beautifully pointed ears and hair that glowed when they got excited. Or scared.

If Lorelle hadn't been so perfectly made to be Rhenn's best friend, Rhenn suspected she might have hated her. But the Luminent girl had proven herself right from the start. She'd happily joined all Rhenn's adventures, and she'd kept every secret Rhenn had ever told her. And perhaps most importantly, Lorelle deferred to Rhenn's leadership.

"What does it unlock?" Lorelle asked.

"A noktum," Rhenn said.

"Senji's Boots, it does not!" Lorelle blurted.

"Hsst!" Rhenn sliced her hand down through the air, looking nervously at the door. Her parents, brothers, and sisters weren't far up the hall. "Do you want them to catch us?"

"A *noktum*, really?" Lorelle whispered wonderingly.

Everyone knew about the otherworldly patches of darkness that blotted out more than a tenth of the Kingdom of Usara, remnants left over from the mythical Giant wars, they said. The Giants of those wars had been so powerful that, even though they'd died out almost two thousand years ago, their noktums still stood.

"Which door does it open?" Lorelle asked.

Of course that was the first question Lorelle would ask. It was the first anyone would ask because, while the noktums were spread at random across the countryside, there was only one place within the Crown City of Usara where actual doorways opened into that tentacled darkness: the Night Ring, where Rhenn's father held contests and feats of arms to entertain the public.

The Night Ring had five deadly doors: the Fire Way, the Dragon Pass, the Daemon Portal, the Night Door, and the Lore Gate, and each opened into a noktum. Huge, locked iron gates made sure no one went in…and also that nothing emerged. In the noktum, it was said, living people drew monsters like candlelight drew moths.

No human who'd entered a noktum had ever emerged. And no Luminent, for that matter.

"Which door does it open?" Lorelle prompted, jolting Rhenn from her reverie. "The Daemon Portal?"

"Not the Daemon Portal, not the Dragon Pass," Rhenn said. "Not the Night Ring's doors. A different door."

"Different?"

"This key—" Rhenn turned the big silver key in her hand, trying again to catch the flickering glow of the lantern on the desk, "— opens a noktum *inside* the palace."

"It does not!" Light shimmered down Lorelle's long, golden braid like a single strand had caught a ray of sunlight, and Rhenn smiled in satisfaction. That glimmer meant Lorelle was excited. Or afraid. Or both.

"Where in the palace?" Lorelle whispered.

With a smug smile, Rhenn pointed at one of the bookcases to the left of her father's desk.

A look of confusion came over Lorelle's face, and the brief glimmer in her hair died. She glanced back at Rhenn.

"You read about it?" Lorelle asked, not understanding.

"Not exactly. I discovered something."

"In a book?"

Rhenn ignored the question and said, "What if the adults have been lying to us? What if they've been lying to *everyone?*"

"What do you mean?"

Rhenn's chest was about to burst with excitement. She walked to the bookcase, removed a thick tome entitled *The Theology of Senji the Warrior Goddess*, and set it on father's desk. Holding up the key, looking directly at Lorelle, Rhenn reached her arm into the hole left by the missing book.

"I don't understand—" Lorelle began, and then her mouth rounded in a gigantic "O" as the bookcase swung silently outward.

Behind it, a dark stairway went sharply downward.

"Gods and monsters..." Lorelle murmured, covering her mouth with one elegant hand. Golden light flickered through her entire braid, and this time it stayed, a barely-perceptible glow.

Rhenn chuckled. "Indeed. We might find both down there."

"There's a noktum down there?"

"That's what Father said."

"Your father told you?"

"He was talking about it with Mother. They almost caught me this morning, but I hid behind the Kuldraha tree." She pointed at the squat, mysterious tree in the corner of the study. It only rose about eight feet into the air, but its wide limbs reached out sideways. Its wide, midnight leaves—limned in moonlight silver—obscured some of the books lining the walls. Mother claimed it was unique, and it was obviously magical like the noktums. The pot itself was made of black-fired clay inlaid with gold leaf. It was five feet in diameter at the top, sloping to about three feet wide at the bottom.

The eerie Kuldraha tree didn't shed its leaves in the fall like normal trees. Instead, it shed one a day, every day. The leaves dried up, crinkled, and then drifted down. When they hit the circular plate atop the pot, which had been fitted around the trunk—the soil beneath couldn't be seen—they clinked like metal, turning into liquid darkness that spread out across the surface, creating a little pool as dark as a starless sky. Father had tried to capture the metal as it hit, but it always turned into that inky black liquid. He'd tried to study the liquid, but if taken more than a dozen feet from the tree, it evaporated. The little tree was a mystery, but Mother had told Rhenn it was one of the Laochodon family's most prized possessions, as well as one of its more tightly guarded secrets.

"You hid in the Kuldraha?" Lorelle asked, staring at the dark pool filling the metal plate beneath its leaves.

"Not *in* the tree, silly. Behind the pot." She pointed. Four feet tall and five feet wide, the space was plenty large enough to hide a ten-year-old girl.

So when Mother and Father had unexpectedly entered the study this morning—when Rhenn was in here reading about the devious Bericourt family—Rhenn had ducked behind the pot just in time. To her surprise, her parents had begun talking about the secret entrance to the noktum downstairs. They'd also mentioned something called a "Thuros," but Rhenn didn't know what that meant.

"I want to see one up close," Rhenn said.

"One what?"

"A noktum, silly."

"No you don't!" Lorelle's eyes got wide.

"Of course I do. I'm a princess, aren't I?" Rhenn raised her chin. "Father refuses to let me see the doors in the Night Ring up close. I need to know about the things in my kingdom."

"*Your* kingdom?"

"Yes, my kingdom. I'll be queen someday, and I need to know everything."

"You have two brothers and a sister in line before you."

Rhenn set her mouth in a straight line. Lorelle, to her credit, flushed. Rhenn hated it when anyone talked about how far she was from the throne, and Lorelle knew that.

"We're going," Rhenn said firmly, "to the noktum."

Lorelle bit her lip, and her hair glimmered even brighter. "It has tentacles," Lorelle protested.

"I know it has tentacles."

"Well, they grab you and pull you in."

"Are you my best friend, or aren't you?"

"There are monsters in there, Rhenn. They *eat* people."

"If you're scared, I'll just go on my own." Rhenn started down the stairway.

Lorelle caught her arm. Her fingers were light, but strong. "I can't let you go down there—"

Rhenn yanked her arm from Lorelle's grasp. "Just try and stop me." Rhenn balled up her fists. It was bad enough when adults told her what to do, but Rhenn lost her temper when children tried.

Lorelle held up her hands pacifyingly. "*Alone.* I was going to say I can't let you go down there *alone.*"

Rhenn relaxed a little. "Oh. All right. That's good."

Lorelle craned her long neck to peer down the curving stairway, as if, if she got too close, she might fall.

Rhenn came up alongside Lorelle, and they both stared into that dark, spiraling hole.

"You're not saying go *into* the noktum, right?" Lorelle asked. "You just want to see it up close."

"Inside the noktum?"

"Yes."

"Lorelle, that's suicide."

"I know. I just wanted to hear you say it."

"We're going down there," Rhenn agreed. "See what they don't want us to see."

Lorelle's hair shone brighter, and her large brown eyes fixed on Rhenn. She picked up the lantern from the desk and held it in front of them.

"Come on." Rhenn went through the dark doorway and down the first few steps. She glanced over her shoulder at Lorelle, and the stalwart girl was right behind her. *Best friend material.*

The light from the lantern cast a long, bent shadow across the curving wall of the spiral stair. Lorelle's slender hand slipped into Rhenn's as the doorway vanished behind them around the curve of the wall. Butterflies leapt in Rhenn's belly, and she clenched the large silver key in her hand, reminding herself that queens weren't scared of the dark.

Rhenn heard a distant thumping overhead, like booted feet. Lorelle stopped and turned back the way they'd come. All they could see was the turn of the spiral staircase falling into shadow below and above where the lantern's light ended.

Lorelle's hand tightened on Rhenn's.

"Rhenn...." she murmured.

A scream ripped through the air, and both girls jumped. That hadn't come from below. That had come from above, from the royal chambers.

And it had sounded like Rhenn's older brother, Whendon.

Rhenn pushed around Lorelle and sprinted back up the steps. Another scream tore through the air. Shouts. Swords clashing.

"Senji's mercy!" Rhenn pushed her burning legs harder—

Lorelle caught up and yanked on her hand, bringing her stumbling to a stop. The lantern slipped from Rhenn's grasp, hit the floor, and crashed down the steep steps, crunching and banging, glass shattering. The oil spattered from inside and caught fire, bathing the right half of the stairway and wall in sudden flames. They shielded their eyes, then spun about as more screams and shouts came from above.

"Stop it!" Rhenn shouted, trying to pry her wrist from Lorelle's grasp.

"Rhenn wait," Lorelle begged.

"Whendon is *screaming!*"

"That's steel. Swords on swords. They're fighting up there!" Lorelle said urgently.

"Someone is hurting my family—"

"Yes." Lorelle yanked Rhenn so they were face to face. "What if they want to hurt you, too?"

"Your parents are up there, Lorelle."

Lorelle jerked like Rhenn had poked a pin in her. Her friend seemed not to have considered that. Her eyes went wide, and her hair shone so bright Rhenn squinted. Lorelle leapt past Rhenn and vanished up the stairs, her light fading with her.

"Lorelle! Wait!" Rhenn shouted, launching herself up the stairs again. Lorelle weighed less than half what Rhenn did, and she just couldn't keep up. Horrible visions flashed through her mind. Whendon hurt. Mother and Father hurt. Lorelle rushing into danger....

Two more screams ripped from the chaos above, the first high and piercing, then dying out as a second one began. Those sounded like Rhenn's sisters.

Rhenn's legs burned as she forced them harder, faster. She burst into the study, which was bright with the light from Lorelle's hair. The Luminent stood at a crack in the open door to the hallway, but she'd stopped there, frozen in place. There were no more screams, but Rhenn heard the booted feet of many men, the creaking and clinking of armor.

Gasping and huffing, Rhenn grasped the door to fling it open when Lorelle stopped her.

Rhenn followed Lorelle's gaze and looked through the barely-open door to the hallway—

Two bodies lay on the hallway rug in a pool of blood. They were long and tall, stretched out as though they'd been cut down while running. Both had golden hair. Lorelle's parents.

"No…" Rhenn whispered, and her heart wrenched. She wanted to charge into the hallway and demand an explanation, but Lorelle hauled her back from the door. If Lorelle had been a human of the same size, such a grapple might have thrown Rhenn to the floor, but because of their weight difference, she only pulled Rhenn back a little as Lorelle's boots skidded on the floor. "Lorelle—"

She clapped a hand over Rhenn's mouth.

"They're dead," Lorelle whispered through a tight throat, as though she didn't believe her own words. "My parents are dead."

Rhenn tried to shake Lorelle's grip off and reached for the handle, but Lorelle yanked back and swept Rhenn's legs out from underneath her. The slender Luminent picked Rhenn up and ran back to the secret passage.

"Let go of me! You don't know they're dead!" Rhenn struggled. Lorelle put her back on her feet, but kept hold of her arm.

"I overheard them talking," Lorelle whispered. "They killed your mother and father. They killed…everyone. Now they're looking for you. And me."

"You don't know my mother and father are dead yet—"

"Rhenn, I heard them! I heard your mother scream."

Rhenn couldn't believe it. Even though she'd seen the bodies, she simply refused to believe it. Things like this didn't happen. You didn't just walk halfway down a stairway with your parents alive and asleep and safe, and then walk back up the stairway to find them dead. They *had* to be alive.

"I have to get to them!" Rhenn said.

"They will kill you," Lorelle said adamantly.

That single statement hit Rhenn like a slap to the face, and she realized Lorelle was right. Somebody had attacked the palace. The stomp of boots and clink of armor. The clash of weapons. The screams of her brothers and sisters….

"But I have to help," Rhenn said in a small voice. "How…can I help them if I run away?" She felt tiny, powerless. She wasn't a queen at all.

"Live," Lorelle said in a broken voice. She was crying quietly now. "You have to *live*. And that means we have to run."

Rhenn looked at the barely-open study door, a thin barrier between them and slaughter. She suddenly realized it was astonishing someone hadn't already burst through.

"We…have to run," Rhenn said numbly.

"Yes."

"But…that's the only way out," Rhenn said.

"No." Lorelle looked at the open painting, at the dark stairway.

Rhenn desperately wanted to believe her parents were still alive. She wanted to fling herself into the hall and search frantically for them, to claw out the eyes of anyone who would dare hurt her family, but she froze.

Rhenn had once asked Father what it meant to be king, to rule over so many people, and he'd answered her.

"When you're a ruler, your life doesn't belong to you. You cannot choose to die selfishly, because your life doesn't belong to you alone. It belongs to those you protect, and you must guard it for those who need you."

If Rhenn's parents were dead—if that was really true—it meant she really was the queen now. She had to look after the kingdom, after her subjects. She had to look after Lorelle.

Rhenn squeezed her eyes shut. She drew in a deep breath and opened them again. She saw the open painting and the dark stairway with sharp clarity.

Her fears calmed, and she saw what she needed to do.

She couldn't spend her time being afraid. She couldn't spend it being angry. She had to be like Father. She had to be smart. To make good decisions. She had to look at what was in front of her with clear eyes.

"They're coming for us," she said in a monotone.

"Rhenn—"

"Those who killed our families are going to come for us," she said, and each word felt like a little hammer strike on her chest. That was the truth. That was what was real. That was seeing clearly.

Lorelle didn't protest this time. She swallowed and nodded.

"But we won't let them. We're going to hide." Rhenn shoved the giant key into her belt and snatched a long, thin dagger from Father's desk, the one he used to slice through wax seals on scrolls.

"Yes. We hide," Rhenn repeated emphatically. The guards in the palace would come eventually; they would kill these horrible murderers. Maybe there was a battle taking place right now, loyal guards fighting fervently to get to the royal wing. Rhenn had to keep them safe just long enough for reinforcements to arrive.

Rhenn took Lorelle's wrist and entered the hidden stairway. She turned and carefully closed the painting behind them. It clicked shut with finality, as though their new world was this stairway, and only this stairway. Rhenn swallowed her fear and led the way down.

The oil from the lamp Rhenn had dropped was almost burned out, flickering weakly up the wall. It barely lit the spiral staircase. They stuck close to the inner curve of the spiral and stepped quickly past the burning oil.

Around and around they went, down and down, until even the burning oil was a dull, orange flicker behind them. Finally, Rhenn stopped. They both breathed loudly in the silence, listening.

A thump came from above, then angry, arguing voices, but Rhenn couldn't make out what they were saying. More thundering noises, as though someone was pulling books from the shelves and throwing them to the floor. Lorelle's hair brightened.

"That doesn't sound...like someone who's coming to help us," Lorelle said.

"Come on," Rhenn said. They wound around and around the staircase, but this time Rhenn didn't feel the exhaustion in her legs. She didn't pay attention to the burn in her lungs. The stairs ended abruptly at another door. Rhenn pushed the latch, and it opened on well-oiled hinges.

The room beyond looked like something out of a myth about the Giants. The stairway ended in the middle of a circular room. To the right, an enormous arch with strange markings upon it glowed in the center, smears of many colors slithering across the plane that should have shown the darkness of a hallway beyond.

Directly ahead stood another archway, this one human-sized and closed with a thick, cross-banded iron gate. The lock was enormous and looked like it was a perfect fit for the tarnished silver key in Rhenn's belt.

"That's…" Rhenn pointed at the larger archway. "That must be the Thuros."

The two of them walked around the circular room. The ceiling was twenty feet tall, and the walls were made of the same dark, chiseled stone as the stairway. There was no other way in or out except the stairway or the iron gate. Or the slithering rainbow Thuros. Rhenn ascended the dais and put her hand on the swirling colors. She half-expected her hand to go through like water, but it felt like a smooth stone wall. There was no way out there.

They approached the iron gate. Lorelle's glowing hair pushed back the shadows until they resolved into dark, oily tentacles. They drifted forward lazily, as though looking for something to grab. Under the direct shine of Lorelle's light, the tentacles turned grayish, fading from the deep black to something that Rhenn could almost see through. The further out from the radius of Lorelle's light, the darker the noktum became, a supernatural darkness that threatened to devour anyone who came too close. It oozed evil.

"Do you see what your light is doing?" Rhenn asked. "It's…I can almost see into it. Do you see that?" Rhenn had never heard of that. Noktums swallowed light. All light. No light had ever pierced a noktum, not even bright sunlight. But somehow the light from Lorelle's hair did.

"I don't want to go in there," Lorelle murmured.

"We're not going in there. We're not even opening the door. We're just going to wait here until the palace guards—"

A loud bang came from the doorway to the stairs. They both jumped. Lorelle's hair grew brighter, and tears welled in her eyes. She clenched Rhenn's hand and looked more scared than Rhenn had ever seen her. Rhenn felt the same way. That didn't sound like guards coming to help them. But Rhenn had to think of something. She had to think clearly. She had to give Lorelle courage.

"All right. We *are* going in after all," Rhenn said.

"Rhenn!"

"Not into the noktum. Just…inside the gate. We'll hide there. They don't have the key, and if we blend with the shadows, they'll never see us. They'll come in, find nothing, and they'll leave."

Tears stood in Lorelle's eyes, like diamonds in the bright light from her hair. "How are we going to hide?" She gestured to her hair, brighter than a torch.

Rhenn pushed the naked dagger into her belt and pulled out the thick silver key. She shoved it into the lock and tried to twist it. It didn't budge. She tried harder. Nothing.

"Help me," she commanded.

Lorelle put her hands on Rhenn's. They both twisted with all their might.

It didn't budge.

Booted steps echoed on the stairway, coming closer.

"Rhenn!" Lorelle whispered urgently.

"Open!" Rhenn commanded, twisting futilely. Tears of frustration streaked down her face. She yanked the stupid thing out and slammed the key into the lock again and again. "Open, open, open!"

Something crunched in the lock, and when Rhenn withdrew the key this time, flakes of rust came with it, sifting and falling to the floor. Rhenn jammed the key in harder and tried to twist it again. This time, it did turn a little, and a little blue flash of light flickered inside the keyhole. Magic!

Lorelle grabbed Rhenn's hands again, and they both twisted, grunting with the effort. The lock screeched, and the key turned. Blue light flashed within the keyhole, tumblers clicked, and something inside clanked. The gate jolted half an inch forward.

The girls hauled on the door, and it ground open.

"What are we doing?" Lorelle asked hopelessly as they went into the tunnel and stood on the other side of the gate.

"Help me close this," Rhenn commanded.

Together they pulled the screeching gate back into place. Turning the key from the other side was hard, but it had loosened up a little. With both of their hands working on it, they managed to lock the gate. If the gate was locked, the murderers couldn't reach them. That was something, at least. It was hard to kill someone with a sword if they were twenty feet behind a steel gate.

"We have to cover your hair," Rhenn said, trying to keep her voice steady. She pulled her tunic over her head, leaving only her nightshirt to ward off the bone-deep cold of the tunnel. "If we cover your hair, they won't see us," she said. Together, they wrapped Lorelle's hair in the tunic, securing it tightly with a knot. The tunnel plunged into absolute darkness, and the hair on the back of Rhenn's neck prickled, knowing how close the tentacles were. Senji, they could be inside the noktum now for all she knew!

"There's no way out," Lorelle whispered, echoing Rhenn's desperate thoughts. "We're trapped."

"We'll be all right," Rhenn said. Surprisingly, her voice sounded strong. She pushed the key back into her belt, yanked out the knife, and held it with both hands.

The booted feet sounded from the stairway louder. Eerie blue light flickered at the bottom of the door.

"They're coming," Lorelle squeaked. The darkness around Rhenn retreated, giving a slight illumination to the tunnel and the gate. At first, she thought it was the new blue light, then she looked over her shoulder and realized Lorelle's hair had become so bright, it shone through the cloth of the tunic.

"Lorelle!" Rhenn whispered harshly. "Your hair—you have to calm down."

"I-I can't!"

The door banged open, bathing the circular room with blue light. An armed man emerged from the stairway, and Rhenn froze, feeling horribly exposed. How had she ever thought they could hide here?

The man peered into the dim room, gripping a bloody sword in his hand.

"What is this place?" he said, his deep voice loud in the cavernous room. Rhenn recognized him. It was Baron Tybris Vamreth!

The bright blue light followed him, growing stronger. A woman in mage's robes emerged, holding the blue light in her palm.

Vamreth stared at the Thuros, cocking his head in curiosity. The swirling colors had pulled his gaze away from the tunnel, and Rhenn and Lorelle. He hadn't seen them yet.

Reflexively, Rhenn retreated and bumped into Lorelle. Lorelle desperately grabbed Rhenn's arms to steady them both. The tunic, which Lorelle had been trying to tie tighter, unraveled and fell to the ground. Bright, buttery light filled the tunnel. Rhenn twisted, reaching down to snatch at the tunic—

She sucked in a breath and froze. Behind Lorelle, the reaching tentacles of the noktum had lengthened. Somehow, they'd sensed the girls, and their tips wriggled like hungry tongues, inches away from Lorelle's legs.

"Your Majesty!" The mage with the blue light said as more armed men poured into the room. Vamreth tore his gaze away from the Thuros and followed the pointing finger of the mage.

This time, he saw the girls.

Baron Vamreth smiled a horrible, smug smile.

"Open it," he said to the mage.

"It's…bound," the woman replied.

"Bound?"

"The key is the only way," she said. "This lock cannot be picked, and it cannot be forced by any spells I possess."

A flood of relief flowed through Rhenn. If they couldn't get inside, they couldn't reach the girls. Maybe that would be enough. Maybe the palace guards would come, and these murderers would have to flee.

"Then what good are you?" Baron Vamreth snarled. He looked over his shoulder at the dozen men who'd entered the room. All of them were looking around. "Crossbow!" Vamreth snapped.

Rhenn's heart sank.

The baron's men looked at him like he'd said something indecipherable, and Vamreth rolled his eyes. "Senji's Teeth, get yourselves together. Somebody give me a crossbow."

After a shuffling moment as murmurs went through the crowd of fighting men, one of them passed a crossbow forward. Vamreth fitted a bolt and turned to the girls.

"You're in a bit of a spot, aren't you?" he said, approaching the gate.

Rhenn and Lorelle's hands clasped together, fingers intertwining. Lorelle began crying softly, looking back and forth between Vamreth and the noktum's tentacles, which had nearly reached them. Rhenn clenched her teeth, and a high-pitched sound escaped her. She wanted to leap at these murderers, tear their throats out with her bare hands. She felt utterly helpless.

"You…" she said, choking on the words. "My parents…"

"Are dead." Vamreth carefully put the tip of the arrow between the slats of the gate and leveled the crossbow at her.

"Nnnnno! Nnnnno!" Lorelle said through her sobs. Her hair brightened like a miniature sun. Vamreth squinted, peering at them as he aimed.

The crossbow twanged, and Lorelle yanked Rhenn backward. "No!" Lorelle shouted.

White hot pain stabbed into Rhenn as the bolt sank to the feathers in her arm. She screamed.

The girls stumbled back together—

A single shadowy tentacle brushed Rhenn's cheek like a feather. It twitched as though in ecstasy…and then all the tentacles lunged for the two girls at once. They coiled around and around the girls. Rhenn's heels skidded on the rough-hewn ground as the tentacles pulled her and Lorelle backward.

The last thing Rhenn saw was Vamreth's surprised expression. Then the entire room vanished as Rhenn plunged into utter blackness…

For the first moment, she couldn't breathe, couldn't think. She felt like she was floating, like she'd been plunged into a cool tub of water.

Am I dead? she thought. *Is this what it's like to die?*

"Rhenn?" Lorelle's frightened voice pierced the darkness.

Rhenn's sense of weightlessness vanished. Her feet hit the ground, and she stumbled, flinging out her arms to catch her balance. Her arm screamed in pain, and she lost her grip on the dagger, heard it clatter somewhere in the dark.

Slowly, the dark retreated around a single glowing light. In the midst of the light emerged Lorelle's face, tight with fear. Her hair *could* pierce the noktum. Rhenn could see!

Rhenn cast about, fingers fumbling, and grasped the dagger she'd dropped.

Lorelle's hair revealed their surroundings in a ten-foot radius. Beyond that, it was just blackness, but they appeared to still be in a tunnel, just as before. Rhenn didn't know what she'd expected. Tumbling forever in a weightless blackness with bat-like terrors trying to take a bite of her? So far as she could tell, this was just an extension of the tunnel, except now everything was utterly dark except for the ten-foot radius of light provided by Lorelle's hair that showed the world in shades of gray. And if that went out…

Rhenn shuddered.

"Keep shining," she murmured. "Don't stop being scared."

Lorelle gave her a look like Rhenn had gone insane. Rhenn forced a pained laugh.

"Where are the monsters?" Lorelle whispered. "Legends say they attack light immediately."

"I don't know," Rhenn said, pushing her fist—still gripping the dagger—against her arm beneath the arrow sticking out of it. It hurt so much, it made her dizzy.

"We should…find a way out," Lorelle said, looking up the tunnel. Behind them, the tunnel ended in a flat black wall. Going back would put them into Vamreth's hands again.

But the other way led deeper into the noktum.

"Yes," Rhenn said, and she led the way. A queen should lead the way without fear. But with every step, she waited for a monster to leap out of the darkness.

Time passed as the tunnel wound on and on. Abruptly, the cave widened, and they reached the end of it. Lorelle's light grew suddenly brighter as they looked out onto a flat landscape. Her light now reached twenty feet out, but Rhenn could also see a kind of sky overhead. It was dark gray instead of black. A stand of trees began to her right, and all of them seemed to be made from darkness. No greens or browns, only shades of gray and black. Black tufts of grass grew just outside the cave atop the dark gray of the ground.

The girls stood there, staring, for a long moment.

Lorelle looked over at Rhenn. "What do we do now?"

"I don't know—" Rhenn stopped herself. No. She was the queen now. She didn't get to "not know" what to do. She cleared her throat and stood up straighter, though the pain in her arm lanced through her. "An hour ago we were children, but we can't be children anymore. We survive. We live. That's what we do."

A flicker of hope crossed Lorelle's face. It encouraged Rhenn, so she continued.

"We start walking." She looked to her right. "Into those trees. The noktum…south of the city… it runs through the trees. Everybody knows that. So we walk until we find the edge of it. It can't be far."

"How do you know that's the right direction?" Lorelle asked, pointing at the trees. "How do you know that's northeast?"

"Because…." Rhenn hesitated. "Because the palace is at the western edge of the city, right up against the wall." Rhenn dredged up half-forgotten memories, things she knew, and things she'd been told, linking them together like a chain. "If we'd come out to the east, we'd be under water. To the north or south, it'd be plains. So that's the Laochodon Forest," she said with conviction. She pointed at the trees. "Which makes *that* north. And the noktum barely comes as far north as the city. Which means we won't have far to go to get out—"

An insidious purr drifted from overhead.

Rhenn craned her neck to look upward, and her breath caught in her throat.

A long, sinuous creature crept into the light of Lorelle's hair, coming down the cliff above the cave entrance. It clung to the rock face six feet above them. Its sleek, black-furred body was longer than both girls stacked on top of each other, with claws that crunched into the rock and looked strong enough to crush a person's head easily. The thing had a large, black nose at the front of a blunt muzzle, and beady black eyes on either side of its round head.

It peeled back fuzzy lips to reveal fangs as long as Rhenn's dagger.

"Nnnnooo…" Lorelle keened.

The thing leapt upon her.

It happened so fast, Rhenn didn't even know the creature had moved until it landed on her friend, driving Lorelle to the ground with a thump.

Rhenn screamed in rage and jumped on the thing's back, stabbing wildly with her knife. Rhenn's parents had died tonight. Her brothers and sisters had died.

This monster couldn't have Lorelle, too!

The thing shrieked. It whipped about, giant fangs snapping at Rhenn. She leaned back from the snapping jaws, but she kept stabbing. The teeth barely missed her arm and closed on the arrow sticking out. The beast thrashed, yanking on the arrow, perhaps thinking it was part of Rhenn's body.

She screamed.

The arrow tore free, and the force of the creature's yank threw Rhenn sprawling to the ground. The enormous fanged otter slithered into the air—hovering! It forgot Lorelle and leveled its deadly gaze on Rhenn. Rhenn scrambled to her feet, gritting her teeth at the pain, and held the dagger before her protectively with her good hand.

The thing's short legs folded back against the long body as it hovered. It seemed to be preparing to launch itself like an arrow.

Lorelle rose up behind it, blood trickling down her forehead from where the thing had scored with its fangs. She raised a fist-sized rock clenched in both hands. The monstrous fanged otter sensed her and twisted.

She brought the rock down on its nose. Something crunched, and black blood spattered the ground.

It twitched, floating backward, and Rhenn charged, stabbing the dagger into the beast. It sank to the hilt, and the creature screamed.

Apparently, that was enough for it. The beast whipped back, flying away. It shot up into the sky, wriggling through the air like a water snake through a pond. It went up and up…

…and into a cloud of beasts just like it. The throng of monsters writhed in the sky like a mass of black worms.

"Senji's Spear…" Rhenn murmured, and Lorelle gaped.

"Run, Rhenn. We have to run now!" Lorelle said.

They turned and sprinted into the forest. Rhenn spared a glance over her shoulder, through the gaps in the branches, and saw the horde of creatures turning their direction.

"They're going to catch us," Lorelle said.

"Not both of us," Rhenn huffed. "You're fast enough. Run ahead, Lorelle. Make it out of the—"

"I'm not leaving you!"

"Go!" Rhenn cried. "Find the edge of the noktum!"

Lorelle hesitated, then leapt ahead like a bounding deer, outdistancing Rhenn in seconds. No sooner had she vanished into the trees than her voice floated back excitedly.

"Rhenn! It's here! It's right here! Hurry!"

Rhenn heard branches cracking behind her. Feet pounding, lungs burning, she glanced backward and glimpsed the massive fanged otters tearing through the forest to get to her. She ran harder, gasping for breath.

Lorelle's light glowed ahead. Rhenn headed for it. Trees whipped by in a blur, Lorelle's light flickering between them, and then suddenly Lorelle appeared. She stood before a flat black curtain that wound through the trees: the edge of the noktum.

Lorelle gripped her rock. She stepped forward and threw it hard at Rhenn's head.

An insidious purr sounded just behind Rhenn's ears at the same moment—

Lorelle's rock just missed Rhenn's head and smacked the creature in the eye. One fang scraped Rhenn's neck as the creature howled and jerked away.

Rhenn reached Lorelle at a full sprint, and they dove through the flat black curtain.

They burst into a bright world beneath stars and a silvery moon, and the two girls tumbled across the ground. Though the curtain of the noktum was flat from the inside, on this side it was covered with those insidious tentacles that quested toward them, seeking to draw them back in.

Lorelle pulled Rhenn to her feet, and they staggered back, out of reach.

They held onto each other, staring at the lazy tentacles, waiting for the fanged, floating otters to burst through. But they didn't.

Compared to the dull gray light inside the noktum, it seemed like the sun was shining here. Rhenn could see everything: the green and brown of the pine trees, the green grass beneath them, even the wall of the city through the branches, with the tall Night Ring and the towering palace poking high into the sky.

Heart thundering, Rhenn clung to her best friend. They watched the tentacles, safely out of reach. Rhenn expected the giant fanged otters to burst through and finish them off at any moment.

But the creatures never emerged.

Finally Rhenn said, "So…that was a really good throw with the rock. I think you have a true talent there."

Lorelle looked down at her and laughed. That single laugh turned into two, and then they were both laughing. The laughter became uncontrollable, they staggered back into a tree, and fell to their butts, still holding hands. They laughed and laughed until it became sobs, and they just held each other.

The sobs eventually turned to sniffles, and then to silence.

"What are we going to do?" Lorelle finally asked in a small voice. The question rang loudly in Rhenn's mind, too. Their families were dead. They'd escaped a bloody coup. They'd escaped the noktum. She could barely comprehend all they'd just done. But now that it was over, they still weren't safe. Where could they go now? To one of Father's loyal dukes or barons? How could she know which was which? She'd thought Baron Vamreth was loyal.

Rhenn stared at the forest. The crying had left her feeling hollow. The storm of fear and grief inside her had blown itself out. She just looked at the tentacles of the noktum, at the trees, and at the Crown City of Usara in the distance.

A ruthless calm settled over her. Below the fear and grief, a molten layer of rage bubbled in her soul.

Yesterday, if Rhenn had found herself alone in the woods with no parents to protect her, she'd have been terrified. No food. No shelter. Wild beasts.

Strangely, she wasn't afraid now.

She thought about Baron Vamreth. In one murderous instant, he'd taken away everything that mattered to her. Everything except Lorelle.

Rhenn wanted to charge back up to the city, knock down the gates, rage into the palace, and kill Vamreth, kill all his murderers.

But a queen had to see clearly. Two girls against an army that had just sacked the palace? She would only be giving Vamreth exactly what he wanted: placing herself and Lorelle under his butchers' knives again.

"What do we do now?" Rhenn repeated Lorelle's question steadily, glaring at the palace.

"Yes," Lorelle said.

"We just went into the noktum, and we emerged alive. We've done the impossible," Rhenn said. "And if we've done it once, why not twice?"

Lorelle glanced at the palace, then back at Rhenn. "What...do you mean?"

Rhenn drew a deep breath and let her anger flow into her, making her stronger. She let it burn away the last of her fear and grief like a rising sun. "In a handful of seconds inside the noktum, we learned secrets no one else knows. Your hair illuminates the noktum. The monsters within can be fought. They can bleed. What other secrets might the noktum give us if we search?"

"You mean go back in?" Lorelle asked incredulously.

"Yes," Rhenn said. "Not now. But soon. Now we learn the secrets of the forest. We make this our home. And then we take the noktum, too. We use its secrets."

"Take the noktum...." Lorelle said, as though trying to understand. "And...what'll you do with these secrets?" Lorelle asked.

"Take back my kingdom, of course," Rhenn said.

"You mean, use the noktum...as a weapon somehow?"

"What a weapon it would be," Rhenn murmured.

Realization dawned on Lorelle's face. She pressed her lips together in a firm line and nodded. "Yes," she said, and Rhenn's heart felt warmer. Whatever else happened, Rhenn wouldn't be alone. And she knew if she wasn't alone, she could do this. Somehow. She could do the impossible. She could make Baron Vamreth pay for what he'd done.

"Together," Rhenn said.

"Together," Lorelle echoed.

* * * * *

Todd Fahnestock Biography

Todd Fahnestock is a fantasy/sci-fi author of the bestselling *Tower of the Four*, *Threadweavers*, and *The Whisper Prince* series. He was the winner of the New York Public Library's Books for the Teen Age, a finalist for the Colorado Book Award in 2021 for *Tower of the Four: The Champions Academy*, and a finalist in the Colorado Authors League Writing Awards for the past two years, for *Charlie Fiction* and *The Undying Man*. His passions are fantasy and his quirky, fun-loving family. When he's not writing, he teaches taekwondo, swaps middle grade humor with his son, plays *Ticket to Ride* with his wife, scribes modern slang from his daughter, and goes on morning walks with Galahad the Weimaraner. Visit Todd at ToddFahnestock.com.

* * * * *

The Caveats of Salish-Bozar
by D.J. Butler

A Tales of Indrajit & Fix Story

The office door was closed, and no one answered when Indrajit knocked.

It was early morning, the sky a gray and sunless slate reflecting the shrill accusations of the wheeling gulls. The *Duke's Mistress* smoldered still, alongside the wharf where it lay at anchor. Indrajit and Fix had set fire to the ship the day before; really, Fix had done it, throwing an oil lamp onto a hulking, tentacled man named Squite. Indrajit and Fix had recovered four punched and knotted leather straps, each the length of a tall man's height, from Squite and his companion, the poetess Oritria, at the behest of Oritria's father, a merchant named Forfa in the Serpent Sea trade. Indrajit and Fix had gotten quite battered in the encounter, and Squite had lost a number of limbs, and also eyestalks. They'd last seen Oritria facing off with a four-armed, scaly man named Chark, and then Indrajit and Fix had returned to their inn-room headquarters to lick their wounds and lie low for the night. Now it was morning, and they'd come to Forfa's office to return the straps.

Only no one answered, and the door was locked.

Indrajit scanned the docks, squinting at each jar-lugging steve-dore and loitering seaman to make sure he didn't see the face-tentacle beard Oritria and Forfa both had.

"We've already been paid," he said. "It's hard to care too much."

"There's the ethical question," Fix said. "We need to return the texts to him." Forfa had claimed that the punched and knotted straps were writing, of all things.

Indrajit grunted. "Remarkable. I've just discovered an actual use for writing. We could leave him a note saying we have the straps, and to come back to our place to get them."

"Oritria's still out there," Fix pointed out, "and we know she can read."

Oritria had written her poetry on a wax tablet. "She might read the note and come after us, you're saying." Indrajit rubbed his chin. She'd intriguingly known a number of Blaatshi Epic epithets. She'd even chanted lines to Indrajit about his own death, like a warrior in the Blaatshi Epic. It had been both disconcerting and fascinating. "I'm not so frightened of her."

"She might bring that pile of bladed rope with her," Fix said. "Squite."

Squite was a Yeziot, a race that it turned out resembled giant piles of living green rope, with blades on the end of each strand, and eye-stalks in the middle of the heap. Until Fix had lit the ship on fire, it had looked as if Squite might singlehandedly kill Fix and Indrajit both, putting an end to their young jobber company, the Protago-nists.

"Good point." Indrajit examined the office building. It was a sin-gle-story cube made of mud bricks plastered white, with a tarred roof. It had shuttered windows on all sides, and the shutters were closed. "Then we'll just have to break in."

"And leave the strands here for Forfa?" Fix asked. "Does that really absolve us of our duty?"

"In light of the possibility that the Yeziot might this very minute be crouched on that rooftop, ready to pounce on us?" Indrajit drew his leaf-bladed sword Vacho and examined the shutters. "It resolves the ethical question for me."

He eased Vacho's blade between the shutters. The steel was fine and thin; it wasn't great for the blade, but it needed sharpening anyway. He slid the weapon up until he found the latch and pushed it open.

He looked up and down the wharf; no one was watching them.

"Shall we just toss them in the window?" he asked his partner.

Fix sighed. "Let's at least go inside. I'll leave him a note."

"Wait by the door," Indrajit told him. "I'll let you in."

He hoisted himself up onto the windowsill and into Forfa's office. He saw the same sagging shelves as the day before, the same ledgers, the same counter.

But today, Forfa himself lay dead on the floor. His head was almost entirely severed, the white bone of his spinal column showing through the wound. He lay in a dried puddle of his own blood, his face tentacles stained brown.

"Frozen hells." Indrajit pulled the shutters nearly closed. "No more Serpent Sea trade for you." He opened the door and pulled Fix inside, shutting and barring it again after.

"Well, no wonder he didn't answer," Fix murmured.

Indrajit sheathed his sword and pulled the knotted leather from the pocket of his kilt. "We were paid in advance. We can leave this and walk."

"Who killed him?" Fix asked.

"Does it matter?" Indrajit tossed the straps onto the counter. "People are killed in Kish every day. Welcome to Kish, watch your back! Robbers killed him. Blackmailers. Muggers. A former business partner, an old lover, someone he cheated in a card game. It's not entirely crazy to think that maybe his daughter killed him."

"Or her tentacled lover."

"We have no reason to think they were lovers." Indrajit shuddered. "But yes, maybe the Yeziot did it."

"Maybe he was killed for the texts." Fix folded his arms across his chest and raised his eyebrows.

"That should warn us to stay away from the written word in the future," Indrajit suggested. "Even when the writing in question is a knotted thong. And if someone is willing to kill for whatever's written on those straps, I say let them have them. I don't think any written words are worth a man's life. Not Forfa's life—and certainly, to be clear, not mine."

"You raise an interesting point," Fix said.

"Yes," Indrajit said. "Now let's get out of here."

"Whoever killed Forfa may be looking for the texts, and he may think we have them."

"We'll leave the thongs *here*. The killer can have them."

"The killer has already been here." Fix tapped Forfa's shoulder with the toe of his sandal. "He, or she, didn't find the strings. He's not coming back."

"You're saying we have to watch our backs." Indrajit shrugged. "I knew that already. What do you think I am, new in town?"

"I'm saying that we should investigate the texts," Fix said. "Knowing what they are will help us understand why someone would want them, who that person might be, and will help us defend ourselves."

"Before I met you," Indrajit said, "I never had to think about books. Do you know that? I didn't read them, didn't see them, wasn't troubled at all."

"Your life is so much richer now."

"I miss the days of my poverty."

"Besides," Fix said, "a murder on the wharf? The Lord Stargazer has the contract to keep the peace down here. Even if you and I aren't ethically obligated to investigate the murder, we can do Bolo Bit Sodani a favor, and I'd like him to owe us one for a change."

"The translucent bastard." Indrajit grunted, then gathered the leather strands back into his kilt pocket. Also, it occurred to him, Forfa had said that Grit Wopal had recommended hiring them. That meant Wopal was Forfa's friend, and Wopal was head of the Lord Chamberlain's Ears. In that capacity, he sometimes gave Indrajit and Fix sensitive work for the Lord Chamberlain. It couldn't hurt to find out why Wopal's friend had been killed. "Okay. But why do I have the feeling I'm going to regret this?"

"Well," Fix said slowly, "maybe it's because we're going to have to do research."

"The Hall of Guesses?" Indrajit sighed.

"I don't think they'll let us in," Fix said, "but I have a hunch they wouldn't be able to tell us anything, anyway, and there's somewhere else I want to try first."

* * *

"This is the ashrama of Salish-Bozar the White?" Indrajit gazed on the edifice in question. It was an unadorned, blocky building of gray stone with an extra wide entrance. He might have taken it for a warehouse if Fix hadn't identified it for him.

Also, it was located in the Spill. The city's main temples were in the Crown, the district of palaces, government buildings, and large institutions. The Spill was mostly occupied by merchants' shops and the related buildings: inns, taverns, apartments, warehouses, stables, factories, and so on. And, apparently, the ashrama of Salish-Bozar the White.

The two Protagonists stood in a light drizzle across the street from the ashrama, in front of a pungent shop selling tea and spices.

"Why doesn't your god have a proper temple?" Indrajit asked. "What's an ashrama?"

"He's not my god," Fix said. "The Selfless of the ashrama raised me."

"Very selfless of them." Indrajit nodded.

"And Salish-Bozar is worshipped in the dedication of the thoughts of his acolytes. The ashrama is where the worshippers live, meet, and work."

"The Useless and the Minuscules."

"The Selfless and the Trivials."

"Right. And you're thinking that some of these worshippers of Salish-Bozar may have dedicated their thoughts to these knotted straps, and may be able to tell us something about them."

"Exactly."

"But doesn't that force us into another ethical question?" Indrajit asked.

Fix frowned.

"If some Trivial's knowledge of this knotted-rope matter helps us, say, solve a murder," Indrajit said, "or save our own lives, then it's not useless information, and we've revealed that the Trivial's efforts have been in vain. We strip away the sacral value of his knowledge."

Fix nodded. "We'll have to talk about the matter indirectly. Maybe it's best if I do most of the talking."

"As in the Paper Sook." Indrajit yawned. "Interest rites and funding sinks and so on."

"Interest *rates* and sinking funds. Never mind, follow my lead."

Fix headed to the ashrama's gate, and Indrajit came one step behind him. In the gate, sheltered from the steady falling mist, stood two women in dirty white robes. One was a long-snouted, lavender-skinned Zalapting, and the other was a coppery Kishi like Fix, with short black hair. They made a gesture of greeting by splitting their fingers left and right, and Fix repeated it back to them. Indrajit tried, couldn't get his fingers to move in quite the right way, and finally just bowed.

"We've brought a gift for the White," Fix said. "A mystery found in the world."

The women's faces lit up.

"The world and all its mysteries," they said together.

"May we see the Selfless Bonk?" Fix asked.

"Come this way." The Zalapting opened a door within the gate and led them; her Kishi companion stayed on door duty.

"What's a Bonk?" Indrajit whispered as he walked down a hallway behind Fix. At first he took it for a narrow hall, but then he realized that a wide hallway had been subdivided by running tall, free-standing shelves down its middle, as well as by standing shelves against both walls. The shelves stood, pregnant with scrolls and codices.

"Bonk is a person's name," Fix whispered back. "The Selfless Bonk is the head of this ashrama."

Indrajit nodded.

The Zalapting Trivial left them in a shaft-like room that was narrow in two dimensions, but rose up three stories to the height of the building. The room's ceiling was a skylight; water leaked in around the edges of the light and trickled down the plaster of the walls. A thin man with skin so pale that Indrajit thought he could see the man's organs sat cross-legged on a small mat on the brick floor. He had large, shell-like ears, no hair, and skinny shanks wrapped in puffy pantaloons.

"Fix, my son!" he cried.

"Are you kin to the Lord Stargazer?" Indrajit blurted out. He'd met the Lord Stargazer once, and the man had been similarly translucent. "Or the same race of man, anyway?"

The Selfless Bonk grinned, revealing a complete absence of teeth. "I'm kin. Wonderfully, that knowledge is useless to you, as I have absolutely no influence over my cousin, Bolo Bit Sodani."

"Why is that wonderful?" Indrajit asked.

"Because today you've learned at least one useless piece of information," the Selfless said. "That's one step on the road to a mind of complete and restful contemplation, in tune with the glory of Salish-Bozar."

"Be careful," Fix warned Indrajit. He greeted the Selfless by kneeling and bowing to the floor, making the split-fingers gesture as he did so.

Indrajit tried to imitate the bow, at least.

"I have a theory," Indrajit said as he climbed to his feet, "though this may be useless information."

"A theory isn't actually information," Fix said. "It's an attempt to *explain* information."

"Tell us your theory," the Selfless said.

"You're not a religion about information at all," Indrajit said.

The other two men both looked at him as if he'd said something shocking. Maybe even rude.

"Salish-Bozar is really a god of beauty," Indrajit said.

Fix scowled.

"What do you mean?" Bonk asked.

"Information that's useless is information that no one understands," Indrajit said. "Which means that it's not really information at all. Or it may as well not be information. It's just patterns, or images, or parallels. What you like is weird patterns, strange things that should have an explanation, but don't. Or the explanation is unknown. Pretty colors, shining lights, weird syllables, forgotten tongues. You like the strange beauty of the world."

Bonk stood with the spryness of a child and took Indrajit by the elbow. "Have you considered a life in the ashrama?"

"We've brought a gift," Fix said, shooting Indrajit a sour look. "We asked to see you first to find out which of the Selfless or the Trivials we should share it with."

The Selfless Bonk seated himself again, smiling benignly. "Tell me the mystery you have seen."

Fix gestured to Indrajit, who brought the knotted lengths out of his pocket.

Bonk's face lit up. "Ah," he said. "I've seen such strands before."

Fix nodded, a satisfied look on his face. "Are they studied by one of the Selfless?"

"Yes. If you leave them with me, I will pass them on."

"We can't leave them, unfortunately," Fix said.

Bonk's smile collapsed. "You have a use for them?"

Fix hesitated.

"No one has a use for them," Indrajit said, "but we promised to give them to someone. Only we thought we should show them to you first. Perhaps you could make a replica, or draw a picture. Aren't they beautiful?"

The Selfless Bonk sighed and shook himself like a dog sloughing off worry. "Do you remember Meroit, Fix?"

Fix nodded. "I remember the Trivial Meroit well. Does he still sell his paintings in the market? He worked hard on the geometric patterns of damage caused to stone buildings by rubble. The falling directions of ruined walls, the cuts made by wind as opposed to the cuts made by water."

"Until the risk merchants of the Paper Sook learned of his work." The Selfless shook his head, eyes drooping heavily. "They delighted in the knowledge, which they said would allow them to write more precise risk-selling contracts. They offered Meroit large sums of money and employment in the Paper Sook."

"He didn't take it?" Fix asked.

"He tried to take his own life instead. Years of study wasted, because it turned out the subject of his study had practical value. We had to watch him closely for months, to stop him from simply walking into the sea."

"Perhaps he should have been an artist," Fix murmured, "and left the mystery of the world to others."

"So the study wasn't *wasted*," Indrajit said, "it just wasn't the right kind of beautiful for Salish-Bozar."

Bonk bobbled his head, a gesture that circled around and became a nod. "But then, on one occasion when we thought we had to rescue him from the waves, we found him staring in great fascination at the sea-kelp."

"Ah." Indrajit nodded, as if remembering the beauty of kelp.

"Meroit undertook then to learn all he could about the kelp," Bonk said. "Its thickness at different depths, its length at different times of the year, the changes in color and texture the plant undergoes at different proximities to the habitations of man. And, in particular, man's sewers."

Indrajit and Fix nodded. Fix seemed genuinely interested, but Indrajit had long since degenerated into a state of complete pretense.

"To the astonishment of the entire ashrama," the Selfless continued, "the Lord Archer turns out to have large kelp farms. They're on the southern coasts, managed by Fanchee sea-farmers, and none of us were aware of them."

"You're focused on useless information," Indrajit said, "and kelp turns out to be useful. No wonder you were astonished."

"It feeds many people." The Selfless shrugged. "Meroit had memorized ten thousand pieces of information and was preparing to defend his knowledge and seek to ascend to Selflessness when one of the Lord Archer's Fanchee came and offered him a job managing kelp plantations."

"How did Meroit take that?" Indrajit asked.

"He ran to the Crown and climbed the Spike. The only thing that stopped him from throwing himself off and plummeting to his death was that a group of dried goods merchants up there preparing to consecrate their annual accounts to Spilkar saw him."

"They saved him?" Fix asked.

"They saw him running up and assumed he was a criminal come to rob them." Bonk frowned. "Their bodyguards subdued him."

"Lucky Meroit," Indrajit said.

The other men nodded.

"The good news for me," Indrajit added, "is that I've absorbed several hundred useless facts about the life of Meroit this morning. I'm well on my way to becoming a Selfless!"

Bonk frowned, and Fix shook his head.

"Caveat number seven," the Selfless said. "The deeds of no man's life can ever be considered useless."

"Wow," Indrajit said, "you guys are really strict."

Fix glared at him.

"Sorry," Indrajit said, "bad joke. Please continue. I think we had yet to hear about how Meroit became involved in the study of knotted thongs."

"I don't know how that happened," the Selfless said. "You can ask Meroit himself if you like. But after the incident on the Spike, he took to his pallet for a month. When he arose, he showed me the first of his knotted strands, to be weighted."

"Weighted?" Indrajit asked.

"Caveat number three," the Selfless said. "All useless facts shall be accounted according to the weight assigned to them by the Hierophant Selfless."

"Bonk is not merely Selfless," Fix said, "he's the Hierophant Selfless, the senior priest of the Ashrama."

Bonk shrugged modestly.

"I understand." Indrajit stretched out one of the strands with his fingers. "And someone has to decide how many facts can be extracted from a strand such as this."

"Length," Fix said. "Weight. Elasticity, strength. Number, size, and position of knots and piercings. Color, texture, taste."

"Sure," Indrajit agreed. "So Meroit wouldn't have to commit ten thousand of these things to memory. But how many? A thousand?"

The Selfless Bonk flared his nostrils and arched his eyebrows. "That number is within the sole purview of the Hierophant Selfless to decide."

"I don't want to argue," Indrajit said. "Just trying to understand. The beauty of the world interests me. And the beauty of the followers of Salish-Bozar the White, too."

"Caveat number four," Bonk said. "No fact about the organization of the followers of Salish-Bozar shall ever be deemed useless."

"Makes sense." Indrajit nodded. "That and the deeds one prevent an aspirant from *creating* ten thousand useless facts."

"Exactly how many of these strands Meroit shall have to know will depend on the strands themselves," Bonk said. "But it will be nearer to one hundred than one thousand."

Indrajit nodded. "Wonderful."

Bonk chuckled. "The mystery of the world is indeed wonderful. Fix, do you remember where Meroit sleeps? I believe he's there now, reflecting on the mystery."

They took their leave of the Selfless. They passed through a long chamber containing cubbies full of stones, sorted by color and size, along the walls. At a staircase at the end, Indrajit expected to climb, but instead they descended.

Beneath the ashrama spread a maze, winding and radial like the roots of a tree. Indrajit followed Fix along a narrow, low-ceilinged root that ended in a circular room bristling with doors.

"What is a Fanchee sea-farmer?" Indrajit asked.

"I assume Fanchee is a race of man," Fix said. "Do you not know any epithets for them?"

Indrajit didn't. "We're not under the building anymore," he observed.

Fix shrugged and knocked on a door. Without waiting, he opened it.

Inside, a lone man sat on a straw pallet. He had a bulbous, root-like head, pointed and covered with thick bristles of hair, and impaled by a bulbous, root-like nose. His skin was a weedy yellow, and what seemed to be his ears were two little flower-like buds attached beneath his jaw. The buds curled forward and swiveled slowly to face the direction of any sound as he listened. No eyes were visible in his face.

A lattice of wood crossed the room just below the ceiling. From it hung dozens of knotted and punched leather strands. The four strings in Indrajit's pocket would have fit instantly and perfectly among them. The walls were hung with paintings of complex buildings. They looked like temples, with multiple stories, windows, gables, and columns, each scene dotted with dozens of men and women in togas of various colors.

"Are we not disturbing meditation?" Indrajit murmured.

"Meroit!" Fix bellowed.

Two black beads rose to visibility from beneath the surface of Meroit's skin. "Fix? Have you returned?" The voice was dull and blurred, the mouth a tiny crescent in danger of being filled entirely, should the nose ever slip from its position.

"Not in the way you mean." Fix made the Salish-Bozar greeting gesture, and Meroit repeated it instantly. "We wanted to come show you something. A gift for the White."

Meroit held very still. "What?" His voice was tiny.

Fix gestured at the strands hanging overhead. "We came across four of these, and we're trying to understand them. I thought the ashrama might be the right place to come, and I was right."

"Well, you know, I…I don't *understand* them," Meroit said.

"If you understood them," Indrajit said, "they wouldn't do you any good. Wait…is there a caveat that says helping one to achieve the status of Selfless doesn't count as being useful?"

"There is," Fix said.

"That's the second caveat," Meroit added.

"See?" Indrajit grinned. "I'm getting the hang of this."

"Next thing you know, you'll be reading," Fix said.

"Let's not go crazy." Indrajit cleared his throat and addressed Meroit. "But you've got quite a collection there. Forty? Fifty?"

"Something like that," Meroit agreed.

"The Hierophant Selfless suggested you might be up for consideration when you get to a hundred or so," Indrajit said.

Meroit nodded. "May I see yours?"

Indrajit fished a strand from his pocket and handed it over. Fix shot him a quizzical look, and Indrajit winked.

Meroit took the strap in hand and ran it through his fingers slowly. He started at one end, where there was a triple knot, and caressed the entire length from that end to the other. His lips moved slightly as he touched each knot and divot. Once or twice, he backtracked to run his fingers over a particular section a second time.

"Where did you find this?" he asked when he'd finished.

"We came across it in a brothel," Fix said quickly. "So many corpses from a fight that had just happened, we couldn't even tell who'd dropped it."

"How about you?" Indrajit asked. "You have fifty of these. The Trivials of Salish-Bozar can't spend *that* much time with harlots."

Meroit turned a slightly darker shade, and his eyes sank into his puffy flesh almost to the point of disappearing. "I found the first one. I...don't remember where. On the beach. And then I put out the word that I'd pay money if people found more of them. They just come to me."

"You don't worry that putting the word out causes people to *make* these for you?" Indrajit asked. "There's got to be a caveat there, somewhere."

"I think I can tell the real ones," Meroit said.

"What do you mean, *real* ones?" Indrajit asked. "Real strands of knotted leather? I can make you a thousand real leather strips; just give me a week."

"I mean strands that weren't just faked for me. That would have existed without me." Meroit shook his head. "You know what I mean."

"One thing that has to really worry you," Indrajit said, "is that you can't be sure there will be enough of these for you to get to your ten thousand useless facts."

Meroit nodded. "The path of the White is hedged about by peril."

"So you can't tell us where these come from," Fix said, "or even where they're usually found, can you?"

Meroit chuckled. "Just the useless knowledge here, I'm afraid."

Indrajit noticed the question that Fix was scrupulously avoiding: *you can't read these strings, can you?* He kept his own mouth shut, too.

"You said you had four," Meroit reminded them.

"The others are back at our room," Indrajit said. "We just brought the one."

"Room?" Meroit asked. "I mean, ah, are you sleeping at the ashrama?"

"We're in an inn," Fix said casually. "Doesn't have a name, actually, but it's next to a big camel merchant off the Crooked Mile."

Meroit tried to hand the string back to Indrajit. "I see, I see."

"Don't you want to write something down?" Indrajit asked. "Paint a picture of the string, count out its knots or something?"

"Ah, yes." Meroit rummaged around in the corner behind his pallet and came up with a roll of paper, ink pot, and pen. He stretched the string out across the floor and laboriously scratched a series of marks on the paper, presumably recording all the information the Selfless Bonk had said he would have to know.

Indrajit stood humming an old tune and raising his eyebrows at Fix.

When Meroit had finished, he handed the strap back to Indrajit. "When can I, ah, see the others?"

Indrajit and Fix shrugged at each other. "Next week?" Fix suggested.

Meroit's hand shook. "No sooner? What if I come to your room to look at them?"

"No rush, right?" Indrajit said. "You're still dozens of strings short of your hundred. Besides, we're not actually going back now. We have to be elsewhere."

"Deeds of derring-do for the Lord Chamberlain," Fix said. "Makes me miss the days of contemplation in the ashrama."

"You never missed us." Meroit laughed. "Did you marry that lady of yours, Fix?"

Fix shook his head slowly. "I did miss the ashrama, Meroit. Still do. And I'm afraid the lady went another way."

* * *

"Meroit's not telling us the truth," Indrajit said as they left the ashrama. "At least not the whole truth. Did you see the way he trembled?"

"He's not telling us any of the truth," Fix said. "He can read that string. He read it right in front of us."

"That's what reading is supposed to look like?" Indrajit asked. "Moving your mouth like that?"

"He's not a very *good* reader," Fix said.

"We should tell on him," Indrajit said. "We tell Selfless Bonk he's reading messages, and that guy never makes Selfless. They'll probably throw him right out of the ashrama. How many tries do you get before they kick you out?"

"He started at the end with three knots," Fix said. "Do all four have an end with three knots?"

Indrajit pulled the string out and looked. "Yes."

"He's reading messages," Fix said. "They're secret, and he's hiding them in plain sight by pretending he's studying some kind of mysterious phenomenon. Maybe he does pay people to bring him strings they find, and those who want to send him a message just leave the strings lying about."

"This sounds like thief- and assassin-craft," Indrajit said. As he said it, he turned his head slightly to one side. His eyes, set far apart in his head, gave him good peripheral vision. As they ascended the hill above the ashrama, toward the long street called the Crooked Mile, he saw a flash of red and yellow scales behind them.

Just a flash, and then whatever it was dipped out of sight.

"I would say spies," Fix suggested. "This sounds like a system for transmitting stolen information to foreign powers."

"That makes it a matter for Grit Wopal." There was altogether too much reading and writing going on here, and Indrajit was happy to have what looked like a way out.

"Let's learn a little more about it first," Fix said. "Let's be sure we're bringing him something real."

"How did you guess that we should go to the ashrama to look for information?" Indrajit asked.

Fix hesitated. "I go back to the ashrama from time to time. I'm generally aware of what the Trivials are researching. I thought I remembered seeing one of these strands there."

"You go back...because you miss it?" Indrajit asked.

"That's not it."

"Because you think the woman you love might go back there looking for you?"

Fix shook his head. "Almost, though. I...just feel close to her there. I can remember my times with her. And it's safer than standing outside her house at night, watching her bedroom window."

"Well, if Meroit is going to try to seize the other three strings, surely he'll do it now." Indrajit yawned. He'd missed most of a night's sleep, in pain after battling on the *Duke's Mistress*. "He'll think we're elsewhere."

"You should go back to the inn and lie in wait, then," Fix suggested. "See what turns up. Don't get into any fights unless you're sure you can win."

"When do I not win fights?" Indrajit asked.

"Just be discreet. I'm going to go back to the docks."

"What for?"

"I want to dig around a little into Forfa. See if he was real."

They parted ways, Fix turning left at the next alley and heading to the water. Indrajit reached the Crooked Mile and followed it straight down. He stopped twice to pretend he was shopping and look for pursuit, but he didn't see anyone.

The rain stopped, leaving a cool afternoon with a general blanket of humidity lying over the city, begging for a breeze to lift it.

At the nameless inn that served as the Protagonists' headquarters, he avoided the front door. He reasoned that if Meroit came or sent someone to search their room, he might ask the innkeeper before trying to break in. So instead of alerting the innkeeper to his return, Indrajit climbed a bakery that backed onto the inn. From the bakery's roof, he dragged himself over the wall and onto the roof of the inn's stables, then forced his way up the corner of the building onto the rooftop. Lying on his belly, he peered over the lip of the roof and watched the door to their chambers from the inside.

He also watched the courtyard and the stables; anyone looking up from that direction would be hard pressed to miss seeing him, lying on the roof.

He tried to think about the events of the day before, and this morning, but in his fatigue and recumbent position, he quickly dozed off.

A loud click awakened him. Peering into the room, he saw the lock on the door rotate, pulling the bar from its socket in the wall. He held his breath as the door pushed open, and then bit his tongue as the four-armed, red- and yellow-scaled man named Chark entered.

Chark had been some sort of officer on the *Duke's Mistress*, the ship he and Fix had burned down. Indrajit had last seen him locked in battle with Squite the rope-monster.

Which Indrajit had taken as a sign of Chark's non-involvement. So what was he doing here?

Indrajit eased a few fingers back from the edge of the roof without losing his view of the interior. Chark proceeded to toss their quarters with a vengeance. He shredded mattresses, ripped off table legs, pulled at loose bricks, and even shattered the chamber pot. He came away looking dissatisfied.

For the first time, Indrajit was happy he'd agreed to let Fix put their money in a bank, rather than leaving it hidden in their rooms.

Chark had torn apart two spare kilts belonging to Indrajit and was circling the room from the beginning, as if for a second look at everything, when Indrajit heard voices at the door. They were muffled, and Indrajit couldn't make out words, but Chark heard enough to make him bolt for the window.

Indrajit pushed himself slightly farther back and gripped the hilt of his sword, ready to draw and fight if the scaly man climbed up the wall. Instead, Chark dropped down into the courtyard. Indrajit kept out of sight until he heard the scratching sounds of the man's taloned feet running, and then he peeped over just enough to see

Chark's back disappearing out the stable doors, running toward the Crooked Mile.

He looked into the Protagonists' chambers as the door opened again.

"Oh, my," the innkeeper said. "Oh, my."

The person standing with the innkeeper was Meroit. The little Trivial seemed not so much disturbed as annoyed. "I take it this is not just bad housekeeping?"

"Something has happened," the innkeeper said with a gasp. "I don't know. I can't. Maybe you shouldn't."

"Maybe I shouldn't wait here for my old friend Fix the Trivial," Meroit said, nodding. "He'll have enough to do to clean this up without dealing with me, too. Perhaps I can leave him a note?"

The innkeeper leaned against the wall, gasping for breath and nodding.

Meroit walked through the chambers. Indrajit watched him through one window and then a second; the little acolyte of Salish-Bozar didn't leave a note at any point, but searched briskly through the trashed remains of the rooms.

Looking for the other three knotted thongs.

"Thank you," Meroit said to the innkeeper. He produced a couple of copper coins. They didn't stop the innkeeper's hyperventilation, but they produced a smile and a nervous laugh.

They closed the door.

Indrajit had never in his life more than this moment wanted to be able to write. If he could have left Fix a letter, it would have said, *Meroit came and I'm following him.*

But Indrajit couldn't write. He climbed down through the window into their chambers. He found an inkpot, but couldn't find any of Fix's scraps of paper—they were probably on his person. So he located the biggest scrap he could of his slashed pallet. He spread the fabric out on the floor, and using his own finger as a rough pen, he drew a picture of Meroit. Root head, root nose, beady eyes. Surely Fix would recognize the picture.

Then he drew a rough picture of himself, a man-shaped image who was mostly stick, but had a long, bony nose ridge and held a leaf-bladed sword. He did a careful job, he thought, of drawing himself following Meroit, even though he hacked out the entire picture, both images, in under two minutes.

Then he took a cloak from the mess on his floor and hurled himself down the wall into the courtyard. He took the ink bottle with him, not entirely sure what he was going to do with it. Stepping around fresh camel dung, he crept to the door to the street in time to see the little root-headed man in dirty white walking away down the Crooked Mile.

Indrajit followed, wrapping the cloak about himself to hide his distinctive facial features. Mercifully, the cool, damp afternoon meant that many other pedestrians on the street were hooded.

He splashed a line of ink with one finger on a door post as he started out, at the level of his own eyes. He wanted to stop and draw a little picture of Meroit, but there was no time for that.

Then he slouched, kept his eyes down, and tried generally to make himself smaller and less conspicuous as he followed the little acolyte across the Spill.

It wasn't difficult. Meroit looked over his shoulder from time to time, but he did so awkwardly, bouncing and stopping before he looked back. Indrajit was able to adjust his position, drifting back, pulling closer, or turning sideways, and he was confident Meroit didn't see him.

He'd have liked to be able to trade off following with Fix, and he blotted his path with ink dots as he went. His trailblazing earned him glares and kicks, and more than once an evil eye. A grain merchant even shouted, "Witch!" and chased him past her shop, but if Meroit heard, he didn't turn around.

The Trivial left the Spill and headed into the Dregs. The shops ended at the wall, replaced abruptly with gambling dens, taverns, bordellos, squalid tenements, and ruins. Indrajit nodded warily at the Jobber crew handling security at the gate—he recognized them as some of Mote Gannon's Handlers, Zalaptings, a Luzzazza, and a Thûlian powder priest. He and Fix had an uneasy truce with the Handlers, who'd tried to kill them, and he would've preferred to run into them with Fix at his side.

He didn't look closely to see whether the Luzzazza was missing an arm (which would have been Indrajit's fault), or if the powder priest was a woman under all the swaddling (which would make her the priest he'd wrestled with in an earlier scuffle). He just put his hand on Vacho's hilt and hoped for the best.

But the Handlers bared their teeth, spat on the ground, and let him through.

Meroit walked into a seedy coffee shop and took a seat at a small table. He sat with his back facing the street.

Was he hiding his identity? Was he waiting for someone who expected to be able to sit with his back to the corner?

A server consulted with Meroit about his coffee, and Indrajit looked for a place to hide. The coffee shop squatted in the corner of a small, muddy plaza. Indrajit backed into the opposite corner of the square and positioned himself on the far side of a cart selling fried tamarind. He bought a handful, wrapped in flat bread and topped with hot sauce, and took his first bite while watching Meroit.

A sharp point poked him in the back. Then a hand pulled Vacho from its sheath.

"Pull down your hood," a thick voice muttered, "and turn around. Slowly."

Indrajit swallowed his mouthful of tamarind and complied. The man holding a knife on him was green-skinned, noseless, and had a thicket of tentacles falling from the lower half of his face. Indrajit sighed.

The crowd on the street continued drifting sluggishly past, ignoring the knife in broad daylight. *Welcome to Kish; mind your business!*

"The only reason I don't kill you now is that I want you to tell me who you are first," the green-faced man hissed.

Then he collapsed.

Fix stood behind him, a rock in his hand. He tossed the rock aside, took the knife, handed Vacho back to Indrajit, and dragged the green man to his feet.

"Right," Fix said. "You yourself already explained why I haven't killed you yet. Start talking."

The green man spat in Fix's face; Fix dragged him past the tamarind seller and thumped his shoulder blades against a mud-brick wall.

"Did you arrange this meeting?" Indrajit asked. "Or did the Trivial?" The green man turned his face toward Indrajit, and Indrajit clapped a hand over his mouth. "No spitting." He wolfed down the rest of the fried tamarind and flat bread.

The prisoner growled.

"Meroit did," Fix said.

Indrajit looked up and down the street for any sign of Jobbers who might interfere, and saw none. The Dregs was notoriously under-policed, though, and organized criminal gangs sometimes stepped in to fill the gap.

"Here's what we know," Fix said. "You're Fanchee."

When had Fix learned anything about the Fanchee?

"You and Forfa are part of the Fanchee clan that farms kelp for the Lord Archer," Fix continued. "You've been sending information to our friend Meroit in the form of knotted ropes. The fact that he's a Trivial makes it easy; you leave the strands in public places, and people take them to the ashrama, knowing they'll be paid. None of your people gets exposed to Meroit, or vice versa. Only now some of the messages have gotten lost, and Meroit wants a meeting. What's the information about? Is it about the farms themselves? Or is there some secret information about the Lord Archer or his other holdings you're smuggling out?"

Indrajit removed his hand. The Fanchee only hissed.

Indrajit grabbed the Fanchee's face tentacles and yanked; the Fanchee yowled and squirmed. Fix dragged the green man down a narrow alley, stepping over two drunkards in a puddle.

Indrajit looked over at the coffee shop to be certain Meroit was still there, and then joined Fix.

Something nagged at the back of his mind, and he couldn't focus on it.

"Who pays you?" Indrajit barked.

"Good question," Fix growled. "Who gets this information? Pelth? The Paper Sultanates? The Free Cities?"

The Fanchee laughed. "Why do you think I would know?"

And then Indrajit understood.

He shook his head. There was no point in interrogating this Fanchee. "You've given away everything, you fool!" Fix shot him a quizzical look. "We've got an appointment, Fix. Time to leave this pawn."

Indrajit pushed the Fanchee to the ground and turned away, dragging Fix with him.

"What are you doing?" Fix asked. "What do you know?"

"What do *you* know?" Indrajit shot back.

"Forfa's body is gone," Fix said, "but I checked those ledgers, and they aren't about the Serpent Sea trade at all."

Indrajit nodded. "Forfa was lying to us from the beginning. And he was using someone else's building. Any idea whose building that is?"

"No. And I asked around the docks to see whether anyone knew Forfa, and no one did. But when I described him, several people called him a Fanchee."

"I have a bet," Indrajit said. He directed their footsteps uphill toward the Crown. "I bet that building belongs to the Lord Chamberlain."

Fix was silent for a moment. "You think this spy ring we've stumbled upon is part of the Lord Chamberlain's Ears. And that it's spying on the Lord Archer."

"Yes," Indrajit said.

"How does Meroit pass the information on, and to whom?"

"My guess is it's something indirect, like the knotted strings." Indrajit shrugged. "Does he still sell his paintings? Maybe the paintings are a way to pass the information on."

"Likely." Fix's voice was flat.

"It would be deeply ironic if the Lord Chamberlain's spies killed us," Indrajit suggested, "since we also work for the Lord Chamberlain. So to avoid that unfortunate fate, I want to shortcut all the confusion and just deliver the four knotted strands to Grit Wopal himself."

They climbed through the gate into the wealthiest part of Kish. They were heading for the Lord Chamberlain's palace, which wasn't the only place to find Grit Wopal, but it was a good place to start.

"Tell me why you think this," Fix said.

"Your problem is that you read," Indrajit said.

"Your problem is that you *don't*," Fix responded. "I almost didn't arrive in time to save your life because I couldn't figure out that terrible triangle-headed cartoon of yours was meant to be a picture of Meroit."

"It's an excellent likeness," Indrajit said.

"It's an excellent likeness of a bulbous root."

"Meroit looks like a vegetable. Anyway, it took me a minute to recall the information, but as we were discussing the situation with our Fanchee friend back there, I finally found the spot in my memory palace. It's a little protrusion of earth, framed by rounded gray stones and lapped at by the water."

"What?"

"My memory. I had to consult it, but I found the information I was looking for."

"Your memory is a picture?"

"Yes. Isn't yours?"

Fix shook his head. They turned down a side street—in the Crown, there were no true alleys—and headed for the tradesman's entrance to the Lord Chamberlain's palace. "Go on."

"And I saw there a picture of Grit Wopal recommending us to Forfa."

Fix stopped and stared at the Lord Chamberlain's door. "Yes," he said slowly. "Forfa said that Grit Wopal recommended us to help recover these knotted strands."

Indrajit knocked at the door. "I don't think that's a coincidence. I don't think that was one old friend recommending a reliable service to another as a kindness. I think Wopal was sending us in to repair a breach in one of his spy rings. Without telling us."

The door opened. Inside stood Grit Wopal, a short man wearing a yellow turban.

"It's about time," he said.

* * * * *

D.J. Butler Biography

D.J. (Dave) Butler has been a lawyer, a consultant, an editor, a corporate trainer, and a registered investment banking representative. His novels published by Baen Books include the *Witchy War* series: *Witchy Eye*, *Witchy Winter*, *Witchy Kingdom*, and *Serpent Daughter*, and *In the Palace of Shadow and Joy*, as well as *The Cunning Man* and *The Jupiter Knife*, co-written with Aaron Michael Ritchey. He also writes for children: the steampunk fantasy adventure tales *The Kidnap Plot*, *the Giant's Seat*, and *The Library Machine* are published by Knopf. Other novels include *City of the Saints* from WordFire Press and *The Wilding Probate* from Immortal Works.

Dave also organizes writing retreats and anarcho-libertarian writers' events, and travels the country to sell books. He tells many stories as a gamemaster with a gaming group, some of whom he's been playing with since sixth grade. He plays guitar and banjo whenever he can, and likes to hang out in Utah with his wife, their children, and the family dog.

* * * * *

About the Editors

Rob Howell

Rob Howell is the publisher of New Mythology Press, the fantasy imprint of Chris Kennedy Publishing, a founder of the Eldros Legacy fantasy setting, and an author in the Four Horsemen Universe. He writes primarily epic fantasy, space opera, military science fiction, and alternate history.

He is a reformed medieval academic, a former IT professional, and a retired soda jerk.

His parents discovered quickly books were the only way to keep Rob quiet. He latched onto the Hardy Boys series first, and then anything he could reach. Without books, it's unlikely all three would have survived.

You can find him online at:

- Website: www.robhowell.org.
- Eldros Legacy: www.eldroslegacy.com
- Amazon Author Page: https://www.amazon.com/-/e/B00X95LBB0
- His Blog: www.robhowell.org/blog

* * * * *

Chris Kennedy

A Webster Award winner and three-time Dragon Award finalist, Chris Kennedy is a Science Fiction/Fantasy author, speaker, and small-press publisher who has written over 30 books and published more than 200 others. Get his free book, "Shattered Crucible," at his website, https://chriskennedypublishing.com.

Called "fantastic" and "a great speaker," he has coached hundreds of beginning authors and budding novelists on how to self-publish their stories at a variety of conferences, conventions, and writing guild presentations. He is the author of the award-winning #1 bestseller, "Self-Publishing for Profit: How to Get Your Book Out of Your Head and Into the Stores."

Chris lives in Coinjock, North Carolina, with his wife, and is the holder of a doctorate in educational leadership and master's degrees in both business and public administration. Follow Chris on Facebook at https://www.facebook.com/ckpublishing/.

* * * * *

Excerpt from

Khyven the Unkillable

Book One of Legacy of Shadows
An Eldros Legacy Novel

Todd Fahnestock

Available Soon from New Mythology Press

eBook, and Paperback

Excerpt from *Khyven the Unkillable*

Two knights threw open the door of the tavern, and the scent of last night's rain blew in with them. Khyven heard their boots thump on the rough planks, heard the creak of leather and clink of chain-mail as they shifted. He sat with his back to them, but he didn't need to see them to know where they were.

The room went silent. This dockside drinking hole didn't see knights very often, and their appearance had rendered the entire place speechless. That was respect. That was what being a knight meant in the kingdom of Usara.

They paused just inside the threshold, perhaps hoping to spook the fearful, but Khyven wasn't a jumper. He had more in common with the newcomers than those who fled from them.

Ayla, the pretty barmaid sitting across from him, looked past Khyven, her eyes wide. She had been a lively conversationalist a moment ago and he'd been daydreaming about what it would be like to kiss those lips.

Now she looked like an alley cat who'd spotted an alley dog. Reflexively, she stood up, the wooden stool scraping loudly on the floor. She froze, perhaps realizing belatedly that when the powerful—the predators—were in the room, it was best not to draw attention to yourself.

Khyven heard the metallic rustle of the fighters' chain mail and Ayla's face drained of color. He envisioned the alley dogs turning at the sound, focusing on her.

She needn't have worried. They weren't here for her or any other patron of the Mariner's Rest. They were here for Khyven.

He had killed a man in the Night Ring two days ago, and not just any man—a duke's son. The entitled whelp had actually been a talented swordsman, but his ambition had outstripped his skill. And the Night Ring was an unforgiving place to discover such a weakness.

After Khyven had run the boy through, Duke Bericourt had sworn revenge. No doubt he had been waiting for an opportunity to find Khyven alone, vulnerable, to send in his butcher knights.

Men like these, sent to enforce a lord's will or show his displeasure, were called butcher knights. Usually of the lowest caste— Knights of the Steel—butcher knights didn't chase glory on the battlefield or renown in the Night Ring. They were sent to do bloody, back-alley work at their lord's bidding.

Khyven took a deep breath of the smoky air, sipped from the glass of Triadan whiskey, and enjoyed the fading burn down his throat.

The booted feet thumped to a stop next to his table.

"Khyven the Unkillable?" One of the men spoke, using Khyven's ringer name—the flamboyant moniker the crowd had laid upon him.

Khyven glanced over his shoulder. Indeed. He had guessed right. The pair were Knights of the Steel.

There were three castes of knights in Usara: Knights of the Sun, Knights of the Dark, and Knights of the Steel, which was the lowest caste and the only one available to most lords. The pair wore chainmail shirts instead of full plate, conical steel caps with nose guards instead of full helms, and leather greaves and bracers.

As predicted, they wore Duke Bericourt's crest on their left shoulders.

There was a code of honor among knights—even butcher knights. Except in cases of war, civility was required before gutting a man, especially when there were onlookers. Often a knight would give a flowery speech—including the offense he'd been sent to address—before drawing weapons. This was enough to justify murder.

Sometimes there was no flowery speech, but a knight would always at least say their victim's name. If the victim acknowledged their name, that was all it took to bring out the blades.

Khyven didn't give them the satisfaction. He took another sip of his whiskey and said nothing.

"Did you hear me?" the knight demanded, his hand touching his sword hilt.

If Khyven had been a normal ringer—a caged slave thrown into the Night Ring to slay or be slain for the sport of the crowd—these men would probably have forgone their code of honor and drawn their swords already.

But Khyven wasn't just any ringer. He was the Champion of the Night Ring, and the king had afforded him special privileges because of that fact, like a room at the palace. Khyven had survived forty-eight bouts, the longest string of victories since…

Well, since Vex the Victorious had claimed fifty, won a knighthood and become the king's personal bodyguard.

Steel scraped on steel, bringing Khyven back to the present. The second knight drew his dagger and placed it against Khyven's throat.

Ayla gasped and backed away.

"You think you're protected," the second knight growled in Khyven's ear. "You're not."

Of course, if Khyven didn't acknowledge his name, there were other ways for the butcher knights to start the fight. If Khyven attacked them, for example, they could retaliate. The powerful could always push a victim into a corner when they needed to. That's what the powerful did. Khyven had learned that long ago.

That was why, when Khyven had won his fortieth bout and his freedom from the Night Ring, he'd continued fighting, risking his life in every bloody bout. For the prize at the end of ten more bouts. For the power that would come with it.

When Khyven won his fiftieth bout, he would be elevated to the knighthood, just like Vex the Victorious. And no one would look at him as a victim again.

The blade broke the skin, just barely, and a bead of blood trickled down Khyven's neck. His pulse quickened. The familiar euphoria filled him, the rush of pleasure that came with the threat of death.

The euphoria brought vision, and Khyven saw with new eyes, his battle eyes. He saw his foe's strengths and weaknesses as a swirling, blue-colored wind.

"You are Khyven the Unkillable," the man breathed in his ear.

Khyven chuckled.

The second knight's face turned red. He slashed—

But Khyven was already moving.

* * * * *

Get "A Reluctant Druid" at:

https://www.amazon.com/dp/B07716V2RN.

Find out more about Jon R. Osborne and "A Reluctant Druid" at: https://chriskennedypublishing.com/imprints-authors/jon-r-osborne/

* * * * *

Excerpt from

Responsibility of the Crown

Book One of The Endless Ocean

G. Scott Huggins

Available Now from New Mythology Press

eBook, and Paperback

Excerpt from *Responsibility of the Crown*

The sky was so big.

She had never been so high up on her own. Thousands of feet, it must have been. She felt as if she could fall forever in the endless blue that was the ocean below and the sky above. Already, she had to strain to pick out the bronze and violet specks that were Elazar and Merav.

Senaatha aimed for the fighters, and they bored in, lines of death shooting from their wings. Suddenly, she seemed to stutter in the air, beating her wings irregularly. She dropped, climbed, and dropped again.

She's throwing off their aim, Azriyqam realized. Consortium planes were fast, but they moved in long curves. They had no wings to beat—*how do they turn?* she wondered—and so they weren't capable of the fast changes in direction a dragon could manage.

Or a half-dragon. The planes sliced through the air on either side of Senaatha, and she whipped her neck around, flaming, but her fiery breath fell short of her targets.

They must be going a hundred miles an hour, thought Azriyqam.

Her heart sank. It was obvious, even to her, that the weapons on the aircraft reached much farther than Senaatha's flame could, and they could use them while going at full speed. Senaatha didn't dare—she'd fly right into her own breath. Even worse, the planes would not get tired. Already, they were looping around for another pass. Senaatha labored for altitude, but the aircraft climbed higher still, nearly to her own height.

Height. She strained against the thin air, found a weak thermal, and rode it upward. The planes settled in for their attack run. Again, the deadly lines of gunfire lashed out.

Two tiny figures dove into them. Elazar slashed downward, Merav flying practically at his wingtip. They twisted between the lines of light and danced in front of the oncoming plane. It veered in the air, yawing and rolling to avoid a collision. Slowing.

Senaatha breathed flame as it passed by her at a distance of 50 feet. The airplane emerged from the stream of flame spinning wildly, a comet of fire trailing black smoke, every surface ablaze.

Then the second plane's guns punched heavy bullets through Senaatha's right wing.

Blood flew like mist from the wounds. The dragon screamed. Engine roaring, the plane broke off in a tight turn. Its pilot had seen what had happened to his companion, and he didn't want to chance closing with the dragon, wounded or not.

He would come back to finish the job from farther away. Senaatha was in a flat glide. The bullets hadn't cracked her wing spars or she'd be falling out of the sky, but there were ragged holes in the membranes of her wing. If she strained it too hard, she'd rip it apart by the sheer force of her passage through the air.

The plane turned. Merav and Elazar beat for altitude, but she could see they were on the wrong side. They couldn't get between her and the plane, let alone be ready to dive. Then the pilot would unleash his deadly guns into Senaatha's helpless body, sending her and her human passengers into the Endless Ocean below.

It was up to her.

Already, the plane was lining up.

Azriyqam winged over and dove.

* * * * *

Get "Responsibility of the Crown" now at:

https://www.amazon.com/dp/B095CLDVMD/.

Find out more about G. Scott Huggins and "Responsibility of the Crown" at:

https://chriskennedypublishing.com/

* * * * *

Made in the USA
Monee, IL
03 December 2021